the
'idiot spy'
(the series)
book ten of eleven

between heaven & hell

c. benjamin lattimore

between heaven & hell
Published: March 2023
Printed in the United States of America
ISBN: 978-1-7334945-9-5

a lattidreamer™ publication
© C. Benjamin Lattimore, 2023

to my bride, Marisa
Your commitment to my work is immeasurable!

ACKNOWLEDGEMENTS

to my children, Christopher, Monica, and Courtney and my grandchildren, Isaiah and Desmond. A profound expression of love to my sister Mary E. and my brother Darryl A. and to all of my nieces and nephews. Yet again, and again, a shoutout to my true friends, Maurice E. Cheeks and Reginald W. Wilkes!

special acknowledgements to Marisa and Jill.

ethereally, lots of love to Mary Alice, Walthro M, Barbara Ann, and Walter Eugene. To my friends Gordon Gant, Joseph Bongiavanni II, Monique Gorham, Rahsaan Stevens, Mrs. Marjorie C. Cheeks, and to my newest guardian angel, Franco Harris (# 32)

CHAPTER ONE

It was a beautiful day in the outback, Ben Beckmire descended to his knees, asked Courtney for her hand, and inquired, "Will you marry me." Her reply was unpretentious, "We're already married."

Ben Beckmire proclaimed, "That was then and there! I am asking you here and now, in the land of the unconventional, in the home of my forefathers, I ask you with all my heart and soul, to commit all of your love and affection once again to me, as I will do to you, in this place of spirits, for you are my lifeline. In asking for your commitment, I proclaim, and explicitly state, that no one from my past, my present, or my future will divert, distract, or persuade me from keeping my commitment to be the best partner and husband, on this earth!"

As everyone's eyes and attention were on Courtney, and as she looked towards the billabong, she saw The Great Saltie rise into the air, and fling a pouch onto the sand. As people turned around to see what was causing the commotion, all they saw was the giant tail of The Great Saltie, descending into the billabong.

To everyone's surprise, the person bending over to pick up the pouch was the Holy Father. As everyone fell to their knees, the Holy Father peeped in the pouch and whispered, "Oh my." He quickly pleaded for people to rise, and to pay homage to the resident of the billabong.

With a quivering voice, the Holy Father proclaimed, "I just witnessed the largest manifestation of greatness, and it must be a spirit of sorts because no one attempted to run away. I have only been here for a couple of hours, and my time on this island continues to restore my faith in mankind, knowing that none of us are aware of all of the wonderful and magnificent things that exist on this earth."

The Holy Father paused, and continued by saying, "Please pardon my interruption. My little friend, Ms. Beatrice texted me, and informed me that Mr. Beckmire was marrying Mrs. Beckmire once again. I emailed her back and told her that I was sad that they didn't invite me to the wedding. Ms. Beatrice in turn wrote, and I quote, "Spirits will marry Mr. and Mrs. Beckmire, and I guess that will be okay, but as the Holy Father, don't you think that you should be here to make sure it's done right?"

The Pope took off his spectacles, and said, "Please ignore my interruption but I thought that this would be a good learning experience for me. My being here is somewhat of a secret, and people in the Vatican are once again roaming the catacombs looking for any sign of me. I'm here with people who understand what the world needs, and it is not always done in the spirit of, or the teachings of the church. I am also here because my friend, Ms. Beatrice, invited me, and I'm going to bless this wedding after her other friend Wajickee, who she says is really, really, old, has performed his ceremony."

Ascending from behind the Pope and his people, a little hand reached out, and waved to the crowd. It was little Ms. Beatrice who grabbed the Pope's hand and led him to the front of the ceremony. She said, "I have a blanket that you can sit on. We usually find a spot on the ground and make it ours for a little while." Everyone laughed.

The Pope meandered around a spot, and said, "This looks like a good place to sit. Will you join me Ms. Beatrice?"

# # #

The ceremony was off the chart. The sounds of the didgeridoos and drums could be heard from the various tribes that were paying homage to the ceremony across the outback.

# # #

Prior to the evening ending, the Holy Father asked Ben Beckmire if he could arrange a short meeting with himself, and that fellow named Wajickee?

Sitting close to the water's edge, Ben Beckmire and the Holy Father sat watching the shooting stars. The Holy Father stated, "My son, I could not bless you during your wedding ceremony because you have half of hell waiting on your arrival. In the case of your beautiful and brilliant bride, I made an exception, realizing that she too has a few souls waiting on her arrival. Secretly, I pray for your survival because it is you and your group who keep the world safe from that monstrous Carbon Factor."

As the Holy Father paused, and consumed more of the delectable drink that he was enjoying, Wajickee appeared, and cautioned, "Slow down my friend, that drink will put you in another dimension, if you're not careful."

The Holy Father stunned by his sudden appearance asked, "How on earth did you so stealthily sneak up beside me, and without my guards having a clue as to how you did that?"

"Holy Father, our little friend is so correct when she says that I am really, really, old. In my world, I have had the fortunate opportunity to be in service to the Beckmire clan, a clan that has always worked for the benefit of the Aborigine people. Now, the modern types, like Ben Beckmire and I, don't always agree on protocol nor does he follow simple mandates. I have been in service to his, great, great, great, great-grandfathers, and they all have challenged my spiritual existence. The Beckmire next to you has been unequivocally my most challenging assignment. By the way, Holy Father in the morning you will not remember this meeting, but you will figure out how to handle certain aspects of your flock that are quite annoying.

# # #

In the morning Ben Beckmire and a small group of people escorted the Pope and his people to the airport. In the hangar, the Holy Father descended to his knees, and whispered something to Ms. Beatrice. She in turn muttered something in his ear. He smiled, rose from the kneeling position, made the sign of the cross, and said, "You, my little friend, are special, and you will help my flock overcome the exigencies of the Carbon Factor, and help us help people save themselves." He proceeded to kiss Ms. Beatrice on her forehead.

# # #

The group voted unanimously to add an extra week to their hiatus. That extra week was spent between Bora Bora, Morea, Papeete, in Tahiti. One might have thought the only thing the group did was play, drink, eat, and lounge around.

That clearly was not the case. The Sabbath was their day for personal reflection, relaxation, and yoga. Yes yoga! As the group aged, flexibility became a critical item that was needed for each person, if in fact, they were going to aggressively perform the tasks of keeping the world and each other safe.

At the end of week six, John Lee was the only person who had elevated levels of cholesterol and blood pressure. His boyfriend, Jilkes, was prescribed Embrel for his rheumatoid arthritis. Somara and Yeshida made sure that their menfolk followed the prescribed regimen and took their medications religiously.

# # #

Once back in the outback, Darryl and his crew met up with his uncle's group to discuss the many challenges facing them. Darryl indicated that a congressional committee was in the process of issuing a subpoena for the one and only, Sergeant Benjamin Beckmire. Darryl also informed his uncle that if he didn't show up for the hearings, that he would be held in contempt, and a federal warrant for his arrest would be issued. His uncle indicated to him that it would probably come down to those busy bodies in Washington issuing an arrest warrant. He indicated that there was no way in hell he was going to show up in Washington, DC for a hearing when there are those who think that he is responsible for the demise of two previous sitting United States Senators, as well as a plethora of other possible charges, including the selling of the Carbon Factor to a known foreign enemy of the United States of America. Darryl suggested to his uncle that he should never step foot on US soil again, because the entire federal government would be after him. His uncle stared at the billabong, and asked, "Did we get all of those diamonds out of there?"

Darryl, uncharacteristically, shouted, "Uncle, let the horseshit go. This matter is as serious as it gets. They can send a battalion of soldiers to find you, and us. Now, I know you are the leader of this community, but you are in a place where I have a lot of power and influence. I need you to pay particular attention to what I'm saying because if you refuse to accept certain conditions, then I will make sure, you never leave the outback; ever!"

Beckmire screamed at the top of his lungs, "Have you lost your fucking mind? Have you sided with the enemy? How could you deceive me, and sell me out?"

Wajickee showed up, and placed his hands on Beckmire's shoulder, and whispered, "Here, my friend, your nephew is electric. He has sheltered his feelings on many things out of respect for you. He can see things that even I can't as a spirit. Disregard what you may consider an affront to your position and listen to what he has to say. There are some, back in your place, who would like to shoot your planes out of the sky, and conclude all that is precious to you, including those grandbabies of yours. He has seen this, and that is why he is sticking his chest out to you. He has a heavy burden to carry if your people are to end this thing, alive!"

The Sarge dove into the billabong and noticed that the residential Salties were behaving aggressively. He calmly swam to the shore, and Darryl said, "Uncle, I am simply devastated because I spoke to you in such a manner. It was as though, someone else controlled my tone and words. You must listen to me, and at least consider my suggestions since I've had too many dreams about you and the team members that you will lose."

Beckmire looked at Darryl, dried himself off, fell face down in the sand near the billabong, and began to cry. It would be three or so minutes before he was able to have a conversation, with his nephew. Darryl looked at him, and adamantly stated, "Me and my people will follow you into hell if that is your decision, but there are other opportunities for many of us to survive that trip to Hades, and continue with our lives without ever being hunted. I gave you information, and you reacted without asking about conditions, places, who would attend, and other options. I am telling you right here and now, that me and Wajickee can influence a lot of outcomes, separately and jointly on this soil. However, in America, that statement of work, ain't true. I have dreamt of the day, have seen it over, and over again, when you no longer have confidence in me, and that leads to a sad conclusion of all that you have built. Uncle, I need you to follow a script that I'm proposing for gaining the favor of a group of powerful people who can at the stroke of a pen, exonerate you and all of us from any crimes that we have allegedly committed."

Beckmire asked, "Why is it that you are giving me this information at this point in time? You of all people knew how to reach me."

"Uncle, I am not as savvy as you or your people are. When I get information or see things, I must analyze, debate, and develop a solution. When you need to act, you just, well, you just act crazily. I admire that in you, but I also like the fact that I will spend more time trying to figure out alternatives which can be detrimental because time is always critical to everything we do. I beg you, please forgive me for increasing the decibel level of my voice when I addressed you earlier but the information that I have is critical to our continued success. I beg your forgiveness."

"Nephew, I gave you a task to accomplish and apparently, you have gathered critical details that I need to understand in order to make a decision that impacts us all. I recognize that here, you and Wajickee are my brain trusts. Let's look at this event as a casual misunderstanding by a resourceful nephew, and a reluctant uncle. Can we do that?"

The two men began to discuss the issues at hand, as well as the best strategies for securing the entire community. Darryl suggested that if they decided to agree on a strategy that his uncle would appear at the hearings, then he would use Sue Lyn, Monica, Luana, and himself, as advisors. Darryl adamantly stated that the rest of his team needed to stay in the outback, and that way if things were a ruse, the group could decide just how to free him. Beckmire laughed, but Darryl failed to see the humor in it.

After a long and complex discussion, Beckmire said, "You know I have dreams when I'm here. You also know that in my dreams, someone from Australia or in my family, betrays me." Darryl looked away, but quickly turned around, and said, "Uncle, you might be suffering from a lack of faith. You should see your elders. Go on Walkabout and Dreamtime and ask that very question. That is a question that you must figure out on your own. All of us from Australia, are your support system. I don't know where that dream emanated, but you must answer your own questions. As you know, faith, is a huge thing in this part of the world."

"So, nephew, what are you recommending that I do. Are you suggesting that I turn myself in, and be held in a cell for contempt for not answering questions that link me to the murder of thousands of people? Are you suggesting that I negotiate a different location than Washington DC to meet with the proposed people? What exactly are you suggesting?"

"Uncle, I have no suggestions at this time other than to obtain a 'no hold' statement from those in charge. Uncle, I'm suspicious of this invitation on many fronts. First, every person we have encountered from that organization called the government, has had their hands out, or worked in some illegal place. Second, I, like you, have seen them manipulate us to do their dirty work, and then ultimately accuse us of committing a crime. No, Uncle, I don't trust any of those people and, therefore, I have not solved how we pull this thing off. My primary task was to get your buy-in relative to considering the idea. I must now ponder all the possible things that can go wrong, and who will be the person hung if anything happens to you. I have a lot going against me on this one, but I have the support of my wife and Michael. Speaking of Michael, he flatly asked me if I had lost my fucking mind. After I attempted to explain what the outcome would be, he began to loosen his concern that I had lost my mind. Uncle, how many more battles can you and your guys fight and win before rockets will be launched, and tanks will be utilized to reduce us to small pieces? I'm looking for a solution that will exonerate everyone from our yesterdays."

"Nephew, suppose I agreed with your proposition, when will this event take place?"

Darryl, cleared his throat, and replied, "Are you free in the next three days?"

Beckmire yelled, "Have you lost your brain? Are you, my Judas?"

"Uncle, those are hurting words, especially since a small bite from that spider near your foot, would conclude all of our concerns for the moment."

Beckmire moved his foot, and essentially ignored the spider. Darry said, "The senators would like to have a session that would last no longer than twelve hours. In that session, they will attempt to ascertain your culpability in the bombing in Massachusetts, as well as have conversations about the demise of two sitting United States Senators. They are also curious as to how our group can afford three jets and have ten pilots on our payroll. I demanded that they send me a list of their questions, and that if you come, this will not be an open invitation to query you about missing mercs who died on lands owned by our associates. The last thing on their agenda is to question you about the Carbon Factor. They want to know if you or any member of our group, sold the formula to any foreign power for payment? All these things are easy answers for you. Oh, and Uncle, they have the NSA, FBI, and the CIA all attempting to figure the composition of the Carbon Factor from the residue of the bombings in Springfield, Addis Ababa, and near the North Korean peninsula."

"Wow, these people are terribly busy. How were you contacted, Nephew?"

"Mike still has contacts in the sewers, and what's interesting is that someone from on high reached down in their world and made contact. The messages got forwarded until it hit home, home being me, and Mike."

"What are my chances of surviving this mess?"

Darryl looked towards the billabong, and whispered, "Believe it or not, they're pretty good if we can implement our security plan, just in case that group decides to try to hold you on contempt charges or attempt to add other charges that were not amplified in their questionnaire, to your current list of items in the inquisition."

"Nephew, I really must be slipping. I thought I gave you and your team the assignment to find additional information on the Carbon Factor. How on earth did you wind up in DC, and you and Mike speaking with people in the sewers?"

"Uncle, I was going to save that for last, but it has been suggested that the explosions that were set off in Springfield, Addis Ababa, and near North Korea, were not the Carbon Factor, but were aberrations of it. It has been rumored and, therefore, the sudden interest in you and your group, that intel is floating around that on a magnificent holiday, the real Carbon Factor will be introduced."

"Do you have any idea as to where it will be introduced?"

"Uncle, I do! There is chatter that there will be a three-pronged approach to the magnificent celebrations, in Los Angeles, New York City, and Washington, DC!"

## CHAPTER TWO

Prior to dinner, Wajickee and Darryl were seen talking to Ben Beckmire. Darryl wanted to delay the announcement of certain information until he had near perfect protocols for making sure his uncle was not held over and/or tortured. Wajickee indicated, that at dinner would be a perfect opportunity for Ben to deliver the information, and try to diffuse his people from boarding airplanes, and preparing a defense for him. He said, "The more information they have, the more confident they feel about you Darryl, and then they might just agree. However, good luck with that one, because that is not how they roll."

Darryl replied, "Yeah, that's my only concern. They're not going to sit back, and watch their leader get on a plane, go to a hostile place for interrogation, without them being somewhere in the background ready to cause a distraction, free their man, and take refuge in another country. That is where I believe my dreams about planes being blown out of the sky originate. Things will go bad, they will attempt to free my uncle, and people will believe that the root cause of this mess, was blown completely out of the sky."

Beckmire said, "Why don't we take the temperature of the group, and decide if we can let them in on a secret that will take me away from them, and may result in my being incarcerated for crimes against the state? I mean selling bomb making formulas to known enemies of our government, extorting millions of dollars from the government for a product that was never delivered, and for failure to report and pay income taxes, might just be enough. However, there is the case of allegedly murdering two sitting United States Senators, and for the murder of several thousand mercs. Now that's not to mention the bombing of Springfield, Massachusetts, and the murder of thousands of citizens, or the fifty other counts of international terrorism, and most of all, lying to the Holy Father. Now that should really cause them to sigh and wish me well. What do you guys think?"

Wajickee responded, "Heck, if that's all you've done, then you deserve a medal from the spirit world. No, my friend, your people will understand the choices that must be made, and the integral part that they will play. They will also understand and make suggestions, but all will realize that the action on your part, will get the group closer to the end of running, and the beginning of enjoying life without oversight, and people trying to kill them. By stating this premise now, will give the group resolve and time to consider not so attractive plots to join you. I will make sure that everyone understands the importance of your mission."

Ben Beckmire smiled at the wise sage, looked at Darryl, and asked, "Nephew, each time I think you've given me all of the information, you come up with more depressing thoughts. Is that all that you have to share?"

"Uncle, there is a small matter that I neglected to inform you of because I didn't understand how it measured up to all of the other things that you're going to be accused of. Some time ago, one of your people gutted the niece of the ranking member of the committee. Now I was informed that they weren't that close but, nevertheless, that's the last piece of data that I need to share with you."

Beckmire scowled at Darryl, and said, "If I have to spend a single day in prison, then you my nephew, had better find a new planet to live on."

As soon as he made that statement, a fish jumped high out of the water followed by a monstrous sized saltie, a rare sight since reptiles are not known for breaching the water.

# # #

Ben Beckmire walked over to where Courtney was playing with the twins and a couple of children who were hearing impaired, and asked, "Honey, when you have a moment, I need to talk to you about a serious matter." Courtney saw the look on his face, and asked Rashida to come and watch the children for a moment.

As they walked towards the billabong, he held her hand, and said, "I know exactly what you're going to say, and how you're going to say it, so I need a different reaction from you this time, my love. Darryl found out that there is the potential of a subpoena being issued for my arrest for the commission of several crimes against the government of the United States of America. If I don't show up, then they will send the real military to arrest all of us. I am being accused of extorting the government, murder, sedition, failing to pay taxes, conspiracy, consorting with a known foreign enemy of the government, the murder of two sitting United States Senators, more sedition, and the murder of those thousands of people killed in Springfield, Massachusetts. Now, the good news is that if I do this, we may be able to go to our home, and live like normal human beings."

Courtney, looked at him, and said, "I'm coming with you."

"That's exactly what I can't have you do. I am going to ask Monica, Luana, Sue Lyn, Darryl, and secretly Larry to come with me. What I didn't tell you is that Darryl and I have had the same dream, a rescue mission that ends with a plane being shot out of the sky. I'm going to talk to the team at dinner and give them my take on the situation. I trust my nephew, and this action is encouraged by Wajickee. I need you to keep my guys here and impress upon everyone that any rescue attempt will lead to several deaths, a thing that I'm not prepared to handle. This is the only way this can happen, and if you want to grill my nephew after I have the talk, then so be it, but I need you to keep the crew on the ground, and here in the outback. If any of you steps foot on American soil, you will be arrested and, therefore, corrupt my chances of figuring out what in the hell they want us to do. Why do they want to talk to me now, is the question, and I think I know the answer! Our guys in the sewers have heard a scary rumor that what happened in Springfield was an experimental device or devices, and not the Carbon Factor. It is also rumored that the Carbon Factor will be used at magnificent events in New York, Los Angeles and Washington, DC. I have three days to gather additional intel about this kangaroo court, who is in control of the formula, and whether I can get my ass out of there without being arrested. Honey, I need you here, and safe. Please don't make it any more difficult than it already is for me. This is a heavy load, and I must do the hefty lifting, for the sake of our community."

A crying, Courtney, held his hand tight, and just watched as the sun began to set, and as its glow was reflected on the water, she said, "I'll be here waiting along with everyone else for you to return. You know if they arrest you, all bets are off!"

#

At dinner, the mood was festive and loud. The children played hard with each other until it was time to eat. Ms. Viola said a prayer to bless the food. She indicated that a strange wind was about to blow, and that people must listen, obey, and not gather arms against a mighty foe. Of course, those words received the attention of everyone, and after the prayer, John Lee asked Jilkes, "What she mean by that?"

Jilkes replied, "Just hold your pigs in their pen my friend, someone else will do some talking, and then we'll have clarity about her words."

Ms. Viola's words actually dampened the mood of the feast until the Sarge stood up, and said, "Tonight, we are going to enjoy food, fellowship, a few drinks, and then I will send you all to bed with my sermon. So, until then, enjoy the meal that was prepared by the villagers."

Courtney asked the Sarge, "Did Ms. Viola steal your thunder, and how did she know?"

"No, darling! She prepared the floor for my arrival, but to answer the second part of your question, I think Wajickee and her have found a medium for connecting, if you know what I mean."

"Ms. Viola is old, isn't she?" Courtney asked.

"Baby, she ain't cold," the Sarge replied.

#

After dinner, there was a sense of anticipation in the air. The Sarge stood up, and said, "First, I'd like to thank Ms. Viola for preparing the mood for my discussion with you.

How she knew there was an ill wind blowing, I'll never know but, nonetheless, I would like to thank her."

Courtney stood up and suggested that parents with little ones should take them over to Ms. Viola's daycare center.

Five or so many later, the Sarge announced, "People, I'm going to cut right to the chase. I have been accused of killing two sitting United State Senators, the deaths of thousands of people who perished in Springfield, Massachusetts, for consorting with known foreign enemies of the United States of America, for the sale of state secrets, for the murder of thousands of mercs, for extorting our government out of billions of dollars, for failing to pay taxes, for selling bomb making materials to terrorists, for as many as fifty international terrorist acts, and for lying to the Holy Father."

John Lee stood up, and yelled, "You did more than that!"

The Sarge smiled, and said, "Oh, yeah, and for the gutting of a ranking member of the kangaroo court's niece!" The laughter ceased, and a quiet came over the camp.

"Ladies and gentlemen, my nephew, from our sources in the sewers, has informed me that I have three days to appear before a Senate Select Committee, and if I fail to show, a warrant for the arrest of everyone here will be issued, and the military will be asked to assist in our capture. My nephew is still trying to figure out our options but moving forward, I will need the assistance of Monica, Luana, Sue Lyn, and Darryl. As a sleeper, I will enlist the assistance of Larry who will scope out where I'm held, if I am held, and the best way of breaching the place that holds me."

John Lee stood up, and the Sarge vehemently, told him to sit down.

He said, "As the leader, of this community, my command is that none of you people will set foot on American soil until

I have an understanding about what is going on. Warrants for arrests will be issued for every single person including the children. You will not commandeer any of our resources and attempt a suicide mission because that is what it will turn out to be. I need this group to follow orders, obey my command, and listen for news from the sewers and Larry about what must happen. Oh, and by the way, my illustrious nephew has indicated that the bombings in Springfield, Russia, Addis Ababa, and near North Korea were a different type of ordnance, and not the Carbon Factor. My nephew has indicated that rumor has it that the Carbon Factor will be introduced at magnificent events in New York City, Los Angeles, and Washington, DC. Listen people, my decision with input from my nephew and Wajickee, is not up for debate. If my appearance is successful, it will allow us to move into our homes, and live a normal life without having to look over our shoulders. On another note, if this goes wrong, and they lock me up, please take care of my nephew! Again, this situation is not up for debate and, therefore, I will not entertain comments or suggestions. Tonight, I'm going to take a walk with my bride, and show her how much I love her."

#

Prior to Darryl asking Mike and Michael to head to DC, Michael told Ayesha that he had to head back to the states, but that she and the children would be fine and if she needed anything, to see Dr. Beckmire. She once again placed her hand on her heart, and looked to the heavens. He smiled and placed his hand on his heart. Ayesha reached for his hand and placed it on her heart. Michael slowly reached for her hand and placed it on his heart. They both smiled, and Michael gently moved towards her cheek to kiss it. Ayesha turned her lips so that his lips would meet hers, thus was the beginning of what was to become a dynamic relationship.

# # #

Mike said to Carla, "Sweetheart, Darryl has asked me to head to DC in advance of his uncle arriving, to do some scouting and information gathering. I know we haven't spent a lot of time together, but realize this, I love you more today than I did when I first saw you."

Carla emphatically stated, "You had better get the work done, and come back here without a scratch. Be careful, and I love you!"

# # #

Once in DC, the two men went to different banks, and turned cash into debit cards. Mike made a call to his contact, and a meeting time and place was established. He told Michael that they should probably stay in a moderately priced hotel and stay off the grid.

The two men checked into a Homewood Suites that guaranteed them breakfast as a part of their stay. They had one SAT phone but knew that it was to be used for emergencies only. Both men watched TV, and eventually fell asleep in their adjoining rooms. At 2 am, both men were awakened by the fire alarm. As they opened their doors to check for smoke, two men breached each of their rooms, held them at gunpoint, and restrained them by using wire tires. One of the men scanned each room for listening devices and determined that they were bugless.

The men never said a word, and seemingly were waiting for someone else to show up. Three to five minutes later, two gentlemen walked into the room, and one of them said, "Sorry about the theatrics, but there is a net over the entire city." He had his people leave the room. Once they were out, he asked, "Is your man considering honoring the request?"

Mike looked at Michael, and asked, "What request are you referring to?"

The man responded, "Doing business with those guys in Minnesota."

Mike announced, "No, he's decided to help the people in Compton."

The guy looked around the room, and said, "Nice to finally, meet you. We weren't sure of your friend and, therefore, we played the game that we had agreed upon just in case this was a setup. Listen, I don't have a lot of time, but I suggest that you guys vacate this place in the morning and come live below the city for the next few days. You're wide open, and you're strangers coming from of all places, Australia where a certain person is known to be and be from. After you enjoy your breakfast, come to 1st & K Streets, Northeast, catch separate transportation, and me and my guys will pick you up." He asked, do you guys have weapons?"

Mike answered, "No, but we have debit cards totaling $6k, and we can get more tomorrow."

The guy responded, "Excellent!" He knocked on the door, and a man walked in with two boxes that contained new weapons and filter paper for the stock. The main man said, "I'll have people watching you, whatever you do, don't use that SAT phone, use this flip phone if you have to reach out to me. Gentlemen, I will see you tomorrow at noon. Oh, and by the way, leave all of that shit you brought with you in the room as if you're going to be returning."

Mike asked, "Do you want the debit cards now?"

The guy replied, "What's your thought on that? Of course, I want them now because we need to buy some new computer equipment to keep track of all the shenanigans that go on in this town. Until tomorrow, lock and load those weapons, but put the filter paper on the stock before you begin to handle them. Good night gentlemen."

Michael said, "Damn, that was precise. I'm glad it wasn't a termination meeting. They completely had us by the balls."

"Yeah, and I didn't like the feeling of that at all. Listen, I have two beds, let's occupy one room, and that way, perhaps we won't be caught off guard again."

# # #

At noon, at 1st & K Streets, Northeast, an uber, and a lyft car dropped their passengers off near the intersection. Two men, independently, began to walk through the tunnel heading towards North Capital Street. A quarter of the way through the tunnel, a door opened that was the access to lots of cables. A man appeared from a hidden door on the left. The two men were ushered into a new and different world, one of vets who were down on their luck, who had wives that wanted support and divorces. They stepped into a world of hurt, and of those who would gladly give their lives for this country.

As they descended further into the bowels of the structure, Mike asked the guide, "How long have you been operating down here?" The man looked at him and continued to lead the way. After approximately descending sixty or so steps, they came to another door, and that is when they saw one of their visitors of last evening.

The man said, "I'm acting commandant of this facility, and I welcome you. My name, which I purposely didn't divulge last night, is Captain Rheingold. Let me give you a tour, but first express our deepest appreciation for all that your group does for our vets. That training facility in Southeast, and the scholarship fund is truly God sent. What we try to do down here is capture our people before they commit crimes, or are institutionalized. What I mean by that is, when our guys come back, usually the family veil has been penetrated by an outsider and, therefore, our guys are subject to use their training and execute someone, including wives and children, and then take their own lives. We try to catch them, train them, retrain them, and provide them with additional benefits that are a direct function of your generous foundation. Now, in addition, we sometimes hear things of value because we have our people operating in some highly classified areas. As an example, and as you well know, we have run interference for you guys on any number of occasions. We have provided you with timely information that had you not received, outcomes could have been adverse for your group. So far, the relationship has been based upon the 'quid pro quo' doctrine. Our commanding officer wants a relationship without any favors expected by either side. We know what those people upstairs are trying to do with your commander, and we don't like it. We know you guys didn't start this fight, but you might have to finish it for our government."

As Rheingold paused to take a swig out of a bottle of water, he said, "Listen, you people are the perfect answer, and that is why they trumped up those charges against the Sarge to make sure that they got his immediate attention. They want the Sarge here to guarantee that if they give him free reign without any more so-called handlers, that you guys will attend to the Carbon Factor issue and conclude a few people who are about to sell it to foreign governments. After they demonstrate the difference between what happened in Springfield, Addis Ababa, near North Korea, Mali, and close to Moscow, they will realize that it was not the Carbon Factor. We believe that we have intel on those responsible for those dastardly deeds, but we keep drawing blanks on who may be in control of the Carbon Factor formula."

Once again Rheingold took a swig of his water, and stated, "Okay, I know I'm doing a lot of talking however, I think I know what you guys are here for. You're here to make sure that if that kangaroo court goes awry, that you can get your man safely out of here without being in a plane that will be shot down. The commanding officer is currently meeting with people to make sure that the details and guidelines for questioning are according to the script, even though, a family member was horrifically dispatched allegedly by your group. Now, am I correct?"

Mike responded, "You are absolutely correct because those who would slam the gavel down on a sentence for the Sarge, would be placed under a scope. Now I'm not threatening anyone, but if our guy is mistreated or abused in any fashion, there will be a reckoning, for everyone involved."

Captain Rheingold replied, "Damn, you just threatened a boat load of senators."

"No, Captain, I didn't threaten anyone. I simply stated that the people who handle our insurance policies will want an accounting of what happened to our guy before they issue worldwide contracts for those involved. That is hardly a threat. It's more like a, ah, you know, an announcement!

That's it. We're just announcing what will happen if this turns out to be a ruse."

The captain looked at Mike, and said, "You were once down here trying to survive, is that right?"

"Sir, with all due respect, this place saved me from Lucifer, and myself. I owe you guys a lot, and on our board, I'm your champion and your financier."

Rheingold smiled, and said, "I appreciate your candor, I love the fact that you speak for us with that generous foundation, and I will inform those involved, that if there is any chicanery, that all fees have been pre-paid, and the outcomes are whatever they may be. That does not sound as threatening as your comments, but it will require people to understand what's at stake! Okay, let's move on to more tactical arrangements. As you know, there are some leftovers that you guys only partially handled. We believe that the one that was operated on is now a functioning bionic man. The other handler, well let's say, he has garnered some significant, ominous, and internal assistance.

Oh, by the way, he cleaned your cleaners, every one of them?"

Michael inquired, "Why did he do that? After all, they are a service to all kinds of righteous people."

"Apparently, they helped you escape at some point in time, and more importantly, the one was with the other, and had been for decades," Rheingold stated.

Michael asked, "What the hell is that supposed to mean?"

"Well, Walter and Utz were long time lovers!"

Mike responded, "Oh, my goodness! Is there anyone in this town that is not involved with someone else who is investigating the same situation? Wow, this place is as incestuous as the largest rat hole. Okay, that is valuable information, and since we haven't implemented the relationship agreement, I will champion, based upon the 'quid pro quo' doctrine, that the foundation add another million dollars to the scholarship program."

Rheingold yelled, "Hell yeah! That's what I'm talking about. Doing business with people who work hard to help people help themselves." He then screamed throughout the tunnel, "Listen up people, our friends from the outback will present a proposal to their group to add another million dollars to our scholarship programs!" There was a thunderous response in the tunnels that probably echoed up to the streets.

Michael said, "I can't let him punk me in that fashion. When I get back, I'm going to advocate that the training programs need another million dollars to add current and relevant trades to the mix."

Rheingold screamed, "Listen up people! In addition to the new scholarship proposal, the other gentleman is going to request that the foundation add another million dollars to our training efforts!" The sounds from the echo effect was almost deafening.

Mike and Michael, after accepting accolades, thanked the people. Michael said to Rheingold, "You are literally living underground in a damp, smelly environment that's probably unhealthy. Have you considered trying to do what you do where the sun shines, and you see buses and planes drive by and fly over?"

Rheingold's head dropped, and he announced, "The smell is manufactured. The dampness that you think you feel is controlled by our engineers. Going above ground would defeat our purpose because if you noticed all those cables when you came in, you saw the source of our information. I'm going to share with you some highly classified data. From these tunnels, we can access twenty-three distinct locations around the city. We do twelve on and twelve off, thanks to your generosity, to share information that would compromise our services to our vets, and to Americans who try to keep this country heading in the right direction. My commanding officer would consider my actions treasonous, but would also thank me for at least having advocates broach expanding our programs for our vets."

Mike responded, "My friend, the only way we discuss this place is if we find ourselves fighting for the freedom of our leader, and we just so happen to be on 1st & K Streets, Northeast."

Rheingold laughed, and said, "I have four-armed people watching your backs. They won't appear like they did last night, but they will always offer to shake your hand with their left hand. Keep that in your pocket and realize that they are there to help."

Mike thanked him and offered a normal handshake. Michael said, "He is probably thinking about his wonderful wife. Forgive him."

Mike asked, "Forgive me for what?"

Michael replied, "Left hand my friend, left hand!"

CHAPTER THREE

A small jet landed in San Diego, California, and was ushered into a private hangar. The hangar was secure, and customs officials conducted their business of examining paperwork, passports, declaration forms, and doing personal interviews. Darryl who was questioned about his frequent trips to and from Australia, flatly asked, "No crime in being able to move about as I feel, is there, mate?" The customs official stamped his passport and smirked at him.

The Sarge, along with Darryl, and Larry, jogged around the hangar until the plane was ready for refueling. The plane was led outside the hangar and refueled. The three men continued to run around the hangar while Luana, Monica, and Sue Lyn assumed various yoga positions.

An hour later, the jet prepared to take off. One hour and fifteen minutes later, the jet was airborne, and heading for a small airport in Maryland. Larry made a quick call to Mike on the SAT phone that he failed to answer. As agreed, Larry called him back in exactly ten minutes, and the two talked on cell phones for thirty seconds. Larry asked Mike, "Good or bad?"

Mike answered, "Cautiously in between."

#

Five hours later, the plane landed in Maryland, and was greeted by Mike and Michael, along with four people watching their backs. The two men entered the plane, and presented each person with small caliber weapons, and extra clips. Mike said, "This is a little welcoming package, only to be carried outside of DC. Do not bring any semblance of a weapon into DC. We will have ample security I hope, from our friends from down below. Our friends believe it would be impressive if you sported your dress uniform at the hearing tomorrow morning and, therefore, they have gone through the expense of gathering enough material to make you a uniform."

Michael said, "Sergeant Beckmire, it is a trimmed down version that was confiscated from your old home and modified to fit your greatly reduced frame. We were not sure of your reaction and, therefore, we took the liberty to buy you a suit that civilians wear. Your choice but both will fit, and both will make you look formidable, and garner admiration."

"Michael, remind me to fire your buddy when I get out of this place. Come here people and give me a hug and tell me what I'm up against."

Mike and Michael informed the Sarge about the use of the SAT phone and, why they didn't utilize it to keep him abreast of what was happening. Michael told the Sarge that Mike had literally threatened every person involved in the hearing if a gavel went down remanding you to be held over. Beckmire cautiously inquired, "Now, what does that really mean?"

Mike replied, "Words requiring interpretation were presented to the chairman of the panel suggesting that the format be implemented as agreed upon, and that if there are any deviations, distractions, accusatory/inflammatory statements, and/or abuse, that each person would be viewed through a scope."

"You, told those people that crazy shit? Damn, I haven't gotten to the hearing, and you have threatened sitting United States senators. Hell, I'm in trouble!"

Michael said, "Sarge, we didn't tell anyone any such thing. However, it was intimated that an international insurance policy would be enacted if there was any deviation from the set agenda, including any abuse from the alleged family member of the woman that one of our members so proudly gutted."

Monica interrupted the séance, and said, "We need to get to the hotel, freshen up, eat and go over what signals we will use, and their inverse meanings."

# # #

The hotel was a moderately priced chain with four adjoining rooms on the third floor, along with three dummy unoccupied rooms on the opposite side of the floor. Of course, Darryl and Sue Lyn shared a room, Luana and Monica shared a room, Michael and Mike shared a room, and the Sarge had a room to himself. It was early, and room service was provided to the empty rooms across the hall, and eventually picked up by the guys, and brought to the right rooms. After a brief session with the Sarge, Monica said, "Remember the signals that we practiced. You're not to use them but we will either draw them in shorthand or point to the microphone, in which case you click the button to off, and keep your hand over the unit."

The Sarge said, "I'm not my own attorney. I have two beautiful, smart, and honorable individuals to help me navigate these waters, and a non-legal brain to pick out trouble spots. Don't worry ladies, no matter what, before I answer simple questions that seeming aren't so simple, I will delay the response, and seek advice. I'm not doing this alone. I have you guys, and by the way, regardless of the outcome, you three are so special to me."

# # #

At 0730 hundred hours the following morning, the group descended to the lobby, and had coffee and muffins. Michael and Mike were outside talking to the man who presented them with weapons. The two men were preparing to examine the vehicle when they were told that four of their underground neighbors watched each vehicle throughout the night. After scouring the area, Michael walked back into the lobby, and said, "People, it's time to roll."

In the meantime, Mike was given an earpiece, and was told which channel to hail on. When Michael came out of the building, he was given an earpiece as well.

# # #

At 0830 hundred hours, the group pulled into a secure lot near the Rayburn building and were ushered into an awaiting minivan. As they got near the building, they could see a beehive of activity going on, and the Sarge vociferously stated, "Stop the damn vehicle. I specifically said, no press!"

The van driver replied, "Sir, the press is here for one of those people who is involved with the president. We're going underground where you will be searched, and a colleague of mine will escort you to your private hearing room."

#

At 0903 hundred hours, the committee was called to order, and the chairman looked around the room, and saw that it was comprised of staff, members, recorders, and security. The chairman introduced himself and thanked the group for coming from Australia to participate in the hearing.

The chairman gave a fifteen-minute overview of his understanding of why the hearing was being held, and what might be some of the outcomes derived from it. He said without further ado, "I would like to start the hearing with the wise gentleman from Arkansas."

"Welcome Sergeant Beckmire. Let me first state that I was a fan of yours until you or one of your people, butchered my niece. Beckmire slouched a little in the chair, and Luana signed, 'erect.' Now son, let me say this, I've never held a hearing with someone who killed someone I loved even though she was as evil as the damn devil himself. When I found out about what she had been doing, and the things she did to people, well anyway, let me just say, thank you. Mr. Chairman, I yield my time to the closing speech because I know exactly what I need from this honorable man."

#

For one hour, the accolades and testimonies of what magnificent work Beckmire's group had done, overwhelmed the hearings. The chairperson asked that lunch be served in chambers so that they could continue with the hearing. At 0100 hundred hours, the doors opened, another senator walked in, and apologized for missing the hearing, but was happy that some food was left for him.

He took his rightful seat, and the chairmen nodded to him, and he said, "Gentlemen, once again I apologize, but I was participating in a request by the administration to add more agents to the president's security detail."

A staff person whispered something in his ear, and he continued by saying, "Now, Sergeant Benjamin Beckmire, you have been accused of so many crimes against your government that it would take me a full hour to read each crime, the conspiracy charges associated, the statutes, and the penalties. I'm not going to do that, and as a matter of fact I'm just going to list only those that concern this committee."

He looked at the paper in front of him, and said, "You are accused of consorting with known foreign governments and enemies of the United States of America, to provide them with something called the Carbon Factor for an enormous amount of money. You are charged with the killing of thousands of people in Springfield, Massachusetts. You are charged with the murder of two, not one, but two, sitting United States Senators. You and your group are charged with extorting our government out of millions of taxpayers' dollars, for selling bomb making materials to known terrorists, for as many as fifty-five, um, this has grown by five since I saw it last night, international acts of terrorism, and the easiest to prove of all, is your failure to pay income taxes. Now that's a lot of damn charges, wouldn't you agree?"

Prior to the Sarge responding, a senator got out of his seat, and put a note in front of the senator who thanked the person. He then said, "Oh, I forgot about the charges for killing several hundred mercs. Damn, son, you and your people have been busy as hell. How many are in your group, five hundred or so?"

The Sarge's voice boomed, and then he backed away from the microphone, and said, "Sir, we have approximately forty-eight or so members in our community."

"Is this community like a cult or something?"

"No Sir! We are comprised of old vets, some new wives, my nephew, and people who work for him in the outback, people we've helped along the way, family, and friends. We don't do no dancing or worshiping stick idols."

"Oh, I see. How about those Native Americans that make up your group? Do they worship stick idols?"

"Sir, if they do, I haven't seen them do that."

"Tell me why you or one of your people gutted my colleague's niece?" Luana signed the Sarge, paused, and responded, "Not sure about that allegation since I personally didn't see it. I did see that your colleague's niece left her calling card at one of my associate's home in Alabama."

"What did the card say? Did it say call me when you get a moment?" The senator laughed, and so did a few others. Monica touched the Sarge, and he took a deep breath. The Sarge responded, "No, Senator, it did not. As a matter of fact, her card was pinned to my associate's woman's dress as she was hanging over the banister in his home, and all of her inners were placed in his refrigerator. Now, any further funnies, and my time here will be up."

The senator stood up, and yelled, "This is not your jungle. This is where laws of the land are made, and you my friend are about to be held in contempt!"

Another senator stood up, and said, "Senator, read the last page of the document, and that will show you that the Sergeant is here by invitation and, therefore, he can leave whenever he desires to. I suggest we take a five-minute break and meet at the Chairman's seat for a short briefing."

After two minutes, the senator making the accusations, said, "Are you telling me that someone threatened this body on behalf of the Sergeant? Hold on one damn minute. Sergeant Beckmire, are you aware of a threat issued to this group by some of your followers?"

Monica and Luana both signed a message, and he smiled. The Sergeant then said, "Senator, I am respectful of these United States of America, and the bodies appointed to legislate, and govern it. If you want to hold me in contempt for a message that I heard about, but do not have a clue as to where it came from, then Sir, please do. Me and my people don't issue threats. If I had issued a threat, Senator, you would already be dead. We don't telegraph our actions like some of the people on your payroll so often did. No, Senator, I didn't issue the threat, and I don't know where it came from. When I inadvertently heard about it, I knew it was going to cause me concern." The Sarge paused for a moment, and then asked, "I'm sorry, may I say something else?"

"By all means!" said the chairman."

"I thought I was invited here to discuss an impending threat against three large cities; New York City, Los Angeles, and Washington, DC, and to try to discern who may have the actual formula, and to catch those involved."

"We were told that you knew who the culprits are."

"Senator, I don't think the same people are playing in the same game. Springfield, and the others to me, were experiments that got better each time. The monster planning the other three detonations, well, I believe he or she has access to the Carbon Factor, and I believe that is a whole new dilemma."

"Sergeant, we hear that you and your people have the formula and have concocted the necessary bombs to carry out the 'magnificent event threat'."

"Senator, again, we don't have any such knowledge or the wherewithal to develop such a weapon and, furthermore, why would we want to kill our own people? Grant it, we've allegedly had various aspects of the Carbon Factor in our possession, and even attempted to give it to one of your past senators, who was in cahoots with my cousin, and a secret society that crossed continents, but maintained one basic principle, and that was to destroy those who are a burden on advancing societies, no matter their race."

"Suppose we gave you full immunity from everything that will happen from this moment forward, would you help us, and work with our agencies to stop the alleged impending disasters?"

"Senator, I would not because the next issue, you will hold me for, will be all sorts of crimes that we did not do just like you articulated when this meeting started."

"Suppose we dropped all of those bogus charges that were read earlier, would you help our federal agencies?"

"Senator, we are old people who just defend better than a lot of other people. We don't work well with others because they don't know how we work. Me and my guys survived Vietnam by doing some really dastardly things for our country, the same country that now wants to hang us for defending ourselves against paid mercenaries."

"Sergeant Beckmire, what will it take for you to help us get this thing under control?" Beckmire cut his microphone off, looked at Monica and Luana's hands below the table signing out what would appear were instructions, but were, dollar signs, planes, ships, and other frivolous notions. The

Sarge turned around, and knew the microphone was off, and began to talk. One of the senators suggested that he cut the mike on. Beckmire turned it on, and boldly said, "I don't trust the government that I bled for and fought for. You commission people to bribe, steal, and kill innocent people. We want to help but we don't trust what you're offering. You want to clear me of things we haven't done yet, and hold me accountable for things of yesteryear. I'm not sure where that leaves me and my people."

"Sergeant, tell us, what would make you feel as though you were being held harmless, and that all those unsubstantiated, historical charges are just what they are, uncorroborated? Would that endow you with a little trust for your government?"

The Sarge stared off in space for a few seconds, and said, "Senator, you and your staff should develop get out of jail cards for me, and my people. Those cards should look like the badges those agent fellas carry in cases, with a photo, signed by someone high up in the justice department. This thing must look and be real. Now, if you really want us to start to work on this, if I were you, I would begin this process immediately. I do have another question that I would like to ask. You guys have entire agencies, FBI, CIA, NSA, Secret Service, and a thousand other specialized groups. Why can't you employ all of them at once to figure this out?"

The senior senator said, "Yes, Sir, we have all of those organizations that are now involved in a leadership crisis, have been politicized, and that almost breaches the bounds of anarchy. This is driven by the commander-in-chief, and his continued policies to discredit agencies in public and privately. The agencies stick to their mandates, the Carbon Factor has been secretly dubbed by this president as a media stunt stimulated by that other party with the intent to divide the American people and conduct a coup on his presidency."

Another senator said, "Suppose we can have this in play by tomorrow evening, will your people start the process prior to having paperwork in hand?"

"Absolutely not, Senator. Get me the paperwork, and upon entry into the country, we will go through customs in San Diego, and your people should be there to greet us, deputize us to some degree, provide us with the necessary identification badges, and licenses to carry, and to kill. This can, and will probably get messy, but if you know of any good dry cleaners who are mobile, we would like to interview them in the interim. Senator, remember, the way we do things is not based upon any codes of operations; we don't do manuals. We get it done, and sometimes we do it in a messy fashion."

The Sarge looked at Monica, and then Luana, and said, "Senators, I'd like to change the subject. When I leave here, I'm going straight to the airport, and will fly to Australia. We will spend thirty-six hours there and return with our entire tribe. We have great intel at work trying to isolate a behavior, and recruitment scheme. In all honesty, senators, despite this hearing, and the false charges, me and my people were never going to cut and run, and watch our country destroyed from the inside. Our constitution is our guide, and despite that others believe that they are above the law, we will hold everyone accountable to the fundamental principles articulated by our founding fathers, as well as ourselves. We are patriots, and we will die patriots in the defense of this great nation."

A member of the committee replied, "I guess you patriots are doing rather good with government property, you know those new jets you have. I guess flying first class all the time at our expense would make me patriotic as well."

The Sarge paused for a few seconds, smiled, and replied, "Senator, the planes that were sent to the Midwest to end our lives, well those planes were turned over to us. We declined ownership of them because they were filled with explosives. Our planes are a function of our foundations, and our commissions from the diamond and gold mines in the outback. No, senator, we don't like flying as it is, and we damn sure don't like flying with explosives on board."

"Well, who has those planes?"

"Senator, we have our own aircraft. I hope you haven't lost two big planes like your people continue to lose substantial amounts of money!"

# # #

The hearing was adjourned, and the Sarge didn't wait around to engage in small talk. Once on the elevator, he told his people, we're out of here, and on our way back across the pond. I certainly hope the pilots are legal."

Once out of the garage, the van stopped for Larry, who asked, "How did it go?"

"They're going to deputize our group to finish this mess, and hopefully catch the culprits before the Carbon Factor is detonated in real time," the Sarge indicated.

Larry said, "While I was just hanging around outside, I was struck by the high number of trucks sporting 'I T' or Information Technology on them. Shouldn't the government use a single 'I T' provider or at least have its own division to handle issues? I mean, I saw at least five different trucks with various company names on them. Why wouldn't the government utilize its own people to work in a place like this that is full of high-ranking elected government officials? Something is spooky about what I saw."

The Sarge was still answering questions from the committee in his mind, when Luana said, "Disrupt the communication systems, and you control the environment."

The Sarge asked, "Luana, what did you just say?"

"I said, disrupt the communication systems, and you control the environment."

The Sarge asked, "Larry, what did you say about 'I T'?"

"Dad, I inquired about why there are so many trucks with 'I T' from all kinds of companies. Seems to me, if I were the government, I would only use my own people to do telecommunications work in my most sensitive buildings."

The Sarge said to the driver, "Sir, please turn this vehicle around, and take me back to the Dirksen Building. Wait, stop over there where that Capitol Police officer is standing."

The Sarge got out of the van, walked over to the officer, and told him where he had been, for how long, and what it was about. He then vehemently asked, "Why would the government utilize so many contractors to deal with matters of communication?"

The officer said, "Sir, I don't know what you're talking about."

The Sarge said, "There are at least five trucks with different 'I T' names on them allegedly providing a service to one of our most sacred places. Something is wrong with that picture."

The officer beckoned another officer over and told the Sarge to stay put. He made a few calls, the person he called made a few calls, and the alarm/alert button was sounded.

One hour later, fifteen Russians who spoke perfect English were being held. The Sarge made a call to one of the senator's office and told him that they should not worry about those who have tried to help but be on the lookout for those who would hurt innocent people for no apparent reason. The Senator asked, "Are you still in the area?"

"I'm across the street with two of your Capitol Police who I presented the information to."

"May I speak to one of them?"

"Absolutely, because they think, naturally, that I'm complicit in this matter." The senator spoke with the officers, and asked them to follow protocol, request replacements, and escort the individuals to his office.

Once in the senator's office, the Sergeant was welcomed with open arms, and applause. It turned out that the Russian agents were not only reconfiguring the building's operating systems but had installed several undetectable relay switches that scanned for key words such as, nuclear, Russia, cold war, aggression, China, North Korea, and many others.

The Sarge unaware of what was happening, asked the senator, "What's this all about."

"Sir, I'm now convinced that you and your people are much more diligent than our contracting agencies who apparently have a gap between offering a contract, and evaluating who the contractors are, and if they have any affiliation with foreign governments. You my friend, waltzed into our home, and immediately saw roaches, rats, and more importantly, snakes."

"Senator, can you have your people get us out of here without any press taking a picture of us? That would be unbelievably bad for us."

The senator spoke to his chief of staff, and whispered something in her ear, and without saying a word, the office returned to normal, and everyone knew to delete any pictures if they so happened to have taken one.

# # #

The van driver asked, "Sir, wherever you go, do you have such an impact? Are you a movie star or something?"

The Sarge looked at him, and wondered if the man was being funny. He replied, "No man, that was a fluke, and one that could get us killed if it were leaked. We don't have a problem, do we? Did you happen to take a picture when I wasn't looking?"

"Sir, we're not allowed to have personal phones with us when we provide this service."

"Thanks, dude. I appreciate you, and if I ever get this way again, I'm going to insist that you have a burger with me. Thanks for your service."

The Sarge turned to Luana, and asked, "Did you get his photo?"

"You know I did!"

## CHAPTER FOUR

When the weary group's plane began it's descent into Sydney to take on fuel, Luana exclaimed, "Oh, my God!" It is simply wonderful and beautiful as she viewed Sydney Harbor from the plane. She asked Darryl, "How did so few, conquer the many?"

Darryl dropped his head for a moment, smiled, and replied, "My people are clannish, divided, backwards, and each had their own spirits, and those spirits, according to tales, demonstrated the same characteristics that many leaders today have, supposedly knowing all, but knowing truly little. What's so sad, is that they could have united, and ran those devils off, but those in the interior thought that the foreigners wouldn't bother them and, therefore, felt safe in their environments until the white man showed up all over Australia. In one of the caves in the village, I'll show you historical drawings of how the Europeans conquered all of Australia. We didn't look like them, dress like them, speak like them, eat like them, or worship the same deity. Therefore, the conquerors raised their flag, and it continues to sway in the breeze today."

"How sad. I wonder if that could happen today?" Luana inquired.

Darryl responded, "Unfortunately, in some areas, that old clannish mindset is as prevalent today as it was many years ago. Some of our tribes are so remote that they rarely encounter other people. They stay to themselves, exist off the land, and tell stories of great battles that were never fought. Evolution has skipped at least two generations in some places.

"Now, that's amazing, Darryl. Perhaps, once we finish with the Carbon Factor situation we can investigate as a group, and at least study ways to bring fringe groups into the twenty-first century. It will be a challenge, but I can't imagine anything as important as educating people and making sure they can benefit from science and technology. Those two things aren't all bad."

# # #

As the pilots went through their checklists, they were reminded to collect all weapons from the group. Beckmire searched his body and felt a weapon that he thought was a part of his anatomy. He smiled, and said to Larry, "Nice to have you on this trip with me son. When I reached around, and felt this thing on me, I had forgotten that I was carrying a weapon. I think I'm going to need some stress relief, yoga, and a distraction that won't let me forget that I'm carrying a damn weapon."

"Pops, your work assignments have all required you to don a weapon; Vietnam, Philadelphia Police Department, our work on drug dealers, and now, this, the Carbon Factor/'idiot spy'. I don't think its unnatural, but I agree with you, we need a stress relieving program. I guess you get used to running, squatting, walking, eating, and everything else with it on your body, and the mind communicates that it's okay to have it."

# # #

When the group exited customs, their entire clan was there to meet and greet them. John Lee exclaimed, "That be the last time anything like that happens. It ain't natural for you to be away from us without us having any chances of helping you out of a jam."

"I missed you to, John Lee. Nice to see you, and the rest of the group." His eyes dead reckoned on Courtney, and he headed straight for her. He bypassed a lot of people to get to her. He picked her off the ground, and said, "Mrs. Beckmire, I love you more than life, and the entire time I was talking with those people in DC, it was my vision of you that kept me calm, and from going overboard and beating the shit out of one of them especially when they thought we were still in command of those planes that had all of that dynamite on them. Damn baby, it feels like it's been an eternity." They kissed, kissed, and kissed some more.

Beckmire hugged his grandkids and told them how much he loved and missed them. When Monica exited the plane last, she kissed Mallory, and Elton, and inquired about the whereabouts of Margo. Mallory looked at Elton, and said, "Son, don't move from this spot."

Mallory and Monica walked out of his hearing range, and she asked, "Where is my daughter?" Mallory pointed to a corner window in the airport, and from a distance, Monica could see an image, looking out of the window. She beckoned for Elton, kissed him again, and said, "I need you to be stronger than me, and your dad. I'm going to gather your sister." She kissed him once again and walked towards the image sitting in the window.

When Monica arrived where Margo was sitting, and crying her eyes out, she said, "I hope those tears are about me, and not some boyfriend." Margo leaned into her arms, and said, between almost hyperventilating, "I thought we did something wrong, and you left us with our dad."

"Margo, when are you going to get over that childish thought. I told you that I would never leave you guys or send you back to that horrible place."

"You just got back from somewhere. That's called leaving."

Monica thought for a moment and realized that the child was correct. She realized that she may not have communicated exactly why she left because she thought that they had crossed that bridge of insecurity and had concluded any issues relating to it. Monica then said, "I think I'm going to cry, and not sleep tonight because my own daughter doesn't trust me. I think she thinks that I lie to her, and Elton, a thing I would never do because they are my children. I thought I had ended that issue."

"I watched you get on that plane, and I thought, I would never see you again. I thought it was happening again, and I thought we did something wrong, but I couldn't figure out what, and I think dad likes Elton more than me."

Monica hugged Margo, and said, "This is my last time having this conversation with you. My husband, and I, love you guys, so very much. I thought you realized that our jobs require us to travel a lot, and to sometimes carry weapons. Listen, baby, this world is mixed with good, and bad people. You guys just happened to luck out and get the two best people on the planet. My husband adores you, and figures that you understand him already. However, his attention to your brother is because he may need a little more work, and socialization than you, my darling. We are yours, and we sure as heck hope and pray that you are ours! We sincerely hope that you won't give us back, and that's why sometimes we try so awfully hard to make sure you guys are okay, and that you love us.

# # #

At dinner that evening, Ben Beckmire started his talk with a recap of the events in Washington, DC. He told the group that they would leave the outback in two days, and head for San Diego where they all would be deputized into a special governmental agency that would allow us to carry weapons, do investigative work, arrest people, as well as have a license to terminate. He explained to the group that all the false charges against them would be dropped, and they could mix amongst other civilians without worry of being arrested. Someone started to clap, and others joined in as the group realized exactly what that meant. After thirty or so seconds, the clapping and yelling reached thunderous proportions.

The Sarge said, "I was wondering if you people were drugged, or something based upon your initial response to what I said. People, we do this right, and we're free as a jaybird. If nothing else I said this evening, I thought that would increase your heart rate."

There were some individual discussions taking place when the Sarge asked, "Does the entire group need to hear what you people are whispering about?" There were no further deliberations.

The Sarge then said, "I would like to spend a few minutes going over exactly what we know about the Carbon Factor. As an example, does the Carbon Factor formula include four

separate devices, or is what was used in Springfield, near
North Korea and Addis Ababa, another kind of dirty bomb.
Now, if those four separate detonations, which drew all things
that utilized hydrogen into a massive device is a variation on
the theme of the Carbon Factor, then I think we're screwed
when it comes to New York City, Los Angeles, and
Washington, DC. Oh, and by the way, Larry, with his astute
self, asked a simple question that led to an evaluation of, and
the subsequent arrest of fifteen, perfect English-speaking
Russian agents working in the Dirksen, Russell, and Hart
Senate Office Buildings. They also installed devices in the
Cannon and Rayburn House Office buildings. I thought there
were three House Office Buildings."

Mike yelled out, "Longworth House Office Building."

The Sarge thanked him, and asked, "Why wouldn't they
apply their trade to all of the buildings unless, they have
already been there, and done that."

Darryl stood up, and said, "Uncle!" He was rudely
interrupted by Mike who said, "Darryl, sorry, but Sarge, if that
variation on a theme device, you know the ones used in
Springfield, Addis Ababa, and near North Korea needed four
devices, perhaps the Carbon Factor only needs three, and if
three times two equals six, the blast radius will be sixteen
times greater than what happened in Springfield. Somewhere
along the line, someone involved in this mess said, "it's a
matter of math." I don't know who, but I've been thinking,
and trying to figure out how those small devices destroyed
thousands of lives and devastated that city. Well, the answer
that occupies my dreams on a continuous basis, especially
when we're here in the outback, is that the Springfield
detonation was an experiment. In other words, Springfield,
and those other places were tests designed to lead us away

from the next strikes, Los Angeles, New York City, and Washington, DC. Sorry Darryl, but my dreams have been consumed with what I just stated."

Darryl looked at Mike as if he wanted to shoot him, and exclaimed, "Those are my exact dreams while I'm on foreign soil. I mean, he's having them here, and I have them when I'm over there. This is not happenstance, Uncle, this is modern messaging between two unlike vessels, however, both are brokering the same basic meaning. To take this thought further, if I were you, Uncle, I would call that Senator, and tell him that the Longworth building is key to any kind of detonation in Washington, DC. I would tell him that I'm on my way with people who don't believe in waterboarding, but a much more effective interrogation technique."

The Sarge looked at his people, shifted his head from left to right, and eleven individuals joined him where he was standing, as if automatically. He then looked at Larry, and blinked his eyes, pointed to Carlos, Mike, and Michael. He then stomped on the ground, and looked at Zanthius and Asiram with a look that suggested, 'what are you waiting on'? As the group swelled, the Sarge said, "I need you people to go back to your tables, I have another way of handling this situation." He walked over to a couple of the elders and asked if they could entertain the children while he discussed certain matters with his group.

After all the children were removed from the immediate area, the Sarge stated, "Oh, my God! My, my, how we've grown into such a huge group. A few of us, just returned from over the water. However, what I'm hearing from Mike and Darryl, clearly describes a situation that will have catastrophic results. Okay, Jong, is the big plane ready, and are our pilots legal? Second, I'm not going to get into leaving the women and children behind, because that shit just ain't going to work this time. By the way, Jong, do we have a plane in Miami?"

"The big plane is always ready, we have lots of pilots, they are always legal. Yes, we have a plane, and pilots in Miami. I suggest that we head out of here tonight, land in San Diego, get legal guns and badges, head straight for Maryland, and have the other plane meet us to take the women and children to *the Sanctuary*. Do you like my plan?"

The Sarge continued, "At least we have a real security detail there that makes life a little bit easier to swallow when I'm not near my woman. Anyway, Darryl, are you and your people ready to fly back east?"

"Uncle, me and my people wouldn't miss this adventure for all the tea in China." He looked at Michael, and asked, "Ain't that right, Michael?"

Michael smiled, and stated, "Boss, where you go, I go, and I go happily. You have done good by me and my friends, and we're as loyal as puppies to you and Sue Lynn. Oh, I'm sorry! We are loyal to the group, and Sergeant Ben Beckmire."

The Sarge said, "Nephew, I need you to get me a secure line to Washington, DC. I need to talk to one of those senators. Son, I need this now. I'm afraid that DC, is a bomb waiting to explode.

#

Later on, after connecting, the Sarge said, "Senator, hi, this is Sergeant Ben Beckmire, we met many hours ago. Anyway, here is my request of you. I need you to authorize the shipment of at least, hold on Senator." The Sarge looked at Asiram, and asked, "How many decapitations do you need before a person begins to want to confess his first sin?"

"Daddy-in-law, you know I don't do that kind of work anymore. I'm a mother of three and, therefore, I am forbidden by my husband, your son, to participate in mayhem anymore."

"Damn it, Asiram, answer the question."

"If you have four, by the time number two has seen the chaos and violence, number three will begin to tell the tale, and number four will summarize the entire event."

"Ah, thanks baby girl."

"Sorry Senator, as I was saying, I am requesting that you send me four of those people who were parading as 'I T' types in your buildings. I need you to randomly select four of them and place them on a plane that will meet my plane in San Diego. I know this is a strange request, but when you work with me, things will always seem strange, but we get the results that normal agencies can't get and use primitive means to get them. Senator, we just arrived in Australia, and we need to have those people waiting on us as soon as we arrive in San Diego. Listen, we believe that somehow, the Longworth building is the hub of their design, and whether they're using the Carbon Factor or a deviant to exact pain, something is going to be detonated. We need four people to cut the truth out of, or all of you in DC are going to die."

"Sergeant, you appear to be a war monger. I don't believe we have been compromised."

"Senator, with all due respect, we think the Longworth Building is the hub. Those people you caught doing 'I T' work, all just happened to be Russian agents, and you consider me a warmonger. I think we need to rethink this relationship. I think I'm talking to a ghost, who doesn't realize that foreign agents have compromised their very structure, and security.

Senator, I'm sorry to bother you, perhaps you're correct, and I wish you well." The Sarge hung up the phone and mumbled, "Damn fool."

Two minutes later, the Sarge's phone rang, and it was the senator who said, "Four individuals will be airborne within the hour heading for San Diego. Sergeant, I'm a politician, and one who is not completely sure of your actions. I was told to ask if you thought the facilities should be vacated?"

"Senator, I'm here in Australia preparing to head back to Washington, DC. I don't have enough intel to suggest that you vacate those facilities. However, I will suggest that you not waste time when I call you for a direct action. We want them in San Diego because we're not sure of a timetable and, therefore, we can save five hours by doing some initial investigatory work in San Diego because we're going to need to refuel. Senator, we're trying to cut down on time by meeting those people halfway, and that gives us a head start on the investigation. I'm hoping we caught them in time, and that we can locate any listening or other spy type devices. Most importantly, I'm hoping we can discern their end game. I mean are they suddenly trying to accomplish world domination by demonstrating knowledge of the Carbon Factor or some facsimile. What is their end game? Senator, that is our concern!"

"Mr. Beckmire, all of your people will be processed, photographed, and presented with official US Government credentials that allows you to carry a weapon, and unfortunately, end life when necessary. I know you are concerned about your people being photographed, and that is why the equipment is simplistic, and does not allow for a digital footprint. It will be like going to the carnival years ago and crowding into one of those booths and taking your picture. Does that create a problem for you Mr. Beckmire?"

"Senator, we usually take out insurance policies on those who we do business with. It would be inappropriate to subtly, or otherwise, threaten a sitting United States Senator. Oh, and by the way, we had no part in the demise of your two compadres who died. I hope you never have to see us or our associates, who we endowed to fulfill contracts on those who attempt to cause problems for us. I'm hoping Senator that you are a man without a lot of bugs in your place, and who no one can hold hostage. I trusted the senator who dared to be president, who subsequently hung us out to dry, authorized mercs to kill us, and our children. Had she not met the kind of death that she did, one of the groups who we entrusted her demise with, would have made a public statement about her in the worst possible manner. I say all of that to say, Senator, don't dance with the devil unless you know how to tango!"

"Mr. Beckmire, thanks for the heads up. I can assure you that you and your people will never visit me because what I'm trying to do is save our nation, its people and most of all, our democracy."

CHAPTER FIVE

Ms. Beatrice had a secret pen pal, who she communicated with frequently on her computer. They would talk about school, the importance of learning, setting goals, having faith that one could achieve those goals, and then establishing lifelong objectives for being a good person. He would give her interpretations of things that were in the bible and would explain to her in detail their relevance. Beatrice, in turn, would state that sometimes things grow old, and have no meaning or not much meaning, like my old dolls, games, and even the church. Beatrice on several occasions asked her pen pal, how could men put those explosive vests on the children. The Holy Father admitted that some people are evil, and do not follow any of the teachings of the church. Beatrice never accepted that as an answer and pressed the Holy Father for a definition that she could understand at her age. As the Holy Father attempted to answer the question, he finally admitted, and said to her, "Beatrice, I cannot explain why some people are unkind, and hurt others. I have hopes that in time, the world will be full of people like you, who show love and understanding for all of God's creatures."

The Holy Father, at the conclusion of their session typed, "I need you to tell your Uncle Ben to call Ben in Rome. He will understand. I look forward to hearing more of your questions as time moves on, my precious little friend. Don't forget to tell Uncle Ben to call Ben in Rome."

As the day was about to end, and after Ben Beckmire toasted everyone, and spoke about the challenges that lie ahead, little Ms. Beatrice stood up, and said, "Oh, I forgot to tell you Uncle Ben, to call Ben in Rome." Everyone looked at her with amazement, and Chakes asked, "Beatrice, what did you just say?"

"Dad, I told Uncle Ben to call Ben in Rome."

"Honey, why did you say that?"

"Dad, before I finished my session with the Holy Father, he asked me to tell Uncle Ben to call Ben in Rome."

"Honey, when did you talk to the Holy Father?"

"Dad, I've been talking to him ever since we left the Vatican. He gave me his card. He sends me prayers, well wishes, and I tell him that all will be well because we have God on our side."

Luana said, "So, Beatrice, is that who you spend your private time on the internet with, the Holy Father?"

"Mom, you guys were there when he gave me his card and told me to stay in touch. He is sad about the status of the world, you know, people killing people for no apparent reason, and he would like to see a world full of people like me, and the other children who love all of God's creatures."

Beckmire jumped in, and said, "Sorry to disturb this internet security thing, but I must ask Beatrice what was said, once more."

"Uncle, the Holy Father asked me to tell you to call Ben in Rome. He didn't say anything else after that. We usually pray for a stronger and better world, and then we say ciao!"

Beckmire said to Chakes and Luana, "There is a significant issue that's about to happen around the world. The Holy Father is a person who I trust, and have faith in." He looked around the room, saw Mary Alice, but didn't see Jong. He asked, "Mary Alice, where is your husband?"

"He's in the loo, he'll be back."

Mallory, Zanthius, and Asiram walked over to Beckmire, and Mallory asked, "What the hell is going on?"

"Someone roust Jong, out of the loo!"

# # #

When Jong arrived, Beckmire asked, "Do we have a secure line that I can call Rome on?"

"Yes, we do, your majesty! Would you like me to secure it?"

"I need to call Ben in Rome, according to Ms. Beatrice." Jong saw the urgency on his face, the perplexing use of Beatrice in the same sentence, and hustled expeditiously to his hut to secure the phone.

When he arrived, he had Wajickee in tow. Wajickee said to Jong, "When the sun breaches that hill in the east, I want you to meet me at the billabong. The stress you're putting on those limbs of yours is beginning to show. You're limping twice as much as before. You must trust your leader, and share things with him. Although he has no powers here, he can surely raise the flag, and one of us, the real Aborigines, will try to provide him with guidance."

# # #

It had been twenty-five minutes since Ms. Beatrice told the group about the message from the Holy Father. Beckmire called Ben in Rome, and was told, "You and your tribe should head here before you head to DC!"

"Why Ben?   It's obvious that the Russians have compromised systems, individuals, agencies, and perhaps the Oval Office itself," Beckmire expressed.

"Well, I'm just a tourist, and my sources have alleged that the things the Russians are touting in America, are simply firecrackers. The Holy Father has called upon the faithful in that nation to respond to the strategy being implemented in your country. By now, you know that the Holy Father and Ms. Beatrice have enjoyed secret educational sessions, where they both share things that are a mystery to each other.   Ms. Beatrice said, "do unto others as you would have them do unto you."   We need a little technical assistance, and then I'm assured that the thing they developed will be pulled from your very structure of government. As you know, the Holy Father hears of things, and sometimes acts on certain information.

Ben paused, and bellowed out, "Ben Beckmire, there are three types of Carbon Factor devices; the one that was tested in Springfield, Addis Ababa, and close to the North Korean peninsula. The ones that the Russians have surreptitiously placed in Washington, DC, New York City, and Los Angeles. Yes, it will cause damage and loss of life but not nearly as much as the product that the Holy Father has in his control. Now, Ben, this is not a matter to discuss with your people. This is for your ears only, and if you must discuss it with anyone, it is Ms. Beatrice. Now Ben, the real product, the one that Helga, and the great doctor discussed, is in the hands of the Holy Father. Your boy, Zanthius had a copy of it, and it was authentic."

Beckmire started to ask a question, and Ben Hackney, said, "Ben, let me finish my story. As a matter of fact, we are at the point where transmissions can be intercepted. Hang up and I'll call you back in a few minutes."

Five minutes later, Ben Hackney called the Sarge back, and said, "I need your entire troop here in Rome in the morning for a photo op. Also, at such time, the real Carbon Factor, that your son, and your group had in its possession, has strategically been placed throughout a country called Russia. You will not get on your planes and head to Washington, DC. You will get on your planes and fly over DC, and land in Rome, after your work and stopover in San Diego. Therefore, my friend, you and your people have one hour and forty-five minutes to board your jet and head this way. If you miss the timetable my friend, you miss controlling the outcome of the event. Ben, I don't cry wolf, often. I'm crying wolf, lion, crocs, gators, rattle snakes, box jellyfish, and every other kind of beast that can hurt you. This is the deal, now do your thing, and get you and your people here for a session with the Holy Father. He looks forward to obtaining more inspiration from the child called, Beatrice. You and your people owe me! Do us all right and get here! Catch you later."

## CHAPTER SIX

When the group's plane landed in San Diego, a sleepy Sarge summoned Jilkes and John Lee, and stated, "I'm going to need you two to accompany Asiram and Zanthius to do some extraction work. This process should conclude before the plane is refueled, and we're supposed to be on our way to Washington, DC. Is that a problem?"

Jilkes looked at John Lee, who replied, "Oh great master, we be doing whatever you want us to do. We will be there to assist, as well as persuade those involved to provide us with concrete information or suffer some sadistic ass shit from your daughter-in-law."

Jilkes looked at the Sarge, and said, "You know, I don't participate in decapitations, but on this occasion, and for the good of the nation, I will cut a tongue out, if I don't feel that it is giving me honest information."

The Sarge said, "We all owe you two a lot of accolades, but we also owe those women of yours trophies, and medals for dealing with the two of you. How lucky you two are. I mean, you met those ladies under, what I would consider suspicious circumstances, and both of you were able to convince them to marry you. How weird is that? A couple, of old dogs, meet two young puppies, and marry them, and live happily ever after. Come on now guys, let's be honest, the two of you don't look like up-and-coming movie stars. You are battle hardened, yet you were able to meet, and I hope those babies are yours, seduce, fall in love with, and marry two amazing human beings. I love those ladies because they are genuine, and they love and honor you two knuckleheads. How crazy is that?"

The two men looked at the Sarge, and Jilkes, asked, "So, what is it you really want us to do? Don't know why you go through that song and dance when all you have to say is what the hell you want us to accomplish."

John Lee chimed in, and said, "This seems like you're about to run a con on us before we have a chance to understand what the hell it's going to cost us. Is that how you want to relate to us simple people from now on?"

#

Asiram, Zanthius, Jilkes, and John Lee were processed first, and presented with their official government identifications. They entered an isolated hangar that was operated by the San Diego Air National Guard, flashed their IDs, kept their sunglasses on, and told the three men who escorted the four men, that they were relieved of their responsibilities. Asiram, took the hoods off the heads of the men, they squinted, and one said, "That was a long plane ride."

Zanthius walked over to him, pulled out his weapon, shot the man in both legs, and then placed a round in his head. He then said, "Unless, you want to suffer the same fate, you will not speak unless you are asked a direct question. There are no other rules except the ones we have in play, and you don't know what game we're playing."

Asiram looked at Zanthius, opened her eyes as wide as possible, and then said, "Hi guys, I think that good looking hulk over there got your attention. He is your easy out because he'll just shoot you in the legs, and then place a bullet in your head. Now, the real monster in the house is that other hunk over there with that nappy blonde hair. Now, he has gutted men and women from their private parts to their brains and have taken a bite out of their hearts before they died. Now, I am the easy choice because I don't do a lot of drama. I go right for the balls! If I'm having a difficult day, then I split the shaft right down the middle, and let people have the greatest orgasm ever, death by penile bleed out. Okay, the mystery man, that good looking brute with muscles to sell, well he just breaks bone, after bone, after bone! Okay, who wants to go first?"

The remaining three men were petrified. The one in the middle, lost control, and urinated in his pants. Asiram saw the weakness in the man, and asked, "Did you spill something on yourself? She then looked at John Lee, and said, "He's soiled, but it won't matter to you while you're gutting him, will it?"

John Lee replied, "I have one get out of jail card. That card be getting you out of here, on a plane to the destination of your choice with $50k in cold hard cash. Now, that be going to that there person who gives me the most information. Now if the material is stuff, I be already knowing, then the bone breaker comes to do the work on you. Those are the only instructions that are available."

The guy who pissed himself, announced, "Control the communications, and you control the country. Integrate communications with detonation signals, and you change the flag. We have changed the signals, and we're in control of your communications from your highest authorities. Whatever is said, in all but one building is being relayed in real-time, to Mother Russia. You see piss and think weakness.

I see a full bladder. No one here will talk no matter how many head shots you do."

At that point, John Lee threw that huge knife of his, it dug into the guy's tennis shoe, and he said, "I be betting a hog's ass that I can make you squeal in less time than it takes me to say Mother Russia, three times." As the man screamed at the top of his lungs, John Lee asked, "By the way, how that foot be feeling? Now, I'm going to bet you that once I slam this here knife into that other foot of yours, you'll tell me how to extract rubles from your account, and everyone else's in this room. Would you like to make that bet?" The knife slit the tendon between the big toe and the rest, not catastrophic but the place for a real bleed out.

John Lee extracted the knife from the man's foot, and emphatically stated, "This is going to hurt like hell!" He slammed the blade into the guy's shoe sitting next to the person he was talking to, and screamed, "Oh, shit, I missed! Do you have anything to say before I miss your foot and hit his foot? Maybe, or maybe not."

In agony the words that came out of the man's mouth were non-forgiving. He screamed, "When Mother Russia raises it flag on your White House and Capitol, I will find you, and will repay the pain 100-fold!"

John Lee looked at the man, and replied, "That there going to be really hard because I'm going to be able to hear your dumb ass coming in your cart." He then hacked the man's other foot until it dangled. He said to the man, "I can have our doctor save your foot, sorry in your case feet, but you can't threaten me with that there Mother Russia shit. Boy, you be in pig land, we don't do threats. You got less than three minutes before I must amputate that there foot of yours. What's it going to be?"

The man, after looking at his bleeding foot said, "In the Longworth building, we control the communications. In the Rayburn building, we control the signal as well as the detonation of the Carbon Factor."

Asiram stepped in front of the last man, and gently asked, "What do you know about the Carbon Factor?"

"I know that in thirty-days, Mother Russia will raise its flag on your White House, and your Capitol building, without firing a single shot or missile."

An incensed Asiram, with a scalpel in her hand, began to slice the man in a random and violent manner. When Zanthius grabbed her, she said, "His arrogance is beyond my comprehension. We need to end this, head east, and try to figure out what they've been able to install."

Jilkes said, "John Lee, I want you to gut this one in front of his comrades, and let's see who develops the rapid tongue. I'm betting my money on the pisser."

John Lee approached the man, and said, "I hope your buddy be clean because you're about to share more than a needle."

John Lee sat in front of the man, and said, "I need a couple of minutes to mentally get into what I must do. Please, don't go nowhere, I'm just going to meditate for a few minutes, and then I will make sure you see me take a bite out of your heart. Oh, you ain't got no kind of new germs, do you?"

John Lee thanked the Pig Heaven and asked it for guidance. He turned to the man, and said, "Now this is how you fillet a human!" He slammed the knife down near the man's private parts, and the guy let out a scream, and yelled, "Screw it, I'll tell you everything that is going on, just no more torture."

Asiram said, "Smart move my friend, he usually does not stop after his meditation. Tell me about the timetable for all your plans. Is it ninety days or what?"

The guy looked at his comrades, and then at Asiram, and said, "In all honesty, things are already in place. The earlier stated timetable is a hoax."

Asiram interrupted him, and asked, "What does it mean that things are already in place?"

The guy once again looked at his associates, and stated, "A different crew has already placed the Carbon Factor in its respective locations. We're the wiring guys, someone else has the detonator that is independent of anything that happens to our work. Three different, and independent crews were assigned with various responsibility centers, the wiring, communications wing, and the product placement crew. No one knows who the detonator is. Each crew arrived in your country at various times to do their work. Our work is communications, and less important in the scheme of things. However, the others, are the key to Mother Russia's success, and eventual invasion of your country. Forces are already here, resources are accounted for, personnel have been strategically placed up and down your east coast."

Zanthius interrupted the man, and said, "This sounds like a Marvel Comic script. You don't have the necessary resources to invade our country."

"Sir, what would you consider the necessary resources? Are your referring to personnel, equipment, money, or weapons?" The man inquired.

"You pick one, and I'll address it," Zanthius replied.

"Sir, we don't need any of those things. The various placements of the Carbon Factor across your vast country will require your government to think about consequences, and come to terms, with the request of our leaders. You may not know this, but a nuclear version of the Carbon Factor has been developed and is in play as we speak. It is our doomsday weapon that will seek out your missile silos, and create a self-destructive consequence, in each one. Sir, America, has already been invaded, corrupted, and led by members of our system."

# # #

A full recording of the interrogations was forwarded to Washington. Sergeant Beckmire gave his estimation of the timetable, but also indicated that he and his group had been summoned to a, to be announced location, on matters specifically related to the Carbon Factor. Beckmire emphatically stated, "Senator, you are the only person with this information. It is in your best interest to protect our movements and know that we are operating on your behalf. We have a contact that can leverage the actions of the Russians and create a stalemate situation."

"Sergeant Beckmire, I trust you and your people. I don't approve of your methods, but I must say, they are quite effective. I will find a way to get you an alternative device for communicating with me. Goodluck and God bless these United States of America."

## CHAPTER SEVEN

In Rome, the group's plane was towed into a hangar where Ben Hackney met them. The two Bens hugged and strolled away from the group where Ben Hackney cut through the chase, and said, "They have you guys by the balls. They have as many as fifty devices planted around your country. That New York, DC, and Los Angeles, noise, is just a ruse. They have their stuff placed in middle America around those missile silos, the net effect would be a wasteland once those things are detonated. Now, here's the kicker, the Holy Father, by the way, is excited that his new best friend is coming to see him, Beatrice that is, and has a more devastating plan that he needs your help in implementing in Russia and a few other places. You will never cross into Russia, but you and your people will be photo-bombed in key cities in Russia. There will be before and after pictures. The before pictures will be of you and your people carrying large bundles, and in the after pictures, you will be without them. In the meantime, the Holy Father's people will be planting his version of the Carbon Factor throughout key places in Russia, at two hundred or more sites. My problem with all of this Ben, is that I think the Holy Father, in what I'm considering is a show of strength, is willing to blow Russia off the fucking map!"

"Ben, that is some crazy shit. Would he do that?"

"Ben Beckmire, he is the Holy Father, and a different one at that. His reasoning is sometimes based upon the dark side of religion, and that leads me to believe that my friend, and leader, the Pope of the Catholic Church, will annihilate what is known as Russia, if within the next twenty days, they haven't retrieved every aspect of the Carbon Factor that was planted in America."

"Jesus, Ben, this sounds like the beginning of Armageddon and quite frankly, extremely diabolic! Shit, a poor ass Russia that wants to take over the world, an unstable ass president of the United States, and a Pope who disappears, and no one can figure out his whereabouts. This is as crazy as it gets," Beckmire stated.

"No, Ben, the crazy part is that you and a few of your people are going to head into Moscow or Paris, in twenty-four hours, and have a sit down with the Russian leadership. Now, this is even more crazy, for you Ben. After you finish your one-way discussion with the Russians, you, and your crew will take on fuel, and head for Hawaii. You will spend forty-eight hours there, and then you will board your plane and head to Beijing where you will have the same conversation with the Chinese."

"What's the purpose of that, Ben?"

"Ben, the Russians, and the Chinese have aligned, and both are involved in the placement of the Carbon Factor in America. Now, the Holy Father, has implemented a nuclearized version of the Carbon Factor for that part of the world, and is quietly determined to, if necessary, to rewrite the notion of world order."

"Ben, are you on some new kind of drug? What the hell is our real reason for being here?" Beckmire inquired.

"See there, I knew I had you going, but the Holy Father is going to express, personally, what he needs you and your people to do?"

#

At the Vatican, the Holy Father saw Ms. Beatrice, and rapidly moved to where she was. He got on his knees, kissed her hand, and said, "Oh, my little friend, it is so good to see you again. I enjoy our messaging, and I must admit it is with your inspiration that I'm able to enjoy life beyond that of the Holy Father. Thanks for giving one Ben a message from the other." He rose from his position and loudly exclaimed, "My spurious flock of varied persuasions, welcome to God's house. I had a meal prepared in honor of our Lord and Savior, Jesus Christ, for you weary travelers." He looked at Ben Beckmire, and then at Ben Hackney and asked, "Did you tell him what I need him to do?"

"Holy, Father, I did, however, he was reluctant to believe me, for he thinks your resolve, is somewhat, of a made-up story by me, and frankly feels it borders on ah, a path that clearly isn't Christian in nature."

"Well, I can assure him and you, my resolve is as demonic as those who would perpetrate or consider annihilating millions for the aggrandizement of a few. Yes, mi amigo, I, when in the devil's mindset, play with his tools. Come now, let's break bread before we get into descriptive details." He looked to his left, and saw Ms. Beatrice, and said, "Oh, Ms. Beatrice, I have a special seat for you if it's okay with your parents."

As the group was being served, a cardinal, hurriedly, approached the Holy Father, and whispered in his ear. He then, as quickly as he appeared, disappeared.

Five or so minutes later, the same cardinal scurried up to the Holy Father, and whispered a rather long message to him. The Holy Father threw down his napkin, apologized to the group, and headed to an office. He inadvertently bumped John Lee's chair and touched him on his shoulder. He apologized and continued on his way. Fifteen or so minutes later, he came out of the office, beckoned Ben Hackney, and Ben Beckmire to join him.

As Ben Beckmire and Ben Hackney joined the Holy Father, he swore, "I will bury both nations if they continue with this madness. My people are aware of the events that are happening at this very moment and are challenging me to make a public statement relative to man's ability to destroy man. Meanwhile, the 'fricken' timetable has been artificially established for exactly ten days from today. I had given us a tight window initially, with at least fifteen days for most rational individuals who are planning on taking over the world, to consider an alternative. How wrong was I, therefore, this negates your forty-eight-hour rest period in Hawaii. Oh, and by the way, they are using a little puppet in South America to assist in this matter. I have that one under control. People must realize that the Catholic Church has been around for a long time and has encountered all kinds of people interested in ruling the world. As such, and having realized how the world would be divided, the church conjured up doctrines to respond to mental midgets who want to rule it. In the service of our Lord, we have placed nefarious devices throughout the world, especially in those two countries. As the leader of this church, it is my responsibility to be willing, able, and committed to end aggression in the most profound manner known to modern man."

The holy father paused, smiled at Ben Beckmire, and aggressively stated, "As half-brother to Lucifer, as you have called me, Mr. Beckmire, I will commit to doing good even if I have to pledge to do dastardly acts of which no man has ever witnessed. As we approach their timetable for considering the beginning of Armageddon, we will use you and your people to thwart all possible actions. Your images will be displayed on cameras in and around both countries of interest, of course on varied days entering facilities with boxes, and exiting without packages. In addition to your photographs and DNA, Mr. Beckmire, thousands of other non-descript individuals will be seen all over those countries entering facilities with boxes and exiting without. This will lead those in charge to expeditiously attempt to track your movements, as well as the others, and attempt to recover the packages. Mr. Beckmire, please forgive me, but when you and your people stopped in Japan, to acquire the formula to the Carbon Factor, we took the opportunity to super-impose your images on people inside of China."

"Holy Father, are you telling me that we're the sacrificial lambs, in this feast?"

"Yes! Indeed, you are, my son! Ben Hackney has thrilled me with stories of your group against insurmountable odds. He told me how your cousin had you cornered in middle America, and you people were able to escape into a tunnel and live to fight another day. He also told me how you people modernized the farm, and the ranch to include computer-controlled-firing capabilities. Mr. Beckmire, the entire world trembles at the sound of your name. That person in South America has an entire army guarding him after it was told that he was on your hit list. That oligarch in the country near here is guarded by a newly created secret police service, and that guy in the far east, well, he has set up his office and home on a nuclear weapons development base. You people are the bomb!"

"Holy Father, I don't understand what one thing has to do with the other. The world is out of balance, and you, supposedly a voice of peace, love, unity, and coexistence, are playing a dangerous game with 'nuts' who want to blow America to hell. This is not a game! These people are committed to detonate the Carbon Factor in America."

"Son, as the Holy Father, I am prepared to decimate any country that unilaterally attempts to overthrow another by using a cheap and dirty bomb, for the purpose of expansionism. This will not and cannot happen under my watch! Therefore, I am willing to go down in history as the most villainous Holy Father that has ever existed. Those who have the Carbon Factor, truly don't know my reach and resolve."

# # #

Approximately, twelve hours later, Beckmire and his main team watched as their super-imposed images were broadcast live on Russian TV. They were amazed at the technology that allowed complete images to be manufactured, positioned, and disseminated in various cities across Russia, including Moscow, St. Petersburg, Kazan, Samara, Chelyabinsk, and others. Two-day old footage showed the Fab 10 + 2 entering strategic sites in Moscow on random camera systems. The systems crashed for three minutes, and that created concern for the actions of the foreigners. Those same images were projected in other cities, as well. The images were so real, that it captured Beckmire, winking at one of the cameras.

The Holy Father said, "Images of you and your group were broadcasted across China, ten days ago, using a combination of, Darryl, I believe is his name and his newly created Fab 10 + 2. Mr. Beckmire, Ben Hackney has been a consort to the Vatican for many years, and we're praying for his recovery. Ben was recently diagnosed with cancer, and people want to move him into hospice. I keep telling Ben that his work is not done yet, and as a matter of fact, on your return trip to Australia, before you visit those in charge in China, and give them a road map of where one hundred nuclearized Carbon Factor products are placed, you will escort him to your forefather's land, where a new special friend of mine, Wajickee, will ease all that burdens him. Yes, Mr. Beckmire, Wajickee, through my little friend Ms. Beatrice, has been communicating with me for some time. Our perfect medium, one who is innocent and godly, Ms. Beatrice that is, holds that royal place. She is many times her age in knowledge and world events, and advises us by using simple mannerisms, to stimulate deeper thinking by me in the real world, and that ghost of a friend of yours who has walked the earth for centuries. He dare not make you aware of the fact that he was working with me, because you would have doubts, and it is now that you must be clear of mind, my friend. After you complete that mission in China, you will take a vacation, and show my friend, Ben Hackney, what the other part of the world is like. I know you probably think I'm the real devil, but believe me, and trust me when I say this, since meeting you and your people, and that darling little Ms. Beatrice, I have formulated a hands-on-policy. The history of the church was to never overtly, and directly interfere, but attempt to finds ways to mediate through public mediums when the world needed saving from itself. Listen, my son, you will do this, because it is the church that continues to provide a veil over you and yours through prayer, and deific intermediation. We are never far from those things that seem to happen to your group. You will go with you Ben Hackney on this adventure, and I assure you, none of us will live forever, but you will live, my son, free from anxiety and pain."

"Holy Father, have you considered how you will thwart the Russian and Chinese, participation in this matter?"

"Oh, yes, my son! I neglected to tell you, that you, Darryl, Asiram, John Lee, and Jilkes will commandeer a helicopter, and fly near the Disneyland Paris Resort, in the city of Paris, Ile-de-France. There on one of those cowboy rides, you will meet several high-ranking Russian foreign ministers, I will give you pictures of them. I will provide you with a package to present to them, and you will give them your SAT phone number, and indicate that they have a total of twelve hours to begin securing the one hundred packages placed in America, or three hundred devices will go active in twelve hours and ten minutes later in Mother Russia unless they have their people completely remove the products distributed across America. He will attempt to hedge his bet, by indicating that he has no knowledge of what in the world you're talking about. You will respond by saying, neither does the three hundred, ground immersing devices, that tunnel deep down, and hone-in on active signals, and detonate things in their homes, thus rendering the land useless, for thousands of years. Really, the time period is forever. I'm sure, he'll look at you funny, and say some nonsense like, "you and your people are those old people from Vietnam. I suggest that you retire because this game is bigger than you old guys." The Holy Father paused for a moment and said, "That is when you will say, "I know, but tell those three hundred devices planted, strategically, in your country, that bull-crap." At that point you will get up, and say, "the clock begins in twenty-four hours. After that, you'll be on your own." You will also tell them about the other problem that you have, a habit of losing your phone. Also, stridently state that their entire country had better pray that you don't get forgetful. Suggest to them that they know how old people forget things. You, Mr. Beckmire will say no more, other than repeat the twenty-four hour start time, and the twelve-hour and ten-minute, end time. If there is no movement by the Russians, then God have mercy on all of us. Your scenario with the Chinese is the same, other than there, my people placed, I believe, a total of five-hundred devices."

"Why so many there, and I thought it was two hundred devices in Russia?"

"Racist members of the church argued for a stronger show of strength and resolve with those people in Asia. Mr. Beckmire, the Carbon Factor is nothing new. We have scrolls that are hundreds of years old, showing how to capture carbon, expose it to hydrogen, and from there, watch the multiplying effect of what happens when an unlimited source of hydrogen is introduced. What happens periodically, some brilliant scientist or chemist, plays around with the Periodic table, and discovers how to make another horrifying way for man to eliminate man."

"Holy Father, first, I'm in awe of being in your presence, and second it requires me to hold my tongue, whether I agree or disagree with you. Having said that, I'm not comfortable with you making personnel assignments on my behalf. I don't agree with your politics, and détente. I say, we snatch those people you identify, and we use a little, ah, 'knuckle therapy' on them."

"Mr. Beckmire, what is this thing called, knuckle therapy?"

"Holy Father, let's just say, it's our way of persuading reluctant people to accept their condition, environment, and realize that it can only get worse from that point."

"You mean you're going to torture them?"

"Sometimes, we don't have to do anything other than suggest that John Lee or Asiram will gut them from their private areas to their brains and have a bite out of their hearts before they die."

"Mr. Beckmire, that's not possible or probable."

"Holy Father, it is both possible, probable, and it has been done by a member of my group."

The Holy Father proclaimed, "That John Lee! He is a most enigmatic character, but he is contained by Jilkes. I find his entire demeanor confusing and exciting. He sounds like he is from another era, but he has the uncanny ability to turn a square into circle in terms of knowing what to do."

"Holy Father, how do you know so much about my personnel?"

"Son, prior to your getting involved in this spy mess, I was fascinated by your reported war feats. I have been watching you, as well as watching over you, for many years. I don't condone killing, but you people were placed in a war like environment where you had to kill or be killed. I must admit, the entire Zanthius thing, escaped me and my people, and we have since put a new person in charge of that division. Also, your friend, and mine, Ben Hackney, tells me stories all the time, and I realize, some may be contrived, about you and your people. I am confessing to you that I have a dark side to me, and your exploits helps me acknowledge it, but I make sure that I do the best that I can do, as the Holy Father. I know, it's an extreme juxtaposition, but I suffer every single day with the knowledge that I can be both sanctified and malevolent. When you inquired if I were the half-brother of Lucifer, things began to happen to me, as my mind raced to and from dynamic situations and relationships. The dynamic situation is with you and your band, Mr. Beckmire, a group of people who have slaughtered a boatload of people. The relationship aspect of this entire matter, rests on my ability to believe in you and yours yet destroy the world in the end. Mr. Beckmire, I am both, his brother and he, all in one."

The mood changed and the Holy Father began to weep. As he prayed for deliverance, he also confessed that the child, named Beatrice, would be a game changer for them in the future. He told Ben Beckmire and Ben Hackney that she, in simple childlike terms, acknowledged the death dealing group that they are. She once wrote me and said, "people are always trying to hurt us. In the mid-west, bad men placed jackets on the children that were like firecrackers. Everywhere we go, guns are always around. I heard the Sarge tell the adults, we will burn in hell before we let anyone ever place those things on our children, again. My mom loves me so much, as does granny, and my new dad. He is the best because he always asks me to make a choice. He says, life is about choices, and people make good ones and bad ones. He always ends, with, I want my little flower to make those choices that may be good or bad but leads her to a higher understanding. I always ask him what that means, but he says in time all will be clear."

"Gentlemen, I am weary, and I need your support and guidance. Your presence will confuse those who do not know you're in Rome and will further confuse those people in the east who think you're somewhere else as well. Mr. Beckmire, my disclosure of who I may potentially be, is a cross between having someone in your sights with a weapon, and pulling the trigger, a thing you are well familiar with."

"Holy Father, again, I must ask questions before I commit my group to becoming the puppets of another lord and master, whose agenda is way above our pay grade. You are the head of this church, and you're attempting to orchestrate an alignment with a group of people who kill people, agreed that in most cases, deservingly. I'm going to cut right to the chase, why the heck us?"

"Hell, son, I haven't found anyone who delivers a message better than your group. Oh, and by the way, if you're going to kill someone, kill them, and don't leave them maimed like your great, great, great, great grandparent did. I know the entire story, Mr. Beckmire. Your cousin, Walter E. Lassiter, is the bionic man, who lives with one last request, and that is to kill everyone, and everything related to Ben Beckmire."

"Holy Father, death is a matter of degrees. I recognize his work, and that is why he's the last person I will kill before I go straight to hell!"

"Son, that is exactly where you and your followers will go. I will pray hard for the children, but as for the adults, hell, oh yes, hell is where you will all go. And when you get there, I will welcome you, and present you with medals for hopefully, saving the world. Please, enjoy the food, you will be transported to a secure location and your plane will head to Asia. One last thing, you all will die, as will I, but some will be horrific, just be mindful of that fact, my son."

"Again, Holy Father, I must bite my tongue, for what I want to say would be considered highly disrespectful."

The Holy Father looked at Ben Beckmire, and said, "You were going to say some shit like, "You're just a man anointed by other men, without any direct contact or connection to heaven. Am I correct?"

"In a manner of speaking, yes. My language would have been a bit more caustic. I'm a believer, but I also kill people, and have desecrated every conceivable commandment. My salvation is that me and my people are saints in the eyes of some, and that gives us a righteous platform to speak from. You, on the other hand, are condemned from the start because of your flock, their proclivities to like the altar boys, and each other, a bit too much. We all have our dragons and demons, Holy Father, but yours are more pronounced, and public. They surround you like servants waiting for the exact moment to drop poison in your drink or create an unforgiveable scandal. Me and mine, well, we are the scandal, and we play it well. Holy Father, if we survive this ordeal, I want you to perform a mass for me and my people, and in an earthly fashion, provide us with absolution. Holy Father, we all sin, and the substance of our sins is a self-developed definition, that allows us to move from one day to another, with a smile, knowing full well, we have committed major sins, and continue to do so."

"My son, things will move from moderate to nuclear when it reaches stage four. You will perform an immaculate reception, much like my football hero, Franco Harris. Go in peace, my son. We must pray for each other." He looked at Ben Hackney, and asked, "Do you feel adventuresome? I need you to accompany Ben Beckmire, head to Australia, and after he finishes that business with the Russians in Paris, sit in the waters of one of the many billabongs, and either be eaten by a big croc or saved by the Great Saltie."

"Holy Father, one Ben messing up things is enough for the world!" Ben Hackney stated.

"Okay, I want to spend prayer time with Ms. Beatrice, and then you guys can go on your merry way. Ben Beckmire talk to her sometime, and you will find your burden lessened by the small words uttered by her. I may be mortal, but I have heard the Lord, speak through that child. Mr. Beckmire, after you've had time to reflect on our conversation, I'd like to know what you really think. Right now, you're wondering if I'm the real Holy Father, based upon my diabolical thoughts and responses to the matter that ails us at this present moment. I will do what the church has installed me to do as one of my functions, and that is to bring civility back into the world or destroy those countries that have another agenda that is not in the best interest of a Christian community. I love my Lord and God, and I will not watch the world go to hell in a handbasket! I might send a communique to both leaders and see how they react.

CHAPTER EIGHT

After convincing the Russians that their plan was as dead as dead can be, the group headed for Asia. The pilots decided to take on fuel in California before making the long trek to Hawaii. Captain Carla came out of the cockpit, smiled at Mike, and hurried into the restroom. Everyone could hear her barfing. Mike unbuckled his seat belt, asked Ms. Viola if she would watch his child, and rushed to the restroom. When Carla finally opened the door, she said, "Damn boy, I think I'm pregnant again!"

Mike escorted her back to his seat where Ms. Viola touched her stomach, and said, "Praise be to God! You be pregnant again girl, but this time, you had better make room for more than one."

Courtney and Monica, with Ava following behind, left their seats, and went back to make sure that Carla was okay. Ms. Viola said, "Ain't nothing you people can do now, this child is pure and pregnant. Halleluiah!"

Courtney gave her a quick exam and didn't notice any signs of a fever or any other illness that would cause a person to throw up so violently. Monica asked, "So, Ms. Viola, what makes you think she's pregnant and that she's not throwing up from eating something bad?"

"Girl look at her. Didn't you hear how she be barfing in the restroom? Anyways, that's the sound of a baby being formulated. I know that sound anywhere."

Monica shook her head, and proclaimed, "Hogwash!"

The back of the plane became quiet, and Courtney said, "Monica, that's a little harsh, don't you think? After all, Ms. Viola has been on the money on several things. Why are you being so publicly rude? Even if she's wrong, that's not how we act in this village."

Monica looked at Courtney, then at Ms. Viola, and broke into hysterics. Mallory left his seat, and asked, "What the heck is going on?"

Ms. Viola said, "Your wife is unhappy because she never felt the anxiousness of pregnancy and childbirth. Don't worry, she and I will have a long talk, and we'll make this thing that bothers her, something of the past."

Mallory escorted Monica and Courtney back to their seats, and her son asked, "Mom, you, okay?"

She mumbled her words, and said, "I am dear, I'm just a little weary of this flying. Mommy will be okay."

# # #

The group's plane landed in Honolulu where the group decided that they wanted to pay homage to those sailors and marines who were trapped on the Battleship Arizona when the Japanese attacked Pearl Harbor. The group was smuggled out of the hangar into vans by members of the Catholic Church. Ben Hackney orchestrated the cloak and dagger arrival, as well as the group appearing to be separate at the historic and final resting place of the Arizona. Monica explained to her children that over eleven hundred people are encased in that ship that is resting beneath where they are standing. The kids were curious as to why the Japanese people would kill all those soldiers. Monica knew it was going to be a long day and decided to defer the question-and-answer period to her capable husband.

# # #

Jong on the other hand, felt that bad karma was in play, this being a place where a relative was killed, unknowingly, by a family member. Yes, Jong had a family member that was a bomber for the group that descended on Pearl Harbor, he also had a family member that was serving as a medical assistant in the hospital on Pearl Harbor.

After an hour and one half at the site, and in the memorial hall, the group was reconstituted, and ushered back to a gated hotel on the outskirts of a military base. Ben Beckmire said to Ben Hackney, "You're not looking too good Brother. What can I do to ease your pain? How about I have Courtney look at you, and perhaps prescribe a mild sedative?"

"Ben, you send that fine lady to care for me, and you might be looking for a new wife."

"You're funny, my brother. Seriously, let me have her look at you. She is more than a pretty picture, she is a helluva doctor. By the way, me and my people are feeling naked. Any way to get some clean clothes?"

"When you enter your room, you will find a package that will make all of the adults comfortable." Ben Hackney looked at his phone that was beeping, and yelled, "The Chinese want to meet in an hour. They must have watched the film of you people, and others entering strategic places with packages, and leaving without them. Shit, do you think Courtney can give me a booster shot or something to give me the energy to handle a stressful meeting with the Chinese?"

"Ben, I'm sure she'll do whatever we need her to do. If you're not feeling well, perhaps we should postpone the meeting."

"Ben Beckmire, no matter how I feel, you must handle the meeting. You know what you must do."

Ben Beckmire looked at Ben Hackney, and wondered how his relatives would handle this situation. He came up with one conclusion! They would simply say, "get your shit out of my country, or in excess of five hundred ordinances will begin the systematic annihilation of your country. You and the Russians have an uncertain timetable to make this happen. As a matter of fact, your timetable is half that of what was presented to us."

Ben Hackney said, "Earth to Ben Beckmire!"

"Sorry, Ben. I went on a trip with my relatives, and they gave me the information that I needed to handle this part of the equation. My only problem is whether or not to trust the Holy Father!"

"Do you remember the first time we met? Anyway, we met when you and Elton Jolly came to meet with the Chief of Naval Operations. He gave you guys the fluff, invited you on that aircraft carrier, and gave you a ride on a submarine, but he didn't answer the moving forward question such as how to develop a partnership, and move more minorities into that elite branch of the military. You and I were young guys, but I was a spy assigned to the Vatican. Do you remember when I saw you in St. Peters Square, and got you access to the inner most secrets of the Vatican, I knew then that our paths would cross again. And they did, in that bar when you beat the shit out of half the people in it. Anyway, my brother, from that point forward, I said to myself, "whatever he needs, I'll have his back." Insofar as trusting the Holy Father, you heard exactly what I heard. I mean he damn sure didn't sound like the head of the Catholic Church. No, sir! He sounded like the head of a death squad, and I believe that he will do exactly as he stated, set off horrific devices in both countries, and then go and have a brandy, and smoke a cigar. I'm not sure if trust is the correct word, but I am more suspicious of him now, more than ever. He is a matter-of-fact kind of guy, and the fact of the matter is that he'll order his minions to create a smaller world."

"Damn, this has become a desperate situation, and I have to interpret the mindset of the head of the Catholic Church. Ben, chill out for a minute, let me find Courtney, and have her give you a shot, and then we'll focus on the meeting," the Sarge said.

"Just to piss them off, I would have Jong, John Lee, and Jilkes attend with us," Ben Hackney stated.

"Why Jong?" The Sarge asked.

"I think you're in for a helluva history lesson my friend," Hackney announced.

# # #

Conveniently, and in the same hotel, members of the Chinese delegation were sitting in the lobby. Ben Hackney knew who they were and decided that they should enter a van to have the discussion to avoid prying cars.

Once the group was settled in the swiveling chairs facing each other, the interpreter said, "Cutting through the bullshit, how many devices are there in our country."

Ben Hackney looked at Ben Beckmire and nodded. Ben Beckmire said, "Cutting through the bullshit, how many have you placed in America?"

The interpreter began to belittle Ben Beckmire until Jong, said, "Sarge, that little motherfucker called you the gay guy with big muscles, and a tiny dick."

The Sarge smiled, and said, "If this meeting is about dicks, then you call me after one of the one thousand units has been detonated." He rose from his seat, and the interpreter reached out, and grabbed his arm. The Sarge instinctively placed a hold on the man's hand that he will never forget. The Sarge then said, "Never touch a gay guy with big muscles, and a tiny dick!"

From the least likely person to be the leader of the group, a man of small stature said, "Sergeant Beckmire, that comment was designed to throw you off guard. I am called Waun, and these are my associates. Please, have a seat."

After the Sarge sat down, Waun said, "Ben Hackney, is it possible that I can meet with you, and Sergeant Beckmire, without all of this calvary?"

Ben H looked at Ben B, and they agreed. Waun asked his people to leave the vehicle. He then pulled out a device that would allow their conversations to be cryptic. Ben Hackney pulled out a device that would scramble signals attempting to enter or leave the van. The three men laughed, and Ben Hackney said, "These are troubling times, and several countries are on the brink of total extinction."

Waun replied, "My leader has engaged in bad joist with an enemy/friend that can't be trusted. I am here for the sole purpose of trying to enter détente. We received a message that indicated that there would be a small demonstration of a device that has been installed in a strategic place in my country. My question is simple, how can so few be in so many different places at the same time?"

Ben Beckmire smiled at him, and said, "I have a few questions that might answer yours. How many dialects are spoken in your country? How many religions, or varied beliefs are worshiped? Before you answer, I'll give you an idea. There is an institution that has followers in every part of the world. That institution has placed in excess of one thousand devices throughout your country. The devices are designed to methodically render your entire country, human less!"

Waun looked at Ben Beckmire, and said, "That's a lot of responsibility!"

"Not for the person who oversees the placement of the devices. I'm not sure if he is Lucifer, or an agent of the Lord, but from my last conversation with him, he's going to give you a little demonstration if I read the meaning of his comments correctly."

Waun looked away, then back at Beckmire, then back into space, and finally asked, "What will be the loss factor?"

Ben Beckmire said, "I'm hoping it's not person based yet, and that the demonstration is restricted to uninhabited land, of which you have many."

Waun asked, "Would your benefactor do such a thing?"

Ben Beckmire said, "Waun, my benefactor frightens me more than any enemy I have ever faced."

"Ben Hackney, you know the person, what's your take?" Waun inquired.

"Waun, I thought I knew the person. The conversation Ben and I had with him makes me wonder. If I were a betting man I would say, he's going to do a one way out, and then multiply the effects and impacts until the five-hundred nuclearized devices kick in."

"What are you talking about nuclearized!"

"The shit you placed in America, well, let's just say, it's a joke. The shit he apparently placed throughout your country, is the real shit. He's not going to hold a fucking news conference before he begins this thing. You and the Russians picked the wrong time, and the wrong fucking prince of peace, to fuck with," Ben Hackney responded.

There was a long silence after which, Waun asked, "When might this begin?"

Ben Beckmire replied, "I think your question should be, when might this end!"

Waun was about to respond when there was a hard bang on the side of the van. Ben Hackney opened the door, a Chinese delegate entered, and announced quietly to Waun that there had been a detonation in an outlying area. His demeanor changed, and prior to the delegate leaving the van, Waun, in a strident manner, yelled, "It's begun! There was a detonation in a small area that has no residents. Cutting once again to the chase, China will extract any devices that it may control from your soil."

Ben Beckmire said, "Your fate is connected to your new partners. You can't quit in the middle of a mutually developed scheme, and request absolution. You must convince your partners that the tide ebbs and flows in all directions. I assume they received the same kind of email from the diabolical prince. Anyone else, I might have reservations about. This one, well, will see his mission through. This one is not to be fucked with! Insofar as I'm concerned, you know the importance of reaching a lifesaving decision by removing all devices from all American territories. If a single device is discovered, Armageddon will be the response. In addition, you will present them for an accounting aboard the vessel that brought them to America."

# # #

Way out in the hinder lands in Russia, a small but noticeable detonation occurred, and got everyone's attention. There was a challenge to the detonation, and a defiance of the light-hearted explosion. The atmosphere changed significantly when the Russians were informed by the Chinese, that the idea, and implementation of nuclearized devices had been put in play and secured throughout the Russian interior.

The Russians were adamant that the person controlling the detonations was incapable of moving beyond this small, but noticeable announcement of his intent.

When the Russian delegation that met Ben Hackney and Ben Beckmire in Paris, made their report to the high command, they realized the urgency of what was happening, and exaggerated the number of devices alleged to be placed, throughout the country. A top general asked, "How could they have installed that many devices in our country without being detected. It's those same old men from Vietnam, no way on earth they could have penetrated our security, and more importantly, place nuclearized materials."

As he pondered a response, he said "I'm not Catholic, and I don't believe in all that mess they try to teach, between groping each other, and innocent children. I say we send him a lasting message!"

# # #

In Moscow, enough radon gases was emitted to trigger an alarm. Alarms began to go off all over the country, recording low levels of radioactive material. In each large city, Geiger Counter type devices began to acknowledge the presence of radiation. Conversations between the Chinese and Russians indicated that each country was experiencing the same results of minimum radiation emissions.

Waun said to his counterpart in Russia, Sassa, "We are in the process of deactivating our devices in that country, and we have begun to extract them. I suggest that you do the same because the small detonation in your southern area was a wake-up call, and now the emission of radioactive materials will be followed by normal Carbon Factor materials, and then you will face the nuclearized versions that are apparently near missile silos in your country and mine. I know we both thought he was a weak person, but after having an insightful conversation with Ben H and Ben B, I'm convinced we have awakened a madman who will not hesitate to send our countries into a deep freeze, therefore, that plan is dead from our perspective. Our task now, is to try to remove all of the devices he and his predecessors, have installed in my country for decades. More important to my government, is to figure out, how so few could have pulled this scheme off. I say, they couldn't, and my country is full of people who are loyal to another kind of God. From the locations of the emissions, these areas could not have been infiltrated by foreigners; no, this activity took place long before you and I were born. In my conversation with both Bens, it was a slip or a direct line of information, that the Carbon Factor has been in the hands of that institution for centuries, and they hedged their bets against growing governments and economies that were led by the few."

Sassa replied, "Then are you suggesting that India and Pakistan are victims of the same issue?"

"Sassa, I could give a shit about them. My concern is that we wanted to bury the red, white, and the blue, and another flag has risen to put us in check or deep freeze. They have their own issues, mine, for now, is to protect and secure my country at any cost!" Waun acknowledged.

"Waun, what is the timetable?"

"Sassa, did your people talk to Ben H and Ben B? If so, they should have an idea of when things get messy. From my conversation with the two, as well as an interpretation of what was being said, I felt that no action by us would be met with a reaction, and each reaction grows proportionately larger than the last. We have had a small detonation, and the release of insignificant amounts of radioactive materials. Do you need a road map, my friend?"

"I see your point, and I must discuss this with the high command," Sassa replied.

"Sassa, you're playing with a madman with worldwide access. The time for discussion has ended. It is time for action, and so far, the madman is ratcheting up each response. It was a wonderful idea. We failed to think about alliances, and the red, white, and blue, has an unknown one with the power to conclude millions of lives. We concede, we are off the grid once our devices have been accounted for."

# # #

Twelve hours later, the Russian hierarchy was still trying to implement its plan as opposed to retrieving and accounting for the devices that were installed in various US cities. Thirteen hours later, a significant detonation was conducted near Siberia, that got everybody's attention. It was as though Mother Russia stood still and reflected on the future of its society.

Sassa placed a call to Waun, and said, "We just had a massive detonation near Siberia."

"I know my friend. You must act now, or the next one will be in a populated area. He is mad, and I thought about an assassination, but his reach is too far. If he is hurt, his followers will release Armageddon!"

"Waun, how do we concede?"

"Start extracting your devices, truck them to the same port where you will find my vessels being loaded. Do not play with Lucifer, dressed in a holy outfit, for he is truly a combination of all that is good and evil, and he exists between heaven and hell!"

## CHAPTER NINE

Courtney said to her husband, "Your friend does not look well at all. Honey, I would be surprised, if he lasts the trip."

"What, is he that sick?"

"Ben, he is beyond being sick. He should be in hospice."

Beckmire made his way back to Ben Hackney and saw that he looked bad. He nudged him, awakening him, and asked, "Are you going to make it to Australia? You're not looking good at all man."

Ben Hackney tried to regain his faculties, and replied, "Don't worry about me friend, I'm not going to put any bad joist on this plane. By the way, it's spectacular. I was thinking a few minutes back, I can't think of a better place to die, than in the outback, with a person who has remained my friend over the years."

"Ben, you're not coming here to die. I hope the calmness, the water, the natural spirits, and people, will have a healing effect upon you. We're about three hours out, hang in there my friend."

Approximately, three hours later, Ben Beckmire walked to the back of the plane to rouse Ben Hackney. As he approached him, he said, "Dude, it's time to get ready to leave this plane, and enjoy the benefits of the outback." Ben Hackney did not move, and when Ben Beckmire touched him, he felt the coldness that consumed his friend. Ben Hackney, died on his way to the outback, a place where souls, spirits, and the Great Saltie lived.

The first thing Ben Beckmire did when alighting from the plane, was to call the Holy Father, and tell him that his friend and confidant had moved on to another world. The Holy Father thanked him and wished him well on his journey. He said, "My son, a lot of what Ben did for the church can be done by you and your people. I thank you, and the world probably, unknowingly, should thank you and your people as well. For had it not been for your interactions with key opponents, things might have been a lot different when we woke up the next morning. Thank you, my son, and please give my brother a proper send off."

A celebration of life was held for Ben Hackney, and of course, Ben Beckmire would be the grandmaster of spinning great tales of a righteous and loving human being. Beckmire spoke of his association with Hackney, how as a result of knowing him, and being in St. Peters Square at the same time, and after hearing his name called, he once again ran into his buddy. As a result of his association with Ben Hackney, he had a chance to see places in the Vatican that are off limits to most. Yes, Ben Hackney was a wonderful human being whose knowledge and understanding of how the world should work, will be greatly missed by Holy Fathers and the world.

#

Two days later, the group took a tour of the diamond and gold mines, respectively, and were impressed by the security, the daily extraction amounts, accounting, transportation, and the investment strategies. On the other side of the equation, buildings to house schools, health care clinics, hospitals, a branch of a major university, food, and department stores, were being constructed and all managed by local Aborigines.

In nine specific areas of the outback, a similar plan was being implemented in other Aborigine villages. The classic natural coloring of the Aborigine diamonds was a worldwide hit, and sales were on track to surpass South African diamonds. All in all, the outback began to look like a place where natives could enjoy the benefits from the various mines, maintain their culture and beliefs, and become a part of the 'haves, and not the have nots' because they had credit cards, checking accounts, debit cards, savings accounts, and a little bitcoin.'

#

The Russians attempted to leave three strategically placed devices in three major US cities. Less than thirty miles from a populated major city in Russia, a device of epic proportions, exploded. It shattered windows and caused widespread panic.

In America, the Chinese extracted the devices they installed in various cities around America. The Russians, however, tried to negotiate. A secure call was placed to Ben Beckmire. Sassa, said, "Sergeant Beckmire, I want to be frank and honest. I'm not admitting that we have devices planted in your country, but let's just say, for argument sake, why would

I remove the devices we have in your country without you not removing supposedly a number of devices from my country?"

"That is a great question, and one that I will take up with those in charge. However, Sassa, if you didn't remove the entire lot of your devices, from what I'm guessing, a detonation will occur near a very populated city. The question you should be asking is whether that is the kind of thing you want to experience. I'm sure the person in charge is doing a thorough accounting, and if there is a discrepancy, a detonation will occur for each un-accounted device, and after the fourth, a nuclear device will be exploded. Your choice my friend, but there will not be a discussion, just a reaction."

As Sassa was about to ask Ben another question, he was interrupted by an associate who gave him the news that a huge blast had occurred outside of a major city in Russia. His head slumped between his legs, and he said to the Sarge, "We may have missed extracting a few devices from your soil. Please, communicate to those in charge, our humble misgivings, and give us forty-eight hours to remove them."

"Sassa, your tone sounds desperate, my friend. Did something happen?"

"There was an explosion near a heavily populated city."

"Were there any fatalities?"

"I'm not sure. I will let you know. At this time, I must break protocol, and acknowledge that there may have been as many as three to four devices un-accounted for."

"Is it three, or is it four?" The Sarge asked.

"I believe it's more like five," Sassa replied.

"Sassa, you, and your countrymen keep playing with a charlatan who will deal you four kings, and then throw out a royal flush. His next move will be devastating."

"Can you give me forty-eight hours to remove the remaining devices?"

You have twenty-four, and then it's out of my hands. Why would you play poker with the devil, and let him deal the cards? You, my friend, will suffer more after each dumb move you make. I will call him, but if he's in hell, then you can kiss your ass goodbye. If he is in a heavenly mood, perhaps he'll delay another detonation. When we first met, I told you that I didn't know who this person is, and that in so many words, I couldn't understand how he became Pope. He will destroy your country if you don't act swiftly."

"Please call him and tell him about our oversight and plead for understanding."

"Sassa, why would I plead with him on your behalf? I gave you and your counterparts, fair warning about the nature of the person you were dealing with. Your arrogance may just have cost you a significant part of your country."

"Sergeant, with humility, I am asking you to at least inquire, for the sake of many Russian citizens who don't have a clue as to what we were trying to do.

Beckmire thought about what was said, and decided to attempt to bribe Sassa into going on record and admitting the atrocities that the Russian government was planning to commit. Beckmire said, "There have been several detonations of devices in your country. The next one will be in a populated city, and the fourth, will be nuclearized. The only way I can assist you, after the fact, is by you admitting publicly, exactly what your government's intent was, in placing those devices throughout America. If you do that then I will make the call. If you do not, then, I'll see you in hell, my friend!"

Ben Beckmire hung up the phone, and was approached by Mallory who stated, "That was intense! Who were you talking to?"

"I was talking to a group of non-believers, the Russians. They left as many as five devices in the states, and somehow, our benefactor is aware of them, and set off a device near a populated city in the hinterlands. From what I discerned from our benefactor, the next device will be exploded in a populated city, and the fourth device, will be nuclearized."

"How can you be sure of that? That's some potent shit. Who would utilize nuclear materials in this day and age?"

The Sarge looked at Mallory, half-assed smiled, and said, "The Holy Father. He will obliterate Russia without thinking twice."

"Sarge, come now, he is the Pope. His symbol is peace and unity. He wouldn't and couldn't do that. I mean, he's not a nuclear power, nor has he the resources of an army."

"My friend, he is both an army, and a formidable nuclear power.

# # #

An hour later, Sassa called Ben Beckmire, and announced, "My government will never admit to placing destructive devices in and around your country. However, we will admit to collaborating with another government, in what we termed as an experiment to destabilize American democracy. That's the best we can do."

Ben Beckmire said, "Listen, I'm in Australia, and I am going to cut the news on right now. After I tell the Holy Father your response, I'm sure he's going to skip number three, and go directly to number four. Your government may attempt to preemptively strike the Vatican, but the trigger is far, far away. All you would have done is create a world army comprised of the faithful, including those in your own country."

"Sergeant, I thank you, but that is the response of my government." He hung up the phone. Beckmire cogitated for a few minutes, and realized that a statement wasn't necessary, because the world is a better place, if in fact, people aren't aware of the shenanigans of their leaders.

As he started to walk towards the billabong, the phone rang again, and Sassa said, "Sergeant, I will sign such words in public. The leader of the Russian government committed suicide, ten minutes ago. Also, those involved in this mindless and dangerous venture to overthrow a sitting puppet president are being arrested. I can't go back home, and I will probably be on the run for the balance of my life. My family is not responding and, therefore, I'm sure this rebellion is in full swing. I will broadcast that message from a secure location, and then I will attempt to disappear. Goodbye, Sergeant."

In Rome, the Holy Father celebrated mass in St. Peters square. A would-be assassin attempted to eliminate him. He was encased in a bulletproof enclosure that would be his motif moving forward as the Holy Father.

Later in the day, he placed a call to Ben Beckmire, and asked, "Did you give our friend a king like sendoff?"

"Yes, I did, Holy Father. He was sent off as if he were a tribal leader, and accordingly, he was given a royal valediction."

"You're in a part of the world that needs intervention, on my behalf. I need you and your entire group to take a trip to South Korea and spend two days in Seoul. I have a wonderful friend there who could pass strategic information on to the little fat guy who thinks he's in control of the area to the North. I want you, through my friend, to invite him to a place where he has neglected his people, and the land. There, in front of the world, I want to show how he has gotten fat, and his people are starving. He eats like the pig he is, and his people are, famished. In his country, the Holy Fathers of long ago, never thought that he, his father, and grandfather, would amount to anything greater than local tyrants. Today, he tests missiles, barters, and trades with the Iranians, has a boyfriend in the likes of the US President, and is looking for an entry to the world stage. The hermit state should remain as it is. His missiles are toys, and his production of so-called nuclear materials is as erroneous as his ability to feed his people. Once he or his emissaries agree to a, to be announced site, he will retrench into his hole, and he will never be heard from again. His own people will violate the very essence of his body. My predecessors were more forward thinking than I am. His country was placed on a watch list and, therefore, actions or placement of materials were not initially implemented. However, after the Korean War, the church reconsidered its decrees, and decided to place horrific devices in the North and South. My son, you and your people will only have to appear near the demilitarized zone, and from there, my technicians will do the rest."

The Holy Father paused and consumed some type of liquid, and said, "I promise you, I will pray for you and your group as you move towards your twilight moments. After all, you guys are older than me, but I'm not sure who is the most battle hardened, between the two of us. On my side, I could obliterate entire peoples and countries. On your side, well, let's just say, you can do the work that keeps me and my half-brother from destroying the entire world. After you do that little public relations stent for me, I will make a few things go away for you, and finally, give you your cousin, who you should have terminated, rather than decapitated. Bionics are the wave of the future. Never injure a foe! Kill him so violently that the penalty is so horrific, no one will challenge you. When you and your people make your way back this way, I would like you to pay me a visit. I think there is some good we can do together. Will you consider it?"

"Yes, Holy Father, I will make it happen."

"Go with God, my son, and I will see you in a month or so. Nothing urgent, just an idea to keep the world safe from events of yesterday, as well as keep tyrants in check, and make them responsible for their actions. The church will enshrine your people if you do the thing in Korea. We already have your group placing devices throughout his country. He will get the message and rethink his strategy. Oh, one last thing, I know I said that I had that guy in South America under control, well, my resolve was more dramatic than the event called for. I'm trying to implement, a more, ah, human approach, to these issues. I want you to personally visit him while he sleeps. I will set the day, and the time. These are the words I want you to repeat to him, my son,......." The Sarge acknowledged the message.

The Holy Father said, "Thanks, my son! And go with God!" The Sarge thought about all of his previous masters, and uttered, "More like go with Lucifer, and negotiate with his brother the Holy Father, until the truth is discerned, or the lie is convincing.

## CHAPTER TEN

Monica, being a very brilliant jurist, as well as having strong accounting knowledge, tried to understand how the revenue from the sale of oil was used in that country. She developed models based upon what happened in other oil producing countries and couldn't come to grips with the fact that a significant amount of revenue was generated but hyper-inflation, unemployment, and a weak bolivar were causing the rampant monetary issues in the economy. It was noted that spending on the military consumed a large amount of bolivars that otherwise should have been devoted for the benefit of the people, and it appeared that billions were missing and unaccounted for. She reconciled some of the missing loot by saying the process of accounting for the sale of oil was not like selling candy or houses, no, it was more like trying to account for a product that was purchased but was still in the pipeline and hadn't been paid for.

In St. Lucia, where the team would plan their work, Mike said to Darryl, "You know my old boss used to run oil out of this country, and into ports in the US for a shitload of money. He avoided taxes, tariffs, fees, and probably earned an extra $200 on each barrel that was illegally transported. He bragged that he would make at least that amount on each barrel after paying off people at the various points of inspection."

Darryl asked, "In your business dealings, did you ever come across anyone who did business down here with him?"

Mike replied, "Yeah! One of his lady friends lived on this island and provided him with information such as points of entry and exit, as well as the banking considerations that are needed for each tanker that left the port in that country. I accompanied him here once, and what made me curious was the fact that the hotel on the other side of this place is where he and his intermediary would hook up."

"We need to speak to my uncle about this and see how he may want to play this. Let's find him, and share your information," Darryl stated.

#

Meanwhile, the other Michael was conducting hot and heavy online, facetime discussions with Ayesha. He suggested that she explain to the children that she was going to have dinner with him off the island and would return in the morning. Ayesha, on the other hand suggested that he drop what he was doing, and come back to St. Thomas, and have dinner with her.

The two never worked out the travel arrangements but it was decided that, at an appointed hour, they would have serious conversations about moving to the next step in a relationship and what each expected out of it. She expressed to Michael that she was fearful of having conversations of the heart with him because he was the victim of a recent dysfunctional relationship that he concluded. Ayesha thought that it was a metaphor or colloquialism being thrown around, about Michael literally killing the woman he loved.

Eventually, she would get the message, and understand the nature of the group, their mission, as well as their resolve!

# # #

After discussing the highlights of Mike's knowledge of assets his former boss had on the island, Beckmire assigned Jilkes, John Lee, Somara, and Yeshida to investigate whether Mike's information was fact or fiction.

Yeshida, seeking confirmation, asked Somara in their native tongue, "Didn't that witch Malaysia, eventually wind up on one of these islands?"

Somara replied, "She did, and married an incredibly famous person so that if anything happened to her, the stature of their relationship would guarantee an intense investigation. Fortunately for her, and unfortunately for the man she married, he died first, and left her with a lot of money. If she is still alive, I would consider her untouchable now. Perhaps, we should figure out where she is, and seek some modicum of consideration for not divulging some specific intel that we have on her."

Jilkes said, "Honey, when you go deep into your language with your comrades, I feel lonely and left out. I keep you fully informed of what we say, by saying it in a way that you fully understand. Please, again, give us the benefit of knowing what you're talking about when you switch tongues."

Yeshida responded, "Sorry, honey! Sometimes it is easy for us to speak fluently in our language and know exactly what we mean. You guys say things, and they have many meanings, and I consider that rather confusing. Honey, we think we have a contact on this island as well, if she's still alive.

Undoubtedly, she's changed her name, perhaps her looks, but she owes us, bigtime."

"The more information the better," Jilkes stated.

# # #

During the briefing with the Sarge, Jilkes suggested that they include Brown and Okema. The Sarge agreed with the notion.

On the small island of St. Lucia, a place that had changed hands approximately fourteen times between the French and the British, the appointed group fanned out to find any spy type contacts that could give them information about what was happening in Venezuela before they breached the border without consent. In Castries, the capital of St. Lucia, there was only one public internet pub where people went to sell information about things that weren't true or anything else that would earn them a dollar. Okema said to Brown, "If I had to bet money on finding someone from my former profession, that would be the place I would start. As they approached the pub, Yeshida and Jilkes came from one way and John Lee and Somara came from the other. Okema looked at them, and asked, "Don't you think it's going to be strange if we all go in at the same time?"

John Lee replied, "Hell, instead of wasting time, them there people will approach us, and ask for high dollar. The internet is a powerful place where them there spy types gather, according to my bride."

As John Lee, Somara, Okema, and Brown debated about the group's approach to entering the pub, Yeshida saw someone that spiked her attention. She said to Jilkes, "Honey, do you have a weapon on you?" He looked curiously at her, and inquired, "Baby, don't you?"

"Of course, I do. I'm crossing the street. Tell the others to circle the wagon, I think I see an old enemy that might still be holding a grudge."

As Yeshida slowly approached the person of interest, she softly said, "Our last encounter left you with a few damaged parts. I hope you don't try to do something foolish like running or pulling a weapon."

The person, before she turned around, said, "Bitch, this is one time that I wish I had a weapon. Unfortunately, I'm entering my place of business. What are you doing so far away from home?"

"I'm retired, but I still manage to carry a piece. I only see the one hand. If I don't see the other one in two seconds, I'm going to empty this fucking Berretta into you. Do we have an understanding?"

"Oh, we have more than an understanding. This is my new world, away from people like you, and your friends. By the way, where are your constant shadows?"

"They are approaching from many angles and pointing weapons at your ass."

"Oh, my God! When did you learn to use curse words? You sound rather retarded, swearing."

"I still can't see your other hand. Don't make me shoot you in the back!"

"Listen you fucking backstabbing bitch, you fire that weapon, and this entire area will become your battle ground. This is my home, and these are my people. The fucking cops dare not come down here. I'm showing you my other hand, and if you fire your weapon, you will be shot down in the street, like the dog that you are, like you did my friend."

"Your friend had a weapon, and she intended to use it."

"That's a fucking lie. She didn't own, know how to use, or had ever fired a damn gun. Stop trying to give yourself, a self-satisfying notion of salvation for a hideous act committed by your dumb ass. You are a monster, and one day I will provide justice."

Yeshida walked up to the woman, and said, "I am happily married, and with children. If you utter a single fucking word about yesteryear, I will openly shoot you down like a rabid dog. Oh, and by the way, before you ran out of town after I shot our friend, it was acknowledged that she had a weapon, and had every intent on using it. Not on me asshole, but on you! She trusted you, and you played in the swinging pond where everyone fucked everyone else. You gave her some bad shit, she came there to kill you because of that, but her driving motivation was the money you took from your joint safety deposit box. You know, the one where she had two hundred-plus-thousand dollars that disappeared into thin air after you and your crew smoked, injected, drank, and pissed it away. Oh, I see, now all this shit is coming back to you. Okay, listen, this guy approaching is my husband. You fuck this game up, and I'll blow your head off."

When the woman saw Jilkes, she said, "Oh my! You picked a real Black man, didn't you? I would have never thought that you would play in that sand box. Hi, my name is Malaysia. What's yours?"

Before Jilkes could answer, Yeshida said, "This isn't a social call, this is about old business, and possibly some extra cash for you."

Yeshida escorted the woman out of hearing range of the others, and reiterated the fact that she would put a bullet in her head if she spoke of historical issues that she played a part in.

Malaysia inquired, "What do you mean by extra cash, and who are you setting up this time?"

"We need an escort into Caracas. Is that something you might want to assist us with?"

"You must be out of your damn mind. Why on earth would I enter that crazy man's country illegally, while some people are trying to leave the place, and others are trying to oust him, even with the military on his side?"

"I know you're a Catholic. The Holy Father wishes us to discuss matters with him personally," Yeshida stated.

"I ain't that much of a Catholic that I'm going to go into that country, and risk being hung for any number of crimes associated with being there illegally. And besides, why would I help your putrid ass?"

"I can provide you with closure on your friend, and perhaps give you access to the real money that she had that only a few people knew about. You get us in and out of that country, and I'll get you access to the few millions that I know she had."

Malaysia inquired, "If I were to help you, how do I know you'll keep your end of the bargain?"

"You don't! I'm not in the habit of fucking over people, so, I guess my offer is solid. I'll get my offer ratified by the leadership, and if they approve of the idea, then we will back it with our money, up to one million dollars. Do we have deal?"

"I'll have to think about it and get back to you."

"You'll tell me in ten seconds, or we'll make the offer to a few other spy types on this particular island. Your choice, just don't fuck with me, on this one."

"Okay, let me check on a few things, and get back to you. I need to make sure that my reliable folks are in place.

Everyone there needs food, more than they need money. If you're caught with cash, they torture you, and make sure they get it all, leaving you with nothing but a broken body. It's chaos beyond what happened in those places in Africa that we did work in. Okay, I'm going to give you another chance to earn my friendship, don't fuck it up this time!"

"You are such a character. I saved you on too many occasions, and it looks as if you're still living by a shoestring. Are you still getting high?"

"I stopped that shit, six years ago. I only drink, and that has become enough for me. I'm too old for bullshit, freaky people, and strange drugs that have no origin."

Okema said to Yeshida, with Somara in tow, "I see you have friends from yesteryear still trying to play the game."

In perfect English, Yeshida said, "Please go and fuck yourself. We've come too far to throw stones at glass houses. We all have a history, good, bad, or indifferent."

Okema bowed low, slow, and said, "A thousand apologies. I overstepped our relationship by trying to be coy. Please forgive me, my friend!" She then bowed low and slow again.

John Lee uttered to Brown and Jilkes, "Be looking like someone took a foot up the ass."

Brown responded, "Yeah, and it looks like it's my woman. I'm going to pay the price for that tonight."

#

Later as the group gathered, the Sarge was in deep conversation with Darryl, Michael, Mike, Chakes, and McArthur. Also, in attendance was Mallory, Jong, Gladstone, Montomie, Whitmore, and Bernstein, a few of the original 10 plus 2, and a few new members. As Jilkes, Brown, John Lee, and the three ladies approached, Brown said, "I don't like the looks of this situation."

Jilkes responded, "Neither do I. This looks like some really bad shit is about to go down."

When they got to where the Sarge was holding court, the Sarge stepped aside, and acknowledged Brown's birthday! Okema had gifts for him and asked him to make a wish. Brown yelled, "Shit, I thought you people forgot. Not that it matters, because my greatest gift in my entire life was to meet you guys, and then fall in love with my beautiful and talented wife. I love you all, and I would like for you people to take a short walk with me. As the group descended towards the beach, Brown continued to walk until at the water's edge. He exclaimed, "People, behold! I've found Sanctuary # 2!" Everyone continued to look at the water except John Lee. He yelled, I'll be a pig's daddy, this here place be just like our place in St. Thomas."

Jilkes yelled, "Moron, it's just water!"

"Boy you be as obtuse as my dumbest pig. Y'all turn your asses around please!"

When the group turned around, everyone was in awe of what they saw. They saw a similar layout of the beach, an ancient hotel they were staying in, and the cul-de-sac appearance of their property in St. Thomas.

The Sarge looked at Jong and Mallory, and asked, "What are your thoughts on this discovery?"

Jong said, "We need more places like we need new holes in our head."

Mallory responded, "I would like to know the financial side of this equation, but the place doesn't operate as if it has money problems. I mean, it's okay, but with this view, you could attract the rich and famous. I'm thinking, something is not right here. I would like to press Monica into play. She's confounded by the fact that there are billions missing from the sale of oil, both legitimate, and under the table from the other place. I think there is a lot of money laundering going on in this part of the world, and this place seems to be the prime recipient."

# # #

That night, Malaysia showed up at the hotel dressed as a man, and knew exactly what room Yeshida and Jilkes were staying in. She knocked softly on the door, Yeshida peeked through the keyhole, and opened it. Once in the room, Malaysia was surrounded by the Sarge, Mallory, Jilkes, John Lee, Brown, Okema, Somara, and of course Yeshida. Yeshida introduced Malaysia to the group and gave the simple version of their relationship. The exact sentiments were announced to Jilkes earlier, and he was proud of his woman for discussing those aspects of her life.

Malaysia retorted, "Yeshida was like the person to make sure you got home. She never did the things our group did. She is your shining princess Mr. Jilkes. Anyway, I hear there is an interest in gaining access to a certain country, and if it happens successfully, a dearly departed friend's fortune would be turned over to me without any complications. Is that correct?"

Yeshida replied, "Are you fucking crazy? I didn't say that. I said that I would assist you in gaining access to the current information required to access the box since you pissed her off. I never said we would turn over a damn thing to you."

"You curse like a country girl. I was just testing the languages here. Who's in charge?" Everyone raised their hands.

Mallory said, "We have pictures of you as a man, and as a woman. We have a group in Northern Africa that we deal with after we make agreements with strangers. Just so you know what you're getting into, we'll take a $5 million contract out on you, your friends, and any family you might have if you make the tactical mistake of trying to take advantage of us. Here is a signed copy of the agreement by the Omar Group in Morocco, who will take care of any loose ends if you try to fuck us in this deal. I think you're somewhat familiar with them, and the kind of dysfunctional work that they do."

"Nicely played! I need the cash, and I did my research on you people. I'm playing this thing straight up without any chaser! I want to make some money, and not have to look over my shoulder. Can we do this without enforcing penalties for things that I don't control. You people are famous, and a lot of people would like to see you in boxes. I know one, who is alleged to be the bionic man, who would be more than happy to have your heads. As a matter of fact, and for your information, he has a weak ass proposal out on the street that will net those who betray you a portion of your fortune. Any fool knows that you people don't leave your money in boxes, and under the mattress. He's broke, and if not broke, his shit is under duress. No, I prefer to do my business with you guys because the word on the street is that you've never screwed people over a deal that was agreed on."

Mallory asked, "Do you have information that would lead us to the bionic man?"

Malaysia responded, "That sounds like a separate potential contract that could benefit a person with specific information. Wouldn't you agree?"

Brown said, "Let's focus on the ins and outs of the reason why we're here. First things first!"

Malaysia looked at the Sarge, and asked, "Mr. Beckmire, are you going to participate in the discussion?"

The Sarge looked at her, and said, "I guess your intel is pretty good or I'm on a lot of wanted posters."

"I'm not sure what Yeshida has told you, but I'm from the same world as the three new members of your group. Some of us go way back to a time when wild was as wild as one could be. However, some remained as 'goodie two shoes.' Listen, I need to make some money, and you need to meet the ruler or the ex-ruler of that country. He is not going to give up control if the military is on his side. For some odd reason, they stand behind this guy. I think, in addition to their pay, he allows them to develop death squads, to take from the rich, allegedly give to the poor, but keep what they generated for themselves."

"Ms. Malaysia, two things I'd like to express. First, I know where the bionic man is. We may be old, but technology is new. Second, our primary purpose is to ask the person in charge of that country to rethink his position, disappear into the night, and save a lot of lives. We are not his executioners! We are the message board from the Vatican. Our request of you is simple, can you get us in, and out of that place safely. We don't expect you to get us to his bedroom, however, we want to get as close as possible, and our other contacts will secure a bedroom meeting."

"So, Mr. Beckmire, you don't strike me as a religious man. May I ask how you became involved in this new, ah, holy war?"

"We buried a friend of mine in the outback, and the Holy Father asked if we could intervene in this matter and attempt to settle it without the use of force. I, frankly, am not sure who is who, in this developing story. I know that bionic guy is a bad hombre, but I also worry about the person we are emissaries for. He too, seemingly, has the ability to play with both barrels loaded, if you know what I mean."

"I can get you five miles into the interior, and that will cost you $200k."

Yeshida interjected, "Really! I have information that will allow you to access boxes of your former friend along with codes, and the necessary identification papers. I will not pay you a dime, because you and I both know those boxes are filled with a shitload of money. How do you want to proceed? I have several other options, but apparently, you and your place need immediate capital, or the mobster is going to rename it. Now, I will agree to, say, $100k. We will provide you with the access information to what may be millions of dollars or nothing at all. Now this is the deal that I like the most, how about you? Oh, how about we have a word with the competition in the interim and give him a single option. Now, does your deal or my counter proposal make sense to you or are you still trying to nickel and dime us for change?" Yeshida inquired.

"Mr. Beckmire, I like all the tenets of her proposal. When would you like to make access to that place?"

"Are you busy tomorrow?" Beckmire asked.

#

After meeting with his main team, Beckmire and Mallory saw a figure sitting by the water alone, and wondered if it was a member of their team. Mallory said to Beckmire, "That looks like Michael. He appears to be wiping his eyes as if he is crying. Let's take a walk and see what's happening."

When the two men approached Michael, he held his hand out as if telling them to go away. The Sarge realized that there was a problem. He ignored the hand signal and sat beside Michael. Once Michael realized it was the Sarge, he began to cry uncontrollably. The Sarge began to massage his neck. He did not ask Michael what was going on, but realized that recently, he had lost a person that he cared about. Rather than trying to guess what was happening, Mallory asked, "Did we do something wrong?"

Michael looked at him and began to cry harder. The Sarge looked hard at Mallory as if to say, "shut the hell up." The three men sat there for five minutes, and Michael finally uttered, "Ayesha, the woman with the kids, facetimed me, and signed, that my father died today!"

Beckmire exclaimed, "Oh, my God! Oh, my God! We must head to *the Sanctuary*."

"I just got the news. Sarge, your plan for visiting the target, is based upon your team plus Darryl's. There is nothing I can do at home. I know what I can do here. If you can make our mission happen tomorrow, then I will feel better. I will not go home without completing the mission we are here for."

"I know, son. You know your father was a gentleman and a scholar. He was so proud of you, and I'm sure he told you. He didn't approve of your family's action against my associate, but it certainly highlighted a person that could be trusted. Michael, that person is you. You are as important to my nephew as my eleven guys are to me. You are Darryl's, 'Mallory.' Never forget that. You are rich, your family is set for life. You, and my nephew, will become the new Fab 10 + 2. You guys will replace us and continue our work."

The Sarge paused, but continued to massage Michael's neck. He said, "Michael, I have called you son on many occasions. You are an extension of my family, and your father, God rest his soul, will live forever in you. The problem I have with your father's untimely death is that you become our partner in *the Sanctuary*. That means, you don't have to run around the world with us trying to make things good for the poor people. You know Earther and Windom and their families are going to be rich, from that land they own in Minnesota. You, my friend, just inherited a portion of *the Sanctuary*. I personally think, you should head home, and honor your father, a great man that I respected, and admired. I think we can manage this one without you."

"Mr. Beckmire, you don't understand. I need to complete this mission, because that is exactly what my dad would want me to do. Let's take care of this issue, and then I can head back to my family with a clear conscience."

Mallory looked at the Sarge, and said, "We don't know Ms. Malaysia, if we make entry tonight, and if there was any planned treachery, it would throw everyone off. I would like to make our visit happen tonight."

The Sarge smiled at Mallory, looked at Michael, and said, "Son, are you sure you won't be distracted by the death of your father?"

"Mr. Beckmire, I'm a part of your replacement unit. I'm here to make sure you ease into retirement, and that you're not forced! Sir, I need this distraction."

#

As the boats pulled onto an unknown shore, Ms. Malaysia said, "There are two rules! When I say turn left, you turn right. If I say, stand tall, you fall flat on your face. You people are now the proletariat. You have no worth. You do as others command."

Mallory unequivocally stated, "That role is going to be hard for these people. They are elitists, and expect people to wait on them, at every corner. I say that to say, perhaps, we should have role played for a few days until we got the gist of being poor, and without control of our destiny."

Ms. Malaysia quipped, "Oh, my friend, here you will learn in a hurry, or we all will be burned to death." The mood suddenly turned sour, and everyone began to focus on the project at hand.

John Lee astutely asked, "Didn't this here pirate get a vote of confidence from his army? I saw that on Fox news. If'n that be the case, we be going up against a whole army. That don't seem like good pig odds to me." Jilkes, who usually has something to retort to John Lee's comments, stood tall and silent because he realized that Old Country was right on target.

Ms. Malaysia stared at him, and said, "The odds are ridiculously low, and they have reached the negative side of the equation in terms of my safety. If you people are at the fifteen percentile, then I'm at the minus fifteen percentile. If this thing goes moderately wrong, my family, and everyone that I know will be butchered like hogs."

John Lee inquired, "Can't they be butchered like cattle? I like hogs, and some of my best friends are pigs."

"Stay focused! Don't get sidetracked by bullshit," Jilkes stated.

# # #

In Caracas, Venezuela, Darryl's group which included Earther, Windom, Michael, Desmond, and Isaiah, dressed the part, and looked like the locals. On the other side of town, Mallory, accompanied by Jilkes, John Lee, Brown, Yeshida, Somara, Okema, and McArthur dressed like the oppressed. In the middle of town, the Sarge, Chakes, Whitmore, Gladstone, Bernstein, Jong, and Montomie walked into a sleazy bar, and went directly to a back room. It was there that they descended steps into a sewer that would lead them to the palace. From there, a guide would escort them to the laundry room, where they would meet the person who would lead them to a secret passageway into the dictator's boudoir. The Holy Father had arranged for all events to happen seamlessly. Darryl's group and Mallory's contingency plans were clearly for the purpose of providing security for those who encroached the palace.

When the group opened the panel that led to the dictator's bedroom, he could be seen in what appeared to be deep thought. The Sarge walked in front of him, and said, "There are six weapons pointed at you. Three of my people are planting devices around your room to secure our extraction. I come to you with a message from the Holy Father of the Catholic Church."

The Sarge leaned near the man's ear, and recited the exact message given to him by the Holy Father. The dictator grunted, and spit on the floor. The Sarge pulled out his weapon, pointed it at the dictator's head, and then his private area. He whispered to the dictator, "No matter how well you control your people, we can find and target you. You will acknowledge the message I gave you with a sincere reconsideration of your actions, or you will live underground in a bunker for the rest of your life. Even there, my friend, he will activate the real Carbon Factor that impacts the earth, superstructures such as bunkers, and then sever, all possible sources of oxygen. You will respond to the Holy Father in twelve hours, or he will detonate, unfortunately for you, the real Carbon Factor, not that shit that you and others have tried to acquire and have threatened their governments with. His answer is the real deal, most destructive device on earth, superseding atomic, nuclear, and other demonic devices developed to kill humans."

"I don't know who you are, sir. But no one would detonate a device that would trigger a world war."

"You may be absolutely correct. However, my assessment of my employer, who pretends to be the Holy Father, and who I think is Diablo himself, surely is prepared to do that, and more. This Pope is unlike any I have ever read about or have seen. He, to me, is not a Christian, but one who floats between the world of salvation and Armageddon, and between heaven and hell. He, without hesitation, will kill millions, and blame you for that scourge. He will make the many suffer to inflict his wrath upon the few, my friend. You will address the issue I stated to you in twelve hours from 0100 hundred hours. Oh, I was told to tell you that at 0101 hundred hours, a catastrophic explosion will occur in Caracas with your palace being the epicenter."

Jong strapped two devices on each ankle of the dictator, and told him not to use telephonic instruments, or attempt to have someone detach the devices within the next twelve hours.

"I think I will call my guards!" The Sarge cocked his weapon, and said, "I have a funeral to go to. I will blow your head off if you do anything that I didn't instruct you to do as my hostage. I can signal one of my people who likes to gut

people, and then take a bite out of their heart before they die
to handle this situation, it's purely your choice. Don't try to
fuck with me as you do with your people. Me and my people
are non-forgiving!"

# # #

Before leaving the dictator's quarters, the dictator asked,
"Are these device location instruments?"

The Sarge looked at him, then at Jong, and they both
laughed. The Sarge turned to the dictator and said, "I'm going
to give you a heads up! The two ankle devices are designed to
shatter your ankles and signal the four devices that were
planted around your room. It may be in your best interest that
you stay away from cellular communications, in that they
might accidentally trigger the devices. The ankle devices are
statement items. The purpose is to remind you about the holy
father's reach, by shattering your bones. We will always be
near until you do the right thing and relinquish your power.
You lost the election. Go away with the billions you've stolen
and live happily ever after."

"I've never taken a dime, and as a matter of fact, I don't
receive a salary."

The Sarge looked at him, and asked, "Why in God's name
would you need a salary? You people have stolen billions, and
I can prove it. If I prove it, I'll let you go, and let the people
do their justice to your stealing ass. You are a crook, just like
the guy before you. Figure out where you want to live on a
fraction of what you stole because you're going to have to give
back ninety percent if we move in that direction."

"You come to my country, violate my sanctity, and accuse
me of stealing from my beloved people. Sir, I will find you

when this is over, and I will give you the justice that you deserve."

The Sarge looked at the dictator, then at Jong, and told him to increase the sensitivity of the devices on his ankles. Jong pulled up the devices on his phone, and everyone could see the dictator wince from the sudden electrical shock. The Sarge asked, "Do you have any other threats you want to issue to me?" There was no answer, and the Sarge suggested that he avoid people with cell phones as much as possible. Jong blindfolded the man, and the team exited the room through a panel.

# # #

In Caracas as the team prepared to exit, Malaysia asked Yeshida if she could have a word with her. As the two women spoke, it became obvious to those on the periphery that Malaysia was becoming irritated. Yeshida handed her a note with instructions on how to obtain the remains of her lover's booty. Yeshida said to Malaysia, "Before I give you the codes, I want you to admit that you knew your friend was going to kill you, and that I saved your miserable life."

Malaysia lowered her head, and said, "All that was accomplished that night was that I interfered with your potential coming out party, and you saved me from an obsessive, possessive mate. As I look around at where you are today, I can only say, we did each other a favor. May I never see you again, or you me!"

#

In St. Thomas, preparations were being made for the funeral of Mr. Carter. On the flight to St. Thomas, everyone found time to sit with Michael, and express their condolences. The Sarge stated, "As long as I'm alive, I hope you look at me as a father figure. I can never be Mr. Carter, but I can be that figure you might need in the future, son."

Michael broke into tears, and said, "I am concerned that I have become a dark cloud, and I don't understand why. The passing of my father, who when I last saw him, looked as healthy as can be, and then my falling in love with a woman who was in cahoots with a known enemy. Negative things seem to happen whenever I am around." Michael began to sob harder, and Zanthius walked back to his seat, and said, "My brother, I have heard my dad call you son. At first, I was a little jealous, but then I realized that to him you are a son, just like Larry, and me. Think about the future, think about Ayesha, and look at the peace within. Your dad was a good man, his memory, and deeds on that island will last forever. He did a lot for the people there, and somehow, we'll find a way to enshrine his name within *the Sanctuary*. We are all here for you brother, and no matter what, if you need us for anything, we'll be there for you."

"Well stated, son!" The Sarge said.

#

The plane landed and was met by Mrs. Carter's staff. The group decided to forgo the pleasure of the island rum punch, and head straight to *the Sanctuary*. The funeral was scheduled for later that evening.

As the caravan headed into *the Sanctuary*, Michael from afar, could see Ayesha standing near the entrance alongside his mother and sister. His eyes filled with tears. As the van he was riding in came to a stop, he opened the door, navigated the two steps to exit it, walked to his mother, and gave her a hug and a kiss on both cheeks. He embraced his sister and kissed her on both cheeks. He looked at Ayesha, and gently kissed her on the lips. He signed, "It helps me with my emotions to see your beautiful smile. Thanks for supporting my family in the most trying of times. It is noted and appreciated!"

Michael looked at Ayesha who was assisting his mother. Michael thought to himself, "we should be celebrating my father's life. After all, he was a happy man within, but you wouldn't know it if you didn't know him. We should have a party and tell tall tales of this man until the night passes into day."

# # #

After the funeral, the mood was solemn. The group moved from the funeral services to the repass. Ms. Viola prepared her most potent rum punch, and people began to partake in its wonderful taste. As the food began to be served, and as the rum punch continued to flow, Mrs. Carter, uncharacteristically, stood up, seized the microphone, and began to speak softly. Michael and his sister joined her, and gave her the strength to praise, and tell stories about her newly departed husband, and lover. She shared the story of how the two of them met, and how he chased her like a hound dog. She shared how gentle he was about everything he did. He wasn't a confrontational man, and that is probably what got him in trouble with that thieving bank in town she noted. She said, the saddest day of her life was not him dying, but him leaving her because of his dream to make the place, now called *the Sanctuary*, the best place on the island. I didn't support his borrowing from those thieving ass people in town, and he thought I didn't support him. She then exclaimed, "Well, hells bells! Here comes a group of pirates from the mainland who don't steal, propose deals that are too good to be true, and don't ask for a single penny, just honesty and loyalty. Him thought you people were darker than those bankers and decided that he was already in bed with the devil, and that he might as well have sex with him as justification."

The place broke into a loud laughter, Michael and his sister watched as their mother turned this sad occasion into a testament about a great and trusting man. She recounted when Mallory, Jong, and Monica went with him to the bank to pay off his loans. She said, "I know, because I was there sitting in the corner watching everything. I felt good when that little Mr. Jong told the banker, "I want to pay off his account, and I want to do it now! Well, honey, I nearly peed myself. And then Monica told them that she was some kind of highfalutin bank person, well hell, you would have thought that Jesus walked into the place."

Mrs. Carter paused for a moment and then stated, "Chris and I never stopped talking. He told me about the things that my son had to do in order to make sure that certain skeletons never saw the sunlight, and that's when I told him, that I would come back, and help him. I briefly spoke with the Sarge, oh yeah, that big old hunk of a man, and realized that he was a teddy bear trying to make all the kids happy. People, please raise your glasses to a wonderful human being, and husband, Christopher Carter. May his memory endure time!"

# # #

Ayesha signed to Michael, "The children missed you. After you have settled in, and taken care of your family matters, I would like for you to take the children fishing. My heart would be at peace with that image if that is all that you have in mind for us."

"What does that mean?" Michael signed.

"I think I trapped you with pity and needs. After the explosion, and your assistance, we have grown somewhat appreciative of life, luxury, and easy living. I think it's time for us to head back home and check on what is happening with the rebuilding efforts. We have been guests in your home for too long, you must keep your mother and sister in a safe place mentally."

Michael saw Jong, and asked, "Have you heard anything from Franco and his crew?"

Jong bowed low, and replied, "After you have ceremoniously sent your father to the great void, I will update you on our progress. I will not burden you with issues that can be resolved at any moment in time. The passing of a loved one, dims a light of existence for everyone who is family, and those who are truly friends. Bricks and mortar are not important. After you have sent your father on his final journey, I will come to you when the time is appropriate to instruct you on the status of earthly things." He bowed low and backed away.

Michael walked over to where Ayesha was sitting, and comfortably sat between her and the children. The children kept signing him images of fishing, and Michael announced that they would go fishing first thing in the morning. He signed, "You guys have been staying up late. I want you guys in bed early. I will let you bring suggestions to me tomorrow. I also want reading time, math time, and history time. So, we divide our time between fun and learning, and that way, I will always be there for you. None of you are handicapped. You're special, and as such, I want you to be the smartest people on earth."

Michael reached out for Ayesha's hand, and the children went ballistic with their signing. Michael smiled, and signed, "I just want to take her for a walk. If you want to come along, you're invited, but you must stay six feet behind us."

As Michael and Ayesha started walking, all the kids formed a line, followed them down to the water's edge, and sat approximately six feet away from them. Ayesha signed, "They really like you. They also have plans for you that you'll have to ask them about. I told them that I would not be complicit in kidnapping you and making you in charge of our home once it's completed." Michael looked to his side, slapped his hands twice, and told them to move back two feet.

Ayesha signed, "It's too late to show that you're in control. They respect you, and that's all you're going to get. They know you like them, they choose to respect you, and not let you control them. I don't know how that works, but you'll have to figure it out. They also think that you should marry me soon!"

Michael signed, "What are your thoughts about that?"

The question caught Ayesha off guard, and she cocked her head, and politely said, "I don't know much about you, and you don't know a thing about me. Not the beginnings of what I consider a solid foundation for building a future with a bunch of homeless kids who have a few challenges."

Michael signed, "Everything is possible, and it's an attention getter. I don't know about time, but I do know about how I feel. It's not a fantasy, it's a longing to be in your presence all of the time." Ayesha smiled and stared at the water.

# # #

As Beckmire and Courtney finished a marathon session, he sighed and took a couple of deep breaths. Courtney asked, "What's up big fellow? You having a hard time keeping up with me?"

"Baby, that's not what I was thinking. I was reveling in the notion that it is as good today as it was when we met. My compliments to a wonderful human being and wife." As Ben was about to finish his verbal serenade, his SAT phone rang, and Courtney knew it was not good when that phone rang. Ben Beckmire answered it, and to his chagrin, it was the Holy Father. He did not engage in the normal salutations but went directly to the matter on his mind. He asked Ben Beckmire, "Did you give that fellow my exact message?"

"Holy Father, I did indeed. Why, is there a problem with his interpretation?"

"Only that he attempted to have some of his minions assassinate me, and a few of my cardinals."

"No! Are you serious?" Beckmire exclaimed.

"Mr. Beckmire, I need you and your crew to pay him a final visit. Since your breach of his domain, he has relocated his living quarters to one of his military bases, where there is a full battalion on guard duty, twenty-four hours a day."

"Holy Father, we are just a few. That seems more like a suicide mission."

"Sergeant Beckmire, isn't that what you and your people did in Vietnam? Every mission you went on, you were not expected to return. Is this hearsay or am I being fed mythology about you people?"

"Holy Father, those actions were when we were young men. We are beyond the years of trying to do some of the things that we did. Sir, you indicated that the man has moved onto a military base that is guarded by a full battalion of soldiers. We don't have enough weapons and personnel to attempt an event of this size."

"My son, where is your faith?" The Sarge thought for a moment, and finally blurted out, "Holy Father, what you ask, requires a hell of a lot more than faith, and I will not throw my people into a ring where I know there is only death that awaits them."

"Son, faith is a combination of belief and trust. If you believe in God and trust in me, then you should know that if I ask you to commit your people, I will have all the other concerns taken care of. What that mental midget doesn't know is that two-thirds of his soldiers are true believers. They will respond appropriately when asked to turn their heads."

"Holy Father, that's comforting, but what about the one-third who are not believers, and who will protect him?" There was a lull in the conversation. The Holy Father emphatically stated, "Son, that is why I'm calling you. The one-third who are not believers should be no match for you and your people. Now, if you're not sure of your capabilities, and need my people on the periphery, then I will commit my personal guard. This situation must be handled immediately. His minions had the audacity to attempt to assassinate me, and three of my cardinals. He has gone beyond the realm of mental competency, and has assumed that as a dictator, he is invincible! Oh, and by the way, are you familiar with a man named Utz?"

"Holy Father, I do know a Mr. Utz, but he is on the run from the American government, and my people. How is he connected to our conversation?"

"Mr. Utz is your man's most trusted assistant. Mr. Utz is responsible for trying to save the bolivar, and as luck would have it, was able to reduce inflation by several points, and was given the presidential medal of honor. Wherever the man is, Mr. Utz is nearby."

The Sarge paused, and thought quickly about this new information, and stated, "Holy Father, my people are weary. Can I call you back in two hours?"

# # #

The Sarge called Mallory and indicated that he would like to have the entire group meet with him in an hour. Mallory inquired, "What's going on Sarge?"

"I received a call, and a request from the Holy Father."

"Oh shit! Here we go again."

Approximately forty-five minutes later, the group assembled in the dining room where John Lee asked, "Who do we have to eliminate now?"

The Sarge looked at him and realized that it was usually meetings like this one when they decided on someone else's life. He cut right to the chase, and told the group, "I received a call from the Holy Father." Before he could say anymore, Ms. Viola blurted out, "You mean from Lucifer."

The Sarge hesitated, and responded, "Ms. Viola, you and I share the same sentiments. I don't know if he is the Holy Father or Lucifer, or if they're one in the same. Anyhow, the person that we last visited on his behalf, sent his gofers to assassinate the holy father, and a few cardinals. Now, you can imagine the outrage he feels, and he wants to send a concluding message, and he wants us to deliver it."

Jilkes raised his hand, and asked, "Does that mean he wants us to excommunicate him permanently?"

"That is exactly what he wants, but that's not the business we're in. We moved from Allen to my cousin, to Mr. Utz, and now the Holy Father. I'm tired of being handled. By the way, Mr. Utz, is our man's personal shadow. My conversations with the Holy Father have led me to believe that the man is the devil himself. As you know, he had the Carbon Factor placed throughout Russia, China, as well as in North Korea. He has said, without any hesitation, that he would detonate devices in any country, if necessary, and would pray for forgiveness. He is not your normal priest, Catholic, Christian, believer, or Pope. He is a monster that will conclude entire civilizations in order to gain control over dictators and tyrants. His mission is clear; you want to play on the world stage, then you had better have your shit together. This Pope, unlike any Pope that I have heard of, is a tyrant himself, and will do dastardly things to make sure that the world realizes that he is omnipotent! I wondered about our alliance with this person, but Ben Hackney swore by him, and I swear by my departed brother."

Chakes stated, "Sarge, you know we caught him sleeping last time. It won't be easy doing this a second time."

"You are absolutely right. He has moved his residence to a military base where there is a full battalion of soldiers watching his rear. The Holy Father thinks that two-thirds are true believers. I know what you're going to ask. I asked him about the other one-third, and the usually vociferous Holy Father, hesitated for several seconds. He finally admitted only faith would get us through this ordeal!"

"Sarge, you know a lot of us don't practice a whole lot of faith kind of activities," Chakes said.

John Lee yelled, "Me and my African American friend practice faith all the time. It ain't like we got to go to church and hear somebody preach. We just stay quiet and think about the good that we try to do for people."

Jilkes asked, "What are our options on this one. Frankly, I'm not sure of our new handler, but your friend swore by him. Can you foresee a day when we handle ourselves?"

The Sarge looked at him long and hard, and said, "How about we start now and refuse this suicidal mission?" The room became extremely quiet. Yeshida raised her hand, stood up, and said, "The benefits and blessings from the church are surely needed by all of us, when we think about the countless number of bodies we have concluded, and their souls that are roaming around Hades, waiting for us. Mr. Sarge sir, I think if we have absolute intel on this project, the outcome would be a small price to pay for a modicum of absolution from the church."

The Sarge smiled at her, bowed slowly, walked over, and hugged her. He thanked her for bringing attention to the fact that they had suffered, but to date, no one had paid the ultimate price. He announced, "I agree with Yeshida, and I think we should try to plan this action, but also let the Holy Father know, that we're out of business after this event."

Mallory stood up, and asked, "How the hell are we going to get onto a military base in a foreign country with only a few people who can speak the language?"

Jong stood up, and said, "I speak perfect Spanish."

Montomie stood up and began to speak in guttural terms to Jong who said at the end of his speech, "I agree with what he said."

Carlos said, "He spoke badly about your sister, and uncle. Stay with your language."

The Sarge said, "People, please! I must call the Holy Father back in a few minutes and give him our answer. If I say no, it is unlikely we will continue to receive intel from the Vatican. I mean the holy father provided us with that heads up about those military types coming here to arrest us. If I say yes, when will we be able to cut the umbilical cord. Every time there is a situation that calls for our kind of skill set, will he call us at every turn? I wish I could find out if the base had a bunker or just a large area with a lot of people. How about a drone strike? Jong, is that possible?"

"Sarge, anything is possible. I like that idea because it gives us cover and distance, and we don't have to fight a war in the middle of a military base."

Darryl said, "Uncle, Sue Lyn in theory is excellent at launching and delivering the payload of those things."

"Nephew, what do you mean in theory?"

"Uncle, she's a closet gamer, who in her spare time, plays a drone game where precision is the key to winning. Uncle, Sue Lyn wins all of the time."

"Sue Lyn is it possible to launch and control those things from afar, much like the military does?"

"Yes Uncle. You know Amazon wants to use drones to deliver packages. A series of drones could deliver enough ordnances to route the devil from hell."

"Oh my! I'm not sure we want to do that. I like dealing with one of them at a time. Okay people let's see what kind of intel we get back from the Holy Father, and then we'll plan accordingly or abort without reservations. We have been lucky as hell. I sure as hell don't want to have casualties as some of us look to raise our children, and others, pigs."

# # #

The Sarge placed a call to the Holy Father, and the two men talked for over an hour. They spoke of the requested activity, but more in depth about the nature of the group, the adamant and conclusive nature of the Pope, and his disdain for dictators. The Sarge asked the Holy Father, "Would you really have destroyed entire countries if they hadn't removed their dirty bombs from American soil?"

"Son, I'm not a fan, of the people elected to lead your country. Seems like your country is run by a dysfunctional family. Nepotism at every level, and the people have suspicious mental capabilities. The two main characters, Russia, and China, well, let me just say to you, "I'm half Holy Father and half Lucifer. At the point of initially contacting you, I was more Lucifer, and more apt to detonate the real Carbon Factor in both places. I almost decided to do that dastardly deed in the country I need your assistance in, but I have too many faithful's there. I'm still on the fence, but somewhere, unless normal conversations are scheduled about reducing worldwide tensions, there will be a detonation, and the world will know that I pushed the button that few knew existed."

"Holy Father we seek your guidance and absolution. However, we can't be anyone's hit squad."

"My son, our recently departed friend, indicated to me that you were the bridge before the button. I need you to cross that bridge, clean up that mess, before I push the button. After that, and if you fail, then the world will be in crisis. I plead with you my son, to take this mission, and conclude the germ that can begin the idea of Armageddon!" The Sarge became as quiet as a church mouse.

# # #

As the Sarge and Courtney walked along the water's edge, she held his hand and said, "The act of worrying has covered your entire body and has slowed your mental alertness. Would you like to accompany me on a swim from one end of the island to the other?"

"Girl, you know you can't beat me swimming. However, if you want to leisurely make that trip, then I'm up for it. I don't want to embarrass you, and leave you leagues behind."

As the two began their marathon swim, Courtney recognized that the Sarge was struggling with every stroke after about ten minutes. Although the water depth was less than six feet, she didn't want to have to attempt to assist him if he cramped up or something. She swam to him, began to dog paddle, and said, "Honey, this isn't working for me. I'm feeling like this is more of a challenge than a nice long swim. Come on, let's go back to shore."

When they arrived on shore, the Sarge sat down, and announced, "We have four days before we can attempt to do the work of the church. I'm going to have everyone participate in conditioning. We are living large, eating too damn much, and for sure drinking way beyond our normal limits." Courtney smiled at him, gave him a kiss on the cheek, and mumbled to herself, "damn glad we tried that. My man is smart and aware when it's time to leave the burgers alone and pick up the exercising regimen again."

# # #

For two and a half days, the group exercised in moderation with short runs, extensive walks, offensive and defensive martial arts, and a cessation of carbs, meat, and alcohol. John Lee asked Jilkes, "Are you worried about this mission?"

"I worry about every mission because we rarely control the playing field. You remember how they would always have you and me on point, well that was because they were stumbling, big foot people, who had to learn where to place their feet. We saved them, they saved us, and we saved each other. However, the playing field was always different. Think about that place in New York when Larry, ever so cautious, and aware of his environment, fell down a trap door by leaning on a damn tree. Also, think about what we did at the farm and the ranch. Who the hell ever heard of targeting people from afar by using tree mounted weaponry? Listen, I worry about each thing that we do. Secretly, I worry about your country ass because you and I are brothers from another mother. However, on your side of the fence, she wasn't too damn smart or attractive."

"Boy, you be asking for an ass whupping today? However, you be right. All they taught me to do was hate. Hate anybody that had a mouth full of teeth. Hate anybody that didn't look like us. Hate anybody that went to that big school twenty miles down the road, and to save most of my hate for Black people. If it weren't for your black ass, my white ass would be dead. I think if we hadn't had that fight where I kicked your ass, then our noses wouldn't have been sharp like they be, and we could smell them there other fellows in their caves, cooking shit. You know in Vietnam we killed a lot of them fellows," John Lee noted.

"Yeah, we did what soldiers do when placed in battle, we take lives and learn to live with it. You know what's spooking me about this mission, is that we were there in the man's bedroom, and should have terminated his ass right then and there instead of sending him some passages from the bible. Now we must go back to his country, but this time go onto a military base, and deal with him. You think that Pope is trying to assassinate us?" Jilkes asked.

John Lee proclaimed, "He's not a nice person. I don't know much about the Catholic religion, but I always imagine priests to be about saving souls, not trying to kill a whole country. That guy scares me because he is both good and evil, and all in one!"

"Let's get the layout of that place, and study it until we can memorize all of our options for extracting from it," Jilkes stated.

When John Lee and Jilkes entered the dining room, there was a beehive of movement around a table that had been placed in the center of the room. Everyone was looking at maps, weather forecasts, and places to regroup if separated. John Lee and Jilkes joined in the discussions and provided their input. As usual, everyone yielded to their suggestions because for one reason or another, they always got the group out of trouble.

## CHAPTER ELEVEN

In St. Lucia, some things never seem to change. Malaysia was queen of the village, was buying people drinks, and providing them with other stimulants. Yeshida and Somara walked up to her, and asked if they could talk outside. Once outside, Yeshida asked, "How would you like to make 1 million bucks?"

"You must be a simpleton! I wouldn't live to spend it. You're talking about going back into that man's country, aren't you?" Malaysia inquired.

"That's exactly what I'm talking about." Yeshida stated.

"I'll do it for $1.5 million, and not a penny less."

Yeshida smiled, and said, "Not a penny less! That's sad because we're after some money that was hidden by the guy."

Malaysia smiled, and stated, "I will accept $1 million, but I prefer $1.5 because of the risk I have to take. Now, if you're willing to assign a certain percentage of the funds that you seek, if successful, then I would be willing to renegotiate."

Yeshida said, "We'll take that into consideration. We need to be in that country in thirty-six hours. Can you manage that, and extract us approximately twelve hours later?"

Malaysia said, "I will be ready when you're ready. This bad relationship is turning into a profitable one for me, and I apologize for underestimating your sincerity. We can still be friends and forget about the past."

#

The Sarge asked Yeshida and Somara about their intel, and Somara responded, "We just want her to get us in the country. We are not certain about her loyalty or her ability to maximize her profits by selling us out."

"Good thinking," the Sarge said.

The Sarge and Holy Father had talked in detail about the who, what, when, and where. The who, was in the person by the name of Romulus George, who the Sarge had met with Ben Hackney years ago. What, was the team being supplied with a massive amount of munitions. The when would be at 1900 hours, and the where would be on the outskirts of Caracas, Venezuela.

#

The stage was set, everyone knew who the targets were, the dictator and Mr. Utz. The moon was full, and the dictator changed his routine, and decided to visit one of his many loyal lovers. He never imagined that those people working with that guy in Rome, would have the audacity to enter his country again, and try to intimidate him. He thought to himself, "how dare they." As a result of the initial breach, a dozen personnel were summarily executed. The sight of their comrades hanging in the air, gave a new-found meaning to making sure your shit was in order. The dictator was merciless and generous at the same time. His payroll for the military exceeded the cost of all his social promotion programs. He was clearly a dictator who could reward and punish. His problem was he never considered a putsch from the likes of the Catholic Church, using old men from Vietnam.

Malaysia contacted Yeshida, and said, "For another $200k, I will tell you exactly where he will be tonight, and more importantly, that he will have a limited security detail of about twenty personnel.

The dictator's proclivities were much like those particularly important and rich people in America who were charged with crimes relating to sex. This would be his best night in a long time because he combined various stimulants to make himself invincible.

At 2300 hours, a small contingency of soldiers left the base in three armored vehicles, and headed towards a seaside resort that was secretly owned by the dictator. When he arrived, and entered the building, a line of scantily dressed women welcomed him. He smiled at each one, looked at Mr. Utz, and began his selection process. Mr. Utz followed his lead, and off the two men went to enjoy a night of sexual escapades. The information provided by Malaysia was accurate, and worth the additional dollars. She knew several of the women who would most likely be his favorites and gave them each an unassuming ring that was a homing device that would pinpoint their whereabouts.

John Lee and Jilkes had point and noticed that several of the guards were involved in sexual activities themselves. Jilkes and John Lee, assassinated the two men in the middle of their ecstasy, and cautioned the women to be silent, and disappear. They moved quietly through the area, and at each encounter, the two men terminated guards. Michael and Mike were in the rear of the building, and encountered three men, and felled them as well.

Mr. Utz heard the sounds of air puffs that a suppression device would make, ran from the room he was in, and went through a panel that led to a passageway that ended up in a tunnel. He would not be discovered that night.

The dictator was engaged in several stimulating encounters in the room he was in. The Sarge, Mallory, and Montomie opened the door, and caught him in the middle of what could be considered a deviant sexual act by some. The Sarge motioned for the women to leave the room and sit in the hallway. Montomie said to the dictator, "We are here because you sent your minions to assassinate the Holy Father. We are his minions, and we're here to provide you with his intended justice."

The Sarge asked Montomie to translate his words. Montomie translated what the Sarge said, which was, "once you're in hell, you will have the opportunity to meet the dealer of your fate, for he is both the Holy Father and Lucifer, and he resides between heaven and hell."

# # #

The short trip from St. Lucia to St. Thomas was uneventful. Ben Beckmire, after staring aimlessly out of the window, said to Courtney, "Honey, I'm out of this business. From now on, we will work to keep our families together, and turn this craziness over to Darryl and Sue Lyn. Of all the things and lives that I have concluded, this thing with the dictator was rather cold, ruthless, and he had no beef with us. We did the devil's work, on this one!"

# # #

The following morning after everyone had rested and relaxed, and as the Sarge was leading the exercise regimen on the beach, the SAT phone rang. Courtney retrieved it from its charging cradle. She looked at the phone, and decided that she would find the Sarge, and give it to him. On the beach, at the other end of the property, she spotted a group of men exercising. She hastily walked towards the group. She saw the Sarge, walked over to him, and said, "You had a call." He looked at the phone and did not recognize the number. He said, "I'll call after we finish exercising. Thanks, honey!"

Approximately thirty minutes later, the team returned to the resort, and entered the dining room. The Sarge saw Courtney and Monica, walked over to them to say hello, and retrieved the SAT phone. As she handed him the phone, it began to ring again. He answered it immediately, and it was the Holy Father, who said, "Good job last evening, and I'm sorry one of those weasels got away."

"At least we got the intended target."

"Yes, you did! But the bandido pulling the strings is the one who got away. I know you have an interest in capturing him, but son, he is long gone, however, I know exactly how to hurt him, and leave him humble. The unfortunate thing for him is that a lot of the ill-gotten loot is stashed in a bank that you do business with, in St. Thomas. This time, you won't have to dress anyone up to look like someone else when you enter the bank deposit boxes because I will provide you with a copy of both keys for each of four boxes. When you have both keys, no questions are asked. Now, in two of the four over-size boxes that he has in the bank, you will find bearer bonds that should total well over $2 billion. That money belongs to the people. Until there is stable leadership, you will place those bonds in your foundation's boxes. Yes, son, you will be the keeper of billions of dollars that were stolen from the poor people of that country by the famous manipulator, Mr. Utz. If you and I die tomorrow, and there is no stable government, you will pass this burden down to ah, Darryl, Sue Lyn, Michael, Isaiah, Zanthius, Asiram and Desmond. Now, in the other two boxes, well, that was money he stole before he hooked up with the newly departed dictator. I like what Monica, and ah, Mallory, did with that orphanage. I would like you to use a sizeable amount of that loot to update my homes for babies who are left in the window of adoption. I also like what, ah, what's his name, ah, you know the one who signs with that beautiful Ayesha?"

"Holy Father, that would be Michael."

"How many Mikes and Michaels do you have in your charge? Never mind, I like what he and Ayesha are proposing to do with the homeless and hearing-impaired children. I would like to develop a paradigm of that project after the kinks are worked out."

The Holy Father paused, and then said, "Son, I know you think I'm trying to handle you and your people, but I'm not. I can't use my people because I can't be connected to the kinds of things that you and your people do effectively. I promise you one thing, within the next thirty days, I will have a mass with my highest-ranking cardinals, where I will pray, and absolve you and your people of all your sins committed in the name of our Lord, Jesus Christ. I will also pray for you and your people for what I consider, self-defense of your homes, your people, and those children. This I will do my son, without any notion of you doing further work in the name of the Holy Father or the Catholic Church."

The Sarge listened with intent, and said, "Holy Father, me and my people will welcome a mass for absolution for the souls that await us in Hades. Your last request was an assassination, and that is not what we do. Me and my people want to relax, enjoy our families, play with our children, and live in our homes without being on call to do termination work."

"Son, if I call you, it will be to save the world from itself or me! No more intermediary functions. Most perpetrators around the world have tied me to the recent underground communications about complete destruction of countries. I expect a series of assassination attempts from the north, east, west, and south. There are a lot of people for hire in this sordid world. What they don't know, is that I have the Swiss Guards, and secretly you. Your decision is crucial to the direction the church moves in, relating to those who would annihilate countries to assume control. I can let it happen or you can assist me on your own terms, of course. Again, my son, those people were going to kill millions of people until I made my pact with my brother. I said then, and I will say now, "not on my watch." I have devices of all sorts planted around the world, and I will not hesitate to conclude any nation that attempts to aggrandize itself against any peaceful nation. Your choice is simple, you can't hide from a disaster when foreign powers want to conclude your friends and family. Son, I must rest. Whenever I speak with you, you leave me speechless because you broker between good and evil. Those keys will be in your possession within four hours. May God bless and keep us all from tyranny. I would like to continue this conversation in a day or so, my son. Would that be all right with you?"

# # #

At dinner, the Sarge told the group that he had spoken with the Holy Father, and that there was a request in the mix.

As he was about to dive into the issue, he looked around the room, and saw how the children were growing. He looked at Ms. Viola, and said, "My, how the children are growing and developing. Does our constant traveling interfere with their education? Do we do enough to make sure that they are getting the basics?"

Luana rose from her seat, and said, "Sarge, if you track or test our kids by age, you will find that our group will test 2.5 grade levels above the average child their age. We have a regimen that includes, reading, mathematics, and geography that supersedes any lessons on earth because they live and breathe it, along with science. In a normal situation, my daughter, compared to others her age, reads and computes on the seventh-grade level. Rashida's daughter is on the eighth-grade level in both reading and math. Larry and Marisa's twins are on the eighth-grade level, as well. Therefore, if I had to make a comment on our children's education, I would have to say that we are ahead of the game. Now, social interactions are key to the development of humans. Although limited in scope, our children when in the outback and here, have learned to have complete conversations by signing, and they recognize the achievements made by this group, and honor those in charge. We have a good group of children. Oh, and by the way, Monica and Mallory's children came to us reading and computing at a second to third grade level. They now read and compute at the sixth-grade level. Our children make education easy by making sure that each child understands the lesson, and that no child can advance until all children understand the concepts."

The Sarge said, "Thanks be to God. Ms. Viola and Mary Alice, can you do me a favor, and escort the children on a short walk?"

Once the children had left the room, the Sarge said, "The Holy Father is aware of the names of each of us. I don't know how he keeps up with us, but somehow, he is aware of intimate details in some cases. Listen, he wants us to enter a bank in town, remove approximately $2 billion in bearer bonds from two of Mr. Utz's boxes, and deposit the contents into ours. He also wants us to empty two other boxes of Mr. Utz's, with untold millions of dollars, and upgrade homes for children given up for adoption, and he really likes what Michael and Ayesha are doing. Oh, and Asiram, we don't have to make you into someone you're not, because we'll have both keys, identification papers, passwords, and everything else needed to enter the boxes according to the Holy Father."

Zanthius raised his hand high, and asked, "Pops, what on earth are we going to do with $2 billion in bearer bonds?"

"That's a great question, son. We are going to hold them until there is a government or leadership in place that is more people oriented, not oil focused or self-profiting. The money belongs to the people of the country, and the Holy Father is entrusting those very negotiable bonds in our care. He has given the chore to our original team with the proviso that after we are long gone, the responsibility passes to Darryl, Sue Lyn, Zanthius, Asiram, Beatrice, the twins and LaGina. I left someone out. Oh, Michael is the other character. After them, if there still is no stable government in place, the responsibility is deferred to Larry and Marisa's twins, Beatrice, Mallory, and Monica's two children as well as Zanthius and Asiram's tribe. You know as I think about the responsibility for another country's money, I suddenly realize that we must put into place a structure for our ultimate demise. As you know, individually and collectively, we have a shitload of money. As a matter of fact, we still have millions stashed in the farm in

Virginia, and twice as much in the Midwest. Jong, do you have an accounting of the cash stored at the farm and ranch?"

Jong opened his computer, located a couple of files, and exclaimed, "Why you no listen to me!? I told you I need committee to help me count and keep money straight. You no listen, and then you ask me how much we have. Anyway, the farm has $37+ million, and the ranch has $64+ million."

"How much do we have in the various bank accounts?" Mallory asked.

Jong asked, "Is this a finance meeting of all of you, and just me?"

"Jong, get on with it," the Sarge admonished.

Jong exclaimed, "Okay master! In various safe deposit boxes around the country and the world, we have in excess of $200 million in cash and bearer bonds. In the various brokerage houses, we have in excess of $600 million. In the various bank accounts, we have approximately $90 million. The house in Philadelphia that no one talks about has $12 million in the safe, $45 million in gold bullion, $68 million in raw diamonds we collected from one of those crooks, each person including the kids have a cash account or debit card of $100k and each of the original members of the foundation have at minimum $50 million on a personal level. Our investments are a wash, meaning we don't expect any return from *the Sanctuary* or the other investment properties. Oh, I almost forgot, that wire transfer of $80 million from the non-sale of the Carbon Factor is sitting in our Swiss account."

"That sounds like a whole lot of money. We need to start focusing on projects that help people. We surely don't need this kind of money hanging around doing nothing when we could be helping people help themselves," the Sarge said.

"I was planning on presenting a new plane concept to the group. I know we've only had this plane for little over a year, but seemingly, it has a lot of maintenance issues, nothing major, but a lot of minor concerns. Therefore, I have tentatively, brokered a deal for a brand-new Boeing 777 with special characteristics as a result of watching and recording the things that people say they wish they had, while traveling from the outback to the states."

"Thanks for your off the cuff remarks about our finances. You know once we do this job for the Holy Father, Mr. Utz, no matter where he is in the world, is going to put a hit out on us. According to the Holy Father, this was his major stash, and we're about to take and build virtuous monuments with his stolen loot. As I return the meeting back to the basis of my concern, I want people to think about whether we do this thing for the Holy Father or we let Mr. Utz be, in the hopes that he leaves us alone," the Sarge said.

"Daddy-in-law, who I love to death, if I heard you correctly, he stole $2 billion from the poor people of that country. If that is correct, then I suggest that Mr. Utz, pick out his casket before he ventures this way. Daddy-in-law, we didn't go looking for fights, the man I love, your unknown son, kissed a woman, swallowed a capsule, and our world was turned inside out. Our mission has never been easy, and I don't expect it will ever be. I say, we stay true to form, give the heavy lifting to Darryl and Sue Lyn, and we act as, ah, consultants."

"Your comments reflect what Mallory and I have talked about for a long time. We're too old to be gallivanting around like we are young boys. Those days are over, and I want to sit on my porch that those two slum landlords sold me, above market price, I must admit, and just watch that sun set every evening. I want out. I see the look on Windom and Earther's faces, and I know they want out, as well. They want to spend some of that money they are about to earn from that land deal in Minnesota and do some tribal rehabilitation."

Windom raised his hand, stood up, and said, "The look on our faces is that of sadness. We have found a family that does not squabble, is not jealous, is protective of every member of its tribe, and cares about what happens in and to the world. We want to die fighting, and we want to die fighting alongside of you, Sergeant Beckmire, and your people."

A stillness spread over the room. The Sarge walked towards the two men, gave them massive bear hugs, and kisses on the cheeks. He then returned to his seat and began a dialogue with Courtney who motioned for Mallory and Monica to come over. This quiet talk lasted for three minutes when Courtney stood up, and said, "My man, our leader, the Sergeant Benjamin Beckmire, is tired. We will do this thing for the Holy Father, and we will enjoy each other for the next three weeks without any discussion of work, church, or villains. After those three weeks, a full week here, then a full week in the outback, and then another week to spend nights in our own private houses in the country. After those three weeks, we will head to Virginia and make some investments, and then on to Minnesota where we will secure our friends, and make sure all is going well, and then on to the Midwest. Listen people, this meeting is over, and the bar is open!"

## CHAPTER TWELVE

Michael and Ayesha became inseparable. Although no indication of a relationship between them was obvious, it was certain that in time, they too would follow the notions of the group; fall in love and become one.

Michael approached Monica, and said, "I would like to take a plane, and check on the project that those guys from Spain are heading. Do you think this is a good time to ask Courtney, since she's become somewhat of the 'Bey' of the tribe?"

Monica smiled, and replied, "You empower me, broaching your plans to me before moving up the food chain. Listen, Michael, you are such a part of this family, we all believe in you, and we are all still in disbelief about the passing of your father. If you decide that you can do this thing without creating a problem, then go forward."

# # #

The Sarge had essentially been isolated and protected by his woman. She was the leader as he rested and gained his awareness as the 900-pound gorilla in the crystal shop. Michael approached her and told her that he had asked Monica first about heading to South Beach with Ayesha to inspect the project and give her some idea of how they worked. Courtney replied, "Check with Jong, have him bring the smaller plane down from Miami, tell me who your back up will be, and I will consult with Mallory in the meantime."

Like clockwork, Jong was given a two-hour window as to when the plane would arrive. Michael selected Desmond, Isaiah, and Mallory included Windom, Earther, and Mike.

Two hours later at the airport, Michael signed, "I wanted to have a romantic conversation with you while being close to God! I forgot about how we operate. I am happy to make this visit with you so that you can, with your own eyes, see the kinds of things we like to do to 'help people help themselves.' I am still in a tailspin relative to the demise of someone I trusted that could have caused great pain in our community. I saw you, after securing that child, and realized that there was a glow around you that I had never witnessed before. Perhaps I was hallucinating, perhaps at that moment all I wanted was an odalisque, but nevertheless, I have had you on my mind ever since. My problem is, I'm not sure if I'm still in the revenge mode, or if I never really cared for the person who betrayed me, and the group."

Ayesha signed, "Think about it. Out of your entire group, you saved those children, and it was you who could sign, almost, flawlessly. That action was not by chance. This is spiritual, and no matter the pain that was created by the false prophet of love that you enjoyed, the circumstances are what they are. You rescued hearing-impaired children, and others, brought them to a hearing-impaired house whose neighbors think we are all deviants, and misfits. I saw you, and you saw me, and if that wasn't magic in the making then, I don't know what is. Listen, metaphorically, I'm interested in you, I'm not in love with you, however, I'm overwhelmed with your generosity. I will never trade my soul for bricks and glass. My heart is, and never will be for sale!"

Michael watched as her eyes swelled with tears and touched her hand. He signed, so much so soon! That crazy bomb in your city, my dad dying, and a lover who betrayed me. So much so soon!"

"So soon, is never soon enough, when the heart speaks the truth. We shall rest, talk some more, and decide if we should continue on this path. I am not suspicious of people as you should be. I didn't go looking for you to save my children or me, but you found me, and you knew how to communicate with me, and the children. For that, Michael, I owe you a wonderful dinner! She began to laugh, and so did he.

They shared a martini and ten minutes in the air, they were leaning on each other, smiling with the angels, and in the hands of the Almighty!

# # #

The plane landed in Miami at the airport that they secretly purchased that was manned by former military types. Desmond and Isaiah exited the plane, looked around, walked into the makeshift terminal, and was greeted by three individuals. The officious looking person said, "According to our records, you're allowed to land here at any time. The problem is simple, we don't know who you are, and you're not the person we normally deal with. Can you give us some contact information to verify that this is a sanctioned landing, and this plane is not under duress?"

Isaiah responded, "I'll call Jong, and let him know that we need clearance."

"How many are you?" The officious looking person asked.

Isaiah replied, "Nine including the pilots."

The guy asked, "Do you mind if I board the plane, and have a look around?"

"Help yourself. However, I'll have to screen you, and make sure you're not carrying any weapons or contraband onto our plane."

"That's usually the thing that we say! Welcome my brother, sorry to go through that façade, but we're here to make sure that when you guys come to this airport, no matter the time or reason, we're ready to provide security at the highest level." He then looked around, held his fist in the air, and the dots from laser scopes began to light up Isaiah and Desmond. They were immediately extinguished once the officious looking person raised his other hand into the air.

Desmond walked back to the plane, gave the okay sign, and everyone began a quick fellowship with the ground personnel who provided them with the necessary hardware to protect themselves.

Isaiah said, "Not sure we covered the transportation thing. Is that going to be a problem?"

"Not at all. Since we did not get a call for transportation, we put people on standby with two vehicles. All's well, my brother. You're in good hands!"

# # #

Once the group neared the site, Michael said to Ayesha, "I am going to cover your eyes for a few minutes. When the group reached the site, Michael got out of the vehicle first, and greeted Franco. Franco explained to Michael that things were moving slowly because of artificial rules governing the use of acquired property in the city limits. Michael said, "Franco, forget the bullshit, when will it be completed, my friend?"

Franco proudly stated, "Michael, it will be ready, furnished, and stocked with food in thirty days, fifteen days ahead of our promised completion date." The two men embraced, and Franco asked, "How are my friends and partners?"

Michael gave him a summary of events, but was cut short when Franco said, "I'm so sorry to hear about your padre. May we all meet him in heaven when it's our time."

When Ayesha was helped out of the vehicle, Michael uncovered her eyes, and Franco exclaimed, "Momma Mia; La Madonna." He walked over to Ayesha, grabbed her hand, and kissed it tenderly. Michael signed to Ayesha, "He loves beautiful women."

Ayesha signed, "Do you think I'm beautiful, despite my inability to speak to you?"

"We have been talking since we met. It's different, silent, and to me, spectacular. I'm interested in substance and character. Your beauty is pleasing to my eyes, but it's your soul, and character that I want to learn more about."

Ayesha looked at the main structure and began to cry. Michael was not watching her and did not realize that she was crying. Franco nudged him, tilted his head towards Ayesha, and that is when Michael truly fell in love with her. As she cried, he began to cry, as thoughts of his sister, father, and potential lover came to his mind. They embraced, and Ayesha signed, "You must cry until you realize that you did good things for good people. I know the loss of your dad is weighing on your mind, as well as the friend, that betrayed you and your group. Cry until your heart is content. I'm here for you." Franco and the rest of the men teared up as well.

As Ayesha entered her place, and looked at all the improvements, at every turn, she was surprised, and there were a new set of tears. Michael asked Isaiah to fetch her some water. Between her silent tears, she kept signing to Michael the same thing, "Are you an angel, are your people angels as well?"

Later after the realization that this was not a dream, but a conscious state of existence, Ayesha was shown the plans for the properties that had been annexed by Michael, and the group. She signed, "Those people would never sell their properties. Did you threaten them?"

Michael signed, "I never talked to them. The lawyers and bankers had conversations with them. No one in my group discussed buying them out. It seemed like a good idea, especially since there are lot of children who need a home, special services, and people to love them. This is a model that I hope to make my life's work, when I'm between work with the group. I have been studying the plight of the hearing and sight impaired, and they are often thrown away. I would like to create a self-sustaining program that will allow you to offer a service that can turn into support for your new homes and children. I'm not sure what this will look like, but I've already begun looking at foundations that will support self-sufficiency for those with special needs. My group will endow you and secure these properties. The only thing you'll have to be is creative about developing a program that will support your people and make them self-sufficient. I hope you'll allow me to work with you and express my ideas on how to do that."

Ayesha signed, "Are you an angel? If not a real angel, will you be my angel? I worry when you're not around, and

I'm elated when you are. I just don't want to push you into something that may not be in your best interest. I know what I want, Michael and it's to get to know you, and hopefully love you in a way that you'll know that you're the king of my heart!"

Michael smiled, reached for the hand that Franco did not slobber on, and kissed it with passion. He then signed, "My heart is full of sorrow today. Tomorrow and the next day, I hope it leads me blindly to you!"

At the airport, Michael met with the person in charge, and suggested that he lower the temperature of his greetings to those who support, and finance veteran's efforts. The guy looked at Michael, and said, "I wasn't sure who you were. I've never seen you before, and this group is too important to us, and this country to make a mistake by not grilling a stranger, even though he descends from one of their planes. I was never told about you, Michael. I'm a cautious man, as well as my friends who you represent. I would like to call this meeting, and this entire event a wash. I don't need the heat, and I'm sorry for giving you some."

"As I think about it, you're correct. We have never seen each other before, and I guess, I wanted to be important, and so did you. From this day forward, once I've sanctioned it with Jong and the others, I may need you to check on some special people who don't hear or speak. You guys can be mentors, but you must learn sign language. I'm trying to create more opportunities for all of us. I won't speak of this again if you won't." The two men hugged, and then shook hands. Michael, out of habit began to sign, and then caught himself. He said, "I'm Michael. What's your name?"

"My Name is Bob, Bob Tagartmore, and those guys looking at you are Bernardo Wallace, Arturo Washington, Theodore Fields, and the sleepy looking guy is Lawrence Humphries. Guys, when I get back to St. Thomas, I'll have my friend get me books on sign language and send them to you."

"By the way, how is St. Thomas?"

"Wait a minute! You guys have never been to St. Thomas?"

"No, but we hear about it now and then," Bob stated.

"When I get back, I'll check with Jong, and if they agree, and you guys are all clean, I'll send a plane for you. You'll love it, and perhaps being around our group, they will see the merit in you, and begin to think beyond sign language, and getting you involved in our core responsibilities. It's amazing what a few words without testosterone can do. My brother, I will get you guys that vacation."

# # #

On the plane, and after all were accounted for, Michael looked at his people, and said, "Thank goodness we didn't have any issues. I'm thankful that you guys escorted us. Talking with Bob, I realized we have a lot of support people that don't enjoy some of the benefits that we do. I'm going to propose to the Sarge that we give these guys and their families a vacation on us in St. Thomas. We have a lot to be thankful for, and a lot of people to thank for supporting what we do."

#

Courtney continued her regimen relative to her husband. Rumors began to circulate but were extinguished by Monica who politely stated, "We should pray for our leader, and not guess what is going on. I, a friend of both the Sarge and Courtney, am not aware of his condition. However, before we descend into the bowels of stupidity, let's all hope that he is well, resting, and ready to command our next move as a group."

Mary Alice, it was thought, appeared to want to contest the information from Monica, but was pinched by Jong, who said, "He is our bey, what he decides is not your concern. When he comes out of his funk, he will allow us to know what his ailments are if any, or what his directions are, if he so chooses. Never, my love, challenge the source of our survival, and the center of our group. He is the one!"

"My love, I was going to ask her if she needed anything. Where the hell did these metaphors come from?"

Jong said, after feeling embarrassed, "Honey, I was practicing my oratory skills in order to have a sane debate with John Lee. I never understand him, but he too, is the key to our survival."

Mary Alice said, "Yeah, right my noble, loyal, and full of shit husband, who I love so very much!" Jong formed his lips to respond, but realized that he was entering forbidden territory, a place that most men hate because it makes you sleep alone, a thing a wise man never wants to do.

#

A few days later, at breakfast, the doors to the dining room swung open, and there he was, the center of concern, Sergeant Benjamin Beckmire. He acknowledged everyone who was there, went directly to his table, kissed his bride, and many of the grandbabies that were near. He saw Beatrice and Lagina and beckoned them over. He looked at both girls, and asked, "Did you pray for me?"

Beatrice responded by saying, "I pray for everyone, every day."

Lagina laughed, hugged the Sarge first, and then said, "You know you're always in my prayers because I know that you pray for all of us each day or at least on the days that you pray."

The Sarge smiled, hugged both little ladies, and kissed his bride again. Courtney asked, "What would you like for breakfast dear?"

The Sarge responded, "Plain old oatmeal with blueberries. Is that possible?"

The Sarge then looked at the group, and announced, "Today we are going to move billions of dollars in stolen money, from a crook's account to ours, and hold this money in escrow until real and honest leadership comes to office in that country of interest. On another note, many of you have been wondering where I've been for the past week or so. Well, the truth of the matter is, I was in constant communication with the new person who wants to be our handler. I also took the time to allow my wife to treat nagging wounds and cuts that were on the verge of infection. Now, I heard about the rumblings throughout the group, but I'll only say this one time, we have a chain of command. Now, are there any volunteers who want to move as much as two billion dollars in bearer bonds from a crook's account, and into one of our boxes?"

All hands were raised, including Courtney's. The Sarge looked at her, and asked, "Are you looking for a golden parachute or something?"

"No, dear! I'm looking to see what two billion dollars in bearer bonds look like."

Ava, Monica, Ms. Viola, Luana, Mary Alice, and every other woman in the group wanted the assignment. The Sarge knew better than to do the picking, looked at Mallory, and said, "Make the assignments."

Mallory gave him a 'I don't believe you look and shrugged his shoulders.' He said, "Since I have been given this ominous task, the only fair way to consider every potential volunteer is by doing a lottery. Do you all agree to abide by the outcome?" All the women agreed, and he walked over to Mrs. Carter, and asked, "Do you have any of those strips of numbers that are two sided?"

She laughed, and said, "That Sarge sure is shrewd, ridding himself of this snake. I do have such a thing that we use for prizes for guests. I'll be right back." As she headed for the door, Ayesha was entering. Ayesha signed, "Hello, how are you?"

Mrs. Carter pulled out a piece of paper, and wrote, "My dear, I am doing fine. Will you spend time with me and others to teach us how to sign?"

Ayesha smiled, hugged her, and signed, "Your words make me feel welcome!"

Mrs. Carter had no idea what she signed until a voice behind her said, "Mother, she said your words make her feel welcome!" Mrs. Carter hugged Ayesha, and when she backed away, she placed her hand on her heart. The Sarge witnessing this exchange interrupted Mallory, and asked, "Have the sign language classes begun, and if so, how come no one told me about them?"

Mallory screamed, "Sir, you have to be among the living, sir!"

"Funny, smartass corporal. Please, answer the question," responded the Sarge.

"Sarge, the kids have been teaching us at meal functions. Today there is a lesson in signing the alphabet. After your meal, you will be asked to participate."

# # #

Later during the day, the selected members of the group walked into the bank, presented several sets of keys, and were shown to boxes that belonged to Mr. Utz. The rest is history!

# # #

Michael received a call from Franco who indicated that some local union officials and/or thugs, were demanding payment for them stealing their work. Michael instructed him to find out who was in charge, and to give that person the SAT phone number so that the Sarge could make our resolve perfectly clear.

Five minutes later after Michael had briefed the Sarge about the problem with their new project, the SAT phone rang, and the Sarge answered it in a very officious way. He said, "This is Beckmire, and currently I'm on a mission for the Catholic church. I understand that you or your people are threatening my crew who are building out those properties for the hearing impaired. Now, I'm not sure what you want, but once we finish with the church matter, we will be happy to meet with you."

"Listen buster, I don't give a shit......the phone was disconnected. The guy on the other end said, "That little shit hung the phone up on me."

Franco responded, "That means, him and his crew, are boarding their plane to come here, and relate to you personally. Listen, I'm a contractor, and they are my friends, but hell man, you just stirred the fucking devil. You heard about all those dead bodies in Virginia? Well, those be the people who are responsible for them. If I, were you, my friend, I would try to reconnect, but avoid swearing at him, at all costs."

"You think that we're afraid of a bunch of cowboys? Well, let them bring it on. We'll handle their asses like fluffed pillows."

Franco said, "Please call him back. They will emasculate you and your people and gut you from your little head to that big one. You made a mistake by fucking with the 'killing machine'!"

There was a pause in the dialogue, and the union official, Mike Wallace asked, "Does the name Ben Beckmire sound familiar to you?"

Franco acknowledged, "Sir, that is who hung the phone up on you. If you know him, don't make them come here for bullshit. Take your people and that big ass plastic rata and disappear."

# # #

Michael called Franco back, and asked if he could speak with the union person. Franco responded, "Those people took their plastic rata, and left in a hurry. I mentioned the 'killing machine,' and he asked me if the name Ben Beckmire sounded familiar. I told him, that is who hung up on him. They had a thirty-second meeting and left in a hurry. I think we're good for a while. Now, I have a question, we're up to code, and things have been ordered. How much space are you designating for everyone? I mean, is there a code requirement?"

"Franco, I don't know the answer to that. Google it and let me know. Are you referring to space in general or living space?"

"Both my friend. I don't want to board a plane and know that we screwed up by not appointing the right amount of space for each child. I remember reading something like that when I thought about a daycare center," Franco announced.

"Oh, my goodness! I'm going to talk to Ayesha about that. I see this project as a long-term care facility, and it will need doctors, nurses, and other medical specialists. Perhaps we can establish a daycare center where parents can bring their children for extensive evaluations, and stay with their child in our facility, much like the Ronald McDonald House. I'm sure we can arrange a relationship with a hospital or research lab that specializes in the hearing impaired," Michael stated.

"Michael, you have lots of land to expand on. Let's get this aspect off the ground first, and then think it through with your support team, and Ayesha. By the way, if you're not interested in her, I can escort her to Spain with me."

"Adios mi amigo. Speak with you soon," Michael stated.

At dinner everyone enjoyed the meal prepared by Mrs. Carter. It was lamb stroganoff with potatoes, onions, celery, and a sauce to die for. She had overheard the story about how the group came to be and knew that the stories she heard about how spectacular the lamb creation was at the Italian Bistro, were exaggerated. She decided to provide the meal without informing people what it was. ***The Sanctuary*** was aware that there were no food allergy issues of any members of the group and, therefore, she felt confident that this would place her lamb stroganoff on a higher plane than the brothers and their dad, from the Italian Bistro.

Everyone had seconds. In some cases, there were some receiving their third portion. Unexpectedly, Asiram commandeered the microphone and said, "My conejo has done it again. I'm pregnant!"

Luana walked to the mike, and said, "I think I'm pregnant as well." Rashida, Marisa, Gerri, PJ, and Azuree followed her.

# # #

John Lee said to Somara, "We should head for our homes, and see if these newcomers want to buy from Jilkes and me."

The Sarge bellowed out, "You're both slum landlords!"

During the dinner, and right after the final woman acknowledged her status, Okema's phone rang, and it was her former handler. He got right to the point, and said, "We need the help of you and your comrades. We have a critical situation happening with merchant and oil ships passing off the coast of Somalia. We can't escort every ship that travels that route with our Navy. We want to entice certain overlords to try to commandeer two ships carrying over $15 billion in illicit drugs," her handler stated.

Okema said, "We're having a celebration. I'm not comfortable listening to you without my leaders being involved. I will call you back on this number once I have had a chance to speak with the Sarge. By the way, you screwed us on the payment for that last job. You charged us a surcharge for saving your elite from a nasty ending. What was it, ah, twenty-three percent! Your sorry ass had better figure that into your payment offer. Before I speak with my people, you can send me a text with the proposed number. Goodbye!"

Brown asked his wife, "Who was that on the phone? You seemed upset."

"Rich, it was my former handler. He wants us to do a job for him, but I told him that we were in the middle of a celebration. If you can get the Sarge and Mallory to walk away with us for a few minutes, I would like to say what I have to say, just one time. Personally, I don't trust that bastard."

Later after all the celebrations, Brown cozied up to Mallory, and said, "Boss-man, I need to speak with you and our leader, privately."

As the group circulated to congratulate each other, the Sarge happened to eyeball Okema, and realized that there was a problem. His first thought was, "what on earth did that dum-dum do this time?" When Mallory approached him, and asked for an audience, he knew there was trouble afoot.

An hour later on the beach, the Sarge, Mallory, Brown, and Okema met. As she was about to explain the reason for the meeting, John Lee, Jilkes, Asiram and Zanthius approached.

Okema explained the call from her former handler, and showed a text with a number in it, from him.

The Sarge asked, "Is that the same guy who put a surcharge on our bill?"

Okema bowed, and said, "You are correct."

The Sarge boldly, and nastily stated, "Fuck him, and the flag he's under!"

This was uncharacteristic of the Sarge. As he began to walk away, Asiram asked, "So, daddy-in-law, if one of your grandbabies asked for your help after doing something bad, is that going to be your response?"

He looked at her, smiled, then frowned, and said, "You're right my love." He turned to Okema, bowed as low as possible, and asked, "Is this an adventure or a good deed? Frankly, I'm tired of doing good deeds. As I get older, I like adventures, if they're good deeds as well. Okema, I can't correct what I said. However, we're getting fat sitting around here. We need to train for something. What does that scumbag handler of yours, I'm sorry, ex-handler, have in mind?"

# # #

The details of the adventure/good deed were discussed and received a vote of confidence from all of those in the meeting, save one. It was agreed that the idea would be broached at the groups' breakfast in the morning.

Later, when Okema and Brown entered their room, she embraced him, kissed him seductively, and inquired, "My love, why did you vote against that business we discussed with the Sarge?"

"Okema, I'm tired of killing, and having people attempt to kill me. I want to enjoy our family and leave that adventure shit to the young at heart. I'm older, and hopefully wiser. I've hurt a lot of people in my life, and I want out."

"My heartbeat, you want out of the group?"

"Yes! I want to go somewhere with my family, and live life without looking over my shoulder."

"Oh, my goodness! Are you going through involutional melancholia, also known as male menopause? What the hell is wrong with you? You should have gone through that before you gave me babies. Now, do I need to get a lover, or are you going to continue to do death defying things with me, and the group? My husband, my friend, and my lover, I tried to get out of this world, and you dragged me back into it. Hey, boyfriend, put your damn man drawls on, and get over this pacifist mindset. You're a part of the 'killing machine,' and it will follow you no matter where you go."

Brown looking defeated, and friendless said, "Baby, I needed to hear that from you. I know my destiny, but I wasn't sure if you knew yours. I staged my response, and you kicked my butt. I will never abandon you, or the group, and hopefully, I will never have to choose between the two. I love you so much, and still stimulate myself with the view of your walking into that lounge in the Marco Polo Hotel, in Macau. You are my soulmate, and I just didn't want you following me into the lion's den without a true commitment."

The fire burned bright in their suite. The passion and love making would last until the wee small hours of the morning, and in the morning, both would evolve committed, invigorated, and eager to challenge evil wherever and in whatever form it took.

At breakfast time and emulating the first time he spent the night with Okema, Brown strutted into the room like a peacock, as Okema, and the children followed. The Sarge looked at Courtney, and said, "Damn, look at him flow! Remember when Okema spent the night with him, and he strutted into that restaurant in Macau? Check out that walk ahead of his family. Damn that's beautiful!"

Brown walked directly to where the Sarge was sitting, and said, "There was a misunderstanding about my recalcitrant behavior last evening. To avoid a lot of bullshit, just don't consider my hand being raised in the air."

No one paid attention to the amount in the text message. Okema convinced the Sarge not to consider any opportunity, until the surcharge was reimbursed, and that they would charge him a flat fee plus travel, and a kicker if the situation were underestimated. The kicker as explained by Zanthius could cost her handler another $10+ million on top of the $100 million offered for completion.

In his infinite wisdom, the Sarge said, "I don't want to go to war against oppressed people. Okema, tell your handler, we're not the right group for this job. We have a price, but it's not a paltry one. Tell him, we saved him billions, and he paid us minimum wages, no thanks. Wish him well from us."

Okema bowed slightly and retreated from the area. She called her ex-handler, told him the sentiments of her leader, and decided to push him for the return of the surcharge. She asked him, politely, "Are you fucking insane? You cheat us by charging us a surcharge to do business to save your sorry ass. Now you have another problem that you can't handle directly, and you need a group that can discreetly produce the kind of results you want. You my friend are ashes in a crematorium that have already been extinguished. Until you stop cheating the people who help you, may the fire burn so bright and continuously, that your DNA is erased from awareness." Okema hung up the phone and smiled at her approach to her former handler.

Thirty minutes later, Okema's phone rang again. She recognized the number but decided to ignore it.

Less than three minutes later, her phone rang again, and she decided to give it the same acknowledgment as before. This continued nine times, and she finally answered the phone, and yelled, "What the hell do you want from us?"

"I want to pay you $200 million for the proposed job, another $10.5 million that was accidentally charged to you as a surcharge up front, and a bonus of $20 million. I will handle all of the pertinent issues, and be responsible for your, in and out functions."

"If you're going to pay us that amount of money, handle our entrance and exit strategy, then it is unlikely we will trust your process. If we successfully complete the job, why would you want to make sure that we get out of the country successfully? Seems like a win-win for you! If we did the work, and somehow couldn't get out of the area, you would save the crown or yourself, a lot of money," Okema stated.

"As I said, I'm willing to pay it forward?"

"How about it. Do it, and I believe my people will be more apt to help with that issue. I need to remind you, every time you kill a cockroach, you had better find out where he has been, so that you can go and kill all of its eggs."

"Yeah, we are aware of that problem. However, the way you people make statements, people might become a little hesitant to strive for the highest seat or surround themselves with ruthless people to make sure that people like you don't have access to them," her ex-handler lamented.

#

The following day prior to the pre-dinner cocktail hour, Okema and Brown approached the Sarge. He looked at them, and said, "My gosh, you people want to do charity work. Don't you?"

Okema replied, "Oh, yes, Sergeant Beckmire, we want to perform charity duties, at the tune of $200 million plus the $10.5 million in rebates for that surcharge that the person assessed us, and a $20 million bonus."

"That's a lot of dollars. Is he willing to pay that for this job and guarantee an exit strategy for us?"

"Sarge, he's willing to pay it forward along with the surcharge monies exploited from us and guarantees an exit strategy. I'm assuming, he has a lot of shit going on that his people can't be caught involved in."

"Okema, why would we want to protect $15 billion in drugs?"

"Sergeant Beckmire, I'm told that there will be no drugs, or if there are, just enough to draw out the overlords, and have them at least, commit their lieutenants. We surely don't want to go into that country unless we send nukes first, the marines, second, the army third, and then us. That place is a safe haven for pirates."

"Okema, why would he pay us that kind of money for a job that's a mirage?"

"Sergeant sir, I have asked my wonderful husband the same thing. I think that although he says there is $15 billion in drugs on the ship, I'm assuming that there must be $100 to $200 billion in drugs, or sophisticated weaponry on those two ships. Perhaps the real cargo is on another vessel. My suggestion is simple; we rig those ships with enough explosives, that will sink them in a matter of minutes. In addition, my leader, I also suspect that my former handler is a part of a smuggling outfit and, therefore, those ships probably will have as much as $100 to $200 billion in illicit contraband or weapons."

As the Sarge pondered the somewhat suicide mission, he asked, "How do you pay or receive payment for that kind of money?"

Okema replied, "In diamonds, bearer bonds, or a lot of trunks full of cash."

Brown responded, "If the banking industry is crooked and connected, then it's all about paper transfers. No cash, no diamonds, no gold bullion, and no bearer bonds, just paper to paper and account to account."

The Sarge thought about it and said, "In essence, your former handler wants us to provide protection for his treasonous behavior, and piracy. That is not the kind of work that we do. I must admit, being paid forward $200 million sounds fantastic, it also sounds like a complicit number, you know, the kind that says you were in this deal because you are a significant part of the transaction."

Okema thought about what the Sarge had said, as well as the nature of her former handler, and decided that the Sarge was on to something with that bit of wisdom. She looked at Brown, and flatly stated, "I really don't want anything to do with that person. He has proven to me time after time that the only game in town is the one that helps him move up professionally, financially, and I think this is his financial end game at play."

# # #

During breakfast, the Sarge announced the opportunity, and asked for comments or concerns. There were none because the group, although living large and easy, needed the notion of an adventure to keep the blood flowing through the aging veins.

In the dining room, the Sarge dropped his head, and said, "Each adventure creates the possibility of a lot of pain. We are set for life, our kids are set for life, our friends are set for life, and God and spirits have been good to and for us. I want to go to my house in the South, sit on my porch, and monitor all these kids playing in the streets. I want to be the male version of a nanny, or manny, to these babies that are being formed as I speak, and those who are here. In other words, I want peace!"

John Lee stood up and said, "I like what the Sarge said, and I support his retirement."

Jilkes yelled, "Hey dum dum, he didn't retire. He said he wanted to play with all these children. Where the hell did you get that retirement mess from?"

"I just thought he was not interested in the shit he got us into in Vietnam, then with Brown and Bernstein, and then continued with Zanthius and Asiram. I mean, my life is rewarded with my children, and my wonderful wife, who by the way, is also interested in pig farming. But that there thing called adrenaline, and that there other thing called adventure, be the thing that keeps this group together."

Suddenly, John Lee's voice began to quiver, and his eyes began to water, and he burst into tears, and yelled, "That thing called adventure is our blood of life. Without it, we will disappear without a trace."

The Sarge and Jilkes embraced him, and the Sarge said, "One of these days, you assholes are going to let me finish my statements. I said I wanted peace, but I also want the adventure that is monetarily stimulating and allows us to adopt additional programs that help people help themselves. Stay with me, people. Listen, this has been the greatest adventure on the planet. I am still with eleven guys who were with me in Vietnam, covered my back, and me theirs on every occasion. I have the greatest wife, the doctor, who heals, prescribes, and watches each person in the group, a daughter and two sons. In this world, I didn't know I had one of my sons, you know the one who brought us a shitload of trouble, along with his beautiful wife and her wacky mannerisms. She saved us, housed us, and fed us. We expanded our group, look at my nephew, who has a wife and children, and his wife is one of the smartest people that I've ever known. Our pilots, and their significant others, our people in the sewers, Franco, Ms. Viola, and the others including our recently departed founder of *the Sanctuary*, Mr. Christopher Carter. Do you know we have another family in the Midwest, and you know what I want to do? Of course, you don't! I want to send our plane for them right now and let them enjoy what we take for granted. Mr. Jong, will you arrange for that to happen?"

As he paused for a drink, he said, "Now, I am the luckiest man on earth in that I have eleven people who would die for me, and me for them. I have McArthur, Gladstone, Whitmore, Jong, Jilkes, John Lee, Mallory, Bernstein, Brown, Chakes, and Montomie. Historically, we went through hell as soldiers. I am so happy that every day of my life, these people are with me, loyal to me, and each other. This is the greatest gift my God could ever give me. In addition, I have Larry and Rashida who never ask why, but immediately do as I ask. I have all of you, Marisa, Monica, Luana, Mary Alice, Ayesha, Somara, Okema, Yvett, Yeshida, PJ, Alvara, Gerri, Azuree, Isaiah, Desmond, Earther, Windom, and others. We have family in Australia, and Jong has people all over the damn world. Listen, I just want to say, I like adventure, but it comes at a cost. It is that cost that bothers me and keeps me from making decisions about obligating our people for money!" As the Sarge was about to continue his dialogue, the SAT phone rang. It was the Holy Father!

CHAPTER THIRTEEN

Sergeant Beckmire did not immediately answer the phone call from the Holy Father. He and the entire group listened to the phone ring, and finally stop. He looked at the SAT phone and said, "I am a believer, but I will not be manipulated, used as a weapon, and fight battles that should be fought in public with words, and not bullets. The Holy Father, as most of you know, troubles me. I'm not sure if he is truly the Holy Father or Diablo. His resolve is unheard of, for a man of the cloth. By my not answering his call, I want him to realize that we're not for sale, not to be exploited in the name of salvation, and for adventures other than the ones we sanction. He will call back in ten minutes, and I will not answer his call. I will have my cocktails and enjoy the night with my family and friends. I am not sure who is calling, so, I'll just hold the call-in abeyance until tomorrow. Salute!"

#

The following morning, Ben Beckmire's SAT phone rang. As he opened his eyes and tried to discern the numbers on the clock, he mumbled something incoherent, and said to Courtney, "Honey, do you want to go for a swim before I talk to the person that called?"

"Ben Beckmire, I'm asleep, and plan on staying in this position for the next three hours. Please, take your call in the anteroom."

At 0800 hours, there was a tremendous bang on the door! The Sarge and Courtney both grabbed weapons. The voice on the other side of the door said, "Sarge, I need Courtney, Chakes is in a bad way."

Courtney dressed quickly and ran out of the door with the Sarge trailing. When they got to Chake's room, he was on the floor, convulsing, foaming from the mouth, and shaking. Courtney screamed, "Get the van ready for transport. He is having a stroke. She grabbed a pen from the end table and tried to place it in his bleeding mouth. He apparently had bitten his tongue. She told the Sarge, "I need you to open his mouth, and let me reconfigure the placement of his tongue. He is going to bite down with a horrific force. If he catches my fingers, he will bite them off."

The Sarge retorted, "Honey, I got you covered." He strategically placed his fingers in harm's way and told Courtney to secure the pen. No one lost fingers but Chakes was in a bad way. Courtney tried to discern which side of his body would be in trouble and decided that it was not characteristically the left side, but the right side. She yelled, "Sarge, slap the shit out of him."

The Sarge replied, "What?"

Courtney screamed, "Slap him or lose him!"

The Sarge did not hesitate. He slapped Chakes so hard, it appeared as though he fractured his jaw. Courtney said, "Sarge, you may have broken his jaw, but you saved his life. The clot in his head was relieved for a moment, but we must get him to the hospital. The source of the problem must be isolated, and I'm afraid I might have to perform a lobotomy of sorts on him. The hospital here is unequipped to handle this kind of an emergency. We need to get him back to the states, and I mean asap!"

In the meantime, Ms. Viola, Luana, and Beatrice were in shock because the indication that something was wrong was when Chakes yelled at Beatrice for something that she was not responsible for. Ms. Viola told Luana to call Courtney because the scoundrel was not well.

# # #

That night, the SAT phone rang again, and it was the Holy Father. The Sarge saw the number, and once again decided that he was not going to answer it. At the hospital, he said to Courtney, "That was the Holy Father again."

Courtney responded, "Honey, return his call, and see what he wants. If it's something you can't consider, then inform him. After all, you're one man short, and you never go forward without a full complement." The Sarge looked at her, and said, "What on earth would I do without you?"

The Sarge called the Holy Father and was told that his team would probably be better positioned to handle the impending threat if they were in the outback. The Holy Father said, "If you attempt to handle this issue on US soil, you will add the scrutiny of your government, and many things will be unable to be explained. My son, had you answered my call, you would have 48 hours to make haste. As it is, you have hours before *the Sanctuary* will be invaded by authorized military types. When did you openly threaten the leader of the free world?"

"Holy Father, I don't like the guy, but we would never go against the grain, and threaten the President of the United States of America."

"My son, you and I know this. However, you failed to terminate Mr. Utz, you emptied his coffers, he couldn't make rent payment on his property in Paris, and it was sucked up by someone who hates him. You embarrassed an important man, and he is out for blood. He manufactured notes, and audio of you stating that the only way to free this country of tyrants and oligarchs, is to openly kill them!"

"Your holiness, that statement if factual doesn't advocate tyranny. It is simply a statement. Mr. Utz on the other hand, was a lucky man. We will now devote a significant amount of his resources to locating him. I will place his picture in the alleys, tunnels, and everywhere else my brothers are. It will only be a matter of days before we flush him out. I will offer a modest contract for his head, and in the lowest places, people will barter to gain access and destroy, the vermin. In his namesake, we have built an institution for the hearing impaired. It will be expanded to include those who are sightless, from there we will test the model, make sure it's replicable, and we will do this with the funds we extracted from the thief."

"My, son, gather your flock, and immediately head to your aircraft. May God watch over and protect you. I know Mr. Utz will become your main interest, but on your way to the outback when you stop in San Diego for fuel, and to regroup, if you could go to the border and take pictures, I would greatly appreciate it. The truth is being distorted. I need a rebellious group of people to start a campaign of righteousness, in your country. You talk about going to hell in a hand basket, well, as you can see, those in charge are trying to sell your country to the Russians, and some are trying to buy America back from the Russians. It appears to be complicated but, in the end, it all will end in a wash. My fear is that those in Australia, will own the world without competition, based upon the amount of natural resources available to them."

The Sarge asked Courtney if she could stabilize Chakes, and could his body endure the long flight to the outback. She said, "Sarge, the problem is I can't discern the cause of the condition, and whether or not it's a stroke or a blood clot or a thousand other things. I mean, the air pressure might create a problem or any of a million things can go wrong with moving him."

"Honey, a legal military force is on their way here to confront us. The last remnants of Mr. Utz's loyal payroll. We can't have a confrontation at *the Sanctuary*. Do you think we can fly to Maryland, and seek help there?"

"Sarge, if we land at our normal airport, I can make a call, and have some of the best surgeons from Hopkins waiting on our arrival. I can put him in a vegetation state for at least three hours without hopefully, injuring his brain."

The Sarge saw Mallory, and said, "We're out of here in forty-five minutes. I want the wheels of the plane to be airborne then. I'll explain everything on the plane."

As Ms. Viola tried to convince Beatrice that it was not her fault that her dad was ill, Luana said, "Baby, he is a strong man, and he loves you and your brother dearly. You really saved his life by allowing him to scream at you knowing that he has never done that before. He knew that by shouting at you, everyone would realize that there was a problem. Beatrice, your dad is alive because he chose you to deliver the message that he wasn't feeling well. Be thankful to God that he loves you enough to know that you would make sure that someone attended to him."

Forty-five minutes later, all personnel were present and accounted for. Courtney injected Chakes with zolpidem tartrate, that would allow him to sleep peacefully for the next five hours and breathe completely on his own.

Fifteen minutes later, Captain Carla who was in command, received a call from the tower to hold in place. She roared those twin engines and let the brakes off. The plane rocked backwards, then lunged forward, allowing her to pull her vertical take-off once again. The air traffic controller called on her radio, and said, "I'm glad you got my backwards message. With that many military planes attempting to land, I figured they wanted to have a conversation with you guys. Have a safe trip and see you when you straighten this mess out."

Courtney yelled, "I'm going to kill that woman."

The Sarge replied, "Look out of your window. Those are military planes lining up to land. She did us good, baby. She did good by us!"

After the plane had leveled off, Carla came out of the cockpit, picked up the microphone, and said, "I know that take-off scared some of you people, but you didn't see the planes that were about to land as I was taking off. I violated all protocol and safety measures, but I also know that they weren't there on the island to do maneuvers. They were coming for us." She returned the mike to the holder, Courtney started a slow clap that turned into a thunderous recognition of what each family member must be willing to do,   take matters into their own hands without a lot of conversation or approval.

Courtney unbuckled her seatbelt and approached the cockpit. She said to Carla, "Didn't I tell you to give us a warning when you were going to do that mess? Well, anyway, good job, and keep us safe. Thanks, Carla."

Carla came on the public address system and requested that the Sarge and Mallory enter the cockpit. Minutes later when the two men entered the cockpit, Carla said, "I highly suggest that we bypass San Diego, and hold your mission in abeyance for the Holy Father and fly directly to our alternative fueling depot. Those military types that landed, in my estimation, are probably having us tracked. As soon as we get near San Diego, I will engage that three-million-dollar cloaking system and see if it works."

The Sarge replied, "I know you're joking. Right?"

"Sergeant Beckmire, when I talk to you, I tell you what the actual landscape is. I don't make stuff up as I go along. Mr. Jong thought that the cloaking technology might come in handy and decided to invest his personal funds. Apparently, it was one of the projects his late cousin was working on. You are aware that this plane has a carbon footprint on it which makes the use of that technology conceivable."

"Mallory, let's take this meeting to the back of the plane, and call his ass in. Why would he do this without inquiring?"

"Sarge, just like Carla placed this bird into a vertical climb, each person who has to make a decision at that precise moment, must make it with the interest and safety of the group in mind. Listen, you always tell Jong, make the decision, and do what you think is right. Okay, he did what he thought, and spent his own money. Not a bad deal for the group, as I consider it, if it works."

The Sarge looked at Carla, and said, "I need you in the meeting. Have your second in command take over and have your standby pilot assist."

In the back of the plane, the group gathered, and Jong was the last one to join. He said, "I hope no one complained about take-off! It saved us from military."

"How come you develop that alternative language when you think your ass is about to be chewed out?"

"Old saying, 'when you don't know what the problem is, improvise and bring another issue to the table. People will forget first one'!"

The Sarge said, "Cut the shit! Did you spend $3 million on a cloaking system for this plane?"

Jong looked at Carla, then at the Sarge, and said, "I spend my personal money on the people I love. Is that now a problem?"

The Sarge asked, "Does this plane have a carbon footprint?"

"Sarge, it does. Why are you asking me this? The plane is safe, nothing was done structurally, mechanically, compositely, or anything else. We installed a layer on the wings, the fuselage, and the engines. It's supposed to work like those stealth fighters, but our imaging functions are less efficient. If we add another layer of materials, it will give us greater capabilities to stay under the radar, and unnoticed. This is an experiment with a company we own with the technology that's ours, and with the workers who are loyal."

"You must believe in this technology to invest $3 million of your personal money."

"Sarge, I would have placed all of my funds in this project if I knew it would keep us all safe!"

"Okay, remind me to reimburse you for your investment. The question at hand is getting out of the country until we can reset this issue," the Sarge stated.

# # #

At the group's airport in Maryland, an ambulance waited patiently for the plane to land, and come to a complete stop. As soon as it stopped, the ambulance pulled up to the forward door on the port side, and steps immediately began to descend to the ground. Once the steps locked into place, Chakes was loaded onto a stretcher, and his buddies helped him into the ambulance. Ms. Viola remained behind with Beatrice. Mallory, Jilkes, John Lee, Courtney, and Luana squeezed into the small ambulance.

At the hospital, Chakes' vital signs were taken as he was ushered into an emergency room. Courtney filled the doctors in on what had happened, and what she thought was the problem. As Courtney watched the monitors come online, she gasped, "His body temperature is off the charts. That's not a sign of a stroke. Something else must be going on with him. As they extracted vial after vial of blood from Chakes, Courtney went to her homegrown remedies, and told John Lee and Jilkes to fetch her some raw onions. As the doctors in the hospital followed protocol, and tried to deduce the nature of the problem, Courtney began slicing onions, and placing them around Chakes' body. An intern walked in, and said, "Oh, my goodness! That old wives' tale stuff doesn't work. Here at Hopkins, we practice learned medicine, not that medieval stuff you're trying." Courtney mumbled to herself, "yeah, ask the Lack's family about your learned medicine, rookie."

The intern replied, "I'm sorry, I didn't understand what you said."

"Young man, you wouldn't," Courtney snidely remarked.

As the doctors began to monitor the screens, it was obvious that there was an appreciable drop in his body temperature, and the only thing that could be attributed to that development, was the onions. The head doctor said, "Dr. Beckmire, it looks like the onions are working. My grandmother used to tell me about the healing capabilities of onions, but I never had the opportunity to use them, or see them applied. I mean, we haven't given him anything because we don't know what ails him, you come along, and show us up with simple onions. Kudos to you my friend, kudos!"

As the young intern eased near where Courtney was standing, he said, "I learned a lot in medical school, but my most valuable lesson was learned today, and that is, never be too skeptical about applications that you don't know much about! Thanks Doc, you opened my eyes beyond those damn books."

# # #

The SAT phone rang, but this time, Ben Beckmire did not waste time answering it. He exclaimed, "Holy Father, to what do I owe this call from your eminence?"

"My son, are you trying to be funny? I called you to tell you that your photo op on the border would have netted you Mr. Utz. He had a stash there, and I wanted you to be there to give him the holy ghost, and several unmarked bullets. However, I heard about your man, and I'm happy that your people come first, not that I thought any different. However, there is a more rabid set of circumstances coming your way, and will probably breach the very hospital that you're in. There is a group of people who are flying on commercial airlines that are scheduled to land at Regan International Airport, and others at Dulles within the next three hours. They are a composite of people from a triad that you inflicted heavy casualties on, and a group of people whose drugs you stole and destroyed, but whose money you kept. They are being outfitted by yours truly, Mr. Utz. His stop at the border I found out, was to gather enough cash to pay those seeking revenge, and to outfit them with the latest military weapons."

"Holy Father, how are you privy to such delicate details about people, drugs, money, and schedules? Who on earth supplies you with this kind of intel?"

There was an unusually long pause on the phone, and Ben Beckmire inquired on several occasions, "Hello, are you there? Holy Father, can you hear me?"

Finally, the voice on the other end said, "Son, on several occasions, you have indicated to people that you were not sure as to who I am. You have advocated that I'm the twin brother of the devil. You have even gone so far as to question who you are dealing with, and you have even stated that you didn't know if you were relating to the Holy Father or Diablo and, therefore, you were suspicious of both. Now, my son, I have forgiven you for all your negative inquiries, assertions, and I have come to realize that you and your people are my hidden warriors, subject to agreement on assignments. This new fight is not about religion. No, my son, this new fight is about whoever gets their hands on that unabridged dastardly Carbon Factor formula and implements it strategically. They will hold those with long-range missiles, and other antiquated forms of killing people, hostage. As an example, my son, a small breakaway state from Russia could acquire it, and become the new Moscow. Hong Kong could become the master of China. Those cowardly acts in Springfield, North Korea, Addis Abba, China, and Russia could eventually lead to new regimes, including the place that most think is invincible and untouchable, the United States of America. My son, you know that I'm thrilled by your history, and your potential future. Listen, my eyes and ears and my legions are in places that you can't imagine. Be my epic hero, fight my battles that must be quiet, off the charts, and decisive. Otherwise, what you know as your country will become the trading place for another entity. Mr. Utz is a mere mosquito, a simple distraction that buzzes during the night, until you cut the light on, and swat it with an old newspaper. You my son, should trust me, because you are correct, I am both the Holy Father and Diablo! Pick your days and times to discern which one is up and running and trying to destroy or save humanity!"

"Holy Father, if you have a minute, I would like to quickly respond to my designations of you. I heard you state that if the Russians or Chinese attempt to mastermind a coup in America as a result of it having weak and incompetent leadership, then you would not hesitate to obliterate both nations from the map. That seems to me a thing that Diablo would stoop to. Now, on the other hand using corrupted money to help people help themselves, seems more associated with a deity than the devil. Those were the basis for my comments and observations, but they were always with the concluding factor that I didn't know which one was at the plate—Diablo or the Holy Father."

"My son, I know all of this. Now, more importantly, there is a group coming to kill everyone related to you. I know exactly what you're thinking, and here is my suggestion. I would put my faith in God and remove my friend from a hospital that historically has raised suspicion in its treatment of minorities. You can't change the stripes on a Zebra no matter how many sensitivity sessions it attends. If you so choose to leave him in that hospital, those seeking revenge will find him, and use him as a bargaining chip."

"Holy Father, we don't leave or abandon our own. We will all die here in the hospital, or we will all die somewhere else. Chakes will go when we go. No one gets left behind."

# # #

Luana sat next to her husband, and said, "Scoundrel, you convinced me of your perfection, your ultimate love for my daughter, my grandmother, and me. Beatrice thinks that she did something wrong. She is distraught, and I told her that you used her to tell us that you weren't feeling well. Was that true? Even if it wasn't, that was our only indication that you were under duress. You had better not leave me, and our family. I love you so much since the first day you tried to pick up my grandmother. Scoundrel you are, but you're mine, and I need you to help me raise our children. I need you here with me. I love you so very much, and so do the children. Ms. Viola confessed the other day that she is so happy with my choice that she arranged for me."

The Sarge walked in and said, "Luana, you have to make a decision! If we don't leave here in the next hour, we will be under attack by some of our enemies. We can stay here and try to protect our brother or live to fight another day in a place of our choice. However, we place him in great danger by taking him away from this medical facility."

"Sarge, you are his brother, and I am his wife. The life we've chosen is complicated, and always at risk of being terminated. My man would rather have the option of fighting for his life as opposed to dying in a hospital from something that no one can define. I'm afraid that a long flight to Australia would kill him."

"Luana, we're going to take an ambulance and drive to Virginia where we can see the enemy coming and trying to plot against us. If I have your permission, we'll head to Virginia, and figure what we must do from there. If we stay here, a lot of innocent lives will be lost, and we will be blamed. We can't win in this environment. We need to head to a place that we have a modicum of control."

#

As the group prepared to leave, the Sarge made a call to the Holy Father who decided not to answer his call. As the Holy Father watched the phone ring off, he said to himself, "that is why I realize I am human, because I am sometimes as vengeful as a jealous husband." He picked up the SAT phone and called Ben Beckmire back. He said, "I just watched the phone ring off, and decided that human frailties are so much a part of my psyche that I'm not sure if I'm deserving of being the Pontiff. However, I'm here for you. What is it my son?"

"Holy Father, I just wanted to thank you for that extremely truthful conversation and explanation. You must admit, you're not your typical Pope. I discerned the smell of tobacco on you, and the hint of a fine cognac on your breath. I know that you can be one or the other when the moment calls. I thank you for alerting me of the impending danger for me and my group. After we relate to these people on our own terms, I'll place a call to you, and will grant you two operations as long as they are not suicidal."

"My son, I need you and your people for the long run. If there is a suicidal mission involved in our relationship, I will be in the trenches next to you with a weapon, looking for absolution as I lay waste to our enemies."

"That is very comforting, but I hope it never comes to that. Keep my people in your prayers, especially Chakes, Ms. Beatrice's father."

# # #

On their journey to Virginia, Courtney made calls to local physicians that the group had befriended and helped along the way. The hospital in Maryland made the results of the blood tests available to the hospital near the farm. As the caravan of vehicles got closer to the farm, Courtney received a call from the doctor that treated Bernstein and Jilkes who empathically stated, "Your man, somehow, found one of one hundred sea urchins that were being smuggled on the same ship that sank, and washed-up thousands of individual bricks of cocaine in that last storm in the Bahamas. Somehow, those Indian and Pacific Ocean dwellers survived the storm, and found their way to somewhere your man had recently traveled. Our resident looked at the various indicators such as high fever, high blood pressure, stroke like signs, did a worldwide google of potential causes, and came back with those findings. My question is simple, has your man been near or around the waters in the Bahamas?"

A stillness fell over the phone, and Courtney finally responded, "We just left St. Thomas!"

The doctor on the other end said, "Instead of insulin, feed him apple cider vinegar. You can check the notion later, but for now, feed him vinegar, straight from the bottle. This is going to shock his body, but it's going to save his life. Listen, doctor, we are only guessing from this end. The final decision is yours to make. However, my resident swears by his analysis. Take care, call me, and let me know if it works."

# # #

The group stopped at several gas stations and were disappointed they didn't carry vinegar. Luana saw a sign that said, "Kroger's." The group made a beeline to the store and purchased a case of organic and regular apple cider vinegar. The EMS said to Courtney, "You will have to give him the IV. I will lose my job if I do it."

"Not to worry, I plan on doing it. I want the driver to pull over, and I want you two to exit the vehicle until I've completed the infusion. That way, you can't be involved on any level because you had to take a leak."

Luana handed Courtney a bottle of organic vinegar, and she said, "Give me the old school shit. We're playing with an old school player, and he doesn't know much about this organic epidemic."

After receiving a nonorganic bottle of vinegar, Courtney substituted the IV of saline with pure vinegar. She then donned a pair of microscopic glasses and began to scour every inch of Chakes' feet and legs. After ten or so minutes of looking closely at the bottom of his feet, she saw a callus that was as hard as a rock but had been penetrated by the spine of a poisonous sea urchin. She exclaimed to Luana, "I've found the point of entry, and I hope to God that the resident is correct in his analysis. I'm going to cut wide so that I don't break the spine of the urchin off in his foot. Wish me luck!"

Two hours later, a groggy Chakes woke up, and yelled, "Beatrice, Beatrice I'm sorry for yelling at you. I needed your help and realized that you were the only person that could help me at that time."

Luana said, "Honey, calm down! Beatrice is asleep, and you've been out for a while."

"Baby, where are we?"

"You're in an ambulance heading for the farm in Virginia. Seemingly, and as usual, bad guys are hunting us. The Sarge received a call from the Holy Father indicating that people from that triad, and the drug dealers whose money we confiscated, were on their way to collect and eliminate us from future concerns. You my love found an imported deadly species of sea urchin and stepped on it. How in the hell did you do that? Honey, that thing that you stepped on, along with bricks of cocaine that washed up from the Bahamas, were being smuggled into the country. How could you step on one of one-hundred stolen and illicit sea urchins? You are so special that it's freaky!

"Baby, I need you to do me a favor. I don't know or care what time it is, but I need to see Beatrice. I might die soon, but I need to talk to my daughter. Please, I beg of you, bring her to me."

"Honey, she is in one of the other vehicles heading to the farm. We should be there in about thirty minutes or so. I just need you to relax and calm down. You're not healthy, and your breathing is accentuated by stress. Calm down, when we get you situated, I'll bring her to you, and the two of you can chat for as long as you want or as long as Courtney allows.

#

At the farm, Rashida turned all the systems on, and began to look for yellow patterns at the bottom of the main monitor which would indicate movement. There were several spikes that were obviously created by the caretaker, and then there were two spikes, off hours, that recorded uninvited guests. As she moved the cursor to the exact position of the spike, it showed six individuals methodically moving through the woods in the direction of the farmhouse. Each man had a backpack that looked as if it was filled with heavy materials. As the men got closer to the main farmhouse, two headed towards the barn, two headed to the guest house, and two headed to the main house. The cameras from the field clearly showed each group unpacking their backpacks, and strategically placing what appeared to be C-4, around the perimeter of each building. At the top of her lungs, she yelled, "Abandon the buildings." She then hit the alarm button, and everyone knew to not second guess that sound.

Rashida grabbed the laptop that operates the security system, and ran out of the house. People were frantically looking for their mates to make sure that everyone had gotten out of the houses. As she ran towards her assigned vehicle, she saw that all who should have been in it, were there. She looked out of the window, and saw the Sarge wandering around in front of the farmhouse, and told Larry to drive down the road. She got out of the vehicle and ran towards the Sarge, yelling, "What are you doing? You're not following protocol. We had visitors, and they left their calling cards at every structure on the farm."

"I can't find Courtney. Have you seen her?"

"Sarge, go to the ambulance, and you will probably find your wife with Chakes, Ms. Viola, Luana, Beatrice, and the baby."

"What is the problem? What did they leave?"

"Sarge, I'll discuss this up the road. Right now, I need you to go to your assigned vehicle. I've made the decision that the farmhouse and guest house are unsafe. Let's go dad!"

# # #

Once all the vehicles reached the top of the road, and as they turned east on the access road, there were three enormous explosions that rocked the earth. As the group began to race down the road, lights on three vehicles came on, and raced behind the group. The three off-road type vehicles were mounted with hunting lights, and .50 caliber machine guns that started immediately firing at the group. The old soccer mom vehicles were about to be tested to the max.

On the intercom system, the Sarge told Jilkes and John Lee to cut their lights off, run on the car's radar, make a left turn in less than one-half mile, then a quick turnaround, and come up behind the aggressors. Each of the soccer mom vehicles was equipped with bulletproof glass, doors, and two-inch thick Kevlar linings. The rear of the vehicles had three-inch thick steel plates to further protect the occupants.

As Jilkes made a quick left turn onto an access road, then a U turn, he watched as the slower attack vehicles continued to fire and hit the last vehicle without much success. As the attack vehicles began to reload the machine guns, Jilkes turned on his lights, John Lee targeted the vehicles, and slammed his hand down on the fire button. The weapons systems that Jong's ex-cousin installed, fired eight suppressed rounds at each vehicle simultaneously, striking the shooters first, and the drivers second. As each vehicle came to a horrific stop, Jilkes, John Lee, Somara, and Yeshida exited their vehicles, and completed the termination of the attack team. One of the attackers received multiple wounds but did not appear to be life-threatening. Yeshida, wrapped bands on his wrist, and taped his mouth and wounds as best as possible. They threw the individual in the truck, and headed towards the main highway. The vehicle that the Sarge was riding in backed down the road to view the carnage, and he told Michael, to quickly place dynamite in each barrel of the machine gun to render them unusable. As Jilkes and John Lee started towards their vehicle, John Lee yelled, "Wait a minute. Let me look at those bags that are lying in the ditch." As he neared them, one had been ripped by gunfire and it was obvious that there was cash in them. He suddenly felt around the bags and realized that there was nothing but cash in them, and told Jilkes to grab one.

In the vehicle that Zanthius and Asiram were in, she said, "That is the second damn time someone has blown up our farmhouse. Honey, call Clyde, and tell him to be extra vigilant in securing the ranch."

Zanthius, in a meek manner said, "Honey, you don't seem that upset this time. Am I missing some hidden emotion?"

Asiram looked at her husband, then at the babies, and said, "No! As I see it, everything that is important to me is in this vehicle or one of the others. We will rebuild the farm again, but this time, we'll make it larger, safer, more fortified, and friendly for our families. No, honey, I'm not pissed-off like the last time. The last time, I had just met your dad, and people destroyed my house in Philadelphia, my farm, and then my ranch. Now, I was really pissed at that. This time, I have babies, lots of them, and a husband that is always near to help me out. I love you, our extended family, and that is all that matters, my 'idiot spy'."

# # #

During all this drama, Carla made a call to the auxiliary pilots, and told them to prepare the plane for an immediate takeoff. She asked the lead copilot, "Was the plane refueled?"

He retorted, "Captain, the plane was refueled, approximately one hour ago. It is ready, and we have pilots on the ground, keeping a watchful eye out for anything unusual. Those on the ground are legal to fly, and the two of us inside have approximately five hours before we should be in a rest mode. However, we do what we gotta do, and when we gotta do it."

"Is the plane stocked with provisions?"

"Captain, the plane is ready to fly anywhere in the world that you and your people designate. As usual, we keep around the clock surveillance, and all actions in or around the plane are recorded.'

"This I know. Review the recording, and make sure that the plane has not been compromised," Carla demanded.

"My captain, may I inquire what is stimulating this action?"

There was a long pause, and Carla replied, "The farmhouse, guest house, and barn, were blown off the map. Check everything, we're under attack.

# # #

Zanthius placed a call to Clyde with a secure SAT phone and knew that Clyde would answer it immediately. When Clyde answered the phone, he said, "I sure have missed you people. Are you coming home tonight, or are you already here?"

Zanthius replied, "Hi Clyde, it's Zanthius. We're leaving Maryland now and will be there in about four hours. However, it's important that you respond honestly to this next inquiry. Clyde has anyone been near the ranch?"

"Ah, Zanthius, I go there every day to check on the people I've hired to provide security throughout the ranch. I took it upon myself to employ some of the ranchers because as you well know, there ain't no such thing as global warming, and the scientists don't know squat."

"That's funny Clyde. Tell me how this security thing works. I mean are there people in the ranch house on a twenty-four-hour basis or what?"

"Well, Zanthius, it's like this. In the rear of the house, I had them smart nephews of mine build an extension off the laundry room. Now in that 12 x 20 room, every square inch of the ranch is monitored by sensors, by people having to go and physically scan their IDs, and by cameras hidden all over the place. Any direct movement on the 6,000 or so acres is registered, recorded, and spotted by mobile forces. Animals are easily discerned because they don't carry metal," Clyde stated.

"Clyde, I'm asking about security because we're under attack once again. The farmhouse, guest house, and barn were blown to pieces, and we're just making sure that we have somewhere safe to go. Please, increase security, and will you be able to pick us up in approximately four hours?"

"I'll be there with everyone's favorite toy. Safe travels and rest assured, this place is buttoned down like a witch's ass!"

# # #

Five miles away from the entrance to the airport, the Sarge told Jilkes to pull over, he wanted to interview his captive. Jilkes pulled to the side of the road, and John Lee and the ladies, scoured their surroundings. When the Sarge appeared on the scene he said to the captive, "I'm going to ask you two questions. If you don't answer them truthfully, we are going to cut parts of your body off. Now, who hired you to do that dastardly attack on a caravan with women and children?"

"I have nothing to say." The Sarge looked at John Lee, who unsheathed his blade, and slammed it into and through the man's leg. He attempted to scream but was gagged by Yeshida. Since you didn't answer the first question, I won't be asking you any others. You're a dead man, and don't know it."

The man watching the blood spurt out of his leg began to hyperventilate, Jilkes slapped him, and said, "Last chance asshole. Who hired you?"

"In agony, the man struggled to express the name Utz. The Sarge stopped in his tracks, turned around, and asked, "Are you sure?"

"I heard a guy whisper during a strategy session, the name Utz."

"I'm not going to let you suffer any longer." The Sarge pulled out his weapon and fired a round into the man's head.

Afterwards he said, "You attack my family, and grand babies, and I'll conclude your fucking life!"

# # #

When the vehicles arrived at the airport in Maryland, the hangar was dark, and there was no one around. Zanthius said to his father, "Pops, keep the people in the vehicles until we figure out what's going on."

After identification was confirmed, the hangar lights came on, and two pilots came from different directions with machine pistols. The on-ground copilot said, "Sorry about the theatrics, but we're on high alert as a function of information received from Captain Carla."

Zanthius replied, "Listen, we're happy to have you guys as a part of our family. I know what to expect from you guys, but I must admit, I was surprised to find the hangar dark, and obviously no one around. I feared for my family and friends, because we're under attack, and those attacking us seemingly are more determined than any other foe that we've faced. Thanks for your attention to detail, and our security. Is the plane ready to fly?"

Carla got out of her vehicle, and said, "Good job! Where are the other personnel?"

"Captain, they're on the lady fully loaded, and ready for battle."

"Wow, I'm impressed. Let's stop the chatter, get this girl in the air, and figure out how we can assist our family in their time of need." As she scaled the steps, she said to her copilot, "I need the three of you to perform a visual inspection of every aspect of the lady. I mean climb into the wheel wells and check every inch of her body. I'm not going to be the cause of my family's demise. Okay people let's move. While you're checking, I'll ask you to turn over your weapons to some members of the family to take up where you left off."

# # #

The Sarge asked Courtney, "How is our patient, and can he make this trip without a problem?"

"Honey, I'm going to give him a controlled shot of a sleeping drug that I will personally reduce the level to make sure he remains semi-conscious, and alert. I've removed the apparent cause of his problem, but the effects are still beyond my understanding or control. The vinegar was an absolute lifesaver and, therefore, he is able to communicate, and move his lower extremities. However, if you listen to him, he still sounds as though there is an impediment in his speech."

"Honey, you're the doctor, and the best one that I know. You know we have to get the hell out of here, and now, so if he can fly, and Luana okays it, then the wheels are up in the next thirty minutes."

Michael and Mike assumed the watch with the weapons that the pilots had. Michael asked Mike, "When you first saw Carla, did you just go all out for her?"

"I was on one of the planes, and she came out of the cockpit, I knew that if she wasn't married, then she would soon be married to me. I fell in love with her at first sight," Mike confessed.

Michael said, "I have strong feelings for Ayesha, but you know what happened the last time I gave my heart away freely! I'm not sure how to approach her since sometimes I don't understand her, and I'm sure, the same is in reverse, when we're signing. I think that I sometimes sign how I remember, and things are not the same as when I learned to sign. On many occasions, I've probably insulted her while trying to tell her how I feel. It's complicated, but not unmanageable. I just need to do some serious late-night studying to make sure that I am signing what I feel, as opposed to how I feel."

"Michael, you're overplaying this one. Express emotions, not words. Express deeds, like your interest in the project that you're involved in with her. Ask her to be your lady, but don't wait until some bullshit happens, then you're caught up with the problem of the moment, and not the cause of your anxiety, love my friend! It is a horrible feeling that sucks you in, dries you out, and leaves you wondering if the other party is feeling the same emotions. When I first saw Carla, I didn't care who knew it, or who liked it. I wanted that woman to know that I was interested in her. Fortunately for me, it worked, being brazen and confident, that is. I realized afterwards, that could have gone the other way. The one thing I will caution you about, my brother, is to make sure that your relationship, until consummated is kept under the radar. If those attacking and attempting to conclude our presence get wind of this, it could become a bargaining chip for the other side. I implore you to speak with the Sarge and Mallory about this before we become unintended hostages trying to free an unknown lover. You follow me, Michael?"

# # #

The signal was given, and the two men stopped at the bottom of the steps and unloaded the weapons at the back door to the jet. The plane was towed out of the hangar and released. Captain Carla told those on board, "People, this is going to be a quick take-off so make sure those seat belts are tight and low around your waste."

As soon as the tow truck released the plane, and the driver gave the signal, Captain Carla raced the plane to the active runway, and was given a hold order from the tower. She sat quietly for thirty seconds, moved the throttles forward, and released the brakes. The plane lurched, bounced, and proceeded down the runway at an enormous rate of speed, and within a minute plus, the nose was pointing skyward.

## CHAPTER FOURTEEN

Everyone wondered who was the culprit behind the destruction of the farm. After the seat belt sign was extinguished, the Sarge unbuckled his belt, and headed to where Asiram, and the babies were. He kneeled, and said, "Baby girl, I'm so sorry that your place was destroyed again. Do not concern yourself, we will have it rebuilt in record time. I will call Franco and his crew, and have them do an assessment, and the work. They should be finishing up the Florida project. Please forgive me."

"Daddy-in-law, it wasn't your doing. It was that 'idiot spy,' and had he not been so gullible, none of this would be happening, but then we would miss out on bonding with a wonderful group of people. I'm glad we are where we are today because I love everyone in this group."

"I just wanted to tell you that I would have the place rebuilt in record time, and for you not to worry."

"Daddy-in-law, do you realize that we have approximately $20 to $30 million in the safe. At some point in time, we should probably extract it, and put it to use."

"Do you think it's safe?"

"I'm sure it's safe. The tunnels are self-sealing, and where the safe is, well, let's just say, a novice will be blown to bits trying to enter it."

#

The Sarge walked down the aisle, and tapped Mallory, Jilkes, John Lee, Darryl, and Sue Lyn on their shoulders. They immediately got up, and walked to the back of the plane. As he looked at the assembled group, he asked Mallory to get Jong.

When Jong came to the back of the plane, he announced, "I wasn't in charge of that."

The Sarge asked, "In charge of what?"

"In charge of whatever went wrong. You always accuse me of everything that goes wrong. I just want to make sure everyone hears me deny doing whatever went wrong."

"Are you through with the bullshit?" The Sarge asked.

"I am, but I still didn't do it," Jong confessed.

The Sarge looked around, and decided that his main crew plus Zanthius, Asiram, Somara, Yesihda, and Okema needed to be in this meeting. Mallory left the group to summon the others. When they returned, the Sarge expressed his sentiments by saying, "People, we were caught with our pants down, and toilet paper stuck up our asses! First, our man steps on one of one hundred illegally imported sea urchins, and the damn thing is poisonous. Second, the Holy Father gathers intel about an impending strike against us and uses it to align us more closely with him. Now, in dealing with the Holy Father, on any given day, I'm not sure if he is holy or wicked. I know I've said this on many occasions but, I've seen the man flip the switch, threaten to blow two major countries off the map, and kill anyone or anything that does not follow his mandate. He is a force to be reckoned with but considers us his hidden warriors. Okay, so he gave us a heads-up about the impending strike in St. Thomas. Third, some motherfucker blows up my daughter-in-law's farm. Not just the houses, but the damn barn, where those big-teeth horses seek refuge during storms. Okay, Franco and company are in the country, finishing up Michael and Ayesha's project. I'm sure he'll be willing to assist us in reconstructing the farm. Fourth, we're riding down the highway, and people pull up behind us with three off-road vehicles that have .50 caliber machine guns mounted on them. Okay, we run silent and dark, Jilkes and his crew make an inadvertent turn, then a U turn, and come up behind the assholes as they're about to reload. John Lee targets, fires, and destroys the aggressors. Now, if I'm to believe that Mr. Utz is behind this matter, then it is conceivable and understandable. We took his cash, we thought we bankrupted his ass, but apparently, he had enough funds to engage those people."

John Lee said, "Ah, Sarge, we found some bags full of money. I threw them in the back of the vehicle. I forgot to take them out."

"Jong, call your nephew and tell him to retrieve the vehicles, secure the money, wash it, and make an accounting. Hopefully, he is as pure as you are my friend!"

"I no steal money. I'm in love and have babies. I no steal money!"

"Whatever, just attend to the matter," the Sarge said.

"May I speak your highness?" Jong inquired.

"Maybe you would like to slap me again. Is that what you want to say?" The Sarge asked.

"Ah, that was one of my finest moments, my king. However, no such thoughts are running through my mind. A certain corporation had ordered a new version of our plane that has larger engines, more fuel efficient, with an office in the belly of the plane, and capable of using the technology that I purchased. Our current plane has less than 550 hours, and it's almost ridiculous to upgrade at this level. The damn engines aren't even broken in. However, I highly recommend we change the configuration so that the belly can be turned into a full nursery and converted into a meeting space for forty. It's all about conveniences, and since we spend an enormous amount of time fleeing from place to place, I think it is worth the $10 million to upgrade. The manufacturer has a buyer for our plane, and since the order on his new plane was cancelled, he is willing to part with the new model for that price and our new/used plane."

"Thank you, Mr. Amazing. My purpose for this meeting is not to discuss conveniences, but to instill in each of you that we were caught with our pants down by a guy who will do any and everything to kill us and get his money back. After all, it was in excess of $2 billion that we extracted from his dumb ass. That's a lot of money. I would be royally pissed-offed if someone took my retirement funds."

The Sarge paused for a moment, then continued, and said, "The destruction of the farm was not a simple introduction. No, it was a statement that everyone is subject to a dastardly death including our babies. Now, as you know, if we separate, they could use one of us or the children as a negotiation tool. I'm not going to let that happen. If we don't align ourselves with the Holy Father, then we lose an important source of intel, and we can't do that. Mike, I want our people in the sewers to assist us on this one. I want them floating pictures of that bastard all over their network from Maine to Florida, and New York to California. I want our subgroups to network and use the code words, "bearer bonds" for sale." Have them establish an 800 number that records the incoming caller's number. I want our friends below to help us as we continue to help them."

Zanthius, made a call to Clyde, and was told that everything was safe in the Midwest. He thought to himself, "hopefully, there the group could get some needed rest before they headed to the outback to regroup. He thought it was time that they got Franco and his crew involved in this aspect of their work so that they could truly head to the twin-slum landlords' places and enjoy their homes."

"Master, do you want the other plane?" Jong inquired.

"I don't make those decisions. You do my friend," the Sarge replied.

As the lights on the plane began to strategically dim, voices began to lower, moods began to change, and people began to fall to sleep. The Sarge placed his hand on Courtney's, and said, "Damn I love you girl!"

Clyde was at the airport early and had placed security around the field. He explained to his people that an attack had occurred in Virginia, and that the structures on the farm were completely decimated. He told them that they had their fling with crooks, and they let some good people in who helped them over the hump. He indicated that he didn't want to show them his gratitude by letting some snake rear its ugly head up, and strike one of them. He told the group that he needed people to stay alert, and in their assigned places. He stated, "Let's show them we can keep them safe, as we keep ourselves."

When the plane entered the hangar, Clyde backed the school bus across the entrance, and asked people not to dally, but to enter the bus as soon as possible. Once on the bus, the adults were handed their instruments of choice with an extra clip. Once everyone was accounted for, he said, "Ms. Asiram, I'm so sorry to hear about your farm. Thank God he spared all your lives. As you are aware, we had a tough winter. I took it upon myself to hire farmers and turn them into security guards. Therefore, the ranch has 24/7/365 coverage, video of everything that breaches the property's boundaries, distinctions made between animals and foes, and the ability to terminate any suspected intruder without remorse. We will die, before we let foreigners come here, and destroy your home. I have kept a keen accounting of the payments, with signatures, pay stubs, and I issued 1099's to each member of the team. You will be safe here, so relax, and prepare to enjoy a feast of light foods and drinks that will allow you to sleep until you feel as though you want to wake up."

Asiram thanked Clyde and gave him a hug. He was surprised but appreciative. As she turned to walk away, she walked back to Clyde, and gave him a kiss on his cheek.

# # #

Mike and Carla were about to enter their room when his cell phone rang. He answered it, and the person on the other end said, "Oh, I'm sorry, I thought I was calling the library.

Goodbye!" Mike told Carla that he had to see the Sarge because there was an important message waiting on him.

When he reached the Sarge's room, he knocked, and was asked, "Who is it?"

"It's Mike, Sarge, I just received a misdial seeking the library."

"Hold on, I'll be right out."

A few minutes later, the Sarge opened the door, and asked, "What is this library stuff?"

"Sir, that is a critical message from the underground in Washington, DC."

The Sarge got his SAT phone and gave it to Mike who dialed a number that rang off. Two minutes later, the phone rang again, and the Sarge handed it to Mike who said, "What book are you looking for?"

"I am looking for, 'mechanized mayhem'." Hey Mike, it's the colonel. Listen, you guys have pissed some especially important people off. It appears that you removed several billion in bearer bonds from a deposit box in the islands. To be precise, the amount of the take was $3.4 billion in bonds, and $29 plus million in cash. They want the bonds and the cash back or they're going to step up their attacks on every infrastructure linked to you guys."

"Colonel, can you get us intel on who those people we pissed off, beyond that Mr. Utz fellow?"

"He has two partners who are distressed about that alleged seamless event that has cost them billions. Now, the unfortunate thing that I must tell you is that those responsible for the property damage in Virginia, were associated with my group. I know what you're thinking, where's the trust in this equation. We completed a heist that will afford us the ability to rebuild your place. I didn't know about it before it happened, and had I known, I would have told them that the sole reason they're living well, is a result of your largess. Please forgive me, but I have operations all over the country, and we normally don't interfere with how they achieve additional support. Now, the other thing that is questionable is that my people in Virginia, have not been paid, and their main source of contact has turned off his phone. In other words, they blew up your place, there was no loss of life, and they didn't receive a damn dime. The only person who would strike a deal like that is a person who does not have any funds and is using the notion of a promise to pay, to secure workers. However, to your other question, I will text you the names of the co-conspirators against you. Insofar as the cost of the rebuild, we intercepted information about a huge drug deal, and we were able to pick up $50 million in drugs and cash. The drugs were purged at Jong's nephew's place in that expensive vat that doesn't pollute the environment."

The Sarge said, "Colonel, I'm trusting every word that has come out of your mouth. So far, we have enjoyed the benefit of supporting each other. However, and let me be particularly clear, "we don't mess with drugs!"

"Sergeant Beckmire, I am aware of that. We don't mess with them either. Half our guys were strung out on this, that, and the other when they returned home. We certainly have as a rule, no drugs! Look out for my text with those names. If I hear of any new information, I will get back to you as soon as possible. Again, damn sorry about the property in Virginia, but rest assured, we will provide the rebuild money when you're ready to begin the project."

As the Sarge headed back to his room, the SAT phone rang, and when he answered it, the voice on the other end said, "I didn't see that one coming, especially, from a group that you support! I'm speaking of the destruction of the farm in Virginia. You know I have eyes and ears down in that place."

"We thank God that my daughter, and her surveillance equipment worked, and we saw the perpetrators placing the ordinances."

"You have pictures of them?"

"Well, they weren't that obvious, but we did recognize two of them, and realized that they were ex-military. We later found out that they were a part of the group that we support. The person in charge apologized and has promised to rebuild the farm with funds that were stolen from a drug heist. It was a matter of poor communications, and the ability to make some easy and fast cash. I think it was more of a message than an actual threat on our lives because with us dead, they would never find their bonds or their money."

"I agree my son, but remember, I don't believe people think rationally when billions of dollars in executable bonds are missing, and a substantial amount of cash has been taken. I don't see them thinking about sending you a message. Anyway, my call was about giving you information that will really make Mr. Utz angry. I can give you a series of numbers formatted to correspond with Mr. Utz's entire link to the financial world. By using the numbers, you can cancel each one of his credit cards that he's living on, automatically. Can you imagine him not being able to pay for dinner, let alone hiring people to present you with issues? By doing so, you will make him a very desperate man who would do anything to get his fortune back. That way you can draw out the real perpetrators, and not their go between guys. The two people that your people underground are exploring are minions following the instructions of their employers. Now, those are the people we need to catch. My son, I'm afraid that the people whose funds you've taken are extremely high up in your government. I suspect, one person is in the White House, and the other is the Secretary of Defense."

Moments passed without either man saying a word. The Sarge uttered, "What the hell have I gotten my people into?"

"My, son, know that I will be with you in spirit at all times. Be sure to get a copy of the New York Times in the morning. Once again, sorry to hear about the farm, glad no one was injured, and I pray that Mr. Chakes recovers fully. Good night my son."

# # #

In the morning, people began to stir at varying times. At 1120 hours, the Sarge and Courtney were still asleep. Jilkes inquired of Clyde, "Have you seen the Sarge this morning?"

"I have not. He's not the only one missing so far. There are a lot of people sleeping in or getting busy, if you know what I mean."

Rather than prepare breakfast for the group, Gilda and her friends prepared brunch, and the smell of good food cooking will wake up most comatose people. John Lee showed up to the dining room with John Lee II, and John Lee III. Somara decided that she wanted to rest and told John Lee to take the kids for the day. Jilkes found himself in a similar situation and had his boys in tow as well. When Zanthius entered the dining room he had all three children. Monica's two children were unattended as was Rashida's, and all the other ladies. When Clyde finally realized what he was witnessing, he asked Jilkes, "Is there a rebellion going on? I only see the men folk with the children. Are the women upset at you people?"

Jilkes, after noticing the missing mothers, said, "Yeah, I see what you mean. Yeshida and I aren't at the edge about anything, perhaps this is just a coincidence." As soon as he uttered those words, Darryl came with his two children followed by Jong with his two. Less than five minutes later, Brown and his children showed up along with Bernstein and his. Like magic, McArthur with his twins, Montomie with his child. Whitmore and Gladstone came in with their children, and Clyde said to Jilkes, "I think I'm going to ride around the property. I don't want to catch what you fellas be done caught. Have a good day, and good luck!"

When the Sarge, Courtney, Mallory, and Monica entered the dining room together, and saw all the guys with their children, tears began to roll down the Sarge's face. Monica, first to notice him crying asked, "What's going on my leader and friend?"

Courtney jumped in before he could say a word, and asked, "Honey, what's wrong? Are you okay?"

The Sarge looked at both women, and said, "I want to get out of this thing that we've found our way into. Look at this, all these guys with their babies, and obviously knowledgeable about what they're doing. Can you imagine if something happened to one of these guys? Oh my God, I would never forgive myself. We have got to find the light at the end of the tunnel. Look at them. Oh my God, look at them!"

The Sarge dried his eyes and walked from table to table hugging and kissing the children. At the end of his session, Ms. Beatrice handed him hand sanitizer, and said, "PopPop, you hugged and kissed a lot of little children. You might want to use a little of this just in case one of us has a cold or something."

"How is your dad doing today?" The Sarge inquired.

"Oh, he's doing much better. I can't get him to stop apologizing for yelling at me. When you see him today, would you talk to him about it?"

"Yes, Beatrice! I will tell him that he's becoming annoying, and that you want him to stop apologizing."

"If you tell him like that, he will know that I asked you to talk to him, won't he?" Beatrice asked.

"You're right, my love. I will suggest it in another way so that he won't know that we conspired together."

Beatrice asked, "Is that like you and me planning a joke on someone?"

"That's exactly what it's like," the Sarge replied.

#

The Sarge saw Gilda, and asked, "Where's your husband?"

"Oh, he decided to take a ride to avoid the plague that has infected your men. He thought they made some mistakes, and he didn't want to be caught up in the middle of that kind of a problem."

The Sarge began to laugh, and asked, "Gilda, will you call him for me? I want to ride around the ranch and clear my head. Thanks."

#

The Sarge asked Mallory to take a ride with him. The two men walked to the front of the ranch thinking that Clyde should have been back by now. He walked back inside, and asked Gilda to call him again. She called him on the radio but there was no answer. The Sarge went to the rear of the ranch to the information room and asked the two people to locate Clyde. One of the men said, "He told us he was going to go for a ride in the eastern portion of the ranch." As the man looked at all the cameras for an indication that someone or something had passed in that area, they saw Clyde stretched out in the field, and the all-wheel vehicle overturned. The Sarge yelled for Courtney, saw that the bus was the nearest vehicle, and they raced out towards that part of the ranch. As the bus bounced over the rough terrain, Mallory yelled, "Damn wolves are circling Clyde. When the Sarge saw it, he pulled the lever for the airhorn, and blasted a deafening sound that scared the animals away. When they got to Clyde, he was semiconscious, and dazed. Courtney checked him for injuries and realized that he took a hard whack to the head after being thrown from the vehicle. Mallory and the Sarge checked the area for foul play, and traced the vehicle's tire marks to a deep hole that it hit.

Mallory said, "Hell, this is like a sink hole. Looks as though he was full throttle on that thing when he hit that hole, it went down, and he went out. His stubborn ass wasn't wearing the seatbelt which is probably good because it would have broken his neck. Okay, let's get him back to the ranch."

As they were preparing to put Clyde in the bus, Jilkes, John Lee, Gladstone, and Whitmore showed up in a vehicle. Jilkes asked, "Is everything okay? We went on alert since we didn't know what was going on."

The Sarge said, "Good move my brother. We have some heavyweights that we've pissed off. I'll explain it all after lunch. Let's get him out of here. We'll send some of the locals to right that thing and get it back to the ranch."

When the bus arrived, Gilda was the first person to enter it. She looked at Clyde, and asked, "Old man, what have you gone and done? You know this is our night for, ah, you know what!" Everyone in the near vicinity broke into soft laughter, and in the interim, Courtney assured Gilda that there were no broken bones but wanted to take Clyde to the hospital for an MRI and brain scan because she wasn't sure how he hit the ground after being thrown from the vehicle.

#

Later that evening when Courtney and Monica returned, they told everyone that the hospital wanted to keep Clyde overnight to monitor him, and to make sure there were no injuries that weren't immediately discovered. Mallory asked Rashida, "Are you familiar with all of the new additions to security?"

Rashida responded, "I am not, but Gilda is second in command, and is familiar with all the systems, who is on patrol, where they're patrolling, and when they have to check in. Gilda turned each phone into somewhat of a SAT phone by installing an attachment and reprogramming the Smart Phone."

Rashida paused, and asked, "Did you hear what I said? Let me try it again. Gilda wrote an app, studied it, reprogrammed her phone, and now it operates like a VHF radio, but it's controlled by the twelve simple poles scattered around the ranch. If someone runs up in here, and tries to communicate, it will change their channel, and respond in another language. People, we have some brilliant associates, and she promises to share with me how she did it, and why. So, Gilda, how did you learn this stuff?"

"Girl, I've been playing around with this stuff ever since they walked right up on us and placed those vests on the children. I spent, don't tell my husband, $50 of our savings, and purchased two books on coding. I heard on one of those television stations that coding is the key to unlocking any answer in the universe. So, I decided to learn how to code using an old PC that I bought years ago. It didn't work so well at first, but then I decided that I would try to use one of those Apple phones that one of those villains had. My nephew told me that there were new PCs in the hotel that those people who tried to hurt us would never need them again. Now, that thing was like striking a match. I put in my information, and man ole man, it was like unlocking a safe full of new recipes. I told Clyde, and he was furious at first, until I showed him how we can monitor every inch of the property including all properties that butt up against this one. The rest is history. He gave me a credit card, and told me to order whatever I wanted, and not to buy cheap but to buy good old American made goods." Gilda turned around and saw that the entire team had been listening to her, lowered her head, and felt embarrassed.

Mallory said, "That's amazing. Gilda, you can monitor everything that happens, disrupt signals, conversations, and other things from that room, using your newly developed software?"

"Mr. Mallory, I tested that thing one hundred straight times, and each time, my margin of error was under 1%."

"Margin of error under 1%, that's incredible. Will you show Rashida, Juan, Darryl, and Sue Lyn how it works, and how you developed it? I mean, we're all family, and if it's a thing that can be marketed, you will certainly get the lion's share of the royalties."

"Mr. Mallory, I just played around with a problem that we had and came up with something that I needed to make work.

We ain't trying to sell China to Russia, we're just trying to keep those we love safe."

Mallory attempted to understand the analogy, but decided to say, "Gilda, we appreciate you, and all that you and your people do for us. You're an angel."

Rashida said, "We need you to visit the farm, if the powers that be decided to redo it for the third time. We have an automatic weapons system, and I'm sure that you can find a way to make it better. As Mallory indicated, "We appreciate all that happens when we're here, and we thank God for you guys."

# # #

An hour or so later, Rashida escorted her dad into the annex, and showed him what Gilda, who had no known technical skills, was able to accomplish by reading and trying to figure out a problem. The Sarge said, "Damn, she can cook, and code."

"Dad, this is her work. She embellished what we had, and expanded it by using simple logarithms, with old equipment. She missed her calling. She's a genius whose skills have been hidden on a farm in the Midwest. We should capitalize on her work, send it to one of the universities that we support, have them patent it, and have the proceeds go directly to her. Of course, I'll have to ask for her permission, but I think that is what we should do."

The Sarge was about to respond when the SAT phone rang. He answered, "Beckmire here."

"The Pope here!" Was the response on the other end.

"What can I do for you, Holy Father?"

"No, my son. It's what I will do for you. Somewhere along the line, you and your people thwarted a drug deal in Los Angeles, blew up the man's house in Poughkeepsie who sent you C-4, raided the headquarters of the head of a triad family in or around Hong Kong, and a few other horrific things. Now, the person who took over the triad flew to Virginia to exact revenge. Now, we both know that you left town and, therefore, so did your uninvited guests. However, they will land near the Wyoming border in about four hours and proceed to the ranch. If things couldn't get any more complicated, they have joined up with Mr. Utz who is leading them on this mission. Apparently at some point in time, he has been to the ranch, is that not true?"

"That is true, Holy Father."

"Well, my son, I expect that you will handle your business appropriately, and efficiently. Oh, and by the way, I think you have a weak link in your underground information system. Just words to the wise. If the leader suggests that you go left, consider going straight or even to the far right."

"Holy Father, how will we ever be able to pay you back for the hand holding that you've provided us from those who could cause us harm?"

"Not to worry, my son! When the time is right, you'll do the Lord's bidding on several fronts, and in the process, you will save millions of the faithful. Go with God my son and handle your business. I must see to the demise of a couple of treacherous cardinals who are interested in seeing white smoke come from the chimney. I hope they're waiting with bated breath because I will attend to the treasonous in the most despicable manner. You and your people stay safe, my son."

"Thank you, Holy Father. Arrivederci!"

"Look at you, my son, speaking Italian."

#

The Sarge called for an emergency meeting and asked that Clyde and Gilda be in attendance. Word had not fully filtered throughout the group about Gilda's hidden talents. When everyone was in attendance, the Sarge realizing that he did not want to upstage Clyde, in the full meeting, said, "Team, I would like to make two outside appointments if the two people will accept the fact that their lives will be in danger if they agree to my request."

John Lee asked, "Sarge, what kind of appointments, and how do they impact what we are used to?"

"Good question John Lee. But let me make the appointments first and see if there's acceptance." He looked at Clyde, and said, "Clyde, everyone knows that you're affiliated with our group, and that you're a trusted member of Asiram's inner circle. As such, I would like to appoint you head of our local security. Before you answer, I would also like to appoint Gilda as the head of technology. Now in both positions, there are responsibilities that will seem insurmountable, but are fundamental to our continued safety and existence. As you know that guy waltzed right up in here and donned our babies with those suicide vests. I never want that to happen again. As such and, therefore, those are my appointments. Are there any questions or votes against my appointments?"

Rashida stood up, and said, "I support your decision, and hope that you assign me to assist Gilda and her team."

"Rashida, I've appointed her as local head of technology. Gilda will coordinate with you our security issues, and you're the deciding person on actions to be taken." He looked at

Gilda, and asked, "Are you comfortable with accepting this appointment, Gilda?"

"Mr. Sarge, sir, I just tinkered with a problem, but I ain't interested in being in charge unless I report to Ms. Rashida, and she makes the decisions."

The Sarge turned to Clyde, and asked, "Clyde, as chief of our local security, do you have any questions or concerns?"

"No, sir! I'm simply happy to be an official part of the team. I don't see where I'll be doing anything different than before, but yes, I'm happy, and what makes me even happier is the position my wife has been appointed to. Now that makes me really happy!"

"Okay, moving on to another topic. I'm sure you remember the drug deal in LA that we thwarted, and gained a significant amount of cash from, the house on stilts in Poughkeepsie that we destroyed, the bags of money we confiscated, Larry falling down a trap door, the leader of the triad that we eliminated, and the emptying of Mr. Utz's boxes in excess of $3 plus billion. Well, somehow, they have all joined together to annihilate us, and retrieve their funds. They collectively will be landing near the border in a few hours and will make their way here for the express purpose of seeking revenge. They are being led by the one and only, Mr. Utz. He is familiar with this property and is aware of our tunnels. We will plan a coordinated attack that will leave each person who came here seeking revenge at the mercy of diablo. Now, Gilda, Rashida, Juan, and Sue Lyn, you have one hour to come back to me with a plan to cover the entire ranch. Now, Clyde, in an hour, I will need you to give me a plan as to how you will cover their retreat, and hopefully not ours. Okay people, this is not a drill. Ms. Viola, you know the deal, so get the babies and your helpers, and secure them in the designated tunnel in two hours. Make sure the provisions are suitable, and not dated. Oh, and by the way, if at all possible, I want to capture Mr. Utz alive. If there are no questions, we'll meet back here in an hour, and discuss the placement of our people. Thanks!"

CHAPTER FIFTEEN

At 0200 hundred hours, the night noises ceased in the eastern part of the ranch. Clyde radioed that his people were reporting as many as forty individuals on the move. This was confirmed by Rashida who indicated that they were beginning to disperse and circle the ranch house.

Jilkes said, "The super scope has them at 1500 yards or so, they're moving extremely slow, and methodical as if they are searching the ground for trip wires or sensors. Sarge, from what I can see, several are carrying M72 Laws rocket launchers. We have twelve long rifles on the rooftop of the guest house, and twelve on the rooftop of the main ranch house.

Jong's phone rang, and it was one of the auxiliary pilots who told him that five guys tried to board the plane. Four enemy casualties, one securely tied tight, and waiting an interview. Jong told him good job, and to secure the plane at all costs.

The Sarge said over the network, "Sustained hits from those rockets will level this building. At one thousand yards, I want coordinated firing. I want the people at the guest house to take the first shots. I want the second response from the ranch house. I want the same scenario to be repeated until they retreat into the range of Clyde and his people, or they keep coming at us. Do not let them fire those damn rockets. If they've been shot and they move, shoot them again. However, whatever you do, try to save Mr. Utz's ass for me, and the barn."

At 0245 hundred hours, twelve shots rang out simultaneously striking their targets. Immediately following those shots, another twelve shots were fired from the ranch house, and then the actions were repeated simultaneously. Mr. Utz realized that the people from the West were street fighters and didn't know a damn thing about fighting a foe in an open area. He slipped his black hood over his head and slithered back to the staging area. There he was met by a henchman who was his getaway driver if things went south. Once successfully in the car, the driver proclaimed, "They knew you were coming! It was a setup. Do you have any idea who could have tipped them off?"

Mr. Utz, looked out of the window, and vehemently stated, "It was that motherfucker who calls himself the Pope, but I know he's the fucking devil!" Into the night, and on a lonely highway, the two men quietly disappeared. Utz said to his driver, "It's going to be a long ride to Salt Lake City. I have a box there that has at least a half a million in it. That's enough to get us to the West Coast, and there I can access a friend who is holding $2 million in cash for me."

"Boss, it seems to me people have been doubling down on you to fail. What makes you think he's an honorable person?"

"Believe it or not, he's my daughter's real father. He wouldn't deceive me because he knows that I'll have her killed in front of him. I gave him $2 million and told him not to do stupid because I had eyes on him, and besides, if he spent it, I'll enjoy killing them both."

"Boss, you would kill your own daughter?"

"She's not my blood. The bitch I was married to have an affair with a druggie, and to avoid embarrassment, I made a deal with the devil, after the DNA test proved that the child was not mine. I promised that I would cherish her, keep her under my wraps, and send her to the finest institutions, if her mother committed suicide. She was without a soul, and prone to opioids. I set her up in a hotel, and had her lover, take her a special drug that was loaded with fentanyl. He delivered it, recorded her convulsing, and left the hotel dressed as the same woman he walked in as. Wasn't the most eloquent procedure, but it was effective, and my rage was avenged."

"Damn, boss! I'm glad my soul is pure and committed to achieving your end goals."

"I am too. I won't sleep while you're driving. We'll talk to make sure that we rotate the driving responsibility and arrive at the destination alive."

"Boss, apparently, you don't like the Pope."

"Let me tell you about that crazy ass guy," Mr. Utz said. For the next hour and a half, Mr. Utz told story after story about the Pope. None were flattering, but all were entertaining!

# # #

At 0522 hundred hours, the sun made its presence known over the horizon as it slowly brought the world from darkness to light. At 0530 hundred hours, Jilkes, John Lee, Mike, Michael, Bernstein, Brown, and Clyde, headed to the area where the attackers had fallen. Rashida and Gilda kept a close eye for any movement and were confident that most had received conclusive wounds. The two women did agree that there was slight movement from three targets on the radar, but most were concluded.

John Lee asked Jilkes, "How old are you now?"

"What the hell does that have to do with anything?"

"I just wonder whether I'm older than you, which would make me your older brother, or if you are older than me, that would make me your younger brother. No big deal, just something I always think about."

"Why don't you try to make sure that none of the attackers can bring harm to any of us? Now, that would make me happier than you are wondering if you are older than me."

"You're such a pig hater. A real pig farmer would see that I'm in a melancholy kind of way, and that I be feeling concerned."

"John Lee, do you know what that big word means that you used?"

"I do. It be meaning my heart is heavy."

"John Lee, the saying is I have a heavy heart."

Jilkes raised his fist in the air, and everyone fell to their knees. He turned to John Lee, and asked, "Okay pig farmer, what's going on? Are we in danger? Do you sense danger?"

"You be about as dumb as my pigs. I tell you my heart is heavy, and you ask me about being in danger. Anyways, there be a few out there still clutching them weapons, but we'll show them no mercy. If they be having a weapon, then they be catching a bullet."

Jilkes looked at him and gave the signal to advance to the group.

As the team searched the area in pairs, it was evident that Mr. Utz was not among the wounded, or dead. These guys were Asians with lots of tattoos. There were a few isolated puffs from the team's weapons for those who were not going to give up. As the group started to gather the weapons, it was evident that they had a connection in this country because all the weapons were military grade. Clyde was given the task of isolating and burning the remains.

Jilkes asked, "Clyde none of your people saw anyone retreat?"

"We covered their entry point, and their expansion. I was right there the entire time unless he had one of those suits like that group had that walked up on you guys. We didn't see anyone take tail and run."

"Clyde, you never know when we might have to start our own war, I'm trying to figure out what to do with these rocket launchers. If we bury them in the ground one of our growing children might decide to dig it up when we're not looking. I'm thinking we should use one of the tunnels, and perhaps that empty walk in safe to store them. I mean it is cool down there and ventilated. What are your thoughts?"

Before Clyde could respond, there was an echo from an automatic weapon firing, and then bodies falling to the ground. Jilkes, John Lee, Brown, Bernstein, Clyde, Mike, and Michael were blown off their feet by .50 caliber rounds that were fired from an abutting property. The shots came from over 2400 yards away. A few errant rounds hit the house but were on their downward trajectory and caused no problem. Rashida hit the alarm, and everyone knew what to do. She screamed through the intercom, "Men down!" Men down!"

The Sarge ran down the steps, into the security room, and asked, "Where did the rounds come from?" He screamed, "Mallory get Whitmore, Gladstone, McArthur, and Montomie to cover our fallen friends." He then screamed, "Courtney, put on a vest, grab your weapon and your bag."

Meanwhile, Gilda tried to follow the trajectory and smoke trail on her system, and said, "Mr. Sarge, those rounds came from over two thousand yards away. Somebody has gotten their hands on some powerful military equipment. My screen says two thousand yards, but from the measurement of that smoke screen, I'm saying more like 2400 yards away. They might be using a high-flying drone to laser in on our people. Rashida and I will scan the sky and get a definite location of that weapon or weapons."

On the way out of the door, the Sarge screamed, "Zanthius, get your butt down here, take charge of our security."

When Zanthius came downstairs, he asked, "What's all the commotion about?"

Rashida responded, "Jilkes, John Lee, Brown, Bernstein, Clyde, Michael, and Mike are all down from bullet wounds."

The lackadaisical look on his face turned to horror as he instructed Yeshida, Okema, and Somara to the roofs with long guns to provide support for their fallen comrades. The three women were concerned about their mates but focused on the job. He instructed the rest of the women to arm themselves. He asked Asiram, Ava, and Juan to cover the rear of the building. He had the auxiliary pilots to provide cover for the guest house.

When the Sarge arrived at the scene, he fell into a funk to see so many of his men with various wounds. At the ranch house, and on the roof, using Jong's ex-cousins super-scope, Okema yelled, "Got you motherfucker!" With the newly found L115A3 rifles that were picked up off the highway, Okema loaded 6-.338 Lapua rounds into their weapons. She saw three men attempting to launch a drone that was sitting near a weapon that could fire .50 caliber rounds over 2400 yards. On this calm day, she would place three rounds successfully into three individuals, terminating them where they stood. She radioed Rashida, and stated, "The initial threat has been neutralized. I recommend that we get a reconnaissance unit to that site and gather that weapon."

"10-4". I will give Sarge the info."

"Rashida, we need replacements. Our men are down, and we need to go, and see if they're all right."

Rashida paused for a second, took a deep breath, and said, "I need you guys to provide security with those long guns for the people who are going to attend to them, and for those of us left on the ranch. We do not want another ruse played on us, and people walk smack up in here, and do whatever they want. Please, maintain your position until I can get suitable replacements." She looked at Juan, and said, "You're it. Take over for them."

As soon as she uttered those words to her husband, a pale looking Chakes stumbled up to the doorway, and said, "I can't run, but I still can fire a weapon."

"Great! Rashida exclaimed. Okay Juan, help him up to the roof, and Chakes you take the area facing the east side of the barn, and Juan you take the front facing west."

# # #

In the meantime, Jong raced the bus over rough terrain with a cadre of women to assist people to the hospital. For the love of God, each man had a vest on that provided a modicum of protection. However, the sheer nature of the rounds that were fired, penetrated the Kevlar armor, and left some of the group with gaping wounds, broken bones, and concussions from being hit by such power.

As Courtney attempted to figure out who was the first to be seen, she yelled, "Call out the bleeders first, the unconscious second, and the dead third. No time to waste people, get those vests off them, and look for holes and blood. Put gloves on and change them each time you touch someone new."

When the bus arrived, the rest of the group was there with stretchers to assist those alive to the bus. Everyone cried when they saw the lifeless bodies of John Lee and Jilkes, side by side. Each man had sustained tremendous hits in the chest area and were presumed dead. As Courtney approached the two men, she saw that they were not breathing, she began to cry, and with rage in her heart, she struck Jilkes violently hard in the chest, and he gasped for air. She hit John Lee with the same force, but to no avail. The Sarge said, "Ain't no way you're dying from a damn sniper. Get your pig loving ass up!" He slammed the man's chest with such force, ribs could be heard cracking. John Lee sat up for a minute, and then collapsed. The Sarge picked him up and carried him to the bus.

A call was made to the hospital indicating that there were several injured coming in from a ranch with accidental gunshot wounds. Hell, everyone in town knew what was going down, they were lined up to give blood, and do whatever the doctors needed. They knew the people coming for help were the people that gave help, freely and without charge.

# # #

At the sight where the weapon used in that attack was recovered, there appeared to be an old Russian made gun that had been modified by the Chinese. The three bodies lying with large holes in their heads appeared to be Asian. Zanthius, Asiram, Juan, and Gladstone, searched each body for information about who was paying the bill. Gladstone checked out a new vehicle that was fifty yards away from the gun stand and found two bags that contained something that seemed like paper. Rather than run his hands through the bags, he emptied the contents on the ground. Each bag contained money, and a poisonous snake that he stomped to death. He smiled and said, "No honor amongst thieves." He hurriedly threw the money into the bags and joined the group. Zanthius saw him carrying two bags, and asked, "Can I guess what's in them?"

"You should have guessed what was in them before I emptied them. Besides the money there were two damn snakes, I guess they were poisonous."

"Are you shitting me?" Zanthius asked.

"Brother, walk back near the vehicle, and you'll see two smashed snakes."

"No thanks, I believe you. Let's get the hell out of here," Zanthius said.

# # #

At the hospital, doctors, including Courtney, worked feverishly on those who were knocking on the door of death. On three occasions, the team of doctors and nurses thought they had lost John Lee. His heart was shocked on three different occasions. From across the room, Courtney yelled, "Burn him up before you let him die from that wound."

Jilkes suffered a less than catastrophic wound. His entry wound was near his heart but was deflected to the right and exited from under his shoulder blade. He was more comatose than anything.

Of concern to everyone, was Clyde who suffered two separate wounds, one to his chest, and the other to his stomach. He lost a significant amount of blood, and the doctors gave him a 20% chance to survive through the night.

When Gilda arrived, she calmly asked for permission to see her husband so that she could remind him that this was his good luck night. No one knew what that meant except for the two senior lovers. Clyde, who was heavily sedated made no movements or acknowledgements. Gilda began to pray, and somehow blamed herself for not being able to see a weapon that was over 2400 yards from where she was monitoring the activity.

In the hallway, the doctors were reviewing the fragments removed from the various patients and concluded that they were from large caliber munitions. One of the doctors whispered, "I think everyone is going to pull through this thing except Clyde. A combination of age, and sedentary living will be his downfall. The wounds he received were massive and did a lot of internal damage. We could only repair so much without putting the heart under unnecessary strain. I feel for Gilda, he is a good man, and a great and caring neighbor."

The shots that Okema made were record setting, and each was a head shot. The results were that there was not enough of the heads to identify who the victims were.

Later, at the hospital the Sarge saw Courtney, and he asked, "How are my people?"

Courtney looked at the Sarge square on, and said, "We have three people in intensive care, Jilkes, John Lee, and Clyde. If I had to rank them according to my perceived notion of survivability, I would say, Clyde probably won't last through the night. John Lee is bleeding internally from too many places to cauterize, and Jilkes, who with a lot of prayer, and a little luck might make it through the night. Those bullets left gaping holes in their bodies, Sarge. The team of doctors did all that they could, and the rest is up to the individuals, and their Gods."

The Sarge reached out, grabbed Courtney, and pulled her near. Courtney asked, "Where are their wives?"

"They rode here with me, and are scrubbing down, and putting on gowns. They provided cover for us. They are some remarkable young ladies. I love this group, how they come together, and never abandon their positions."

"We'll all have to come together and pray for those three. I believe the others will make it through this without a hitch. Honey, will this ever end?"

"Baby, I can make it end for us. Just tell me that's it, and we're out of here to Alabama to sit in some rocking chairs and watch the sun go down."

"Ben Beckmire stop the horseshit! You know damn well I'm going where my grandbabies go. I sure as hell don't plan on sitting on the porch to watch the sun go down unless that's when we get busy, big boy!"

The Sarge smiled, and said, "As soon as the group is healthy, I think we need to go overseas, and decide our future. This was an unexpected event that has crippled us in so many ways. I mean, when Jilkes and John Lee go down, we're left with a cavernous hole in our defense and offense. I need to call Rashida to make sure all is okay at the ranch. I certainly wouldn't want another game played on us by some devious individuals."

CHAPTER SIXTEEN

After months of surgeries, and hospital stays, John Lee and Clyde left the hospital. Jilkes was released a couple of weeks prior to his friend.

John Lee asked his doctor, "So Doc, do you think I can fly?"

"John Lee, you were shot, you're not a bird, and I didn't operate on you to teach you how to fly."

"You know Doc, you're a funny man, but I like you almost as much as I like my pigs, and my colored friend."

"John Lee, what color is your friend?"

"He's one of those African Americans."

"John Lee, what color is your friend?"

"Him be a Black man Doc, just like you."

"Thank you, John Lee. Now, get your country ass out of my hospital, and stay out of here, other than for checkups."

John Lee got out of the wheelchair and approached the doctor. He said, "You spent a lot of time checking up on me, and I appreciate you. I even heard that you said prayers for me and my friends. I like that in a doctor, you know smart, educated, but also beholden to faith. If you or the hospital ever need anything, don't you hesitate to call me. If you want to take your wife on a vacation, use our place in St. Thomas, call me and you can use our plane, and it's all on us. As a matter of fact, if all you people can arrange it, and get substitutes for yourselves, then please go to *the Sanctuary* as our guests.   I mean, you people helped me and my friends, and nobody died here, but when we came in here, none of us be expecting to leave.   Thanks Doc, and may God bless and keep you, your staff, and this hospital!"

Clyde said to the doctor, "I'll see you in church on Sunday.   Thanks, my brother," the doctor replied.

Jilkes gingerly hugged John Lee, and said, "That was really cool what you did back there.   I'm proud of you boy. You made me feel that humanity had fallen into the fabric of your soul."

"Stop the horseshit and get me to the ranch.   OMG!   Fresh country air!   Ain't nothing like it in the whole wide world."

When Jilkes, John Lee, Somara, Yeshida, Gilda, Chakes, and Luana, showed up to the ranch with Mike and Michael providing additional support, everyone was outside to welcome John Lee and Clyde.   The Sarge said, "John Lee Jones Jr., welcome home my friend.   We all know it's been a long journey for you, but your faith and belief in God, and your friends kept you going, and kept us praying."

John Lee with tears in his eyes, said, "Well, I missed all of you people, but most of all, I missed Gilda, and the other lady's cooking.   No more words, I want to eat some real food."

# # #

It was obvious that the ranch, and its 6,000 plus acres were closing in on the group.   Two days later after Clyde and John Lee were released, the Sarge said, "People, I have two major announcements to make.   People, may I have your attention?"

After the group quieted down, the Sarge said, "First of all, I would like to thank God for sparing the lives of our people who were injured in that last attack. Some of you were not supposed to return from the hospital, but God, and those doctors who gave you so much care and attention, helped pull you people through. It has been a rough couple of months for everyone here, the immediate families, the children, your extended families, and your friends. I gave an order stating that people could not visit you guys on an ongoing basis. I wanted you people to reflect on what happened, and what we do as a group. I wanted you to think about the consequences of doing what we do. There is only a few of our team that has not had an extended stay in a hospital. I must admit, at first sight, I thought we would be burying all of those who were injured. Those bandits modified a weapon, reloaded .50 caliber rounds, and used a drone to target from approximately 2400 yards away. Now, that's some incredible shooting, if in fact you're using an automatic weapon, and you fired close to 150 rounds. Now, while the drone was being attended to, Okema, used the super-scope to locate the menace. From approximately 2400 yards away, using a L115A3 rifle, Okema loaded six .338 Lapua rounds, and made three head shots. Now, that's what I'm talking about. They used a drone, and she used what was available to take that scum out.

Now, the second thing I wanted to speak to you about, is our plane. You know whenever we wanted to have a meeting, we would congregate in the back of the plane. Well, once again, Mr. Amazing, with his ear to the ground, heard about a plane that was built for a company that couldn't make the payments. From what I hear, it has a padded space in the belly of the plane that transforms into a meeting space for as many as 40 individuals. During all of the activities that we have been faced with, Mr. Amazing made a deal on a new plane that is faster, more fuel efficient, and fitted with almost private living spaces. If there are no objections, I would like to take it over the water so that those who were injured can truly heal from the waters in the outback." There was a roaring sound from people who were elated to know that they were leaving the ranch. John Lee yelled, "When we be leaving?"

"When would you like to leave, John Lee Jones Jr.?"

"Ah , Sarge, you didn't have to expose me like that."

"The question remains, John Lee Jones Jr."

"How about tomorrow after dinner. Do you think we could take Clyde and Gilda? Do you think those watching the place can handle things while they're gone?"

Gilda, uncharacteristically, spoke up, and said, "I think we should stay here, and make sure things are okay."

Asiram interjected, "I don't agree with you Gilda. You and Clyde have been doing our business for years, and it ain't about money. We want Clyde and you to experience a place where you can believe in magic, and waters that heal. The ranch is a place, and a thing. What's important to us is people, and especially people who do our bidding when we're not around. It's settled, you guys are coming with us. And besides, you might get some great recipes from the Aborigines that you can try back here. You'll love the climate, the people, and Darryl and Sue Lyn can show you the diamond and gold mines, gigantic saltwater crocodiles, and a world that you'll never forget."

Courtney asked, "Do you and Clyde have passports?"

Gilda replied, "We don't need that to cross state lines, and we've never been out of the country."

Courtney then asked, "The people who provide protection from afar for us, have they been out of the country?"

"Oh, Ms. Courtney, we're ranchers! We can't afford to leave the land."

Monica hearing the interaction, waited for the opportune moment to interject, "Well, we'll coordinate a security company to provide the services for the ranch, and all of you can get on a plane, and meet us in St. Thomas, and relax and enjoy yourselves once we leave the outback, and head that way. I think the leadership would like to do this. Ain't that right Mallory and Sarge?"

Mallory stepped all over his words, and finally realized that things have been terrific with his family, and that Monica had adapted to the world that he operates in. He said, "I'm sure our illustrious leader will sanction this activity, and I whole heartedly support my wife, and Courtney."

The Sarge said, "I don't know why there's so much posturing. It sounds like a great idea, and I too support it."

# # #

Two days later, Clyde and Gilda had their passports. At the airport, the group, and their guests, entered their hangar, and saw their new plane. The Sarge asked Jong, "Is it bigger than the last one?"

Jong replied, "Not really Sarge. It is slightly longer and more aerodynamic, which increases the fuel efficiency as well as the speed. For the last thirty days, Carla and her crew worked around the clock learning the different aspects of the plane. The manufacturer had three of his people stationed here to assist them in the operations of the plane. After the second week of training, Carla and her crew took turns taking the plane through stressful climbs, descents, banks, and landings. The plane's wheels, on take-off, were off the ground a full minute earlier compared to our previous plane. Carla quipped,

"Oh, my God! Courtney is really going to call me for a conference."

As the group toured the plane, the kids being kids were wondering what all the fuss was about. Captain Carla said, "I'm sure the children are really going to enjoy this feature of the plane. Since there were more than 6 children, the captain opened a door that descended into the belly of the plane, rather than using the 6-person capacity elevator. It was a huge room, equipped and decorated with cartoon characters. Everything was made of a sturdy foam material, and large screen TVs were positioned in two areas. When the children were not using it, panels could be opened where pull down tables and chairs that could support individuals weighing in at 300-pounds, unfolded. Captain Carla indicated that the room was soundproof, and the environmental conditions could be controlled from the cockpit, and in the space.

# # #

Gilda whispered to Clyde, "Honey, I'm not sure I want to get on that thing. I'm scared to death!"

Clyde pulled out a flask, and said, "Here girl, have a sip of our happy drink. It'll calm you right down."

Later, after entering the plane, and being assigned seats, "Gilda, looked at all the buttons, and asked what in the heck are we supposed to push, and when?"

"Oh, I'm sure they're going to give us a lesson in how these things work. Just relax, enjoy the company, and the ride. This here is some kind of instrument. I sure as heck hope everything works."

After everyone was accounted for, and in their assigned seats, Captain Carla engaged the intercom, and said, "Folks, do me a favor, make sure your seatbelts are fastened tight around your waist. Once we're airborne, I'll come back on, and give you an update about travel time and weather."

#

As the big bird began to rumble from the throttles being moved forward, the plane shook, and once the breaks were released, proceeded down the runway, and lifted slowly, and majestically, into the air. All systems were in a go condition, and everyone seemed happy that it got off the ground. Gilda said to Clyde, "Oh, my God! Honey look out the window."

Clyde responded, "I don't want to see anything on the ground. I just want to pray that all the things that are supposed to work, do."

#

The plane landed in Auckland, New Zealand, and took on fuel. As was customary, Carla preferred that while taking on fuel, the plane be absent of passengers, even though it was not an industry mandate. In the terminal, Clyde and Gilda were looking at things that would make for great souvenirs, but realized their budget was a little tight. Monica, all seeing and knowing, figured that they didn't have credit cards, or cash. She went to Jong and requested a pack of money for Clyde and Gilda. Jong gave her a stack of money. Monica walked over where Clyde and Gilda were, and said, "Here is some spending change. Don't say no, just say thanks."

As the Sarge, Mallory, and Darryl huddled, the Sarge asked Darryl, "Any news from the mines lately?"

"Uncle, things are progressing well, and people are reporting those who attempt to walk away with products. Apparently, it's becoming more prevalent, but those doing the stealing are dying from various issues."

"Darryl, the mines are for the people, and the villages. They are not for any individual to take a stone and make a profit from it." As the Sarge looked to the other side of the lobby, he saw several men who didn't look like Aussies who caught his eye. He said to Mallory, "Take a picture over my shoulder, and get those guys in it. I hope they're not going to where we are heading. They look like trouble. I hope we're not about to walk into some mess in the outback!"

# # #

From a collection of his resources, Mr. Utz was able to find out that his people had shot six or seven of Ben Beckmire's team. He rationalized that if the information was true, now was the perfect time to strike with a superior group of people. He contacted a friend of a predecessor, Walter, in Sydney, and bartered knowledge about the diamond and gold mines in the outback. He somehow obtained a photo of the diamond that was presented in the first court case about land ownership.

Jong and Mary Alice came out of the respective restrooms for men and women, and Jong inadvertently, stepped on the foot of a man. He bowed and apologized but received a slap to the face. The man said, "Are you fucking crazy? You stepped on my foot you little slant eyed sonofabitch!"

Jong bowed, and said, "I'm sorry, and began to back away. Jilkes nudged McArthur, and Brown, and said, "Oh shit! Jong needs our help. As the three men approached him, he flashed his hands to back off. Mary Alice said, "You must be from hell, no one takes an aggressive position like that towards someone who accidently steps on a foot."

"Bitch, shut up before I slap you as well!"

Jong said, "That would not be an advisable move on your part?'

"And why not, you little punk?"

"If you were to raise your hand to my wife, I would have to whip your ass!" As he raised his head from a subservient position to one of control, the guy turned away, and tried to sucker punch him. Jong slipped his punch, engaged his foot to the man's knee, shattered it, and round kicked him in the head, rendering the man unconscious. His associates started towards Jong in an aggressive manner, and were stopped by a person who yelled, "Let that go! We have bigger fish to fry. That little bugger shattered his knee. Hell, call for an ambulance, and leave his dumb ass here. This was not our mission to engage unassuming individuals who have skills beyond our comprehension. Give him a few grand and be done with him. I specifically told you people not to engage anyone prior to our meeting. Now, this asshole, got his knee shattered by a smaller man from Asia. How fucking embarrassing is that?"

The Sarge's entire team witnessed the interaction and were in position to assist Jong if needed. One of the men in the other group, walked past Gladstone, and asked, "Boy, what the fuck are you looking at?"

"I'm looking at a little Asian man that beat the shit out of one of your friends. That's what I'm looking at. Now, when you see a boy, make sure he doesn't have the ability to kick your ass, just like that little guy did to your friend, and most of all, be sure that he ain't your daddy!"

#

After the plane was refueled, the Sarge said to his main crew, "I'm glad you guys didn't rush over there, and expose our hand to those people. Don't worry, I'm afraid we'll meet them again for a final discussion, or fight. Damn, we're good, and that little Asian guy, who I call Mr. Amazing, is just that; Mr. Amazing!"

#

Hours later, and as their new plane landed successfully in the outback, the Sarge said to Captain Carla, "I will send two groups of our friends to watch our plane from afar, but it is really your chore to make sure it's never contaminated."

Carla replied, "I know Sarge. Never before have I worried about the safety of our group, but it appears that we've created foes from north, south, east, and west, and in doing so, it has multiplied the number of things we must do as a group to secure and protect each other. Please, do not worry about my side of the equation for it is my life as well, that is involved, and all the people who I've grown to respect and love. I took the liberty of hiring a group of individuals who are associated with the people who transport the diamonds. We will keep our normal rotation using our associate pilots, plus your ground crew, and the crew that I hired to further keep eyes on that beauty."

When the group exited customs, a commercial plane had landed, and was approaching the terminal. The Sarge asked Luana and Monica to hang around for a few minutes, and take unassuming pictures of those getting off the flight.

From a window in the terminal, the women could see a group of men who appeared as if they were familiar with each other, walking towards the terminal. They took as many pictures as possible, and then left when the men entered the terminal.

When they boarded the new school bus, they sat in the front near the Sarge, and showed him the pictures they took. The Sarge said, "I am glad that my sense of smell is still surprisingly good. When I saw those people in New Zealand, I knew that they smelled like rotten meat. I wonder what part of the equation they're after; gold, diamonds, or us?"

After the bus pulled off, the Sarge said, "This trip is about us healing our warriors in those magnificent waters of the outback. However, in the interim, we will operate as if there is a threat, which means that in and around the village, each adult will carry a concealed weapon under their garments. Ladies I know you don't like that idea, but I'm hedging my bet until I can get further intel on a group of people who look like nothing but trouble to me."

The Sarge smiled, and then announced, "Now, on another note, the village is expecting us, and they have prepared a welcoming meal from the water. I, for one, sure as heck hope it's John Dory. Oh, my goodness! That would be an incredible treat for everyone. In addition, they have screened the billabongs for hungry predators, and have deemed the waters safe for wading, swimming, and relaxing. As usual, the animals are our friends and, therefore, we won't attempt to hurt them unless they turn aggressive towards us."

Courtney yelled, "Sarge, do you think you can afford to buy me a bigger diamond ring for our anniversary that's tomorrow?" He thought for a second, and muttered to himself, "Oh, shit! Now that one got right by me." He responded, "As a matter of fact, if there are other requests on that theme, let me know because I would like to approach the elders only once, and ask for stones that don't look large and gaudy."

Monica looked at her ring, and said to Mallory, "You have any thoughts on that subject?"

"Monica, I want you to be happy beyond reproach. I know the kids give you all the love that you can handle, but a bauble here and there shouldn't be a sign of ostentatiousness. I like the idea, and we'll put our request in that pot as well."

# # #

Approximately, five miles away from the village, Darryl saw smoke rising from the east. He walked to the front of the bus, and told his uncle that he wanted to investigate the cause of it. He said, "I'll take Windom, Earther, Desmond, and Isaiah. We should be in the village before sundown. I'm simply curious about smoke in that part of the outback. It's unseasonably dry."

The men gathered their belongings, and bottles of water. The Sarge asked the driver if there was contraband hidden in the bus, he smiled, and said, "My brother, we are always prepared to assist you. Row four on the port side, packages of five with four clips. Things are freshly cleaned, oiled, wiped down, and ready to fire. I know your people have those small hip pieces that were issued upon boarding the bus."

"Thanks, and where is Wajickee?" The Sarge inquired.

"Oh, Mr. Beckmire, I haven't been appointed to interact with that level of royalty. I'm sure between where the smoke is, and the village, he will welcome you with all the fanfare that he can muster. He never stops talking about your great,

great, great, great grandparents, and how he was the mentor to the almighty, Great Saltie."

"He is special to my heart and my people, and I still have a hard time believing what he is to me. Anyway, will you help me with row four?" As the driver stopped in the middle of what could be considered a road, he hit two buttons on his control panel, punched in numbers on the tv units, and like magic, hydraulics pushed a bag out of its side. Darryl grabbed the bag, and stepped off the bus, followed by Mallory and the Sarge. The Sarge said, "There are two SAT phones in this group, but I'm not sure you'll get a signal out here."

Darryl said, "Uncle, listen for the drums, the drums are my SAT phone."

"Son, you don't have drums with you."

"Uncle, I know how to send a message. Remember, I was born here. This is my home!"

Sue Lyn walked to the threshold, and asked, "Shall I expect to see you at dinner?"

"Sue Lyn, I'm not scouting, but I am very curious about the smoke that I saw. Aborigine people would never start a fire in a dense area where a slight breeze could blow a spark and burn thousands of acres of land. No, Sue Lyn, these are foreigners, and I just need to make sure that they don't burn down the entire outback."

The Sarge asked, "Are you sure you don't want to take anyone else with you?"

"Uncle, your people need to get to the billabong, and heal those wounds. We're not going to engage, and we're not going to get close, but we will know what is going on, but from afar. Uncle, we got this. Desmond, Isaiah, Windom, and Earther are all runners. For the good of the tribe, we must know what is happening in and around our hood. I will keep you informed. Love you!"

At that moment, Zanthius said, "Darryl, I think I'm coming with you!"

The Sarge said, "Son, he picked his crew for a reason. Plus, I need you to be armed and dangerous because as you can see, I have a lot of my guys in therapy."

"Okay dad! I just thought it would be good for me to get off my butt."

"Son, you, and Larry are going to oversee setting up protection for the camp. Don't worry, we all know that you people have been slacking."

#

Deep in the outback, and near the origin of the fire, Darryl and his group saw what appeared to be a well-orchestrated group of mercenaries. They practiced their hand-to-hand combat routines, knife throwing, and quick termination strategies. From afar, each move seemed to include a thrust to the stomach, and then a strategic slice to the throat. No automatic weapons or other guns were visible. Darryl whispered to Isaiah and Desmond, "Retreat 50 yards, and give me cover." Earther and Windom had coverage from a 100-yards out, or better. As the group daisy wheeled until they were far away from the camp of those practicing their killing skills, Darryl said, "Damn, we need to get back to the village. First, I need to send a message." Darryl started making various bird sounds, and finally ended with the barking of dingoes. Somewhere and somehow, his sounds were repeated until they reached the village.

One of the young men went over to the Sarge, and said, "I have a message for you from your nephew. He says the dogs are hungry. The dogs are hungry. The dogs are hungry!"

The Sarge asked, "What does that mean?"

The young man said, "Danger is upon you. Danger is upon you. Danger is upon you!"

The Sarge looked at the man, and asked, "Can you send a message?"

"Mr. Beckmire, you know that's how we roll. What would you like to say?"

"Tell Darryl I said, "Come home now. Come home now. Come home now!"

The man wandered off into the bush and began to make sounds that resembled an animal in pain. He repeated his message for five minutes, and at the six-minute mark, a return sound reverberated throughout the outback. Darryl indicated that he was three miles out, and they were on the fast track.

Approximately fifty plus minutes later, Darryl and his crew breached the outer defenses of the village and were acknowledged by the Aborigine security force. When they entered the village, the Sarge was waiting patiently for him, and asked, "Did you expose us?"

"Uncle, we watched from afar, and could smell the various Americanized scents of colognes. They appear awesome from afar, and they were practicing hand-to-hand combat maneuvers. I did not see any automatic weapons. All I saw was the men practicing a thrust to the stomach, and a slice across the throat. Everything they did was in silence, I mean no grunts, or celebrations, just a quiet thrust to the stomach, slice to the throat, and off to the next victim. If I had to guess, they're going to hit us in the middle of the night when they think we're asleep."

"How close were you to their camp?"

"Uncle, I would say one hundred yards at the most."

"Did you see any familiar faces, or any indication that they're focusing expressly on us?"

"Uncle, strange question, however, why would a group like that be out here in no-man's land going through movements that resemble killing? I mean, we're the only act in town, besides the mines. Now, the mines are under the protection of our ancients. We, however, are free targets. My first assumption is that they plan to kill everybody they come in contact with that breathes. Uncle, that includes our children. I don't know these people, but I would like to meet them halfway, decapitate a few of them, and then ask questions of the others. From what I saw, I believe they are from the devil's workshop."

"No such thing, nephew."

"That is what they said about our group, no such thing!" The Sarge looked at Darryl, and said, "I need you to get with Zanthius and Larry, and set up our defenses. Mallory and I will check them out after you three agree upon the assignments of people. Remember, my guys are hurt, but they're not blind or cripple. They can fire a weapon, and engage in limited one-on-one interactions with a hostile enemy. I suggest that you place them near sensitive targets such as the villagers, and places where we hide the children."

"Uncle, I have the opposite idea. I would place the injured on the front line, and the capable near the sensitive areas. Either way, if we're over-run, I want an epic final battle to complete our group!"

"So, are you saying let's sacrifice the injured first?"

"Not at all! I'm saying by the time the injured finish with their asses, they won't have the stamina, or the nerve to enter the village."

The Sarge smiled, and said, "You know I'm going to be with my boys!"

"DAH! Wouldn't expect anything less. However, I heard that Jilkes and John Lee were nearly a 100 %. Is there any truth to that rumor?"

"Funny! They are better and would certainly put a whupping on the enemy. If all my men were with me on the front line, I don't believe there would be a breach into the village. I will await the final design by you and my two sons."-

# # #

The impressive thing about the outback is that it's full of life. At night birds chirp, and make noise, animals call their potential mates, packs announce where they are to keep predators away, and humans know to take refuge.

At 0330 hundred hours, the area near the village became extremely quiet. Ben Beckmire and Mallory were perched upon a little hill watching the shooting stars and talking about yesteryear. Mallory said, "It was a hill like this one, but much higher that started the relationship with those assholes. What an amazing journey it has been. I mean mayhem, destruction, corruption, wealth beyond our wildest imaginations, and not a single death. I know we're not that good, and it gives me strength when I'm here to ask for forgiveness while praying for the demise of all those who would hurt us. I know you remember how I used to think that you were crazy when you talked about all that hocus pocus shit! After that first visit here, and seeing that thing breach the water, I became a real convert. I told Monica how different this place is, she laughed, and once indicated that I was smoking the same shit that you do. Anyway, ask her today about her beliefs, and she'll swear by this place, and it's people. It's an epiphany when we're here! Life is good, healing is about us, blessings are realized, and our camaraderie is stronger. Everything that happens here strengthens us into a common belief system. I mean we've never been church going people, but there's no doubt that we believe in the holy ghost. However, when it comes to the Pope, well, let's just say, some things flee from my mind and soul."

"He is a rare bird if I must say so. He can cross the street on you in a minute. That's why I'm never sure about his meanings, and who I'm talking to. He issues threats with the knowledge that he can deliver on them. Now that's some scary shit," the Sarge announced.

The Sarge looked at his watch, and asked, "What happened to the night noises?" He immediately roused his group, and whispered, "Look sharp! I think we're going to have visitors."

At 0400 hundred hours, Wajickee startled the group. He told them that the animals were on guard, and many of those stalking the village would not survive but those who did would live to explain the natural order of things in the outback. Ben Beckmire asked, "Where have you been? I needed your counsel."

Wajickee jerked around, looked at him, and replied, "A Beckmire is never in need of counsel. He or she may need another opinion, but the Beckmire clan is never in need of counsel. Now, what is it you want me to do?"

"Wajickee, I want those in charge of that group to receive a clear passage without harm from the animals. I want to send a message to their master by one of them. I'm not sure who this group is aligned with and, therefore, I want to know who my present enemies are. If it's Mr. Utz, I will send him a clear message indicating that he is now the hunted, and by some of the world's best trackers. I want him to know that our entire existence will be dedicated to finding him. I want him to know that his stolen money has financed this venture."

Wajickee said, "These men are here for wealth. Although aligned with Mr. Utz, they are not working for him on this mission. Instead, he has guaranteed them a percentage of the mines if they are successful in eliminating all the obstacles. These people are much like the break and grab people in your country, who break glass casements, and then steal the merchandise. Mr. Utz was offered a courtesy relationship since he could not pay the people for the work, but instead offered them knowledge of the mines. Being modern day crooks, they thanked him for the location and information about what was being hauled out of the mines and told him that if they ran into you and your group, that they would dispose of you. They told him in no uncertain words that they were about wealth, not revenge. They essentially took his idea, and told him to go fondle himself, but they felt compelled to offer him some crumbs. No, Ben Beckmire, he is not here, and he is expecting a package that will allow him to reconstitute his forces to come after you if these people didn't eliminate you."

As the night noises increased, and the sounds of screams were softened by the sounds of didgeridoos playing, Wajickee said, "These heathens have slaughtered many animals. However, your wish is my command. In a matter of minutes, three men will run into the village firing their weapons. No matter which one you shoot, the net result is the same, they are connected to Mr. Utz who probably feels betrayed by this group. What a loss of life. There are animals devouring thirty-two bodies, all for stones that are falsely monetized."

Beckmire stared at Wajickee, and stated, "Those stones may be falsely monetized as you say but try to convince a woman of that."

"Ben Beckmire, I know that. If you will allow me, I would like to pick out a stone for the lovely Doctor Beckmire. I am aware that she and the other women are interested in having signature stones that are from the outback."

"We will talk about that later. Look at these three guys coming into the village as if they can control it," the Sarge stated.

The Sarge told Jilkes, John Lee, and McArthur to place non-fatal/grazing shots to their legs. No sooner said than done. The Sarge bellowed, "Those were introduction shots. The next rounds will be head shots if you don't lose those weapons." The three men dropped their rifles, and slowly relieved themselves of their other weapons.'

Once it was obvious that they had complied, the Sarge came from behind a small bush, and stated, "I'm not sure why you're here, but I have a good idea." The Sarge looked at McArthur and instructed him to bind their hands. He then said to the assailants, "I'm only going to ask you a question just once. An unanswered question will leave you with a decapitation. Now, are you working for Mr. Utz?" There was a pause, but no one responded. The Sarge told Larry, to gag each man.

After the men were gagged, the Sarge asked John Lee and Jilkes if they were up to convincing these guys to cooperate. John Lee responded, "Anything for you, my leader." He then looked at the three men, and emphatically stated, "This will

not be small body parts being decapitated. I be looking to
sever arms, legs, and eyes, but not necessarily in that order.
Now, our leader asked you a question, and seeing as you
people can hear and see, and nobody responded to him, it be
like a sign of disrespect. Now we don't be doing a lot of that
out here. So, rather than repeat the question, I'm going to do
some work on each of you!"

John Lee dug his favorite knife deep into the third man's
leg and twisted it. In the process, he severed a major artery,
the trauma caused the man to hyperventilate, and push blood
from his body. He then said to the other two men, "Now I be
just getting warmed up!"

The man collapsed and was dragged out of the area into
the bush by Larry and Darryl. Darryl asked, "Oh, my God!
Did you see what John Lee did to this guy?"

Larry replied, "He's just beginning. Listen, Darryl, when
you come after us, and you're not successful, don't expect ice
cream and cake. No, you should expect to die in a horrific
manner. This guy was bleeding out from a previous wound.
John Lee knew that and picked him out because he knew he
was going to die anyway."

The unelected leader, as a result of attrition to the group
spoke up, and said, "You people are real fucking men. Why
don't we do a little one-on-one, and if I lose, I'll tell you
everything I know, including where to find Mr. Utz. Be real
men and fight me like a man!"

The Sarge said, "Oh, I see, you came up in here to kill
women, children, and men, and now you want to have an
honor fight? Okay, I'll give you one opportunity to beat my
man if he so wishes to challenge you." The Sarge looked at
Jong, and asked, "You feel like fighting?"

"Sarge, you know I'm still hurt, but I'll take him on."

The guy said, "I'm bleeding from the leg. So, it seems fair to me."

Jong said, "I'm the cripple in the group. Do you like beating up on handicapped people?"

As the two men squared off, the bandit took up a stance that no one had seen before. Jong asked, "What stance is that?"

The bandit responded, "It's the one that allows me to whip your ass and walk away free!" The bandit made an aggressive move towards Jong. Jong in return flipped forward and caught the man square under his chin with both feet, rendering him unconscious. Everyone was amazed at the action by Jong who said, "I didn't think that I could still do that move!"

Much later when the man woke up, and found himself tied tight once again, he asked, "What happened?"

The second man said, "You got creamed and clocked."

# # #

The two men were a plethora of third-hand information concerning Mr. Utz, in that they had not met him, but had heard from others on the team who had constant contact with him. They explained to the team that their interest was purely financial, and that they did not want to engage them on any level. This mission was only about precious stones that they heard were found here. They swore that Mr. Utz approached their deceased leader with the idea of raiding gold and diamond mines in the outback. The leader was adamant that the mission was about gold and diamonds, and not about taking on Beckmire, and his crew.

The Sarge asked, "How do you know who we are?"

"Sergeant Beckmire, we're ex-military, and we know about most of your exploits in Vietnam, here in the outback, in Virginia, in the Midwest, Hong Kong, and Europe. Now that one with the dictator, we thought you people were on some special kind of drug to go into the man's lair and take him on in his own home. Now that was a gutsy call."

The Sarge looked at him, and said, "I'm trying to figure out what to do with you two. You came here to kill us for diamonds."

The man shouted, "We came here for diamonds, not to kill anyone. The weapons were a show of force."

"What about your training with the thrust to the stomach, and then the slice to the throat?"

"That was exactly what it was, Sergeant Beckmire, training. We wanted to rob this place, and we were told that you people were not in the country. Had we known you were here this conversation would not be taking place."

"You lost a lot of men to the environment, but yet, you two are momentarily still alive."

Once again, the man cut the Sarge off, and said, "Control of that group was lost in New Zealand, when an Asian guy, your guy, disabled one of the mouthpieces for motivating this group. He was a focal point, and when the men saw how easily he was dispatched by a guy half his size, they kind of lost a lot of enthusiasm for this job. The selling point was that you people were not in the country, however, my partner and I reconciled the fact it was you people at the airport. We needed the job, and decided to attempt fate. "

"What am I going to do with you, my friend?"

"Sergeant Beckmire, we're thieves, we're not in the murder business unless there is an outright challenge to what we're trying to accomplish. The thrust to the stomach, and slice to the throat is a part of the training program prescribed for us by a respected Asian fellow. We steal, and that is why we took advantage of Mr. Utz, and scheduled our heist, believing full well that you people were not here in the country."

"When you had the incident in New Zealand, didn't you consider the fact that it could have been us?" The Sarge inquired.

"Sergeant Beckmire, I knew it was you when I saw you speaking to your wife, Doctor Beckmire. I know my opponents, my enemies, and those who are surely a problem for me. I'm the practitioner who studies the key people. My associate, who is bleeding bad, is the designer of the attacks. Now, after watching Jong polish off that fellow, I knew we were going to be in harm's way. The problem was the guy who orchestrated this deal, was one of the first to be attacked by the dogs or dingoes, and after that, we were pretty much leaderless. Sergeant Beckmire, I'm not begging for forgiveness or release. What I am asking is that you give one veteran to another, an honorable discharge, no torture, but a complete and final, conclusion, a bullet to the head."

"Sir, what is your given name?" The Sarge asked.

"I am Lionel Dempsey, and he's Arthur Hood.

"Mr. Dempsey and Mr. Hood, here's the deal! I'm trying to figure out if we are going to kill you, or release you, and make you do something like community service." The Sarge saw Courtney and asked her to look at the wounds.

# # #

Minutes later, Courtney said to Dempsey, "I need you to relax. You received a flesh wound, but your anxiety is causing your heart to pump excessively and, therefore, you are pushing an enormous amount of blood out. I need you to drink this herb mixture and try to relax. If my husband, and his crew haven't terminated you at this point, I bet you more than likely they are not going to."

Courtney looked at Mr. Hood's wound, and said, "Sir, your injury is a flesh wound, as well. Calm your friend down before he goes into shock. Our guys are not going to kill you. If they were, it would have happened ten minutes ago."

# # #

The Sarge returned, and said, "You people are lucky my guys can't shoot straight. Anyhow, I hope you are not trying to hoodwink me with bullshit. Since you came here for gold and diamonds, then gold and diamonds you shall see, but never have. I'm going to place you in the mines so that you can help unearth the very thing that you will never possess. Now, I know you two probably don't believe in hocus pocus, but here in the outback, there be demons. Your group was attacked by wombats, snakes, spiders, and most of all by the dingoes. Do you think that was by accident that so many different predators concluded the lives of those men? By morning, the only bodies that will be visible will be those who were bitten by one of the poisonous creatures. Those who were dingo and wombat meals are gone. Not even bone fragments will be visible. Now, every larceny hearted person that has attempted to steal stones or nuggets has died. This area is sacred, and protected by forces that you can't imagine exist." He then looked at Darryl, and asked, "Did we remove all of the stones and bullion from the billabong?"

"Uncle, we removed perhaps half of them, and then we became involved in activities stateside. Perhaps once these two brigands are healed, we should show them the forces that protect the righteous and devour the nefarious."

"Maybe you're correct, nephew. However, for now, we will make them do community service, and work in the mines. They will see some of the protectors when they're working, which should immediately stifle any corrupt or treacherous thoughts." The Sarge saw one of the villagers and asked him to escort the two men to the billabong, let them soak for thirty minutes, and then treat those flesh wounds with native plants."

#

Four weeks later, all the injured men were close to 100%. The team was running and doing calisthenics. Jilkes had a slight limp that was noticeable weeks ago but through hard work and determination, it was overcome. The two brigands, Dempsey, and Hood, fit right in, and were often used as goffers for menial tasks.

One night after cleaning up, and relaxing outside of their hut, Mallory walked over to them, and asked them to join the group for some piss (beer). The two men slowly walked over feeling the glares from the group. Chakes said, "Okay, you two have been doing shit jobs for weeks. I mean you're working in the mines, cleaning up the place, handling the latrines, and basically marking your time. Now, tell us, what are your long-term goals, and how do you plan on getting out of here?"

Hood responded, "I had planned on running from here to the airport, but realized that when I got there, I didn't have any money."

Dempsey said, "You have to excuse him, he had too many hits without his helmet, when he played football. Anyway, there isn't much waiting for us when we get back if we get back. He's single, and so am I. Nobody knows where we are, and those who know, probably hope that we don't come back. Once we left that mess over there in the Gulf, we've been doing odd jobs, but nothing important. When we heard about this job, well, we thought we could pull it off. We have some buddies living underground in DC, and they told us in no uncertain terms, to stay away from the outback, and if a certain Sergeant was in country, to leave immediately. We apparently didn't heed their warnings, and now, here we are cleaning up your shit."

Mallory asked, "Would you guys like a beer?"

"Yes sir."

"Okay, you know all of our names. Call us by our names. You're not our slaves or anything like that."

"Yes sir."

"Dude, didn't I just ask you to call us by our names?"

"Sorry, but we're slow thinkers."

Jilkes asked, "How do you like handling all of those diamonds, knowing full well that a single one of them could spell your death?"

"We have fantasized about taking them, we may be slow, but we ain't stupid. When we were first captured, the Sergeant asked one of the villagers to take us to the billabong and let us soak our wounds. Well, Sir, I mean Jilkes, I believe I saw the largest thing that I've ever seen in my life. Hood saw it as well. The villager told us that it was the Great Saltie. After that and seeing the snakes and spiders all day long in the mines, we figured that the stones weren't worth the effort."

Chakes asked, "Do you think when it's time to leave, you might try to steal one or two of them?"

Hood said, "Ain't no damn way. Too many things working against us here."

There was a stillness in the air, and Darryl said, "They don't know I know it, but two of my guys are about to go home and claim land that's worth billions." Earther and Windom looked at each other, and Earther said, "How could you possibly know that? We only discussed the matter a few hours ago. How could you possibly know that?"

Darryl smiled, and replied, "You're in my hood, guys. There isn't much I don't know when you're in my hood."

Windom said, "We were going to speak with you later, and ask you for a timetable for our release. We didn't want to seem like we're just cutting and running after you guys saved our families, our properties, our lives, and embraced us as a part of your tribe. We prayed hard on how to approach you, and the Sarge."

"Guys, my uncle will be here in a few minutes, you can tell him, but I'm happy for you, and you know that if you need us to come out to cold-ass Minnesota, then we will. Anyway, I can't think of two more dedicated men than Dempsey and Hood to take your places as a part of my group. Now, that of course must be sanctioned by our leader, but I hope you guys will state any honest hesitation you have in bringing these two brigands aboard, if in fact they want to be a part of our group."

Dempsey blurted out, "I want to do anything that will get me out of the mines, away from snakes and spiders. I'm committed to doing whatever you need me to do, just get me out of the mines."

John Lee inquired, "How about blowing another man's head off?"

Dempsey said, "That's a tricky question. If it is for the protection of the group, and there is a clear signal of hostility, then consider it done."

Everyone looked at Hood, and Chakes asked, "How about you Hood? Can you kill another human being?"

"We did it in the Gulf on many occasions, and we never really understood why we were killing those people."

The Sarge appeared, and asked, "Killing what people?"

Hood became tongue tied when he saw the Sarge, and Dempsey said, "He was talking about the work we did in the Gulf in response to a question relative to our ability to kill another human being."

"Well, can you do it?"

"Yes sir!"

"Why are you guys having this kind of conversation with captives?"

Darryl replied, "Uncle, two of my guys are planning to relocate their families to Minnesota and claim their lands and fortunes. They were going to discuss it with you, but since I asked these two brigands to consider working for me, we got off track, and the conversation became discombobulated when you showed up. To make it short, Windom and Earther are leaving, and would like a timetable from us to replace them. They need to show up, and sign documents authenticating their existence. Oh, uncle, I think it is something that we need to reinforce by being there to make sure that there is no hanky pranky."

"This is so awesome. I just finished a call with the Holy Father who asked me about the plight of the Native Americans. How is this guy getting the information before it's announced to me in my own enclave? Anyway, my answer is, yes, yes, and yes. Now, can I have a pint of piss?"

## CHAPTER SEVENTEEN

Five days later, Michael said to the Sarge, "I would like to call Ayesha on a zoom once we get to the airport. Is that a problem?"

"Son, you know the policy! As a matter of fact, before I let my two brothers walk into a fire, I'm going to do some reconnaissance with complete strangers. Listen, everyone thinks we're heading to Minnesota. We are going to The Sanctuary first for a week, and then on to Minnesota. I want to get the two new guy's feet wet, and make sure that we can trust them. So, say nothing, I will make the announcement on the plane." The Sarge saw the tears swelling in Michael's eyes, and said, "Son, she's a good woman. She is a keeper!"

Later, the Sarge had a private conversation with Windom and Earther so they knew that the group was heading to *the Sanctuary* for a week, but in the meantime, Dempsey and Hood would be sent to Minnesota to scout and snoop around.

#

After Captain Carla made her personal inspection of the underbelly of the plane and gear, she entered the plane, and winked at the Sarge.

The plane was towed out of the hangar, and onto an active runway. Captain Carla reminded everyone to have those seatbelts fastened low and tight. She then said, "Doctor Beckmire, what is your pleasure insofar as the take-off is concerned?"

Courtney yelled, "Fast and thrilling!"

She got her wish. Captain Carla throttled the big jet engines forward, released the brakes, and the jet roared down the runway, and blasted into the sky.

The Sarge said, "Damn, you and her, have got to get over that control thing. She loves blasting this thing into the air, and now you're advocating and enabling her."

"Honey, she is the best. Sometimes she needs to feel the adrenaline flow like we do back here. Anyway, she's pregnant again, and won't be flying us much longer."

"Damn! This has become a baby farm. I'm glad we have a nursery in the belly of this thing. Now that was a huge decision for Jong, and he made it happen. Gotta love that guy."

# # #

Many hours later, as the plane began its descent into St. Thomas, everyone heard the smooth sound of the engines de-throttling. They stirred in their seats, stumbled to the restrooms, and helped themselves to the coffee that was brewing in the automatic coffee brewer.

Captain Carla came on the public address system and gave the group the weather and touchdown time. She also told them to secure those belts, low and tight around their midsection.

# # #

On the ground as the group entered customs, three obviously out of place men in suits were standing inside. As

Michael approached the desk, he handed the agent his passport, and the agent without saying a word, looked him up on the monitor. He then asked a couple of questions, and flashed a note that read, 'Immigration Officials.'

Michael signed to Courtney and Rashida, 'Immigration Officials.'

Courtney whispered the information to the Sarge who said, "This is a ruse! Everyone stay close, and focused. Don't give any information other than you're an American citizen."

When the Sarge passed through customs, two of the men confronted him, and said, "Please, Sergeant Beckmire, follow us to the corner on your right."

As the Sarge signaled that all was okay, he followed the two men to a corner where a third man said, "On the secure phone that is laying on that seat in front of you is a friend of yours. Please say hello to him."

The Sarge said, "This is Ben Beckmire, who am I speaking with?"

"My son, I hope you had a great trip, and I hope your people are better. I'm going to cut through the chase. If you let Windom, Earther, and their families go naked into Minnesota, they will be slaughtered like the other two families that had rights to property there. I am just giving you a heads up. Do your homework before you let them go there. Call me later, my son. Those three men will be getting on a plane to Minnesota and will do some leg work for you. Go with God my son!"

# # #

Mrs. Carter took over where her husband left off. She purchased a bus company for the employees and members of *the Sanctuary*. Together, the establishments purchased three large modern buses to ferry groups back and forth to the airport, and other locations. When Mrs. Carter saw her son, she began to cry, as did he. He said, "Mom, it is so good to see and hug you. Is everything okay?" Where is Ayesha?" Her head dropped, she smiled, and said, "Look behind you, son!"

Ayesha gave him flowers, kissed him tenderly, and signed, "Michael, it has been a long time, but the only thing that has changed, is that I am in love with you!"

Michael smiled and touched his heart. He along with everyone else was given the opportunity to buy a diamond at a significantly, discounted price. He reached in his pocket, fetched the stone, fell to his knees, and signed, "If you will have me as your husband, then I will have you as my wife. I also have changed because I absolutely love you with all my heart." They kissed and Mrs. Carter signed to Ayesha, a thing that Michael didn't know she could do. His mother was so happy that he made the decision to get engaged to her.

# # #

Mallory and Chakes had the responsibility of making Hood and Dempsey successful looking. Each man picked up a support piece from the secret compartments on the main bus that was designated as their bus only. They also picked up a smaller weapon for the newcomers. Mallory told them not to shoot themselves in the foot with the weapons.

Later, at a local tailor, the men were outfitted with suits, jackets, pants, and other essentials that would make them look like entrepreneurs. Dempsey asked, "Do we have to wear neckties? I really hate them because they remind me of a noose around my neck."

Chakes responded, "Naw! You can do more without a tie than most people can do with one. We are putting a lot of faith in you two brigands, and I hope you don't disappoint."

Hood smiled, and confirmed, "You didn't kill us, and we didn't steal from you. So far, I think that we're both going to enjoy this relationship because its built-on honesty and trust." Hood paused for a second, and said, "I don't have a pot to piss in. This is an opportunity for us to be a part of something that isn't crooked." He then looked at Chakes, and asked, "Come to think of it, you people aren't crooked, are you?" Everyone laughed including the tailor who knew the importance of the group to the island, and its people.

Mrs. Carter, that night at dinner, illustrated that *the Sanctuary* and its adjoining partners were smart, organized, cooperating, and functional. The other property owners elected her as their spokesperson and CEO of the properties that the group invested in. It was clear that Ayesha, and she had formed a partnership that would exist beyond any outside relationships including Michaels. At the feast fit for kings, Mrs. Carter first welcomed the group back to *the Sanctuary*, and signed that Michael was now engaged to a woman who epitomized the essence of purity, and true love. She signed, "I am happy that my son fell in love with a woman of substance, rather than a woman of experience."

Michael stood up and began to clap. He walked over to Ayesha, and the children began to make frantic signs of 'he's going to kiss her.' Ayesha grabbed his hand, pulled him salaciously close to her, and signed, "Oh, my God, I love you so much!"

During dinner, the Sarge allowed Darryl to make comments on the impending departure of Windom, Earther, and their families. Tears flowed, and the mood changed because their families had become a part of Ben Beckmire's tribe.

Ben Beckmire stood up, and said, "They are not leaving us, they are expanding our reach, our home, and our ability to help people help themselves. Now, me and my crew are getting better, but we're also getting older. We purchased land and houses from two slum landlords, and just a few days ago, my wife asked me when will we be able to sit on the porch, and watch over all these babies? Although Darryl and Sue Lyn's group do not share the history of my group, it is a group that will grow and learn to recognize each other's strengths and weaknesses. Yes, my friends, it's getting close to the time when I, and these other senior citizens will only be available for advice, and long-gun action. Listen, everyone connected directly and indirectly to this group is essentially rich beyond their wildest imagination. Oh, sorry, those two new brigands, well, they're on minimum wages until proven otherwise. Speaking of them, I'm sending them to Minnesota prior to Windom, Earther, and their families. As I discussed with the Holy Father, there would be a blood bath if Windom, Earther, and their families showed up, unprotected. Two families have been decimated under questionable circumstances. Therefore, I'm sending Hood and Dempsey to Minnesota to snoop around and gather intelligence on who are the bad guys in the mix. The people that met our plane, have already departed to begin the evaluation of the situation. Now I know, some of you are asking yourselves, "why these two knuckleheads?" My response is orchestrated! Why not these two? Should we kill everyone who attempts to kill us? I don't subscribe to that notion, but it was obvious that they knew they were going to die months ago and had the outrageous audacity to ask for a soldier's death, a bullet to the head. Now most of you know that all of our captives have tried to negotiate a way out of their dilemma. These two just wanted to die honorably, a thing that I must admit that I would want to happen to me if the circumstances were reversed. I trust them, I'm not sure why, but I trust them. If in fact they try to do stupid, they are aware that our reach is beyond comprehension when it comes to animals, insects, and my faith in them to deliver a horrific outcome. I do not plan on entering this relationship with threats, however, I raise my glass to them, and hope that you do as well, in welcoming them into our tribe, and our culture. Here, here!"

#

At five in the evening, one of the group's smaller planes, left the ground on a trip to Minnesota. The flight was uneventful, but the two men riding in the plane, thought it was spectacular. After landing, the two men were picked up by a limousine, and it appeared that they were high rollers. Each man was outfitted with a 'black card,' to make him look like a successful businessman, $10k in cash, fancy watches, clothes, and rings.

Without hesitation, they wanted to know who owned the land that the pipeline was going through or around. They were given a loquacious lesson of the area by the driver who was a Native American. He had been instructed by Windom and Earther to show them around and provide them with full knowledge of any information they desired. Dempsey who was hyper, and easily agitated asked, "What happened to those two families that were killed suspiciously who owned property along the proposed pipeline tracks? Is that what would happen to us if we wanted to buy some of the land?"

The driver said, "I'm no spirit, but if you venture near those properties, I will probably have to send your bodies back in boxes, if in fact they were found."

Hood asked, "What's your name?"

The driver responded, "My given name is Litefoot."

Dempsey said, "Litefoot, take us to the area, I want to walk around, let people take my picture, and eventually come looking for me. If we hide, we'll be here for months trying to figure out who the villains are. That's what I think we should do. Are you with me home boy?"

Hood reflected, "We weren't given clear guidelines. We were told to snoop around, act like potential purchasers, and see who comes to the party without an invitation. If we implement your idea, then I think we're exposing ourselves, but that's what I think we should do."

Litefoot said, "I have weapons for you guys. Do you want them now?"

Hood responded, "Naw! It wouldn't look right if we're just looking around, and also packing."

As the two men were driven towards the area where Windom and Earther were from, Dempsey couldn't resist stating how beautiful, and peaceful it seemed. He said to Litefoot, "Where do you live?"

Litefoot replied, "Near where we are going, but deep in the hills."

"You take your limo deep in the hills?" Hood asked.

"No. I just drive this during the day for a company owned by one of the land speculators. It gives me the opportunity to watch from the inside without drawing a lot of suspicion."

Hood asked, "Can you give us any information about the families that disappeared?"

"All I know is that they were both called to the scene of an accident involving their children, and when they got there, they were bound, gagged, and taken off into the night."

"How old were the children?"

"I think they were around seventeen to nineteen years of age. The boys were rather reckless, and often took the two sisters into town to party. They were just friends from what I've heard."

Litefoot said, "Okay, if you look to your right, those red flags represent the proposed route of the pipeline. Now the big problem is that this route would impact and perhaps contaminate the many lakes in the area. Now, two miles north of this point is where Windom, Earther, and the other owners of the land live. Their properties are ideal because they don't represent any danger of a runoff into the lakes. Their properties are in the middle of a gulley that is perfect to contain any fractures to the pipeline. That's why everyone wants them dead. The two families that are missing were offered peanuts for their land. I guess they should have accepted the peanuts, and perhaps continued to enjoy being alive."

A quiet fell over the car, and it was broken when Dempsey asked, "After we finish seeing where the land is, can you take us to where the accident was reported. Oh, and by the way, who reported the accident? Did the police respond?"

"Sir, all I know is that calls were made, and both families took off in a hurry."

"How do you know that? Was someone watching them?"

"Sir, a lot of our people are still victimized by your alcohol, and now your opioids. They sleep where possible, eat whatever they can find, but manage to be able to buy alcohol and drugs.   In other words, there is little faith in the information provided by some people."

# # #

After touring the proposed pipeline area, Dempsey and Hood made themselves highly visible. They took pictures of the surrounding areas and seemed to know a lot about the topography.   As they entered the limo, the driver astutely asked, "Did you guys see flashing lights from the mountains? They watched everything you did."

"Who was watching us?"

"The Indians that live in the mountains that were promised a piece of the pie once all of the land was confiscated."

"Same old shit; divide and conquer!" Hood announced.

"Take us to the hotel, I'm hungry, I would invite you, but I don't think it's in your best interest to be socializing with us."

Litefoot said, "You're right. My last mission with you guys is to give you these clean pieces, and two clips each. A round has already been chambered in each weapon. You should call Windom, and report to him what you've seen. I'm sure they'll probably send a couple of losers to your rooms. I wouldn't touch them or engage them. They are just plants seeking critical information about you before these people decide whether to make you disappear or not."

"Thanks for the heads up! We'll be obvious, eat in the restaurant, and have a beer or two, and see who's watching us.

What time can you pick us up in the morning? I want to take another trip to that area, and make sure that we're seen."

"There is a forecast for snow in the morning. Let's play it by ear. I won't be driving this thing in the morning. I'll be driving my truck since it's my day off, and you people offered me $500 to take you around," Litefoot stated.

# # #

Later that evening, Dempsey and Hood left their adjoining rooms, and headed for the restaurant. They played the old tape trick on the doors. The adjoining room was taped at the bottom with transparent packing tape. The door they left from had talcum powder strewn about the floor in an unsuspecting manner. Their bags were easily accessible as they sat on the luggage rack in each room. The cash the men had was placed in their room safes, along with the weapons. They expected that people would visit the room once they were seen in the restaurant.

In the restaurant, the scene was predictable. Three women at the bar eyed them and gave them suggestive looks. The two men who were at the end of the bar, and almost unnoticeable because of where they were sitting, suddenly got up, and exited the lounge. Dempsey and Hood were escorted to their table by the hostess who also left a note inside of one of the menus. The note read, "your room is being searched, the women are crooked, order your food, and take it back to your room. Someone will contact you about your next steps."

Hood said to Dempsey, "Listen, I'm tired. I want to order something to eat, and head back to the room."

"That sounds like a plan. I don't like flying, and our little plane is getting smaller and smaller, it feels like to me. I want to have a drink, go to sleep, and be fresh for tomorrow."

The two men received their food, paid the bill, and took their food and drink back to their room. On the way out, one of the women said, "Ah, you guys are leaving us? We were just about to ask you to have a drink with us."

Dempsey replied, "Another time, hopefully. We're tired and have a lot of plans to go over before tomorrow. Thanks, and maybe some other time. Good night!"

When the two men entered their room, it was obvious that someone had been in it, and had searched through their belongings. Hood remarked, "Not very smart crooks. Look at the footprints in the talcum powder. It appears to have been the two men that left when we arrived in the restaurant. I bet you if we go back to the bar and look at those two guys who abruptly left when we entered the restaurant, their shoes and pants will tell the story."

"You're probably right. However, we know they were here, and that's to our advantage."

# # #

The following morning, the two men headed to the restaurant for breakfast. This time, both men were packing. As they rounded the door to the restaurant, a man could be seen drinking what appeared to be a Bloody Mary and had obvious powder residue on both pant legs. Hood said, "I should go over there and cold cock that sonofabitch."

Dempsey, always the level-headed one replied, "Naw! Not now, but soon, my brother." The two men proceeded to the buffet and filled their plates with too much food.

When Litefoot arrived, he was questioned at the door by the other guy who was in Hood and Dempsey's room, who also had powder residue on his pants. He said to Litefoot, "What are you doing here today?"

"Those guys offered me $500 to take them around today."

"Where are you going to take them?"

"Not sure, but first chance I get, I'll call you, and let you know where they want to go."

"You be sure to do that. You know who pays your ass, don't you?"

"Yes sir. You do, and I work for you, but I guess I should have called you to tell you that they offered me $500 to drive them around."

"I'm not concerned about the money. I want to know why the hell they are so interested in that area that we want to control? If you hear anything, and I do mean anything, you give a call so that I can bring a crew out there and make them disappear like those two families."

Litefoot looked at him sternly but didn't say a word. The guy said, "You and your family like working for us, right?"

"You know we depend on you because there is no one else hiring around here."

"Okay, don't you forget that. You keep $300 and bring the rest to us. That's the cost of you not asking for permission to do extra work with outsiders. By the way, how did you hook up with them?"

"I didn't hook up with them. They were assigned to me by the dispatcher. I don't know these people."

# # #

Dempsey and Hood finished their breakfast and saw Litefoot in the lobby. They knew their adversaries were not far away and decided to open the flood gates with information about their activities. Dempsey exclaimed, "I need to check on one thing at the site we were at, and then I need to have people come out here next week to assess the environment! Let's get going." As he was walking away, the guy with the talcum powder on his pants cuffs asked, "Are you people into oil?"

Hood swelled up, but Dempsey said, "No, we don't do oil, we just do financing. Why do you ask?"

"How did you come to find out about that specific track of land?"

"Mister, I don't know you, and that question clearly is a NYFB."

"NBFY? What the hell is that?"

"Sir, I don't know what the hell NBFY is. I do know what NYFB is."

"And what might that be?" The guy asked.

"Well sir, NYFB is short for, "not your fucking business." Have a nice day."

As Dempsey turned to walk away, the guy doing the talking grabbed his arm. Hood moved in an offensive manner but was cautioned to back down by Dempsey. Dempsey said, "Where I'm from, that's an automatic invitation to an ass whuppin. I highly recommend that you remove your hand from my arm." The guy flashed his weapon, and Dempsey nodded to Hood, and the ass whuppin commenced. As the other guy attempted to secure his weapon, Hood hit him with a left hook that put the man to sleep. In the meantime,

Dempsey, placed a major ass whuppin on his guy. Before the guy lost consciousness, Hood said, "Never touch my brother. Never touch me. Never touch any of my friends. If you ever disrespect us again, we'll leave you in pieces."

As they entered the truck, Litefoot said, "You know you've just signed your death certificates. Those two are just apple polishers, bootlickers, and yes men. Their bosses are surely going to hear about this, and then they're going to come down hard on you."

Dempsey responded, "Meet us in the back of the hotel. We're going to check out of this place and make it interesting for people to find us." The two men exited the truck, and brazenly walked through the lobby, and to their rooms. They emptied the safes, left their clothes, and walked out of the rooms.

The guy who Hood whipped mumbled, "This ain't over!"

Hood approached him, and said, "You're right! I just called fifty fellow vets who are financing this matter. We'll catch you later."

As the two men re-entered the truck, Dempsey said, "About three miles up this road, I saw a sporting goods store. Is it open?"

Litefoot responded, "It is."

#

The two men resisted buying automatic weapons and decided on the purchase of long-range rifles. They huddled, and realized that they had compromised Litefoot, and offered him $10k for his truck which would soften the fact that he didn't really know them. Litefoot on the other hand realized that his ass was up the creek, called his sister, told her to get their mom, and head for that cavern in the sky.

Dempsey looked at Litefoot square on, and said with emotion, "You can't go back to that place, or to your home. You need to immediately move your family out of this area."

Litefoot smiled, and said, "I told my sister to fetch my mother, and head for a secret cave that she is aware of. I know I can't go back and, therefore, you need to buy another rifle, and plenty of ammo. I suggest that you buy those machine pistols as well the 100 plus magazine holders. Your beating up on those bone fetchers is going to bring an entire army down on you, and now me."

Hood looked at Dempsey, and said, "I guess you got your wish. You know the one where you didn't want to take all year to figure out who was in charge."

"Not funny Hood. You agreed on my strategy. Where is that SAT phone? I need to call Darryl and tell him what we're up against. In the meantime, Litefoot, go back into that store and purchase as much ammunition as possible. Here is $2,000 plus the $500 we promised you for riding us around. Listen, the people we work for will make this right, and you'll be able to live a normal life here once they clean up this mess."

"Dude, I'm trying to get the hell out of here, but I can't leave my moms, and my sis here to suffer for me."

"If our people come to this place, I simply believe there will be one hell of a death toll, and it ain't going to be ours. Listen, get the ammunition, and perhaps a few pump action shotguns for your family."

## CHAPTER EIGHTEEN

In a sleepy little town in Maine, known for its beauty in the fall, it's fishing, and year-round hunting, on this day, Presque Isle would be the center of the world's attention because it, and everyone who lived there, would be obliterated from the map. At 2230 hundred hours, six devices were detonated, and everything that was composed of hydrogen was sucked into a gigantic vacuum. No one in over a 1.5-mile radius would survive the feeding frenzy brought about by the Carbon Factor, and the extra hydronium ion that was added.

Hours later, after the explosion, the Holy Father called Ben Beckmire, and said, "Son, there has been a detonation of the Carbon Factor. This time, the death toll extends 1.5 miles past Presque Isle, in all directions. I gained knowledge of this event but didn't have enough time to call for an evacuation, or get you, and your people there to try to stop it. A priest, who will certainly go to hell, by my very own hands, conspired with a group of brigands to bring attention to his contempt for the word celibacy. This priest had access to original documents kept in the Vatican and copied 90% of the real Carbon Factor formula. A function of illicit drugs, orgies, temptations of the most vial acts, convinced him of the fact that life and helping people, were subservient to what he did in the closets of his life. He sold his soul to the bomber who promised him absolution, freedom, and experiences that superseded any he could imagine. He had no idea that what he was offering was the innocent souls of people and institutions. The next detonation will destroy an entire civilization and country. I don't know what's to come, but this was just a test. My opinion is that it won't happen in America. America is too important to their monetary system."

There was a pause on the line. The Holy Father then said, "Now, on another note, I do not advise you to head to Minnesota. Those two crooks that you absolved of their sins, have everything under control. They have been discovered because of a fight they had with two perpetrators. They have left the city, hooked up with the driver who, by the way, has secured his sister and mother, and they have headed to the hills with loads of provisions, and weapons. Until I can pinpoint the next detonation of the Carbon Factor, I request that you, and your people board your plane, and head back to the sanctity of the outback. I have ten of my most trusted people covering the actions of those two brigands that you didn't slay. It was a beautiful thing when you considered not killing them. God will never forget that action, and those two will prove as important to you as Jilkes and John Lee."

"Holy Father, it sounds as if I have a leak in my organization that reports to you on a daily basis."

"Nonsense, my son! I am the Holy Father, also known as the Pope. A picture is worth a thousand words. You people are famous and, therefore, wherever you go, true believers will report on your movements and actions. Son, I would love to have a direct connection to you. However, it would compromise your excellent decision-making processes, and make me second guess your next move. I honestly don't have anyone qualified to infiltrate a group like yours. The only newcomers are on their way to a cave and are under the close protection of my people. Somehow, and don't ask me why, I suspect the next test will be in Minnesota. My son, please don't query me, I'm just trying to figure out how the devil would approach and focus on this. That pipeline is important to the entire nation, but it also provides a significant weaning from the middle east. Therefore, it should be at the center of our attention because he or she who controls it, and where it flows, will control the universe as others leave way for the Carbon Factor to reign supreme. Carbon is a curse to some, to others, it is the absolute device to control the world."

"Holy Father, how do you gather intel on me, and my people. I can't say I don't believe the Holy Father, that would be blasphemous. However, it is tricky that you know things, and when things are going to happen especially when it comes to my group. And, Holy Father, why do you call my men in Minnesota, crooks, and brigands?"

"Son, I'm just practicing the vernacular that the wicked would use. From the intel my people gave me on Hood and Dempsey, they are thankful to be alive, and they operate without a roadmap, but seemingly effectively. They drew those people out in a hurry, and I hear that the Hood guy, well, let's just say, he put a masterful butt beating on that one guy. Oh, yes, my people were quite happy with the reactions of your two men."

"Holy Father, I'm still interested in knowing about your intel network."

"Son, on our next encounter, I will show you a place in Vatican City that will absolutely leave you speechless. Go with God, my son, but go in a hurry. Leave the islands, and head to the Midwest. There you will find lots of cover, and plenty restful nights." The phone began to buzz indicating that there was no longer anyone on the other end.

The Sarge saw Jilkes and John Lee, and said, "We need to head to the Midwest. The Holy Father said that there was another detonation of the Carbon Factor somewhere in Maine."

Jilkes shook his head, and said, "We're on it Sarge. What time do you want to depart?"

"I want to be at the airport in one hour!"

#

After the plane was in the air, and reached its cruising altitude, the Sarge engaged the intercom system, and told the group that the sudden extraction was highly recommended by the Holy Father. He asked Ms. Viola to escort the children to the belly of the plane, and asked Mary Alice, Marisa, and Alvara to assist in the activity.

Once the children were below, he announced that a device was detonated in Presque Isle, Maine, and that the number of fatalities was unfathomable. He indicated that the Holy Father thought that the next detonation would be in Minnesota but had no intel whatsoever to support his feelings. The Sarge spoke briefly about the value of the pipeline running through Minnesota, and as if he were struck by lightning, he screamed, "That's a damn ruse! Why would you strike a conduit for a product that could be repaired and rerouted? No, damn it! The only logical disruption would be somewhere strategic that has a production function worth eliminating, or at least shutting it down for years. The only place that makes sense is in the Middle East. Minnesota is the travel route to the refinery. They're going to disrupt the production function of the Saudis."

The Sarge secured the SAT phone and dialed the Holy Father's number. After consulting his watch, he realized that it was 0330 hundred hours in the morning. As he started to hang up, a groggy voice on the other end said, "My son, this had better be important, or I'm going to send you straight to Hades!"

The Sarge hearing this information, calmly stated, "Your Eminence, it makes no sense to strike another place in America, and especially, a pipeline in Minnesota. Someone has convinced the world that the devil does not exist. Therefore, the data leads to Minnesota, but the event occurs far, far, away from there."

"My son, you're rambling. What is it you're trying to say?"

"Holy Father, you're not going to believe me." Those were the last words spoken before the phone went dead. The Sarge repeated his announcement, "Holy Father, are you there? Holy Father, are you there? Holy Father, are you there?" Beckmire said to the group, "Oh, shit! I just lost contact with the Holy Father. I think he's in trouble."

As the Sarge walked back, and forth across the room, trying to gather his thoughts, the SAT phone rang. He answered it, and it was the Holy Father, who said, "My son, do not speak of any issues until I can clean the rats, snakes, bugs, spiders, and crooked bishops from Vatican City. There was an attempt on my life by two trusted nuns, and several cardinals. My trusted guards dispatched them all to hell, except the one who was dressed as a bishop, but is a cardinal. We took him to the dungeons and will interrogate him in a moment. My son, I'm going to call you on that number that no one knows about."

Fifteen minutes later, John Lee was convincing his wife that they could make money in the pig business, and not the cow business. As she was about to reply, his cell phone rang, he answered it, and asked, "Who the hell is this calling me at this here hour?"

"John Lee, this is the Holy Father!"

"Oh, shit! I mean, Oh, heck! Let me get the Sarge."

John Lee ran to the Sarge's room and banged on his door. The Sarge yelled, "Who has the audacity to bang on my door at this hour?"

"Ah, sorry Sarge, but that there Holy Father person be on my phone, and I cursed at him, and a few other things."

The Sarge opened the door in his skivvies, and John Lee handed him the phone. He softly said, "Holy Father, forgive us, for we know not what we do!"

"My son, I will not forgive you, for you people know more than most. What was your call about?"

"Holy Father, your idea about Minnesota, to me, is incorrect. The next interruption, I think, is going to be in, of all places, Saudi Arabia."

There was complete silence on the other end of the phone, but breathing was distinctly heard. He muttered repeatedly, "Oh shit! Oh shit! Oh shit! I didn't' see that one coming. Disrupt the real production function, and you disrupt the world's balance. More importantly, a detonation in that area would create a fireball that would last forever, and that no human being would or could survive. Therefore, you create a new Kingdom! The United Kingdom of America, Russia, or China. Oh, shit, this is a dangerous situation. Damnit, you're probably fucking correct. Damn, let me call you back, I need to look at what would be the consequences of such a detonation."

"Your Eminence, depending upon how serious they are about controlling this event, and the amount of detonations that they consider, I can tell you the consequences without looking at a map. Listen, Jordan, Iraq, Kuwait, Saudi Arabia, Yemen, Qatar, the Emirates, Oman, and neighboring areas would be catastrophically impacted by such an event. Now, if that were the case, who would be the likely beneficiaries of such a dastardly event? Well, too many to name, but a lot would welcome such an apocalypse. I would bet on one country, but I reserve the right to be wrong because others would want them to be blamed and destroyed. The devil is clearly at work in this matter. The major question is, how much infrastructure do they want to destroy? The detonations would only join with those things that are hydrogen based and would leave most of the structures in place. However, the threat of a recurring event would cause most governments to capitulate."

"My, son, tell me, do you think the Iranians would be blamed hands down for any detonation? Those who would plan the deed, will place the evidence in very spurious places, and get a lot of innocent people killed. Come now, think about it. They've already been accused of drone strikes to the oil fields. Although their leadership is erratic, the people don't want to engage in a war. Skirmishes are okay, but if they're blamed for the annihilation of neighboring states, Russia, China, the United States, the United Nations, and everyone else would make it a full house by destroying what is known as Iran. This, my son would be called, Armageddon! The very essence of life would be at the crossroads of destruction with the current heads of states, in power. Armageddon will be the new buzz word, my son. After that, alignment, divisions would be territorial. The benefit to the United States is that

Canada, and South America will align with it. On the other side of the equation, Russia, China, and Africa will form an unholy alliance that will engage them in turmoil for centuries until one of them decides to push the magic button. Although huge in mass, disparate in beliefs, ideology, structure, religion, and wealth that becomes a distinct possibility. Will the poor countries align with a poor Russia? I don't think so, and that leaves us with a mighty powerful China. If I, were you, I'd learn to speak Chinese! That's called humor, my son."

"Holy Father, if nothing is done, and if my assumptions based upon no empirical information are correct, how many people stand to lose their lives?"

"My son, from the direct results of the detonation, fallout, contamination of water supplies, rivers, and food sources, I think we're talking about roughly ½ billion people dead from the immediate detonation. Another ½ billion will die from disease, malnutrition, and famine."

There was a long pause on the phone. Eventually, Ben Beckmire asked, "Is this that immaculate job that you spoke of a while ago?"

"My son, it would be immaculate and terminal for you and your people, as I see it. My immaculate job was not in that region, but in South America. With your new wisdom, I hesitate to consider the consequences, but the entire world is at risk if in fact your haphazard deductions are accurate. Can you imagine the fallout from such a destructive act? Listen, billions of people will die, be impacted, afflicted, and abandoned. And, as my final act as pontiff, I will destroy every country involved in this act. My venom would impact them for centuries. You and your people have done a lot of good for this world, yet you've been hunted, accused, shot at, shot, and a lot of other unholy things."

The Holy Father paused, consumed a drink of something, and then said, "Listen my son, I want to have a mass in your group's honor. I want to thank God for the hidden saviors of many souls, and now, the world. My son, you and your people have had a great run! I read that, or heard that in one of those underground magazines, or corrupt sites. Remember, to be effective, I must know what's going on with those who believe in God, as well as those who worship the devil and, therefore, I must, with God's help, visit places that are despicable, horrid, and vial. To practice my religion, I must know what the other side is offering."

"Holy Father, that's between you, and whoever you are on any given day."

As the holy father was about to respond to the comment, a cardinal flurried in, and approached him. The cardinal whispered in his ear, and the Holy Father screamed, "Infidels are everywhere. I need to clean house."

Ben Beckmire stood silent and waited for some instructions. The Holy Father asked, "Will Asiram help me discover who this poisonous group of bishops, and cardinals are?"

"I have one better for you, your Eminence. Let me introduce your captive to John Lee and Jilkes. If they can't make a dead man sing, then it can't be done."

#

A day later, the group landed in Rome. Deep in the catacombs of Vatican City, John Lee, Jilkes, Mallory, and the Sarge followed the elite guards deeper into the bowels of the facility. John Lee said, "I ain't used to being in a place that ain't got no windows. If we go another 30 feet down, we'll be in the middle of hell.   Sarge, I don't be liking this here mission."

"John Lee, I don't like it either. However, we must figure out who is trying to kill our immediate handler. Now, if you can't do this, then I will have to improvise and try to get the job done myself."

"Sarge, it just be too dark, damp, and stinky down here. I guess it's a good practice to kiss my kids and wife every time I leave my room. I don't think I be coming back from this here hole in the building."

"John Lee, shut you know what up! Don't make me whip your, you know what, in this holy place, or the home of the devil. Let it go man, you're getting on my nerves. You know I don't like dark places, and now you have me spooked as well. Just shut the "F" up, let's just get this over and done with," Jilkes lamented.

Five minutes later, the group turned into a catacomb where there was minimum light, and a body hanging on what appeared to be a cross. The Swiss Guards indicated that was as far as they could go.

As the group walked another 30 paces, John Lee, said, "Oh, my God! They still be having the body of Jesus. Let's get out of here."

Jilkes said, "That ain't the body of Jesus, you pig farming moron. That is the person who tried to assassinate the Pope. Listen, if you can't pull yourself together, then I'm going to go in there, and botch this on the first cut. I need you with me on this one brother. I don't like this place, I feel the warmth, and that means we're really close to Hades," Jilkes stated.

The Sarge screamed, "Stop this horseshit! We ain't near hell, we ain't going to hell. Not today anyway, but we are going there. Stop this shit, let's get this done, and get the hell out of here."

Standing in front of the man tied to a cross, John Lee said to the man, "I hope you're not in pain. Please forgive me for what I'm about to do to you. It ain't my choice, but I must do it. Now, if you cooperate, and answer truthfully, I'll be gentle."

The Sarge sternly said, "John Lee, get on with it or give me the damn knife."

The cardinal screamed, "The entire church is against that evil Pope. He will never survive our onslaught. He will die, and he will die soon."

John Lee said, "When you be saying the whole church, just who be their names?"

"Are you a nitwit? I'm not telling you anything. Couldn't they at least find someone with a brain to interrogate me?"

"Sir, I agree with you. I ain't the sharpest knife in the drawer, but I am in a place where if you be moving me, then there be a response. Now, since you be thinking I'm a nitwit, then let this first incision remind you of being born, and that there pain you gave your momma."

John Lee slightly dug the knife into the man's groin, barely penetrating him, and said, "I bet you I got your attention, now. Before you bleed out, I want you to see me cut this thing off that you call a penis, but to me it looks like a little blade of grass."

The man screamed and pleaded for mercy. John Lee asked, "How do you spell that word, mercy?" He then placed the tip of the blade on the cardinal's penis and said, "I'm afraid you might get pleasure from me cutting this thing off."

The man screamed, "Do what you must, God is on my side."

"I'm sorry, God don't be on the side of traitors." Without warning, he ran the blade from the man's ear to his mouth, slightly breaking skin. As the cardinal screamed for mercy, John Lee once again asked, "How do you spell that word called mercy?" He placed the blade at the man's other ear, and the cardinal screamed, Flarrety, Mcgriff, and DePasula. They're the leaders and they know who the others are."

John Lee looked at the Sarge, and asked, "Can we go now?"

The Sarge asked, "May I borrow your blade?" After retrieving it from John Lee he walked in front of the bleeding cardinal, and stated, "You know I have to kill you. Do you have any last words?"

The man gathered his wits, and said, "Please tell his Eminence that he shall eventually be returned to his natural state; that of the serpent. Tell him he is a dead man walking and doesn't know it. You people are the minions of the greatest puppeteer ever! The man you serve is the greatest lie ever told. He is not earthly, or even heavenly! He is the fucking devil, orchestrating skirmishes, creating distractions, detonating the Carbon Factor, and enjoying every moment someone enters his burning lair. Yes, Mr. Beckmire, you've been duped by the master, he will wed one of your children, and consummate his reign over heaven and hell. Your next assignment will be your last, for he will terminate all the adults, enslave most of the children, and burn the rest.

Ben Beckmire stared at the man for over a minute without moving a muscle. Jilkes, Mallory, and John Lee were silent, but recognized that the cardinal had gotten their leader's attention. The Sarge asked, "How many others are involved in this hyperbole? You named Flarrety, Mcgriff and DePasula. Are there others?"

The cardinal who was bleeding, but not profusely, adamantly, and with vim and vigor, stated, "The whole fucking Vatican is afraid of this Pope, and his dual love and hate for heaven and hell. Kill me and be done with it. I am already dead, but my soul is clean. This charlatan will create a barn fire, but he will use countries to do so. His next detonation will create a suspicion on a few countries that will be annihilated by the axis of good and evil. Please, kill me, and end my quest to expose Apollyon. My son!"

"Don't call me, my son. What do you want me to do with this belief that you have?" Ben Beckmire asked.

"You are your own person. You and your people are not easily conscripted into the ways of others, especially those who you suspect are not who they say they are. Remember what your friend Ben Hackney said to you, "this Holy Father is different." And remember what you said to your people about the Holy Father, that you're not sure if he is the Holy Father or Diablo. Listen, you will save me from a horrible existence if you end my life. Otherwise, I will be left here until there is nothing left of me except bone after being devoured by rats, bugs, and flies. Value your people, but remember, he is not who you think he is. Your latest premonition, was one that he planted in your mind, but you ignored it because of your faith, and realized that the real epicenter of his miserable plan is to wipe out most of the Arab states."

"How do you know this?" How on earth could you know what Ben Hackney told me, and what I told my people? I know how you know. Perhaps the real serpent is in front of me and is trying to create a new illusion. And, how do you know about the burning fire, and the blaming of one country? It was just discussed a little while ago."

"Son, you have received manifestations from the master. He will send you on that one-way mission and tell you to go with God! He is correct when he says that you and your entire group will meet their deaths. You've served the puppet master, and now it's time to replace you. Most people who are used by the puppeteer don't last long. The strength that you and your people brought to bear is a clear indication of why he is reluctant to send you into Saudi Arabia. He sees further utility from you and your people but fears the independent thoughts and actions by your group. In the name of all that is righteous, please end my suffering, I beg you!"

Mallory, who was baffled by all that he heard, unexpectedly screamed, "How do we know that you're not the puppeteer, as you call him?"

"Because, my son, I have a soul! Oh, and by the way, the nun that provides the Holy Father with earthly pleasures, is someone that I think you people are familiar with. Yes, Sister Mary, is his absolute pleasure syndrome, and mind massager. She has been a part of this charade from the beginning. I think that she slowly poisoned Ben Hackney as well. He had an absolute weakness for beautiful women who were versatile in providing pleasures, and the fact that she was a nun, a forbidden fruit, provided him with an even greater feeling of accomplishing a masterful seduction. Yes, Sister Mary, oh, I'm sorry, you probably know her as someone else. Perhaps I should say, Sister Helga?" Everyone froze in their place.

"My, son! I know, don't call you, my son. Helga Spengatsenburg is alive, well, and living in Vatican City as Sister Mary who is detailed to the Pope's private entourage. She has entry when no one else does. Oh, and if I'm not mistaken, intel informs us that your son, Zanthius, is the father of her child that she is desirous of retrieving. Your entrée into

Saudi Arabia would concretize her mission, and allow her to finally kill her friend, Asiram, who has mothered the child since he was retrieved from the convent in Spain. In addition, all the women, including Dr. Courtney will be slain by her."

"How do you know all of this?"

"I'm a humble servant who was charged with information gathering. My son, you just don't walk up in the Vatican, and have the privileges that you people have. No, there is a pre-screening process, and I was in control of that function until I uncovered the relationship between Sister Mary, and your little bastard, Zanthius de Lombardo. That was not our mission, our mission was to try to figure out why during certain hours in the night, there is a stillness, and an aroma that comes from the Holy Father's quarters, which is demonic. The various sounds of suffering, agony, as well as lustful sounds of defilement. He has a secure network, and we were trying to figure out what sites he was visiting on the internet that gave him energy, and visions for the following morning. My son, I know when you met Ben Hackney, and where. Your initial contact was at the Pentagon when he was a part of a meeting that you attended. Also, in St. Peters Square you turned around, and saw him after he called out your name. You two embraced, he arranged for you to go on the deep tour of the Vatican that very few have seen and know about. Listen, what Pope has an interest in those who kill for a living? That's certainly not the Christian way. That path seeks the blessing of the Devil, not the Lord. Your man has a fetish for your stories, the details, and the un-glorious deaths caused by your team."

The Sarge said, "Why are you babbling about things in the past that you could have researched? We are not assassins, and we're not going to kill you. That will come from some other person, but not us."

The Cardinal asked, "I want to be closer to my God. Please place my cross in my mouth."

# # #

As the men walked back to where the Swiss Guards were positioned, the Sarge turned to his people, and said, "Not a word of this to anyone!"

On the path from the catacombs, the Sarge instructed Mallory to give the immediate evacuation notice to the women. As they walked towards the light, the Sarge entered a soliloquy with himself asking, "how can mortals intervene between good and evil? It's not like a quarrel between Jilkes and John Lee. This is more about how my group, with the evil we have done, attempts to judge between a man tied to a cross, or one flitting about with expensive and ancient garbs on. This is too much for me to fathom, but what consumes me is the notion that our current puppeteer will marry one of our children. I remember how infatuated with one of our children he became, and she with him, and their apparent texting or messaging. What was the frequency of that, and what were the topics? I'm so baffled, but that cardinal shared many of my latent thoughts. Shit, I need to clear my head. I need to go to the outback, so that I can visit my family, and seek counsel. The problem is whether whoever is in charge will use this opportunity to detonate the Carbon Factor in Saudi Arabia, and how complicit will we be if we're there, or in the outback. It makes no difference our location, they will post our pictures like they did in Russia and China."

As they moved towards the exit of the catacomb, there was a frenzy of activity taking place. Below ground, the Swiss Guards were completely out of range of active communications. After gaining communications, the furor was a result of another assassination attempt on the Holy Father's life. Apparently, a group of bishops, and cardinals, attempted a Julius Caesar like assassination on the Holy Father with him screaming, "Et tu, Brute?"

When the smoke had cleared, three bishops, and three cardinals laid dead in the Holy Father's chambers. His admissions, and declarations of the events were perfect; they killed each other in an attempt to kill him. The Holy Father indicated that the faithful saved him from the predators but were slain during the action. He indicated that, although men of the cloth, they fought valiantly, but succumbed to their wounds.

The Swiss Guards immediately followed protocol, placed the Holy Father into a secure environment, and his only permissible visitor was of course, Sister Mary. After the information had been presented to Ben Beckmire, he gathered his people, and they were permitted to exit the Vatican.

On their way to the airport, the Sarge refused to recount the activities of the day until they were far away from the Vatican. In their midst, and unsuspected by anyone, Ms. Beatrice said to her mother, "I think the Holy Father is not such a good person."

Ms. Viola hearing this, quickly said to Luana, "Honey, let her come over here, and sit by me. I will talk to her."

# # #

As the vehicle approached the airport, Darryl received a call from Hood and Dempsey. Darryl said, "I need you to call me back in 45 minutes unless this is an emergency."

Dempsey responded, "Understood!"

It was approximately, twenty-six minutes when the wheels of the big jet left the ground. As the plane approached its cruising altitude, Darryl called Dempsey and said, "We were in an area where everything that is said, is recorded. How are you two guys holding out?"

From the background, Hood yelled, "We could use some back-up."

Dempsey replied, "He's such a drama queen. We're tucked deep into a mountainside with support and intel coming from nearby natives who are friendly to our purpose. You know, alcohol and drugs sway the way people think out here. What we're seeing is a lot of people saying, 'no to the bullshit.' There is mounting responses, and concerns about what happened to the rightful owners of the properties that suddenly seem to be up for grabs."

"Listen, I'm not sure where we're heading, our leader won't announce that until his seat belt sign goes off. My question and concern are strong, do you need us there asap, or within a few days?"

"Boss, me, Hood, Litefoot, his family, and other concerned citizens have this thing under control, from a distance. What we don't know is who is doing what with the almighty pen and paper. Our surveillance is imperfect because we don't know what is being done legally."

The bell rang concerning the seatbelts, the copilot engaged the communications system, and gave the spiel about the use of the seat belts once again.

The Sarge unbuckled his seatbelt, walked directly towards the rear, and stopped where Ms. Viola was sitting. He descended to his knees, and said, "Beatrice, I would like to talk to you and Ms. Viola in the back. Is that okay with you?"

Beatrice nodded yes, and the threesome headed towards the back. Luana looked at Chakes who looked at the Sarge and suggested that they accompany them. In the back galley area, when the doors are closed, it becomes a secure, soundproof, and private gathering place. The Sarge got on his knees again, and asked Beatrice, "So, tell me how you're feeling these days?"

There was a lull of sorts, and then Beatrice said, "The Holy Father keeps showing up in my dreams. I don't like what I see because it scares me. He always appears with two heads, one is a good head that's smiling, and the other one is scary."

"Thanks Beatrice, we'll talk about the two heads a little later. I just wanted to know what your thoughts are. And don't be afraid because you have your mother, grandmother, daddy, and me, to make sure that you're safe."

#

The Sarge proceeded to the cockpit, and confirmed with Captain Carla that Middle America was their new destination.

On the approach to his seat, he stopped next to a sleeping Zanthius with one of the babies in his arms, and whispered to Asiram that they were heading for the ranch. She smiled, and asked, "Are you going to call Clyde, or do you want me to?"

The Sarge responded, "I'll call him because I have a special request of him." The Sarge passed Mallory and whispered that the next stop would be the Midwest. Mallory responded, "Cool, boss. We need the break."

"Don't know how much of a break it's going to be because some of us will ride the school bus to Minnesota to clean up some stink. I need you to consider the assignments, especially since we have 24/7/365 security around the ranch."

"Why don't you use one of the smaller jets?"

"Not a bad idea, but I think these people are expecting the Charge of the Light Brigade. I want to play this one as low key as possible since our two recruits have already raised the other sides antennae."

"I guess you have a point there. I think the leader should be Darryl. We know what he can do combat wise, this is more of a political/hostile takeover kind of deal. His hands are going to get dirty, but that will indicate his resolve. I mean you could watch the action from afar if you know what I mean. After all, we did assign those two brigands to him, didn't we?"

"That we did do, at his behest since he was losing two of our trusted recruits. I'm not sure that I liked that deal. I mean, in a lot of ways, Darryl is still wet behind his ears," the Sarge intimated.

"Really Sarge? Darryl is a natural leader. He just doesn't call people assholes and demean them at every turn. No, he facilitates meaningful discussions, points our potential flaws, and areas of concern that might lead to someone being injured or even killed. Sarge, he is not a boy, and besides, when he is paired with his wife, the two are unstoppable, and crafty in ways that we don't have a clue about."

"Okay, smart ass, stop the horseshit! Perhaps I'll assign him field command."

"Sarge, please. Listen, between he and Sue Lyn, Earther, Windom, and now the two brigands, there ain't a lot of shit that is going to get past their noses. How about we set up a command post on the plane or bus, and you can monitor the situations and conversations from afar. Give up the reigns! God knows, we need to make sure that there is a leader if we're in trouble and need someone to bail us out. You know just like Larry wouldn't give up the search for his kids, his parents, and his friends."

# # #

On the bus ride to Minnesota, John Lee asked the Sarge, "Do you think it be right letting that cardinal guy put that strip of paper in his mouth that was poisonous?"

Jilkes who is never far away, asked, "Why the hell are you going there?"

"I would have preferred to kill him than let him put paper in his mouth that was poison that was attached to his cross, of all things. That there was disgusting to me."

The Sarge looked at him and said, "John Lee, I'm getting tired of this killing. That is why Darryl, and his crew will be handling issues like that. I want to go to my place in your country ass town and play babysitter for all those kids that are a part of our group. More importantly, why are you asking about that cardinal?"

"I have been dreaming about him every night, and his words come to me the same each night. He calls that there Holy Father the master puppeteer. Not sure what that means, but when he talked about love and hate for heaven and hell, I just got totally confused. Shouldn't it be one, or the other? I mean how can you love heaven, and then hate hell, and then love hell, and then hate heaven? I'm confused, and it's bothering my sleep."

The Sarge started to respond, but was cut off by Jilkes who said, "Let's take a walk to the back of the bus and compare notes."

When the two men were alone, Jilkes said, "What are you trying to do? Are you trying to make the Sarge think harder about the relationship with the Holy Father than he already does? He knows the man is both good and evil, if there is such a juxtaposition, but he controls a lot of what we do right now. What the hell do you want to accomplish?"

John Lee looked at Jilkes with his eyes swelling full of tears, and said, "I want to know who he is. He be tormenting me and giving me thoughts about hurting my family."

"What the fuck are you talking about?"

"My dreams, each night be about me hurting John Lee Jr. Each night it gets more real than the night before. I see blood all over my room. I see my woman hanging, I see Jr., but in half, I see the babies in the tub with a heater that is turned on. John Lee screamed somebody is fucking with my mind. The only thing that be breaking what I see is when I be seeing the vision of me cutting your damn head off. That's when I wake up and realize that someone be poisoning my mind. At first, I be thinking it's that damn cardinal tied to the cross, but he talked about salvation, and the destruction of that there Holy or Evil Father. But night after night, these bad dreams be coming to me all night long."

Overhearing the conversation, the Sarge walked to the back of the bus, and said, "Quiet! You came running to my room banging on my door saying that the Holy Father was on your phone for me. How the hell did he get your number, or did he deduce that the so-called smallest wave wouldn't create disclosure of the tsunami that was about to hit? He thought that you would quickly act on those manifestations he presented to you because you were the weak link. Damn, how dumb is the leader of the above ground group, or the below earth tribe that thinks you're a weak link, and a mental midget. He bruised his own ass on the concrete by selecting you. He should have selected one of the others because you're the strongest pig farmer that we have. He exposed his hand. John Lee, you're brilliant. Listen, the deceased cardinal told us that he oversaw intel gathering. He knew a lot about Ben Hackney, when we met, and our reunion in St. Peter's Square."

The Sarge paused for over a minute, and asked, "John Lee, are you sure you didn't give someone your phone number over there?"

"Sarge, I ain't that dumb. I can't give a number that I don't even know." The Sarge looked at Jilkes, and he nodded affirmatively.

Jilkes jumped in, and announced, "Sarge, we need to put John Lee under house arrest, and keep him away from his family and friends."

The Sarge retorted, "Yeah right! That's really important at this moment, Jilkes. Not funny, not funny at all!"

Jilkes screamed, "He's having nightmares of cutting my head off, cutting John Lee Jr. in half, placing the babies in a tub filled with water, throwing an electric heater in it, and hanging his woman. I don't consider that shit funny at all, Sir!" The bus became extremely quiet, and Jilkes said, "Sir, I wouldn't bring you horseshit about a man that I love."

The Sarge sat down, and began to murmur, "This is too much to comprehend. How can this be happening?"

John Lee responded, "That guy, somehow, has gotten into my head, and is giving me negative thoughts, and things to do, that is repeated each night, the same damn dream, over and over."

"Okay, how do we handle this intrusion?" The Sarge asked.

Jilkes said, "I think the outback is the place that holds many cures for this group. I mean he says each night it becomes more real."

Windom responded, "If we get him in the bowels of the sacred mountain that those two new guys are hiding in, then we have medicines, and natural herbs that will free his mind, and block further attempts. It's a native thing, you guys can't attend because you don't believe in spirits. Darryl will need to be there to bring the power of the outback to assist if John Lee is worthy of their intervention."

Beckmire bellowed, "What the hell do you call the Great Saltie? A picture show for the lost?"

Jilkes looked at Windom, and said, "Where he goes, I go! Make no mistake about that."

Earther said, "Oh, we know that. You are a feeling man and, therefore, your presence would be appreciated because you love John Lee, and he loves you. Your bond is the strongest in the group because it has been annotated, spoken, illustrated, and confirmed. Once we get to Minnesota, we will begin the process. I just need you to witness, and not interpret or disrupt."

"I will follow your mandates. I need you to fix my friend. I love this group, but this guy is my heartbeat. I will die if something happens to him. We share something bizarre and natural that scares me when I feel what he feels."

Ben Beckmire said, "I'm afraid that he is not the only person caught in the middle of this firestorm. I think he has bewitched one of the children and is planning a satanic wedding with her."

Windom vociferously stated, "Sarge, one thing at a time. The way evil operates is usually deceptively predictable, it has somewhat of a script that attempts to lead those involved astray. It develops a medium, a ruse, and a target. From what you say, and Sarge I'm only guessing about this, then John Lee is the medium, or that thing or person that gets the host closer to the object or person it's trying to conscript. This would make John Lee the distraction, or thing ready to commit despicable acts, that would engage the attention of everyone. Therefore, he is also a ruse, and allows the host full access to its target without interference, because everyone is trying to figure out how could John Lee do such a despicable thing to his family. Sarge, the child is the target! Who is the child, Sarge? Is it Beatrice?"

"Why would you ask about her?" The Sarge inquired.

"He was always friendly to her. He provided a special place for her to eat which was next to him. Apparently, he is texting and messaging with her, but that isn't a secret."

"Yeah, you're right. I don't know why I'm not surprised about any of this because when we're in the outback, we've seen some strange things occur including the animals doing battle for us. Not your everyday occurrence."

The Sarge walked to the front of the bus, and asked Clyde for an ETA. He was told another hour, and they would be in the area where Demspey and Hood were holed up.

The Sarge sat next to John Lee, and said, "We've been through tougher times than this my friend. Hang in there, and we'll see this thing to the end."

"This ain't like warfare, Sarge. This is mind control. I mean this dude, or someone is sending me images of things

I'm supposed to do. I need to get this mess out of me before I hurt someone that I be loving."

The Sarge hugged John Lee, and he violently pushed the Sarge off the seat, and screamed homophobic slurs at the Sarge. Jilkes jumped in, and physically restrained him. Windom and Earther wrestled his hands behind his back and placed wire ties on his hands and ankles. The Sarge said, "Something is going on with him. Two seconds ago, he was concerned about hurting those he loves. I reached around and hugged him, and damn, well, you all saw what came next."

The mood on the bus shifted from the task of authenticating Windom and Earther as owners of the land, to who is directing the mind of John Lee. As the group crossed a small lake, and saw the mountainous area, Windom said, "Not long now. I'll tell you when to turn off," Windom said to Clyde.

John Lee appeared as if he were in a trance or something. Jilkes said, "Don't worry you pig farmer, you won't have to go through this alone. I'll be right there, every step of the way."

John Lee growled at Jilkes. Jilkes said to him, "You don't scare me, and that asshole who is trying to manipulate you, well, he's just waiting on a private visit from me. I'll take care of his ass. You can buy two pigs with that information.

# # #

It was a long bus trip from Wyoming to Minneapolis, Minnesota. The Sarge read and attempted to sleep. Clyde had enlisted the assistance of two other farmers to help with the driving chores. Other than stopping for taking on fuel, the modified school bus with a huge engine in it, never stopped running. Although the seats looked like regular school bus seats, they were pneumatic, reclining, and offered Lombard heated massages. John Lee would awaken, and ask the proverbial question, "Are we there yet?"

Around Litchfield, Minnesota, Clyde was driving when the radar detector began to reach a crescendo, and he slowed the vehicle well below the speed limit. A trooper entered the highway with his lights flashing, and his siren blasting. Clyde pulled the bus over and alerted everyone. As the patrolman slowly approached the vehicle, he had his hand on his weapon. When he reached the already opened door, he yelled, "Hands up you old ass soldier!" He entered the bus, hugged Clyde, and said, "Your picture flashed at one of those toll booths. When I saw it, I said, "That old preaching ass man is trying to sneak into my state without letting me know about it. How the hell are you, and who are all these suspicious looking characters?"

"Well, Barrington, this here person is Sergeant Ben Beckmire, my employer, and leader of this group. Guys, this guy, and I were in the military together. I want you to meet Barrington Hunt. That other officer getting out of his car is Jack Brown, another army buddy of mine."

Barrington asked, "Do you need an escort?" Clyde looked at him, and said, "I have two very important individuals on this bus who own land where they're trying to run that pipeline."

The Sarge uttered, "That's too much of a description, don't you think Clyde?" The Sarge thought to himself, "what the fuck is he doing?"

Clyde came back, and said, "Sarge, these two will provide you with information that they can glean from their secure networks. They are distant relatives of mine, and their heritage are Native American genes. In other words, they will protect and serve your guests."

Windom in his native tongue uttered several words. Both men, responded, almost in unison in the language of Windom. Earther rose from his seat, and asked in English, "What the fuck are you doing way out here?"

"This is where we were transferred. It was said that we knew too many natives in the city and, therefore, the arrest rate was significantly down."

Clyde said, "They have native names, but they won't use them while they are in uniform and carrying the white man's weapons."

Jack Brown said to Earther, "Quietly, we have been running back east to make sure those two Yankees in the caves are okay. The limo driver is his cousin, and my uncle."

Earther made some ear-piercing noises, Windom joined in, and the two patrolmen echoed their sentiments as well. It was like a family reunion, all designed to make sure that the native brothers weren't robbed or disappeared before acknowledgement of the facts of ownership of land that would make them rich and endow the American Indian Tribes with many beneficial projects that didn't include gambling.

#

As the group continued towards its appointed destination, Windom said to Clyde, "Pull off the highway at that rock formation on your left."

"Man, that ain't no road."

"Clyde, pull off at the rock formation," Windom calmly stated.

The Sarge yelled, "Hey Clyde, I hope you upgraded the suspension on this bus."

Earther said, "It might last longer if you slowed down just a tad bit!"

The road didn't get any better, but the scenery was spectacular. As Clyde pulled up to the base of what appeared to be a mountain, Windom said, "Turn right into that wooded area, and shut the engine off. The bus will not be visible unless you're right up on it."

"Well, you don't have to see the bus, just look for the tire tracks," Clyde smugly replied. Earther replied, "Not to worry, it's going to rain in 7 minutes."

Clyde responded, "I didn't see that in the forecast." Everyone on the bus laughed except John Lee, who was still battling demons near and far. He turned around and asked, "What's so funny?"

The Sarge said, "Native Americans!"

# # #

As the group entered the cave, Hood yelled, "Hey Dempsey, our reinforcements are here, but they have one of us hog tied."

Once in the cave, everyone greeted each other, and those who had a history embraced. Litefoot said to Windom, "It is good to see you among the living. Those people placed bounties on your head and Earther's. Two families that owned property in that area have gone missing, and that means they're dead. Dempsey and Hood met some of the perpetrators and had a little fight. The timetable for you to authenticate who you are must happen by next Wednesday. I know how we can diminish the numbers, especially with Hood and Dempsey. I mean, they are wanted as bad as you are because of the ass whupping they put on two of their guys."

"My brother, there is time for birds to fly, and for them to sleep. We came with warriors who have fought and are fighting demons who apparently walk between heaven and hell and sit at the epicenter of religion. The one who is in bondage is one of their most loyal brothers whose mind has been penetrated by a powerful demon. We want to take him deep into the cave, exploit this thing, and clean this man up. He's in a bad way," Windom stated.

Litefoot looked at John Lee, and whispered, "You will not remember a thing when you return, warrior."

Windom exclaimed to the Sarge, "This thing with John Lee has to happen now! We're not sure who his landlord is and, therefore, we may have to call many names in our language. Jilkes, will not let him go, and that's a good thing. Darryl should attend because he's somewhat of a spirit himself. Not your ordinary lad from the outback."

"Listen Windom, that guy has saved us so many times that I can't recall. I need you to bring him back to me without any baggage. I need that baggage, and every aspect of it removed for good. Take this person or thing, but bring back, John Lee Jones Jr. Remember, he is as strong as a bull. You might want to triple those wire ties on his ass," the Sarge announced.

#

Unknowingly, the limo driver, Litefoot, was the coordinating person for all the families on the track of land that investors wanted to rid themselves of. He said to the Sarge "I expect that the greed factor is so strong that seemingly good human beings have been sucked into a void of no return."

Litefoot was about to say something else, when the Sarge abruptly asked, "What do you mean seemingly good people are being sucked into a void?"

"Sarge, several of the local ministers have invested in a group that guarantees huge returns once the pipeline is completed, and functioning. The mayor, his staff, and countless numbers of others have a look in their eyes that's not natural. It's as though the whole damn town drank Kool Aid."

The Sarge looked at the man, and bellowed out so that all near could hear, "This is still a distraction. Whoever is orchestrating this fiasco, knows full well that the entire world is watching, and suspicious of missing Native Americans who just happen to own a parcel of land that's worth billions. That's done to keep us focused on this occurring national travesty while they prepare to make destruction in the middle east. My question is, according to you, how can so many people buy into a destructive plan that kills the rightful owners of the land for profit? Unless the water or air is contaminated where those people live, then I'm beginning to believe that someone is playing a mind controlling game.

CHAPTER NINETEEN

Three days later, John Lee emerged from a cavern with an obviously shaken group of people who looked as though they danced perpetually with the devil. He asked, "Where is my babies, and that there wife of mine?"

Jilkes replied, "Dude, they're at the ranch in Wyoming."

"Oh, I see! Where we be?"

"John Lee, we've been in Minnesota for almost four days, and you've been down in the cave for almost three days."

"Why was I in a cave for that long? Did the bad guys catch us? Did they hurt you?"

"No, brother, I am fine. A bad guy did capture you, but you were saved by me, the Sarge, and a few others."

"How they be catching me without you? Where were you when all of this catching was going on?"

"John Lee, I went to the restroom, and when I came back, you were gone."

"Them people done snuck up on me like that. Hell, they must be the devil or something nasty. When will we be going home? I think my woman be mad at me about something, but I can't remember."

Jilkes looked at John Lee, and his eyes began to swell with tears. John Lee noticing this change in behavior asked, "Is your black ass the reason why I got captured?"

"Listen you country ass pig farmer! Did you ever watch any of those movies where the devil takes over a person's body, mind, and soul?"

"Now, why would I be watching some walking dead kind of programs. I get my news from Fox." Jilkes dropped his head, and quietly began to weep. John Lee seeing that his best friend was in agony, stopped the horseshit, and asked, "Did I do something bad to make you mad. I be sorry, you know I don't mean no badness when it comes to you."

Jilkes, who was breathing deep, and full of emotion yelled, "Someone captured your mind, body, and soul." John Lee was about to say something when Jilkes screamed, "Don't say a fucking word until I finish talking." He went on to explain to John Lee the behavior he demonstrated, his visions, and a description of how he was going to kill each member of his family. Jilkes also told John Lee what he had said about decapitating him.

John Lee asked, "Why you be bringing my family into your sick joke?" As he finished his sentence, the Sarge walked over, and said, "John Lee, you got captured by pure evil, and what your brother says is exactly what you kept saying. You said that each night, your visions became more real, and that you cut John Lee Jr. in half, put the babies in a tub, and threw an electric heater in it, and the most bizarre thing, you cut the head of your best friend off."

John Lee fell to his knees, and screamed, "What the fuck be wrong with you people. Ain't nothing you be saying funny. I need to go and see my family. Why would I hurt Jilkes? Jilkes is me, and I be him. I don't like this conversation, and I don't want to have it any longer."

The Sarge asked, "Have you ever seen Jilkes cry like that?"

There was a long pause, and the Sarge said, "Come now, have you ever seen your best friend in the whole world cry like a little baby? I know the damn answer, and it's no. He hasn't slept in four days making sure that what was done to you to cleanse you of the pure evil, was at least in his eyesight, the right thing to do. He is your walking dead because he kept an eye on you for three damn days. We're not playing with your mind, brother. Someone got deep into your mind and soul, and was attempting to use you as a vessel, and your test was to kill your family, and then your friend. This is no horseshit. Look at your wrist. Those marks are from the four individual ties that were strapped tightly around your wrist and your ankles."

John Lee looked at the marks, looked at the Sarge, and then walked to a corner, and retreated within his own body and mind. He crawled up in the corner of the cave and assumed the birthing position of a baby. John Lee was saved from one demon, and retreated to the inner sanctum of his mind that was confused, scared, and lonely.

# # #

Litefoot, Windom, Earther, and an unknown elder emerged from the bowels of the cave. Windom said, "I have heard of spirits and demons, and I have seen some in the outback that baffled my mind, but I've never seen an active demon with such a grip on a strong human being. I'm wondering if he had a sermon with John Lee, or inadvertently touched him, there must have been some kind of contact."

From the corner, Jilkes said, "The last time we were at the Vatican, the Holy Father or Diablo, bumped into John Lee's chair, and touched him on the shoulder."

Litefoot replied, "That's all it would take."

#

The Sarge's SAT phone rang, and he said, "Speaking of the unknown entity, I'm getting a call from the Vatican." He answered the call, expecting it to be the Holy Father, but instead it was the head of his security.

The person said, "Sergeant Beckmire, the other party will be with you in a minute."

A minute or so later, a female responded, and said, "Hello Sergeant Beckmire, I've heard so much about you, and I'm really familiar with your son, Zanthius De Lombardo, aka, the 'idiot spy'."

"Well, I'll be damned! Is this the never dying, but always dead, Helga Spengatsenburg?"

"Sergeant Beckmire, that is the name I use when I'm in the presence of mere mortals, but when here at the Vatican, I'm known as Sister Mary, you know, the same one from the convent in Valencia. Before I discuss the business at hand, tell me, how is my, bambino? Is he tall and handsome like his father?"

"Sister Mary, aka Helga Spengatsenburg, let me just flatly state, insofar as I'm concerned, you were just a vessel, much like your people tried on John Lee. You have no claim, warrants, or legal responsibility for the child and, therefore, I suggest that you move quickly on to the next business of concern."

"My, my, Mr. Beckmire. I would have thought that you would find a more pleasant approach to the mother of your grandchild, no matter the exigencies surrounding the child's safety. Let's move on."

There was a momentary paused, and Sister Mary announced, "The Holy Father has gone missing, and there are those of us who believe that he has infiltrated your tribe for some real-life experiences. It is well known that he admired your rough and tough tribe and appreciated the stories that Ben Hackney used to tell him about your group, may his soul rest in peace. The basis for my call is to find out if he's in your possession?"

There was a hiatus in the conversation because the Sarge looked at John Lee in the corner and realized that there was no way in hell there was an incarnation going on with John Lee. He firmly announced, "The Holy Father is not amongst my group, in any way, shape, or form. There definitely isn't any channeling going on here."

"Why Mr. Beckmire, you act as if you or one of yours has had an outer body experience or is having one. Is that an accurate thing to say?"

"Sister, Mary, that was just me making sure you realize that the Holy Father is not here in any way, shape, or form. How can the head of the Catholic Church, go missing? I mean, he has security everywhere he goes, cameras in every crevice and dark place except in those dungeons where people are apparently tortured. How on earth could he go missing? Perhaps, you should consider that he might have gone home!"

"Mr. Beckmire, what does that statement mean, gone home?"

"Sister Mary, it's just a saying when you're tired of things not working out in your favor, you go home, and sulk. What did you think I meant by the statement?"

"I wasn't sure, Mr. Beckmire. On a personal note, please tell Zanthius to kiss my child each night. Although never being the mother that I wanted to be, I am still the mother. Goodbye, Mr. Beckmire."

The SAT phone went dead, and the Sarge said, to Windom, "The Holy Father knew that we were coming here, he even had people watching Dempsey and Hood. Why doesn't she know that being his alter ego? Seemingly that small detail should have been discussed. Somewhere there's a disconnect."

The Sarge paused, and eventually inquired, "Okay, on to the more immediate problems. Do we wait until they come here looking for us, or do we go into their lair and handle the business?"

Hood started to open his mouth, and Dempsey capped it. John Lee uttered, "I want to know what he be thinking?"

Hood said, "I'm sorry about being impetuous. I think that the people doing surveillance are just jokers, much like me and Dempsey. Now, I would go and get a few of them, bleed one out, so that the other one can see our resolve, and then we'll know whose door to knock on. Those are my sentiments, Sir."

Jilkes smiled at him, and said, "Sounds like something a certain Sergeant that I know would do."

John Lee laughed, and said, "I be liking these boys. They don't cut their words in half. They say what they be feeling."

The Sarge looked at the two men, and asked, "Which one of you started the fight?"

Hood announced, "It was me, but I didn't start it, I finished it."

"Okay, then I'm going to go into town with you and Dempsey. Jilkes, John Lee along with Windom and Earther, will have our backs. Gentlemen, that means, you got to bring the iron to this fight. If we walk in with knives, and they have shotguns, then I think we lost this one because of failure to prepare with the correct equipment," the Sarge intimated.

Litefoot announced, "I don't think you'll have to go to town. There are four guys with weapons roaming around in the valley looking for something. How stupid can they be to come out here and wander around. They must have a vehicle nearby because they're going to lose daylight in fifteen minutes."

The Sarge borrowed the binoculars and viewed the men looking for something on the ground. Windom and Earther also had binoculars and watched as the men desperately tried to find something. Litefoot said, "There are only several places they could have crossed into this mountainous area. We can leave from the rear of the cave and be behind them in twenty minutes without breaking a sweat. It's all downhill, and as the mountain curves, we curve right up behind them."

The Sarge said, "Load up with machine pistols and handguns. Jilkes, I want you and John Lee to take the long guns and move to that ridge to the right of the entrance. Put distance between yourselves as I may want you to pin them down as we show up behind them."

#

As the men departed the hidden entrance to the cave, and made their way to the rear, John Lee lightly grabbed Jilkes by the arm, and asked, "Did I really say those things about my family and you?"

Jilkes responded, "Why do you want to have this conversation now? I think we need to focus, and make sure that whatever we do from that ridge, we don't endanger the Sarge, and those guys."

"You're right, but I just can't put it in a cracker box and close it up. I be needing to figure this mess out here," John Lee replied.

Jilkes looked at him, and asked, "Are you feeling, okay? Do I have to watch my back?"

"Now I be fixing to whup your black ass. How you say some dumb shit like that to me? We ain't figured all that mess out yet, but I be needing you close to me at all times. I'm scared to death. I don't know what be done got into me that I be talking about killing my family and cutting your black ass's head off! I got to address it, or it be my main focus. You get what I mean?" John Lee asked.

"I'm sorry, but when you were that other person, you scared the bejesus out of me. That blank look in your eyes, you know the one you usually have, but this one was 10 times scarier, and caused me great concern. You were not the man I've spent most of my adult life with. You were a demon, you were demonic, you were hellish, and you were scary. I didn't sleep for three days making sure that your transition, if there was such a thing, was done properly, and that you came back to me like you once were, a total pain in my ass."

"I love you too!" John Lee softly stated.

#

Two days later, the press began to question the lack of appearances by the Holy Father. A high-ranking cardinal who was having a tryst with a well-known magazine editor, leaked that the Holy Father hadn't been seen in five days. As the editor finished her work with the cardinal, she told him that she was not going to see him again because she felt that she was compromising his ability to ascend to the papacy. As the tears rolled down her face, her last words were, "I wish I had never met you, and fell in love with you. You have been my heart, soul, and my friend." As she walked out of the door, she patted her eyes, pulled out her mirror, adjusted her hair, smiled, left by the rear door, and entered a car driven by her new lover.

On the seventh day, the Swiss Guards conducted a complete search of the Vatican and its tributaries. The Holy Father was not to be found. Sister Mary called the Sarge again, on the SAT phone, and stated, "Mr. Beckmire, the Holy Father is still missing. Do you have any idea where he may have ventured off to?"

"Helga, that is one of the names you go by, isn't it? Anyway, as I said before, he may have gone home.

"Mr. Beckmire, my name is Sister Mary, and I find it disrespectful when you call me by my given name, as opposed to my Christian name."

"Wait, is this name changing, game changing, and cloth changing, a regular function of Helga Spengatsenburg or Sister Mary? Listen, I'm confused because you swore a life of celibacy, but had a child with my son. Even after repenting, you're the Holy Father's thang. So, Helga, Sister Mary, or whoever the hell you are, play one game consistently, and I will address you according to the rules of that contest. Right now, you're a chameleon!"

"Mr. Beckmire, you're an insulting ogre! However, I do understand your lack of faith, and your inability to believe that people can change. The basis for this call is to solicit your assistance in finding the Holy Father."

The Sarge screamed, "Stop the horseshit! He ain't no Holy Father, and you know it. He is the medium between

Heaven and Hell, and you're his nanny. If anything, tell me how to rid the world of this transgression that you support."

The phone went dead. Helga, or Sister Mary hung the phone up.

# # #

As the day began to transition into night, a coordinated set of warning shots were placed near the feet, of the people searching the area for some unknown reason. It wasn't until John Lee placed a round into the hand of the person who appeared to be in control that those being targeted realized that they had to rid themselves of their weapons. From the rear, the Sarge's booming voice announced, "If we find a damn toothpick on you, you will be summarily executed."

# # #

The men were blindfolded, and turned around six or seven times until they couldn't stand straight. Once in the cave, Hood said, "Well, I'll be damn. It's the person who started the last fight that I concluded.

The blindfolds were kept on the rest of them, and John Lee found a rock and began to sharpen his knife. The men thought that they were lined up besides each other. They were gagged, blindfolded, and the Sarge's group had sound suppression devices covering their ears.

The Sarge said, "I'm only going to ask a question once, and if the information isn't satisfactory, then I will place a round into the nearest person to me. Okay, rules have been clearly articulated, and now let's begin the game!"

He looked around the cave and saw that his people had protection over their ears, and was satisfied that this might work without needlessly, slaughtering people who were trying to earn money. He said, "Who among you is the leader of this group?" No one acknowledged the leadership role.

The Sarge said, "I'm going to give you guys a pass on that one. However, my next questions will be answered. Okay, what is your mission, and what were you scouring the area for?" There was no answer, and the Sarge motioned to John Lee to discharge a round.

The Sarge said, "Get that bleeding body out of here. Drag it to the edge of the cliff, and just push it into the gulley. The animals will have a feast on his ass. Now, my next question is again, who is your employer?" No one answered, and the Sarge asked, "Which head should I blow off next?" Suddenly one of the men screamed, "I'll tell you who they are, and where they are."

The Sarge replied, "Take the other two out of here, put rounds in their heads, and throw them into the gulley."

A voice announced, "I'll tell you what you need to know, and I'll tell you who is in charge of us." The next guy, realizing that everyone was snitching, decided to say, "I have pictures of their group meetings, the principals, the money managers, and where the illicit cash is kept."

John Lee stated, "Now I like what I be hearing from this here fella. Me and Jilkes will take him for a walk to see what he has to say, and show."

Approximately twenty minutes later, the group reconvened with the people they separated, and interrogated. The captured men were surprised that no one had been killed. Beckmire quickly, and affirmatively stated, "We have pictures of each of you. Our network is worldwide. If you join up with those carpetbaggers to enrich yourselves and your families, then you will watch your families die first. Disappear until this mess is over. If you give a heads-up to anyone, then expect the worst from us. These are not threats, they are the absolute resolve of our people. Those pictures have been forwarded to our underground network, and as such, $200k contracts have been initiated on you, and your families. Now, take leave, but don't go where we're heading unless you have a death wish!"

#

Outside of the Church of the Everlasting, on the outskirts of Minneapolis, a select flock of individuals who had the Lord in their hearts, but 'Benjamins' on their minds, entered the house of worship. As the minister offered an opening prayer for health and safety, he slyly asked that the coming bounty be clean, and plentiful.

The Sarge hearing this request to the heavens, cleared his throat, and in a roar yelled, "Blasphemy! Blasphemy! How can you pray for a clean bounty when its dripping with blood? How can you meet in a place of reverence to discuss a dirty investment? More importantly, how can you prepare to receive blessings that are not yours to accept?"

The minister shouted, "Who on earth are you, and what are you doing in my church?"

"I thought this was a house of God, not a house owned by a single man. If you must know my name, then it is Ben Beckmire, and those weapon toting fellows stationed at each exit are my associates."

"Sir, you brought weapons into the house of the Lord?" The minister asked.

"Sir, this is only the house of the Lord, in appearance. This is a place without a soul or a belief system. This place is no different than the casinos on the reservations, or the whore houses near them. You pray for bounty that's not rightfully yours, and you're willing to commit sin after sin to obtain it. I'm not here to preach to you about sin or salvation because yours will be in the reckoning. I am here to tell you that the quest that you've committed to, is one of death and despair. You and your families will be summarily terminated if you continue down this road. The rightful owners of the land that you're trying to steal, in the name of the Lord, are now protected by a force greater than any that you could imagine. Now, we're here to make sure you understand that the force that protects the owners of those lands is neither forgiving nor understanding. Any involvement in this scheme moving forward will conclude in your death. Now, there will be many legitimate opportunities to provide a service for a reasonable fee for the development plans that a majority of the funds from the lease, mind you, not the sale, of these lands will produce. I am the messenger, my associates are the force that will conclude families, friends, and associates. If we come back to this place, neither your police nor the national guard will be able to protect you."

The Sarge gave the preacher a vitriolic look, and said, "The building that you commandeered for your after-church activities will be destroyed in approximately 15 minutes. You will no longer entertain those who willingly or those who are coerced into servicing your wicked needs. This place you call the Lord's house seemingly is just for you white people. Therefore, tomorrow, you will pack your belongings, and leave this area by sundown. If the sun sets, and you're still in this area, you will be engulfed in flames because fire is the calling card of the one you serve!"

The Sarge dismissed those in attendance except for the minister. He said to the man, "How many others are involved in this scheme, and who killed those families? Now, you might want to try to lie your way out of this, but this is when your objective starts to not work out for you. I need you to turn around and look at the massive stain glass window that has an alleged rendition of Jesus Christ on it, and it is directly behind your pulpit. If I detect a lie, we will fashion a cross, nail you to it, extract your eyes, and let you bleed out. I know you were a part of the apprehending of those families, and their ultimate demise. I know, you didn't physically touch them, but you plotted their deaths in the name of 'Benjamins.' So, this is where you decide how you want to die or live. Who is the mastermind of this chicanery?" The minister lowered his head, and uttered the words, "I am!"

The Sarge said, "I didn't understand what you said. Repeat it please."

"I said, I am the mastermind, the architect, the financier, and the root cause of those people being slaughtered. There are no layers above me. This was all my doing."

"Preacher, the actions taken against these people were skillful, financial, and final. Are you telling me that you had time between your crooked ass sermons to assemble an action plan to first, rid the people of their land, second, to encourage an unholy alliance amongst your parishioners, and your mayor, who you brought into this plot, and third, to commit murder? I'm sorry preacher, what divinity school did you attend?"

"I did have some outside assistance in developing the plan," the minister admitted.

"Who might that have been?"

"I met a woman who was convincing, captivating, sexy, manipulating, and evil. She convinced me of connections that couldn't fail, and that if I backed out now, it would be at the cost of my life. She filmed me in compromising positions and acts with different people."

"What do you mean different people?"

"Listen, they were different," the minister replied.

The Sarge studied his face, and surmised the answer, but wanted to hear the minister confess it. He said, "Different is a matter of life and death for you. It's your choice, but you will answer my questions, or you will be hung in the portal of that stain glass window."

"She drugged me, and when I was cognizant, she showed me pictures of my involvement with both sexes."

The Sarge knowing the answer said, "I don't understand what that means. I want you to say exactly what happened!"

The minister began to weep, but the Sarge wanted answers, and yelled, "What the hell does that mean involved with both sexes?"

"Please, just kill me!"

"This woman, where can I find her?"

"I have no contact information for her. She shows up with directions, demands and threats."

"What did you call this woman?"

"She said her name was Sister Mary!" The Sarge reeled backwards, and was supported by Hood, who asked, "Are you okay boss?"

The Sarge looked at Hood, and said, "The devil has wings, and vessels. We need to get back to the group." The Sarge looked at the preacher, and yelled, "Sunset; be gone or have a fiery death!"

###

Once back in the cave, the Sarge gave instructions to Litefoot insofar as what was to happen to the minister of the church. He looked at Windom and Earther and said, "You're expected to show up on Wednesday to authenticate who you are. The other families are coming out of hiding and are planning to do the same thing. I don't like that idea. I want to be at that place in the morning before it opens. I want Monica and Luana here tonight, so Jilkes, call Mallory, and have him put the two women on a plane for here. Have him secure them with Brown, Bernstein, McArthur, and Gladstone. Tell Rashida and Gilda to place the ranch on high alert and tell Zanthius and Asiram to be extremely diligent about the children."

###

Two and a half hours later, Monica and Luana walked into the cave where the Sarge was. Monica asked, "Who is the decorator?" Everyone laughed. After introductions were made, the Sarge asked "Monica, "Did you bring the legal papers for Earther and Windom?"

Luana looked at him, and asked, "Do we look like two-ten cents attorneys?"

The Sarge said, "I would be stupid to answer that loaded question. I'm sorry, it's just that an old nemesis has been doing the devil's work in this area?"

"Who might that be, Sarge?" Monica asked.

He looked at the two women, and said, "You would never believe me if I told you."

Luana said, "Sarge stop with the guessing game, and tell us who's in town."

"Helga Spengatsenburg, aka, Sister Mary!"

Monica screamed, "Oh, hell no. Ain't no way she can be working for both the Vatican, and these crooks? What's the expected outcome? I mean, this is probably going to be worth hundreds of billions of dollars, but I don't see the payday for her."

"She hoodwinked the preacher in town, seduced him, captured him in extremely compromising situations, and he sold the package to his wealthy flock. They in turn are complicit in murder, because two families have disappeared who own land on the path of the pipeline."

Windom announced, "Daniel and my daughter were given a package to hold for one of the missing families. I never thought much about it, and they don't have time to think about it either after having the twins. When we get back, I'll inquire. The wife loved Mysteir because they were without children, and my daughter told her that she was her second mother."

#

The following morning, Litefoot drove Dempsey, Hood, Brown, and Bernstein into town. He dropped them off in pairs at different points but near the county courthouse. The men saw a restaurant and decided to grab a bite to eat. As they entered the place, the first person they saw was the guy that Hood had a fight with. The guy threw his hands in the air and walked out of the restaurant. Dempsey said, "I hope he's not going to snitch, and bring the heat down on us." No sooner had he said that Litefoot walked into the place and gave the peace sign. Litefoot sat at a table in the corner by the window and kept flashing the peace sign.

At 0908 hundred hours, Litefoot saw the blue school bus coming down the street, got up, and left the restaurant. Brown and Bernstein staggered out next, then Dempsey and Hood. Hood said to Dempsey, "We need a high vantage point. This ground level layout is not in our best interest. We can't check for people on the roof tops. I don't like this."

"Chill out brother, the two intended targets are sitting in the window, and the windows are bulletproof."

"Are you crazy, it's a yellow bird bus, painted blue. It ain't magical. It's just a damn regular school bus."

At 0930 hundred hours, the Sarge and several of his team exited the bus flashing badges in the air. He yelled, "This is a federal government operation, and any persons attempting to obstruct these proceedings will be prosecuted to the full extent of the law, if they so happen to live. At the top of the steps of the courthouse, the Sarge turned around to see if he saw any flashes of light from the most advantageous places and realized that those involved were more likely to be trying to figure out how to avoid jail time for the murder of one of the families.

Luana, and Monica were followed by eight individuals, and they presented the clerk with the petitions. The clerk asked for the records so that he could make copies. Luana, said, "No need, here is a clean copy so all you need to do is stamp, date, and sign."

The clerk said, "There is a lot of interest in these papers. Just saying!" After 15 minutes of minutia, the clerk came back, and said, "I have certified that these properties belong to you, Mr. Windom, and to you, Mr. Earther, the names given to you by your forefathers. By my doing this, it certifies that the tracks of land in the quadrants listed in the deeds are on Native American land, and that only Native Americans can file documents stating ownership. I'll probably not have a job in the morning, but you, and the others won't have to worry about those thieving sonsabitches trying to steal your land."

Earther said, "You will always have a job. If not here, we can set you up in Australia, Spain, the US Virgin Islands, and many other places."

# # #

On the ride back to the ranch, Hood who was curious about the response of the Sarge when he heard the name Sister Mary, stumbled up to the front of the bus and asked, "Sergeant Beckmire, may I ask you a question? Who is Sister Mary?"

The Sarge rose from his chair, and everyone thought that a confrontation was in the making. He escorted Hood to the back of the bus and motioned for Dempsey to join them.

In the back of the bus, the Sarge expressed to the two men, the nature of their group, the battles they had fought, the people who had betrayed them, and the various handlers who had used them. He told them that Sister Mary, aka, Helga Spengatsenburg, was involved with his son before he knew that he had another son, in this world. He told them that she assisted his son in escaping death, and making his way back to America, from Switzerland. He also told them that she had a child by his son, and that she had allegedly been killed, buried, and burned to death on many different occasions, but somehow, managed to rise from the dead, and reap more havoc. He told the two men that she had been instrumental in the acquisition of a devious device known as the Carbon Factor, a bomb that uses the byproducts of carbon, and when combined with hydrogen, creates a highly destructive explosion. The Sarge indicated that everywhere she shows up, there is death and destruction. He told Hood and Dempsey that the massive explosion at the NBA Hall of Fame was the result of the Carbon Factor, or a derivative of it, and that he was sure that she was somewhere around when it was detonated. He indicated that she is a spy, a sister of the cloth, a coldblooded murderer, and a fornicator. He said, "Oh yes, Helga Spengatsenburg, aka, Sister Mary has been at the heart of our adventures for years, and every time that she is professed to be dead, she somehow miraculously rises from the dead to create more mayhem. When I heard her name in that church it just made me realize that she is always several steps ahead of us, and that's a dangerous thought considering her penchant for death and destruction. Oh, she is also the consort of the Holy Father in the Vatican." The two men shook their heads, and Hood said, "I hope we never meet her."

Dempsey asked, "Why, if we did, what would you do?"

"I wouldn't know what to do, that's why I hope we never meet her."

The Sarge looked at the two men and thought how similar they were to his young recruits in the military. He asked, "Has anyone talked to you two brigands about your pay?"

Both men smiled, but it was Hood who said, "No one has said a word to us. I thought this work was a function of us staying alive in that we met under dubious circumstances."

"I agree, but you two have turned out to be as solid as a rock, and Litefoot told me how you guys handled yourselves in the absence of constant supervision. Anyway, when we reach the ranch, you, me, and Darryl will have a conversation to discuss your compensation or actually your earnings. You're a part of a billion-dollar enterprise that helps people help themselves. If you feel that you don't want to continue on this journey with us, then we'll front load you a quarter of a million each, and you can be on your merry way."

Hood asked, "A quarter of a million of what?"

"A quarter of a million dollars," the Sarge responded.

Hood said, "Come on Sarge, we don't have $20 between us, and now you're throwing numbers like that around us. Please don't play with our simple minds."

"Son, I would never embellish the truth to con you. If you want to take the money and run, then we'll set you up with an account, and you're done with this business model of ours."

"Why can't we have the quarter of a million dollars, and stay with the group? It ain't like we got wives and children waiting for us to unwrap Christmas presents," Hood stated.

"Guys, here's the deal. If you want to stay in this fold, and if Darryl has a role for you, then you're subject to make more than that. Darryl is in charge of the diamond and gold mines in Australia, and you've seen the products of the mines, and apparently you didn't try to take anything because you're still alive."

"Sarge, we ain't going anywhere, and we don't have no need for that kind of cash. However, if you'll help us invest it, and account for it, then we would be much obliged. Just so that you know, we'll take any assignment that you give us. If it's a problem morally, we'll let you know. We just don't want to be a part of killing children," Dempsey stated.

"We don't kill children! We protect them," the Sarge vociferously proclaimed.

#

At the ranch, and after a late evening snack, Earther and Windom met with members of their families to talk about what had happened in Minnesota. The two men began the discussion by thanking the spirits near and far for the Sarge, and his clan. They told the members of their tribe that had it not been for the compassion and trust of the Sarge and his people, they probably would be buried in unmarked graves.

Earther then stated, "We have made a lot of money working with this group, and we'll earn more when settlement is made on our bordering properties. It is important that we approach this matter, at least from our two families, as a single unit when negotiating prices." His wife interrupted him, and asked, "Will we use Ms. Luana and Ms. Monica to do our legal work?"

Windom replied, "This is a matter that we want to discuss with the Sarge and Mallory before we make any final decisions. I know the value of those two lawyers, and if I know them, they are going to want us to involve Native American attorneys in this process. Also, I think we should use their investment model, and align as much as possible, our resources with theirs. Let me speak for myself for a minute. Since I've been with this group, I have learned a lot, made a lot of money, and met people who value people over earthly possessions. I personally do not want to stop the adventures. I feel like a little boy when we're marauding, dodging bullets, and returning fire. I know it's dangerous, and at some point, one of those rounds may strike home. I don't care about that because, I am content living loose, without a lot of earthly possessions, but with a lot of love and compassion."

Earther replied, "Those are my sentiments as well, my brother." He looked at Mysteir, and asked, "Did my neighbors who are missing give you and Daniel a package to hold for them?"

Looking a little puzzled at first, Mysteir recounted, "Oh yeah, they did ask me to keep an envelope for them. Why do you ask, Dad?"

"Honey, by any chance, did you open it to see what was inside?"

"Dad, gosh no! That would have been dishonest to do so. Should I go and get it, and open it in front of everyone?"

"Great idea, honey, but in the meantime, I'm going to ask the Sarge, Monica and Luana to join us for a minute."

# # #

When all of the parties had convened, Earther asked Mysteir to give the sealed package to Monica. He then asked Monica to review the contents of a package that were entrusted to his daughter and her husband by the family that is presumed dead. Monica opened the large envelope and found a letter to Mysteir. She scanned it, and said, "I think Mysteir should read this privately, and if she feels compelled, she can share it with the group."

Mysteir, opened the letter, and it began by stating, "So many times I considered scooping you up, and running away with you, just the two of us. Mysteir, from the day you were born, I plotted to steal you. I know, it sounds strange, but I love you so much, and now that we're in this battle for our land, it's important that I give all that we have to someone I love and trust. If you make decisions based upon knowledge of our deaths, and find out that you're wrong, just let us live in peace somewhere with your support and blessings. Do the right thing, and the right thing will be done by you! Oh, and by the way, you will find the paperwork for two other disputed properties that we just happen to have the deeds for. We made payments for them, and they trusted us with their deeds. Now, if they happen to survive the new war with the white man, please do the right thing, and endow them with their deeds, or the value of the properties. I wanted to trust this task with the banks, but I know they will side with the white man and screw us out of what is legally ours. My trust is with you because you are the flower of my heart. Take care my dear, and may the spirits and God bless you and yours forever. Running Water (Nadine) and Crowind (Robert)."

Mysteir wept and was comforted by Daniel who said, "You are such a good person, so much so, people want to take you and run off with you. I am so glad that you selected me to give your heart and love to."

## CHAPTER TWENTY

Exactly one month later, the Vatican had not successfully selected a new leader of the church. The whereabouts of the previous pope remained a mystery, and the investigation was ongoing. It appeared as though he vanished into thin air.

As the weather began to shift to the cold side, the group decided to relocate to St. Thomas for two weeks. It was decided that each person would select a project to work on and dedicate twenty hours a week to designing and/or implementing it.

# # #

Mrs. Carter extended the marina by 150 yards, added waste pump out stations every 20-feet, and the port side slips could accommodate two 225-foot yachts. Some high-tech guru made reservations for ten days for his 450-foot yacht named Octopissy.

As the group began to settle in, a most magnificent sight became viewable. An aircraft carrier, and its support group was making its way to St. John, a neighboring island for a twenty day stay. Everyone was excited because that vision meant that 4,500 to 5,000 men on liberty would be on the island spending money on virtually everything that was for sale, and things that were not. Each island that comprises the

US Virgin Islands was elated that a military vessel of that size was docking in its waters, and that thousands of soldiers with plenty of money, were willing to spend it.

With the good comes the bad! After three days and nights on the island, thirty-two soldiers had been robbed and beaten, three were knifed, and three were violently murdered. In each case, contraband was the advocate.

Ms. Viola said to the Sarge, "Mr. Sarge, we got to go, and clean up St. John. Them military ships are the salvation of all three islands, and we depend deeply on them. Them thugs over there be murdering soldiers, robbing them, and slicing them up. If the military stops bringing those ships to the island, man, we're all in trouble."

The Sarge looked at her, and stated, "You know if we get involved, we'll be between the locals and the military, and some might try to say that this be our program."

"Mr. Sarge, man, I be telling you that we are the only people who can handle this thing. The local police, well some of them be corrupt, and others be turning a blind eye. It be just a few crooks making this problem. If I weren't so old, I would go over there, and kick their butts. But you know I can't do that. Man, I be needing your help on this one."

The Sarge replied, "Let's go, and have a talk with Mrs. Carter."

A few minutes later, the Sarge said to Mrs. Carter, "Tell me about security here. What upgrades, and protection for our guests are in place?"

After a lengthy discussion, and demonstration of hidden cameras, and listening devices, the Sarge asked, "So, Mrs. Carter, if someone says something in confidence to someone else, can you justify that you're not eaves dropping or using listening devices for nefarious purposes?"

"Mr. Sarge, what the humans hear is intelligible, in most cases. The computer synthesizes the information, reports what is questionable and/or what needs further examination."

"Okay, if I were you, I would put extra security personnel on duty tonight, and I would arm them. We're going to go to St. John and kick some ass."

"Mr. Beckmire, I'm afraid it's too late. The murder of those three boys is going to be hard to fathom, and our president ain't going to forget that mess. You clean it up, but be discreet, and hidden."

The Sarge looked at her, and stated, "You seem like a seasoned professional, would you like to lead this charge?"

"Well, I do know where them people from Babylon be hanging out and plotting their murderous events."

The Sarge looked at her, and said, "We need you here. I'm sure Michael knows where they live."

"Mr. Sarge, I'm trying to keep my boy away from that area. He has a cousin, and dear friends who are probably caught up in those atrocities on St. John. My boy took another route, and well, you know, he's a fine, trustworthy, and honest man. Years ago, Michael was the target of a hit because of his righteous nature to tell the truth. That truth would have placed a kingpin over there behind bars for life. Several attempts to assassinate him occurred. Three people over there vouched for him and swore vengeance on anyone trying to kill Michael. In essence, Michael only saw an image, and not a face. Purely circumstantial, but enough to put those nuts over there in a frenzy."

"Mrs. Carter, I'm sure Michael wouldn't have said a word about this to me, and I thank you for the heads-up. I'll keep Michael in a backup and support role. I'll take members of my crew and get as much intel as I can from friends in sewers in DC."

Mrs. Carter pulled up the stronghold of those people from Babylon on her GPS, showed the Sarge the best entry and exit points, as well as an exit through the luxurious Caneel Bay properties. She indicated to the Sarge that there gang was approximately 25 strong, and most of them stayed high.

After the murders, robberies, and assaults on the sailors, shore leave was cancelled, and it was noted that the vessel would be departing the islands in three days after provisions were secured. This was distressing to most of the islanders who called for police intervention, and for arrests to be made.

At 0130 hundred hours, the Sarge's SAT phone rang, it was his friends who live underground in Washington, DC. The colonel said, "You know they hurt a few of our boys, and they need to be stamped out. The only problem is that there is an agent working inside who provides us with tremendous intel. Any suggestions?"

"How do you know we're going to attend to this thing?"

"Sergeant, we know you're there, and we know that you don't like this kind of thing happening because it could spread to your happy little Sanctuary."

"How do we identify your agent?"

"Ave Maria and Hail Mary will be the code. I picked that one because of the never dying Sister Mary."

"Thanks, Colonel. Just what I need, another reminder of that woman. Is there any other intel I need to know about this rabble?"

"Only that they have a master plan, and it includes your Sanctuary. Kill the bugs before they can hatch more like them." There was a disconnect indicating the call was over.

# # #

At 0300 hundred hours, several small crafts were lowered into the water off a rented tugboat. Michael told the captain, "If you have to hang here until the world ends, you had better do it. When we exit that place or not, you make sure our bodies are picked up, and delivered to our boss who will probably nuke the fucking islands."

"Michael, come on man, you know I ain't going nowhere. I'll be lounging around in the water, but I'll have two speedboats in the water ready for an emergency evac if all goes wrong. Also, I'll use my antique Gatlin gun on anyone chasing you, but you have to get me and my crew out of this place if we do that."

# # #

The two watercrafts pulled up to the small beach at the Hotel H on St. John. Sue Lyn and Desmond were their retreat eyes, and long gun handlers. Darryl had previously assigned Mike, Earther, Giuseppe, Windom, Dempsey, and Hood to himself. He changed that configuration, and assigned Isaiah, Jasper, the Tire—John Cheapman, and Harold, to Michael.

Using the coordinates that Mrs. Carter had googled, the group studied the environment in real time. Darryl radioed

Michael, and said, "Your team has the rear. Wait, that looks like a uniform police person perusing the place, as though he is guarding it."

Michael radioed back, and said, "Roger that--Money speaks volumes in this place."

Darryl responded, "Okay, it is 0405 hundred hours. We will begin our purge at 0430 hundred hours. Keep an eye out for other police persons. Let's make sure we disarm them, and taser them to sleep. No shooting of cops unless there are no other options."

At 0415 hundred hours, a vehicle with darkened windows, pulled in front of the house that those accused of killing the soldiers occupied. A man stumbled out of the building smoking ganja rolled up like a huge cigar. The front passenger window was rolled down, and the man smoking dope handed a package to an unidentified person in the car. There was an exchange of words, that couldn't be deciphered by the teams, and then the car drove off. Darryl radioed Sue Lyn, and told her to flatten a tire on the car approaching her position. Desmond took the shot, and hit the tire near the ground to eliminate any suspicion of a bullet. The car veered towards the left and ended up in a ditch. The driver scurried out of the window, and began to yell, "Ave Maria, Hail Mary, be my protector, over, and over again." He helped the person in the passenger seat out of the vehicle. Sue Lyn had no clue as to who either man was, but recognized the call sign of the colonel's man, and had filmed the car arriving, and passenger receiving a package.

At 0425 hundred hours, another car pulled up to the house. When the cop who was patrolling the area opened the front passenger door, he was expecting a friendly face, but it was someone else. The person in the car placed a round in his head and proceeded to give a signal to someone else.

Two minutes later, a full-scale battle was in play with those on the inside gaining the upper hand. It was the result of local residents trying to intervene by eradicating the people who murdered the sailors. They were out-gunned, out manned, and without a plan. It was a virtual slaughterhouse except for the two men in the car. They were taken into the house, pistol whipped, and then questioned.

Michael called Darryl, and said, "This is a cluster fuckup! We need to conclude this issue or retreat, now."

Darryl radioed back, and said, "I'm not sure that all of the players have presented themselves. Let's give it 15 minutes, then we'll go in, and exterminate the vermin. Hold tight and keep a sharp eye out." He called Sue Lyn and told her to apprehend the people in the car.

In the meantime, Sue Lyn and Desmond placed several rounds into the car. An advancing Desmond stated, "We are eight, and we have you covered. Drop your weapons or watch the next volley rip the driver to pieces, and then we'll use you as target practice."

The next message was lay down on the ground with your arms fully extended in front of you. The men complied, and when they saw that they had been captured by an Asian woman, and a childlike looking male, they shook their heads. Desmond double locked their hands behind them with multiple wire tires. Their weapons were placed in a bag, and they were led onto the Caneel Bay property where they were gagged, blindfolded, and turned around several times.

Sue Lyn radioed Darryl and told him that they had the two individuals securely wrapped up. Desmond searched the men, found a wallet and badge that belonged to the Chief of Police.

He said, "Well, I'll be damn. This information says that this guy is the Chief of Police. Radio Darryl, and tell him about our catch."

At 0500 hundred hours, Darryl told Michael to secure the rear and right sides of the main house, and that he and his team would assault the front and cover the left side. As they began their approach, Darryl saw headlights that moved slowly up the road. The car had one occupant and did not look at the house that had interest to them.

Darryl told Michael to proceed, and that they would draw fire from the front and for Michael and crew to come in blazing. He told them to be mindful of the two prisoners that were in the house. At 0510 hundred, Hood and Dempsey heaved stun grenades through the window. The blast disoriented the occupants who were already disoriented from smoking weed. Darryl and his crew began to fire into the building for two minutes allowing Michael and his group to breach the rear of the house. Hood and Dempsey used pistols to handle nearby threats, and in a matter of six minutes, twenty-three bad guys laid with various wounds to their bodies. Most were fatal wounds, those who were alive, were provided with a mercy round.

Later, when the team met up with Sue Lynn, the two hostages were blindfolded, and led to the road. Darryl, Michael, and their crews, made their way out of the rear, and ran a quick mile to an area that led to the property line of Caneel Bay. There they entered rustic vehicles, made their way to Hotel H, into the launches, and back to the tugboat.

The chief of police had filmed his interaction with the person from the drug house on his phone. As Desmond viewed his latest pictures, he logged onto the chief's Facebook page, and shared the entire interaction. Desmond said to the chief, "I would like to see you explain your situation, your car in a ditch, just a half-mile from the action, and you getting a package from the leader." Desmond heaved the phone against a tree and shattered it. They left the two men tied up but with their feet and legs free.

On the way to St. Thomas, the weapons were cleaned, disassembled, and thrown into the water. At 0600 hundred hours, the police were on the scene trying to figure out what had happened, and who had made it happen. From the various bodies from different factions lying near and around the house, it was concluded that it was a gang war that ended with everyone involved, being killed.

On the ride back to *the Sanctuary*, John Cheapman began to hyperventilate, and was rushed to the hospital. A call was placed to the hospital informing them that they were on their way with a victim that seemingly was having a heart issue.

Ten minutes prior to arriving at the hospital, Darryl confirmed, and announced that John Cheapman had died. At the hospital, and after being evaluated it was confirmed that John Cheapman suffered a stroke, and a massive heart attack. Darryl after hearing this said to the Doctor, "I would like to bring these guys back here in a few days for a complete and thorough examination. I feel awful about what happened to one of mine, and I won't let assumptions rule my leadership."

At *the Sanctuary*, the mood was somber. The Sarge met the bus, embraced his nephew and his wife, and said, so that all could hear, "We won the battle but lost one of ours. How could we have known? How could we have known?"

#

At the end of the two weeks stay, Darryl and Sue Lyn were still in a funk about what happened to John Cheapman. Courtney told the Sarge, that he had better get them out of that mood or it could impact their leadership. He said to her, "Honey, I'm his uncle. Please, do me a favor, and talk to them."

Courtney saw Monica and spoke to her about the situation with Darryl and Sue Lyn. The two women saw Darryl and Sue Lyn sitting in the water and decided that this was the best time to break them out of that funk.

Monica said, "Every time my husband leaves me, no matter the reason, I'm afraid that this will be the last time I am going to see him. We've had some close calls, and some scary situations with suicide vests on children, while we were helpless. God made a way, and we entered the tunnels in time to avoid that catastrophe. I say all of that to say, that most of the men in your group are seasoned combat types. If they see you sulking, they might think you're weak. You two need to get on that horse, and be prepared to kick ass, and take names. This ain't no game, and none of us are guaranteed another day."

Sue Lyn exclaimed, "Monica!"

Monica threw up her hand, and said, "Sue Lyn, I ain't God, and only he can answer your question. You two are leaders, and until you abdicate your responsibilities, then you need to act like leaders."

Courtney said, "Monica, I wanted to figure out how to assist them in getting through this, and you go right for the jugular, as usual. Listen guys, she is absolutely correct. You need to exercise your leadership skills, or renounce your positions, and let my husband appoint someone else. I know one thing, Darryl, if you abdicate your position, you will put a stain on the Beckmire name. Come on people, if you want to feel bad, wait until five or six of us have been shot, and you don't have the facilities or the support to save us."

Darryl stood up, approached Courtney, and said, "Auntie, you and Monica are tough ladies. I thank you, or rather, we thank you for the talk, and it's our first loss, regardless of the circumstances, it's our first loss. You're right, we have to move on, and make sure that's our only loss."

# # #

As the group was preparing to leave sunny St. Thomas after breakfast, a vehicle appeared in front of *the Sanctuary*, a very lean looking young man got out of the car, walked towards the reception desk, and said to the clerk, "I would like to speak to a Benjamin Beckmire. I understand that he is a guest here, is it possible that you can attempt to reach him in his room? My name is Jelani Latinmire."

"Sir, we don't disturb our guests. Is the matter critical?"

"Yes ma'am, you could say that. I'm with the FBI, and I need to speak to him. I'm alone, this is not a warrant serving activity, or anything like that, we need him to corroborate some information we received."

John Lee appeared, and said, "I'm Ben Beckmire. How can I be of service to you?"

"Well, sir, I'm actually being of service to you. This is an unofficial visit, but I must let you know that a former ex-agent from a no-name agency has masterminded the resources, and personnel to provide a formidable strike against you, and your people. It appears that you have something he wants, and he has absconded with some heat seeking missiles designed to destroy aircraft, your aircraft in particular."

John Lee asked, "Why on earth would he want to blow us out of the sky? If we have something he wants, then he sure as hell won't be getting it from us. Now, are you the missionary for that there fellow or what be your involvement in this thing from the FBI. Let me see that there badge of yours."

The agent handed John Lee the leather pouch that contained his credentials. John Lee said, "Show me some more certifying documents like credit cards, driver's license, and anything else you might have on you."

The young man reached in his pocket, retrieved his wallet that was fat with credit cards from Walmart, Macy's, TJ Max, Sam's Club, and others. John Lee said, "I think I be liking you because we shop at the same stores. Where you be from?"

"I'm from Raleigh, North Carolina. I moved up to Maryland last January to take this job, and immediately became frustrated with the nonsense that goes on in the bureau. It's unlikely I'll last another year because I have insulted two superior officers, one who had poor math skills, and the other one thought the military should have given him stars for being smarter than the rest of the recruits. I'm tired of kissing it if you know what I mean. However, that's not the reason for this visit, the real reason is to find out whether you guys have any information about who killed those three sailors, and who sliced up those other ones? I don't know if you heard, but there was a massacre on St. John last night. The individuals who were under investigation were slaughtered in their house, and some locals who attacked them, well their bodies were scattered around the property and the road in front of their house."

"No, I haven't had a chance to listen to the news. Was that reported on Fox News?"

"I believe so. Why that question?"

"Oh, that's the only station that I believe in. The rest are definitely biased."

"Sir, the information I gave you is confidential, and if released, will make for my expedient, and dishonorable exit from the bureau. It ain't what it's cracked up to be. Every married guy is either in denial, or in divorce court. I had a girlfriend, and after two weeks of training, she told me that she loved another. Listen John Lee, I know who Sergeant Benjamin Beckmire is. He and his people, including you, saved my grandfather's life, and his business in Spain, for had he lost his business, he would have ended his life."

"What be the business that he be in?"

"He owned a wonderful old hotel that captured the essence of Valencia, but was in disrepair, and crumbling before his very eyes. You guys tore it down, rebuilt it, and he still has full ownership. You used a guy by the name of Franco, and his once shady crew to manage the rebirth. Listen, I don't know what Mr. Utz is up to, but he stole 4 Laws rockets, and two heat seeking missiles. Now I know your group clipped him out of a shitload of money he stole from the Venezuelan people. I also know that he, and his cronies are doing stick up jobs to gather pay for the people they've hired to assassinate your entire group. He has two silent partners who are connected, and allegedly, someone in your group is assisting in sponsoring his notion of revenge. By the way, they have issued Mr. Utz, a life-or-death ultimatum; secure their money, or face their wrath."

John Lee said, "I don't get that. If he kills us all, how does he expect to get his money? Is he just going to walk into a bank, and tell them that the money we have is his?"

"John Lee, that is the billion-dollar question. However, I'm down here about the killing of soldiers on St. John. Your Mr. Utz has a connection somehow to someone in your group. I just happen to know that he is responsible for the theft of rockets, and that you guys are his targets. Tell Sergeant Beckmire when I find out more information, I'll call the hotel. If he wants, he can call me, and we can try to figure this thing out together."

"Why don't you just take my number down?"

"Give it to me, I'll commit it to memory," John Lee announced.

# # #

After a long discussion with Mallory, the Sarge, Zanthius, Jilkes, Darryl, and John Lee, who concluded, "If that there Mr. Utz shoots the plane down, how in pigs heaven is he going to get that money he stole from those people on that island over yonder? I wonder if he be after someone else, and in the meantime get us for all we done did to his ass, and maybe we pissed somebody else off as well, really bad?"

It was as though an eternity of time had elapsed, before the 'idiot spy' screamed, "Oh, shit! I wonder if Helga was somehow connected to one of the many schemes that we uncovered that included a bunch of shady people. Dad, I think John Lee has just solved a huge puzzle. I'll bet you $20 that there is a connection."

The Sarge looked at his son, then at John Lee, and with a look of bewilderment said, "All I want to do is move permanently into my house and watch the children. I'm sick of people who ain't who they say they are, come to assist us, and then stick a knife square up our you know what! At least in the Vietnam, we knew that the smiling and bowing farmer, was the same asshole that would shoot you in the back during the night. This game is so complicated, and I don't know how in the hell we've survived this long with our forever forgiving, accepting, and allowing shit to happen."

Jilkes interrupted the Sarge's babbling, and said, "Sarge, I think there are two sides to Sister Mary just like her other name is Helga Spengatsenburg, and that's the other side. However, I'll bet you if she's the person in the middle of this, both sides will want to protect that baby."

As Jilkes was about to elaborate, the SAT phone rang, and it was the lady topping the discussion. She calmly said, "Sergeant Beckmire, I know you don't have a lot of trust from your side for me, however, I need you to listen carefully, and investigate the probability that what I'm about to say to you is the truth. I know I've done things under various shades of truth, and deceit. I need you to stay put on the island until you can locate Mr. Utz, and the 4 Laws rockets that he stole."

"Sister Mary, or is it, Helga Spengatsenburg? You do realize that the Laws rockets are for close combat missions."

There was a pause on the phone, and Sister Mary announced, "He also stole 2 heat seeking missiles."

"Sister, if he shoots us out of the sky, he'll never get his money."

There was an extremely long moment of silence. Helga Spengatsenburg felt uncomfortable for a minute, and announced, "Sergeant Beckmire, this is not only about money, but alliances, debts, promises, revenge, and family ties. The word on the street is that he is broke and is doing petty stick-up jobs to hire his next crew to kill you. He has feigned that rumor which allows him to operate under the radar."

"Sister Mary, if this is not only about money, then what is it about, and why is it so important that me and mine are dead, to him?"

Again, there was a long pause to the point that the Sarge asked, "Sister Mary, are you there?"

"Yes, Sergeant, I'm here." Once again quiet, and the group began making hand gestures, and wondering what in the hell was going on.

Sister Mary finally exclaimed, "Mr. Utz knows that within your group, there is a baby that was conceived by me, and is being cared for by my friend/enemy."

"Sister, if I didn't know any better, I would think that you're trying to pinpoint our exact location for a strike of your own. You seem to be stalling in responding to why Mr. Utz, is so interested in seeing me, and my group dead. Is there more to this story?"

Sister Mary exclaimed, "Sergeant, there is much more, and the real focus, or target in this matter, is me." There was once again a long pause, before Sister Mary said, "Helga Spengatsenburg killed his entire family, and made him watch! All of this happened after he told, unsuspectingly, one of my minions that he knew I had a child, and it was by the 'idiot spy'."

"Why did you kill his family? Was it just his wife?"

"Sergeant Beckmire, Helga Spengatsenburg killed his wife, two daughters, infant son, mother-in-law, and her husband, and in the most macabre manner possible. Ms. Spengatsenburg is one evil bitch. Therefore, until you find your current nemesis, here on this island, I wouldn't move that plane of yours out of that hangar. He will blow you to hell because of me, and it is rumored that once you're dead, there is a clear route, to the fortune you have amassed as a group. Listen, in this game that you're playing in, please know that there are no loyalties, or boundaries. I will do what is required of me, or the same thing will happen to me."

The Sarge interrupted her, and asked, "Where is the Holy Father?"

"He's in unholy hell at the moment. He'll be back, don't worry. You can't keep him down!" The phone went dead.

After making sure the phone was disconnected, the Sarge said, "Now that's some weird shit. It was as if she were two different people, and that answer about the Holy Father, whew, now that was some scary shit!"

John Lee said, "Don't' let that there guy touch you. Boy, he'll screw up your mind, and make you want to do some damn bad things to people you love."

The Sarge looked at Michael, then Darryl, and said to both men, "I need your people all around town. If it's his mission to blow us out of the sky, then I assume that his ass is somewhere near the airport. If I were he, and I had a bone up my ass, I would lay low on that beachfront property near the airport that has a wicked view of the airport, a beach that's incredibly beautiful, but a facility that is repugnant."

The Sarge paused for a moment to cogitate, and finally said, Darryl you and Michael are well known assets to our group. How about we throw a wrench into the engine, and send the most unidentifiable Hood and Dempsey? I mean nobody knows them, and they act as if they smoked an entire cannabis crop, but neither man gets high. I trust them, but I know I've trusted people before, and they turned out to be rattlesnakes."

"Not those two boys, Sarge. They be solid as a rock!" John Lee professed.

## CHAPTER TWENTY-ONE

The change in the itinerary was communicated to everyone, and no one cared to inquire as to the reason why. The Sarge asked Zanthius, "Have you seen the two new guys?"

Zanthius responded, "Dad, I saw them talking to Larry and Rashida about an hour ago, but there's Larry, and Juan is in the corner over-loving Rashida."

"Where is Asiram?"

"She said she wasn't feeling well, just wanted to relax, and watch a new series on Netflix."

"Son, what's your opinion of the two new guys?"

"Dad, you need to relax, and accept the fact that we didn't kill them, and they turned out to be assets in Minnesota. They stick to themselves, and seemingly spend a lot of time talking quietly on the phone."

"Oh really. I wonder who they're talking to?"

"Dad, you know that Rashida can pinpoint and record conversations on that unit of hers."

The Sarge looked at Zanthius, and a light went on in his head. He proceeded to the corner where Juan was kissing his wife. He said, "Boy, let her get her breath. You trying to smother her? Anyway, baby girl I need your help on a matter. Can I speak to you without that kissing husband of yours?"

The two walked on to the veranda, and the Sarge stated, "That's some glow about you. Are you okay?" He thought for a moment, and said, "Oh, boy! Oh, my goodness! Are you pregnant again?"

"Dad, I am pregnant, and happy." The Sarge embraced her, and said, "I'll keep my big mouth shut until you're ready for me to announce that I'm having another grandbaby."

The two hugged, and Rashida asked, "What did you need me to do?"

"I need you to bug the new guys' room, and I need to know who they talk to on the phone," the Sarge said.

Rashida placed her hands on her hips, and announced, "I am truly your daughter. Oh, my goodness! I've been watching and recording their mess since day one. When they were in Minnesota, Hood met Litefoot's sister Dawn, and Dempsey met a waitress at the diner, Christin. That is who they've been talking to, and their last conversation included inviting them to their next station, securing them a room, and funds so as they were not captives to any craziness."

"That's it?"

"Dad, they are not accustomed to talking with women about meaningful things. They talk small, hesitantly, and like naïve men. If they're crooked, then so am I. We sent them to Minnesota, and they didn't know a soul there. Unless they're smarter than the rest of us, I think they're clean."

"Thanks baby girl, and I won't spoil your thunder until you give me the go ahead. Love you so much!"

The Sarge saw Mallory and asked him to secure Hood and Dempsey.

Later, when the two men arrived, they were literally shaking because they thought somewhere along the way, they screwed up. Hood stated, "If you're calling us out, then we screwed up bad. Before you say anything, we've acted in the best interest of the group, followed instructions, and protocol. I usually do the interpretations. I accept full responsibility for any fracture in our execution."

"What in the hell does that mean, fracture in our execution? Do you speak English?"

Hood began to show signs of agitation, the Sarge shifted focus, and asked, "So, Mr. Dempsey, do you want to add to his comments?"

"No sir, Sergeant sir!"

"Why are you addressing me like that?"

"Sergeant sir, I'm trying to maintain my cool. I'm a little upset Sergeant sir."

"Why is that soldier?"

"Sergeant sir, you gave us back our lives. You gave us a mission, and somehow, we fucked up, but we don't know what and how we screwed up, Sergeant sir."

"Knock off that Sergeant sir, shit. Call me Sarge or Mr. Beckmire. Is that clear?"

"Yes sir, Mr. Beckmire."

"If I didn't know any better, I would surmise that you'd like to take me on in some way. Is that correct?"

"Mr. Beckmire, we don't have 20 bucks between us, and you never concretized our pay scale, and apparently, we did something wrong. I would like to at least be paid before I'm fired."

Mallory broke into an uncontrollable laughter, and yelled, "Hood, I will give you $10k if you can knock him down, $30k if you stagger him, and $50k if you knock him out."

Hood replied, "That would be unfair since I am much younger than he is, and I'm in better shape."

"I'll give you $100k if you can pin him to the ground."

Jong walked in, and inquired about what was going on, after receiving a short story, he walked over to Hood, and whispered, "I don't know what you bet, but I would never go up against him. He is as strong as four men, lifted me off the floor with one hand, walked into the enemy's camp, killed five men with his bare hands, and I could go on and on. I suggest that if you're going to challenge him, do write your last will and testament."

Hood smiled, and said, "I have no intention of going up against the man who is a legend, my leader, the man that owes us some modicum of pay. No sir, I'm just anxious because I would like to have at least 40 bucks between us. Sarge, if I may speak freely?"

"Go ahead."

"You reminded me of my father, and I regressed all the way to that visualization of him about to hit me. Somethings I can't forget, no matter how hard I try. I don't want to tangle with you, I want to tangle for you, but not against you. I might be slightly off balance, but I'm not totally crazy."

The Sarge walked up to the man, and asked, "Do I need to get you help for that condition? Is that something as a group we can work on with you?"

Hood dropped his head, sighed deeply, and stated, "Other than Dempsey, no one has much cared about me living or dying."

The Sarge got closer to Hood, gave him a man-size hug, and said, "Welcome to my family. It is your family as long as you think we're doing the right thing."

The two embraced, shared private words until John Lee appeared on the scene, and stated, "Damn, Mallory, I be thinking that he was your special friend."

The Sarge looked at him, and said, "You are some kind of special, John Lee. However, we all love you."

The Sarge said, "Now that the kiss and tell session is over, I would like to address the reason why you two were summoned. Oh, and by the way, we don't summon dead men. Now, we are all pretty much known by our adversaries near and far. You two, are like our enigmas, chameleons, unknown mentally puzzling, mysterious, and often difficult to understand. By the way, what's going on with these long phone conversations. You want to enlighten us?"

Hood said, "I met Litefoot's sister Dawn, in Minnesota, and Dempsey met Christin at the diner."

The Sarge looked at Jong, and asked, "Where are our other two planes?"

He was informed that one was in Miami, and the other was in New York. He looked at the men, and asked, "Would you like to invite them to dinner at *the Sanctuary*?"

Hood said, "Sarge, we got 20 bucks between us."

"Gentlemen, when I ask a question, answer the question, and don't give me the current status of the planet. Is that clear?"

Both men nodded with apprehension until the Sarge asked, "Do you two want to call them, and see if they're able to take off for three days, and come bask in the sun?"

Hood didn't hesitate, and called Dawn, who told him that she had to work. His head dropped, and the guys could see that it wasn't going to work. She asked him to hold on. Two minutes later, she announced that her boss was granting her the weekend off. Hood told her that he would call her back in ten minutes.

When Dempsey made the call to Christin, she asked him twenty questions about when, where, and how she would get there. He told her that she would be in a secure room, hopefully with Dawn. She responded, "If she comes, then I will feel better and safe. It's not that I don't trust you, but this is the kind of thing that gets an invisible mark across your nose in my community."

Dempsey asked Christin, "Can you hold a minute?" He turned to the Sarge and said, "Please, don't make me disappoint someone dear to me."

"Son, I would never play with your emotions. Tell them that a plane will be at the airport to fly them to St. Thomas for the weekend and return them home. Tell them our group is honorable, and that the men requesting their visitation are respectful men. Tell them their accommodations will be separate, and their choices will be theirs."

Both men lit up like Christmas lights on a tree, turned colors from the excitement, and started giving each other high-fives and hugs.

The Sarge said, "Now, this is a promise. I will break your backs if you offend, abuse, or otherwise treat those ladies without respect. Is that clear, and do we have an understanding?"

Hood asked, "Why don't we invite chaperones to accompany them?"

The Sarge looked at Jong who shook his shoulders, and referred the idea to Mallory who said, "I think that's a decision for the ladies to make."

The Sarge said, "We're kind of getting ahead of ourselves. I need you guys to scour a few places in search of someone who wants to blow our main plane the hell out of the sky. When you were summoned here, and before you both went left on us, the reason for the meeting, was to enlist your services to seek out the asshole that's holding us hostage here on the islands with a couple of Stinger heat seeking missiles. We think we know the ideal place that would allow him to have a full view of all planes leaving the island. It's not as though you can take off from the rocks in back of us, and over the city, no, we take off from the terminal to the rocks, over that hotel on the water with a perfect view, and a shot of everything coming and going from the airport. Also, and crossing issues, Jong, I need you to work out a contract with these two brigands. However, in the meantime, give them each, one of those $10k debit cards."

He looked at the two men, and asked, "Is that a show of good faith, on our part?" Agreement was acknowledged by high-fives and hugs.

# # #

Arrangements were made for their friends to visit for the weekend. In the meantime, the two men, upon checking into their hotel by the water, were quickly eyed by the local ladies. Their pictures were taken, and run through a wanted database, but nothing suspicious turned up. After being assigned to their rooms which were next to each to other, the two men decided to have a drink in the bar. St. Thomas was a good place to try out the islands favorite rum, Cruzan. The two men drank themselves into a contrived coma and were obliged to be easy prey for those with devious intent. Their rooms were searched, and the little cash they had, was taken. The men only had one debit card between them, and it was in Dempsey's shoe. The ladies of the evening thought they were nobodies, broke, and job seeking tourists.

In the morning, after the two men allegedly woke up with horrible headaches, they went swimming in the sky-blue water. When word was sent to Mr. Utz about them, he unceremoniously, instructed his people to kill them. When one of his lieutenants asked why, Mr. Utz drew his pistol, and fired a round into his head. He looked at the other people in the room, and stated, when I give a command, execute it, or suffer the same fate.

#

After swimming and realizing that they didn't have any cash to pay for the room, and food for another night, the two men were at the front desk having an argument with the clerk telling him how their room was torn upside down, how their credit cards were stolen, and their cash was taken. The clerk said, "Well, the good thing is that your credit card company approved your stay for last night. Unfortunately, we can't provide you with continuing accommodations without a valid form of payment."

As the two men talked between themselves, Mr. Utz appeared in the lobby, and his aide told him that those are the two men he ordered assassinated. He looked at them, then at his aide, and said, "Those two don't have a pot to piss in. Why would I kill them?"

Later, on the beach, the two men made a call to the Sarge's SAT phone and told him that his nemesis was present and accounted for. The Sarge asked, "What's your status?"

Dempsey said, "We did that rum thing, pretended to get drunk, and the room was ransacked, and all of our stuff was taken."

"Are you sure you saw Mr. Utz?"

"Unless the picture you gave us wasn't him, then the person we both eyeballed, and who seemingly is in control of this group, and place, is here in the flesh."

While the Sarge was talking to Hood, his SAT phone began to beep indicating that a second call was coming in. He told Hood to standby, and that he would call him back. When he answered the second call, the voice asked, "Do you think it's possible that you, and the 'idiot spy' can meet me for dinner tonight? I'm staying at the Four Seasons on the other side of the island."

For the sake of clarity, the Sarge asked, "Whom might I have the possible pleasure of dining with later?"

"This is Helga Spengatsenburg. Can you make it happen?"

"We currently have plans, but I'll get back to you within the hour if we choose to modify them. Hit you back later."

The Sarge looked at Mallory, and said, "You will never guess who the hell that was?"

Mallory replied, "I have no idea."

"Well, it was Helga Spengatsenburg, and she wants to have dinner with me, and the 'idiot spy'."

Zanthius lowered his head, and said, "Dad, that's not funny. Not funny at all."

"Son, I was not being funny. That was Helga Spengatsenburg on the phone, and she wants to have dinner with you and me later tonight." Zanthius stared at his father while searching for some notion of "bs," but saw none, and knew that this was a chapter of his life that he had to conclusively end.

The SAT phone rang again, and it was Dempsey who said, "We count nine associates with your mark. If you like, we can handle that for you."

The Sarge responded, "Thanks for the offer, but he's mine. His body and soul belongs to me, and I will not be cheated out of my revenge, so stay away from him. I'll have Jong call the hotel, and pay for two more nights for you brigands, and by the third night, I'll be there to pig roast that asshole! In the meantime, I need you two to find out where the Western Union Office is, and we'll send you some cash. Once you're in the office, the clerk, a friend of ours, will hand you a locker key. Make sure when you enter it, no one is watching. I'll have one of our guys put two .9 millimeters in it with two clips, and one in the chambers. Once I find out the address to a proposed dinner meeting, I'll text you guys, and you can do some surveillance, and protect me and my son. It's probably going to be at the Four Seasons on the other side of the water. I need you to watch our backs close up. Stop at the clothing store down from Western Union and buy some appropriate clothes to look like you belong in the place. I will have other members of the team there as well, but you two are my sleepers."

Mallory announced that he would pick the advance team and place *the Sanctuary* on alert. The Sarge inadvertently, told him that Hood and Dempsey would be enough.

When the Sarge told Courtney that Helga Spengatsenburg was on the island, and wanted to have dinner with him and Zanthius, she announced that she was attending. The Sarge dissuaded her, and told her that he would be well covered, and protected.

It was not the same kind of commiseration when Zanthius told Asiram that Helga was on the island and wanted to have dinner with him and his father. Asiram went through all kinds of conniptions, threatening to kill Zanthius and Helga if there was any conversation about the child that was not in their best interest.

#

At the Four Seasons, in a darkened corner, sitting quietly, was Helga Spengatsenburg. When the Sarge saw her, his first thought was, "Damn she be fine!" Helga rose from her seat and greeted Ben Beckmire with a firm handshake. She embraced Zanthius with a close, and feel this thing, kind of hug. Zanthius backed away, and said, "Nice to see you as well. We're not hungry, but we are interested in hearing why you're here on island, and as Helga Spengatsenburg?"

Helga responded, "So much for small talk. How is our child? How is he developing? You were always to the point, lover boy!"

The Sarge said, "I'm not interested in any of the things I've heard so far. Why did you invite us to dinner?"

"Shall we at least have a drink before we enter the world of demons, weapons, betrayals, and demands?"

"Water is fine for me. We don't plan on being here that long. What is your purpose? Has the Holy Father been located?"

"Mr. Beckmire, what Holy Father are you referring to? Are you considering the person from hell, or the one who parades around as the Pope, and the Holy Father? You people have no idea concerning who you're dealing with. You've been manipulated at every turn, and you still don't understand the game that's being played on you, around you, and with you as major players. I'm the key to your salvation, and longevity. However, I don't come cheap."

Zanthius asked, "What is it you want?"

"What is it that you think I might want? I certainly don't want to play Marco Polo with you, that wasn't very lasting," Helga replied.

Beckmire said, "Okay, enough jousting. Exactly, Ms. Spengatsenburg, what are you seeking?"

"I'm seeking righteousness. That's the only thing on earth worth having, righteousness. Can you provide me with that, Mr. Beckmire?"

"I'm only going to ask you this one more time, and then we're out of here. What is it you seek?"

"I seek that which was stolen from me, Mr. Beckmire?"

The Sarge looked at Zanthius in a perplexing manner, and Zanthius aggressively asked, "What the fuck was stolen from you, Helga?"

"My heart and soul?"

"What in the hell are you talking about?" Zanthius asked.

"I want that child, my child, that was stolen by you from that monastery in Valencia. I want that child, my child, who I entrusted with a bunch of money hungry nuns to care for, who sold him to the highest bidder. I want a life with that child, my child, and that Mr. Beckmire is how I become righteous."

Zanthius moved aggressively towards Helga, and was restrained by his dad who responded, "Lady, that just ain't going to happen. There is no way in heaven or hell, you'll get that baby. Legally, the die has been cast. Oh, and don't try that storm trooper shit, and go out, and hire a bunch of mercenaries because we'll provide them with a quick trip to hell, to join the thousands of people who are awaiting our arrival. Lady, you should go back as Sister Mary because Helga Spengatsenburg is out of her fucking mind."

"Zanthius, give me my child by noon tomorrow or watch your entire tribe be destroyed by people from hell. Every place that you call home is rigged, your plane is rigged, your so-called Sanctuary is rigged, and you don't even know how. Do you want me to tell you how?"

The Sarge looked at Helga and said, "Give it your best shot. I hope you don't hold your breath until noon. There will be no transfer of any child to a nut case. Have a wonderful evening."

The Sarge looked at Zanthius who had a look on his face that his father had seen before, and affirmatively commanded, "Don't you fucking think about doing anything crazy. Don't you dare!"

As soon as they turned around to leave the table in the dark corner, twelve well-armed and attired mercs quietly entered the restaurant from all available doors and caught everyone off guard. Laser lights moved methodically around Zanthius, and the Sarge's bodies, through the windows. The Sarge thought that they had been set up, and silently cursed himself for not adding more security.

There was no talking, just a perfect execution of commandeering a place without firing a shot. The leader, with a weapon in his hand, walked up to Helga, bent down, and whispered something in her ear, and smiled at her. Helga smiled back at the person. The leader rose from the bending position, smiled again, and descended to ear level with Helga once again. The person again whispered something in her ear, rose from the bending position, smiled at Helga, and unsuspectingly, fired two rounds into Helga's head, and two others into her heart. The leader turned, walked towards the door of the restaurant, and twirled a hand in the air indicating that they were out of there. At no point did they pay attention to the Sarge or Zanthius. It was clear, Helga Spengatsenburg, aka, Sister Mary had supremely pissed someone off, and they sought, and got revenge.

The Sarge looked at the people retreating from the place, and asked, "Who the hell was that? They literally butt screwed us without any lubricant. How could they get that close to us, and past our people?"

Dempsey looked at Hood, then at the Sarge, and said, "There was something weird about that group, Sarge. Everything about them was pristine. Their outfits were clean, and no one had a distinguishable smell, their shoes were shined, and they acted like robots. I mean, how could they just walk up on us, have the outside covered, and place red dots on everyone? That was spooky if I can use the word."

"How many people came into the restaurant?" The Sarge asked.

Zanthius responded, "Dad, I counted twelve but there were multiple beams covering our bodies from every window, from the outside. I can't imagine how many were outside."

While people were trying to figure out the who and how, Zanthius fetched a pillow from a seat, placed it over Helga's already destroyed head, and fired two additional rounds from his .9 millimeter into it. He mumbled, "I know how many times you've come back from the dead. These were just insurance rounds, that your ass will stay dead, you evil bitch."

The Sarge exclaimed, "Now you've gotten us involved by killing an already dead person! Anyway, if we're such high value targets, why did they just blow Helga's head off, and not take any action against us. We were completely compromised."

Dempsey said, "Sarge, there was something strange about that group of mercs. They just didn't seem like a killing machine. They didn't seem aggressive enough to be mercs to me. Something is wrong with that picture."

The Sarge said, "Whoever they were, they had us dead to dead! I don't give a shit about how they looked, they had us dead to dead."

Dempsey proclaimed, "Gotcha, Sarge! The bottom line is that they could have wreaked havoc on us without us having an opportunity to respond."

Hood responded, "We screwed up again. We had one simple task, and that was to make sure you and your son were safe. We failed on every count."

The Sarge stated "Whoever orchestrated this event, would have succeeded regardless of any attention to detail we might have put in place. They covered us with beams through the window, waltzed into the restaurant, put two bullets in Helga's head, and two in her heart. I'm damn glad we were not on their hit list.   Damn glad because they were extremely efficient. Let's get out of here. Dempsey, you, and Hood see if you can retrieve, and destroy the video. Don't waste a lot of time on it, the only thing my son did was abuse a corpse! Zanthius, collect her belongings, and let's get out of here."

## CHAPTER TWENTY-TWO

Later, when the group arrived at *the Sanctuary*, Mallory, Brown, Bernstein, McArthur, and Gladstone greeted them. John Lee, Jilkes, Montomie, and Jong were positioned on the east side, and on the west side, there was Chakes, Whitmore, Isaiah, and Desmond. The Sarge asked Mallory, "Why so much security tonight in addition to the service we hired?"

"Sarge, whenever Helga or Sister Mary has been around, there has been trouble. I just didn't want to take the situation lightly, and decided to cover all bases especially since you and Zanthius were out of pocket."

"Good thinking, but someone concluded that situation in a permanent way?"

"What do you mean?"

"After hearing her demands that would lead her to becoming righteous, we turned around to leave, and found laser lights all over our bodies. Twelve mercs, loaded for bear silently circled us in the restaurant. I mean they swept down on us without a sound, and the leader never said a word to us, or even acknowledged our presence. He walked over to Helga or Sister Mary, bent down, whispered something in her ear, and they both smiled. The leader bent down again, whispered something else in Helga's ear, and once again they both smiled. He made the sign of the cross with his off hand, raised his weapon, fired two rounds into Helga's head, and two into her heart. The leader turned, gave the circle the wagon signal, and off they went. They never acknowledged us or presented aggression towards us other than the laser beams covering our bodies."

"Sarge, how many times have we heard, and saw pictures of a dead Helga or Sister Mary? If you remember, she was killed in Switzerland, and a couple of other places as well."

"Yeah, I know, but this time is different. The 'idiot spy' decided to fire two additional rounds into her head, to make sure that she was dead."

"No, he didn't!"

"Oh yes, he did. He unsuspectingly, grabbed a pillow off of a chair to cover her face, and with the other hand fired two rounds into her head. On the way back I asked him about his actions, and he said, "I will never let anyone hurt my Asiram. She has mothered that child since we gathered him from that monastery in Valencia. I will die before I yield to her being crushed by a ball from hell."

"Damn, but it ain't over," Mallory stated.

"Remind me my friend. Tomorrow, I'm going after Mr. Utz. I need to meet with you, and Captain Carla. I know he has a snitch in the airport and, therefore, I'm going to set a plan in motion that will draw both of them out. First thing in the morning, we'll all board the plane, at least it will look like it. Oh, I'm going to need to meet with Ms. Viola as well. I'm going to need to be seen boarding the plane, but a few of us will leave from the rear, meet up with the two enigmas, and conclude this thing," the Sarge stated.

"What about the Holy Father or Diablo as you call him? We won't have peace until we know the truth about him. I usually don't buy that crap about mysticism, however, after my first trip to Australia, I realized that the world isn't defined by common sense, scientific matter, or what you think is real or not. I remember wanting to go swimming in that beautiful billabong until I saw that monster. How about the tattoos that everybody received? And how do you command wild dogs, spiders, snakes, and other unknown animals to attack an advancing force? I looked at John Lee, a hard case no matter who takes him on, and he was on the brink of cutting John Lee Jr. in half, hanging his wife, drowning/electrocuting his other children, and decapitating his best friend, Jilkes. Even more perplexing was the writing on Zanthius's organs. Now that was some weird shit! Who writes on a person's organs without cutting them open? Come now, think about it, and that big ass croc in the billabong was more than a notion. I'm afraid to go near the water. This entire mission has been about things most people don't believe in, spirits, demons, and strange animals. Also, who would have thought that a bunch of old ass Vietnam vets could stir up so much trouble trying to help the 'idiot spy'?"

"Yeah, you're right. Let's try to put an end to Mr. Utz before we figure out what's next for the group. Did you okay the plane to pick up Dempsey and Hood's friends from Minnesota?"

"Sarge, they are scheduled to leave Minnesota with their chaperones in two days," Mallory replied.

The Sarge asked, "Did you tell the two guys, and where the hell is Jong?"

"Sarge, there is something going on with him. He's been missing in action, and when you see him, he rarely engages in conversation. I haven't seen Mary Alice in a while. She orders food in for the children, and herself. Something is up, but with those two, I don't pry. You know we don't do that kind of thing. Perhaps, it's time for Courtney and Monica to make a house call? Maybe you can suggest that to her, and then she'll drag Monica into it."

"My problem is that there's a guy at a hotel directly under our flight pattern who wants to blow us the hell out of the sky with stolen heat seeking missiles. You handle the Jong thing for now. I have to try to catch a thief by using a couple."

# # #

Dempsey and Hood got out of the taxicab and walked into the entrance to the hotel. The manager immediately welcomed them and apologized for any troubles they suffered on their last stay. He said, "Your aunt in Maryland advanced payment for a single room. I have taken the liberty of giving you an ocean view room with two double beds, and I was instructed to allow you guys to eat, and moderately have two beverages each for the next sixty days. I suppose that's the point when you two decide what your business is going to be or when you go back home. By the way, what kind of business are you interested in trying to start?"

Dempsey replied, "A ride sharing business, much like Uber and Lyft but tailored to more high-end clients."

"What are you going to use for vehicles, bicycles?"

Hood said, "That's really funny, but you shouldn't judge a book by its cover. We're not destitute. Given the right strategy, if we shift gears, we might buy this place, and put your smart ass in the unemployment line. Give us our keys and be gone." In the background, several sets of ears were listening to the staged discussion, and a voice finally said, "Get me details on those two. I think I see talent that I could use. Call my friend in Virginia and have him check them out. They both laid their hands on the counter, have our man gather the prints, and let's see who these two really are. I don't think they know our adversary. Let me know what you find out. Have them expedite the issue," Mr. Utz stated.

In the meantime, in their room, Hood announced, "I'd like to go back, and kick that desk clerk's ass. We should consider buying this fucking place, gutting it, and building a real hotel. This is a joke, run by a jokester, and operated like a whore house. This looks like the kind of thing we should do. I'm glad you told that asshole about a ride sharing business. We need to investigate, who the hell owns this place, and how to rid this albatross from them." Both men saw the hidden cameras in the opposing corners, and further enlightened those listening to what they were up to.

Three hours later in the bar, Dempsey and Hood ordered beers, and watched through the reflection from the mirror as the desk clerk hurriedly, made his way to the table in the corner. A call came to the front desk that seemingly put the clerk in a frenzy. He walked over to the table in the corner, and whispered something to the two men, one being Mr. Utz. Dempsey and Hood talked about the hotel quietly to each other, decided to leave their drinks, and take a look at the kitchen. When they looked through the upper glass in the door, it displayed a tragically dirty, and nasty kitchen. Knowing that they were being watched, they walked back to the bar, and engaged in a quiet conversation. Dempsey said to Hood, "Despite the conditions of the place, ultimately, this could be a helluva investment. We should consider it seriously, after we rid it of the riff raff."

A preliminary report came back indicating that Dempsey was established and rich, and that he and Hood had been friends for twenty plus years. The report indicated that the two of them were fresh from Desert Storm and performed classified missions. Mr. Utz said to his associate, "One is a rich boy, the other is his friend. Let's have a drink with them and see who the hell they really are."

Prior to entering the bar, Mr. Utz received a phone call. He immediately waved his people off, left the building, started walking on the beach, and appeared to be under stress. The caller apparently said things to Mr. Utz that were of concern to him, and his physical reactions indicated that his strings were being pulled by someone else. One of his two partners indicated to him that there had been too many botched attempts to end the issue that kept them from enjoying the full benefits of Beckmire and his groups demise.

# # #

Much later at the bar, Mr. Utz introduced himself as Paul and his friend as Peter. He said, "Where are you guys from?"

"We're from the states, been in the desert too long, and want to be near blue water. How about you guys?" Dempsey inquired.

"Where in the desert were you?"

Hood vehemently stated, "Don't answer a question with a question."

Mr. Utz looked at him, smiled, and said, "You're absolutely correct. We are entrepreneurs looking for an opportunity to expand our business here on this beautiful island."

Dempsey asked, "What line of business?"

"Just general investments in infrastructure projects that have long term benefits for both the people, and us."

"How about you?"

"We were thinking about buying this dive, firing that snotty nose little bastard behind the desk, until we looked through the window into the kitchen. It is a disaster."

"We know, but the per night rate is cheap, and we're trying to scope out our next move. You know the rates at the upscale places during the season is ridiculously high. By staying here, we add four nights per week on our stay as opposed to staying in style. We don't eat here. We know the kitchen is a mess."

The four men talked, and drank, drank, and talked until Mr. Utz said, "There might be some cooperation between what you're thinking of doing, and what we want to do on this island. I have an appointment at 11 in the morning but shortly after that, I would like to lay some things out, and see if you guys have an interest. My goal is to maximize my dollars, minimize my costs to achieve my goals, and settle for nothing less than doubling my investment in the first six months. In the meantime, I have to collect some funds that were expropriated from me."

Hood stated, "That's an aggressive strategy."

"That's my goal and, therefore, any investments I make have to show me an aggressive return strategy. Listen, I want to live here, do business here, but I don't want to rely solely on locals. I want an international presence. I want to think big, not cautious."

Hood asked, "How about 11:30?"

"That's cutting it too close for me. I'm not in control of the action I have to take tomorrow. It's dependent upon the actions of others and, therefore, I don't want to commit to a scenario that is timewise, uncomfortable."

"Understood! We're in room 123. We look forward to furthering this conversation. Just one question before you leave, are you a part of the ownership of this dive?"

Mr. Utz smiled, and said, "Naw, but you know what, this might be a beginning project that we can mature into a helluva investment. I mean, look at that pristine beach. Let's discuss this tomorrow. Good night, guys."

In their room in the bathroom, Hood texted the Sarge and asked, "What time is departure?"

The Sarge texted back, "11".

Hood texted the Sarge, "Your man has an appointment at that time. See you soon."

# # #

The following morning, the group assembled, and boarded the bus for the ride to the airport. Everyone was aware of the charade that they were a part of. Ms. Viola had arranged for the Sarge, Jilkes, John Lee, Michael, Zanthius, and Isaiah to enter the customs area from the employee entrance, after being seen boarding the plane. From there, they would be escorted to a van that would drive them from the airport. The rest of the tribe was escorted into a holding room.

At 1000 hundred hours, Mallory and Gladstone picked up the rest of the group in a smaller van that was equipped with weapons and disguises. Meanwhile, an extremely attractive young lady working at a concession stand, texted Mr. Utz to inform him that the parties of interest had entered customs and were now boarding their plane. The young woman did not know Mr. Utz's intentions and was happy to earn two hundred bucks for just letting him know that the group was leaving.

At 1015 hundred hours, Mr. Utz, and four of his henchmen entered their van. Inside of the van, were two Stinger missiles, and four Laws rockets. The group drove to a rocky, and deserted beach area, approximately two miles from their hotel. Mr. Utz told one of his guys that they would fire the missiles at the same time, counting down from 5 to 1, and firing after the announcement of number 1.

At 1030 hundred hours, the two missile launchers were uncrated, and prepared for firing. Mr. Utz screamed into the wind, "Never fuck with someone smarter than you, Ben Beckmire!"

At 1050 hundred hours, with the wind blowing easterly, the sound of an empty aircraft's engines could be heard screaming. The plane was on the runway, and was being operated by Captain Carla, and her crew. Mr. Utz received the text that he so desperately wanted; "The plane you described is next in line for takeoff."

Captain Carla proceeded down the runway but diverted the takeoff.

Mr. Utz yelled, "Get ready! The next plane leaving the airport, is our target!" As the two men exited the van, Mr. Utz, and his associate, hoisted the weapons in preparation to fire them. Four shots rang out, incapacitating his associates. As Mr. Utz turned to figure out what was going on, another round tore into his wrist, forcing him to drop the weapon. As Beckmire, and his crew slowly approached him, he attempted to gather the weapon, but received a bullet in his shoulder. Dempsey and Hood came up from behind Mr. Utz, retrieved the weapons, and placed them in a safe mode. Mr. Utz, after seeing them, said, "I should have killed you two assholes when I first met you."

The Sarge said, "They're not assholes, they're a part of my tribe. Listen, I'm not going to torture you, or lecture you, but I would like to know your connection to the Holy Father. You answer that one, and I'll put you quickly, out of your misery."

"You and that guy, whoever in the hell he is, be him the devil or the pope, you two have a day of reckoning to look forward to, you, sonofabitch. My death doesn't end this event. My death only accentuates the determination of others, and by the way, be ever so mindful that family ain't always good family. So, you my friend, can kiss the sunny side of my ass!"

The 'idiot spy' wasted no time, pointed his weapon at Mr. Utz's head, and placed a round into it. His father in complete shock, looked at him, and shouted, "We're going to have to talk about your impetus nature. I wasn't through talking with him. That is not the way we do business. I have seen you do this too many times before, and this, my son, is the last time you will ever raise a weapon and execute a foe who is in my charge. Is that perfectly clear?"

"Dad, that guy was going to blow us out of the sky. He was prepared to kill our families. His ramblings were nonsensical. I felt compelled to do that. I'm angry and have only vengeance to offer anyone who conspires to kill us for profit."

"That was not the question I raised. Is my last statement crystal clear?"

"Yes, dad. I must learn to react based upon your directions, and not assume that because I'm mad, I can just do what I want. However, I will say this Dad, at every turn, death has been stalking us. I promise to achieve a higher-level resolve, and only act upon your commands. That I promise!" Zanthius proclaimed.

The Sarge said, "Dempsey, you and Hood, head back to the hotel, search his room, bring me any documents, and hopefully his computer. Make that clerk that tried to minimize you guys, let you in his room. Slap him around, but don't hurt him. Also, don't try to decipher the papers, just bring what you find in his room to me. I'm sure these aren't the only members of his crew, so be careful. Do you need backup?

Dempsey considered the offer, but said, "If we show up with a new set of characters, there might be a problem. How about having them remarkably close, but not too close?"

# # #

In the back of the van, the Sarge was visibly shaken, and in tears. Mallory noticing his reaction, quietly kept the other members of the van engaged in conversation allowing the Sarge to express those new emotions without every eye in the vehicle on him.

At the turn into *the Sanctuary* properties, the Sarge said to the driver, "Let me and Mallory out here. We'll catch you guys in a few!" Once the van left, Mallory turned to the Sarge, and asked, "What the hell is going on?"

"My son is beginning to like the notion of executing people. He doesn't hesitate, blink, or give a sign that he's going to blow your head off. Zanthius, draws his weapon, and proceeds to execute the subject at hand. Mallory, that's my son. It's not like Larry and me, on a hunt for the scum that poisons our communities. No, Zanthius is well established, funded, married, a father of three, and he acts as though he was given the divine right to provide justice, and be the executioner. I think it's my fault. This cavalier approach to deciding who should live, and who will die, will be his downfall. And besides, what the hell was Utz referencing when he announced, "family ain't always family." Should we be watching 'the idiot spy'? And besides, that's not the first time someone has intimated that notion to me."

Mallory responded, "I am not sure what a man sentenced to death would say to avoid such a conclusion. However, I do know that Zanthius has dedicated his life to those children, Asiram, Ava, you, Courtney, and our group. He will kill anyone who threatens you or the rest of our tribe. I know it's not what you want, but on the other hand, it's what we need. Your task as a father is to temper his actions, direct his emotions, and prepare him to take over once you're no more. Listen, Ben, I too have to sit on the side of the bed in the morning, and figure out, if my body is working. We need to get a bottle of Jack, go down near that fire on the beach, and figure out what's next? It certainly isn't the course of actions we've been on. Between Darryl, Sue Lyn, Zanthius, Harold, Jasper, Michael, Mike, Quick, Carmichael, Isaiah, Desmond, Dempsey, Hood, and Nikelson, I think they can continue our mission, and call on us for technical assistance and training. This has been one hell of a ride, Ben Beckmire, and I'm so happy that I was a part of it."

"Yeah, you're right. This has been an adrenaline boost for a bunch of old guys, who met and came together to fight foreign enemies, that also turned into domestic ones as well. A few wounds here and there, but overall, no real casualties to the old team, and our new recruits, except Cheapman who died from a freaking heart attack. I thank God for his protection and guidance, for without him, we would be entertaining the thousands of souls who are waiting in hell for our arrival. What an existence; pretty remarkable for a bunch of old poor guys who met and served in the *Maiden from Hell's Kitchen.*

## CHAPTER TWENTY-THREE

For the next nine months, the group would travel to the farm, the ranch, *the Sanctuary*, Spain, Alabama, and the outback. After a month's extended stay in the outback, the Sarge at the final dinner in the country yelled, "I need everyone's attention for five minutes."

Zanthius yelled, "Dad, you won't get started until thirty minutes from now." There was laughter, and the Sarge announced, "People, I think it's time that we head to our homes in the south. I personally, want to sit on that big porch of mine, and watch all of these children playing in the streets, riding their bicycles, and having fun until that sun sets on the back side of my house. Oh, and son, you're correct. This is going to take more than five minutes."

The Sarge suddenly became quiet, watched, and listened to the people conclude what they were talking about, and become still enough to hear what he was about to say. It didn't take long, especially after Mallory began to clap his hands. Once silence had been acquired, the Sarge looked around the fire, and to himself, acknowledged the new relationships, and the old ones. He cleared his throat, and said, "I want to first of all thank God, and all the spirits for joining our side, and minimizing our losses. We have been in some confounding positions, and the most we sustained was one loss that was due to a health issue. Practically, my entire team has been shot since our encounter with the infamous, 'idiot spy', aka, my son, Zanthius Beckmire De Lombardo."

The Sarge cleared his throat again, and said, "Many of you don't know that Courtney and I, have another son, who will graduate from the Naval Academy soon. He thought that his parents were not reflective of the people who he would like to introduce to his classmates. That took the wind out of me, it put Courtney in a state of denial that created some short-term mental issues for the two of us. A few months ago, he called his mom, and asked her if she had twenty-thousand dollars that she could give him. He always felt that since I was a policeman in Philadelphia, I couldn't support, provide, and give him the kind of things he needed in order to be in the 'in crowd.' Can you believe that shit? Anyway, Courtney and I laugh each night, and pray for his soul. I guess he thinks Santa pays that enormous bill of his to attend the Academy. Listen my people, my friends, my family, and my saviors, it's time for us to try to live like normal humans, in houses, watering lawns, cutting grass, yelling at the children, shopping for groceries, and buying clothes. Yeah, that's what I'm talking about."

The Sarge took a big gulp of his beverage and said, "Most of you purchased land from the two people who bought the land for peanuts and sold it to us for hundreds of thousands of dollars. That's right, John Lee and Jilkes, are our slum landlords. They still have property for those of you who may be interested. I'm just kidding, I don't think anyone has paid them for the land or for the building of their homes at this point. Is that true, John Lee?"

John Lee replied, "Sarge, I really don't want to be embarrassing anyone, but I would like to have a meeting later to discuss it with those who can't find them there checkbooks."

"Listen, people, it's time for us to live, and that might denote separately from the group. I don't know how to say this but, I guess we're through erasing bad guys, and there aren't many left looking for us that I know of. Since I know that the only person who we can't account for is the Holy Father, aka, the Pope, I'm comfortable that we're good. We were in good graces with the Holy Father. I'm not concerned about any consequences from the church. We did what was asked of us and, therefore, I'm at ease about how we left things with the church," the Sarge announced.

John Lee stood up and said, "I'm not on the same bus with you on that one, Sarge. I be thinking that guy is a really sick person. Think about it, he be representing both heaven and hell. Now, I be wondering how the heck he can do that. I didn't believe in all that hocus pocus until I came to this here place, saw that massive thing in the water, and how those snakes, spiders, dingoes, and other animals acted together to protect us. I be believing that there be some strange things going on here, and I know that there fella from Rome, be very questionable." Nobody laughed because they all knew that some of their experiences were not what could be considered everyday occurrences.

The Sarge said, "In conclusion, but before I conclude, doesn't it feel celestial, not to have someone overtly trying to eradicate you?" There was a thunderous applause. "Those be my sentiments, as well!" the Sarge exclaimed.

## CHAPTER TWENTY-FOUR

Six months later, without any indication that trouble was in the air, Ava and Carlos commandeered one of the smaller jets to take care of personal business in Valencia. She knew her people in Spain would be the source of protection once they were there. On a bright and sunny day in Valencia, Spain, as Carlos and Ava exited her villa for brunch, a car pulled up, two men got out on the passenger's side of the vehicle, and two exited the driver's side. They revealed their automatic weapons, and opened fire on the two lovers, leaving their bodies mangled beyond recognition.

On the same day, but across the Atlantic Ocean outside of Boston, Massachusetts, Carla, and Mike attended her father's funeral on a rainy and miserable day. Their children were secured in the limo by their nanny as the couple braved the rain at the burial site. After the priest concluded the sermon, the coffin exploded, killing everyone in the immediate area.

In Birmingham, Alabama, on the same day, John Lee, Somara, Jilkes, Yeshida, Mary Alice, and Jong, were in line to order their morning shot of caffeine. Jong, who had his back to Mary Alice's, saw two vehicles approaching the store, but continued to move his buttocks against hers. As he watched the people get out of the cars, he realized that these guys were hostile when he saw the first person out of one of the cars covering up a machine pistol. He turned, pushed Mary Alice to the side, and yelled, "Hostiles Incoming."

Everyone turned to see what he was talking about, and in the process, they all drew their weapons. The sight of guns in the store caused a panic, and people began to run out of the store from all exits. The group, stayed in the store, took cover behind walls, tables, and whatever else that offered protection. The brazen gunmen walked into the store from both entrances and were met with gunfire from six different vantage points, and unknowingly, from the rear. Rashida and Juan had made their way to town, saw what was going down, and joined in the fray. Seven gunmen were cut down. Most suffered head shots and chest wounds. The eighth guy suffered two shots to his shoulder and was quickly hustled out of the store.

John Lee went into the back of the store, disabled the camera system, and took the disk. On the way out, he looked at the three terrified clerks, and exclaimed, "Better to know nothing then to guess what happened! Mums the word."

the end

also in the 'idiot spy' series

Available at Amazon and BarnesandNoble.com

www.ingramcontent.com/pod-product-compliance
Lightning Source LLC
Chambersburg PA
CBHW051521250626
47156CB00001B/175